Blood and Oak

A Novel

By Garrett Bettencourt

FREE GIFT!!
The Art of Blood and Oak

Join my Readers' Group email list at
www.bloodandoak.com/gift and get a FREE Art Book!

"The Art of Blood and Oak" brings this classic high seas
tale to life with original commissioned art. The artbook
is delivered in easy-to-print PDF format. You'll also get
exclusive behind-the-scenes details about the
characters and the world. Yours FREE!

For my mom,
My dad,
And my sister,

You inspired me to always find a way

1798

A young United States struggles to survive.
Revolutionary France wages war
with Great Britain.

Caribbean slaves in Saint Domingue
rebel against brutal masters.

Amid this renaissance of freedom, the Barbary
Pirates roam the Mediterranean Sea, plundering
merchant ships at will. The Ottoman princes of
Morocco, Algiers, Tripoli, and Tunis send captains
to raid coastal towns. The corsairs carry off men,
women, and children to hold for ransom or sell
into slavery. Their attacks have raged for three
hundred years, reaching from Italy to Iceland.
Countries must buy peace or face terror.

A sailor's greatest fear is a living death
on the Barbary Coast.

Prologue

The Merchant Schooner *Wandering Hart*
The Mediterranean Sea
Tuesday, June 12th, 1798

"No matter what you hear, my darlings, don't move," Nora whispered. She held back tears as she knelt with her children, Kaitlin and John. On the lower deck, behind piles of crates, bundles, and barrels, only a single lantern lit their faces. Her children huddled in a rectangular hole in the floor, where the natural slope of the ship allowed their father Declan to create a secret space between the cross beams. They would have enough room to lie down and stretch their legs, but little else. "Stay in this compartment. Don't move. Don't make a sound. Wait for me to return."

Footfalls thudded overhead. The pirates barked threats and insults in a foreign language.

"What about Isaac?" Kaitlin wept, her red curls disheveled. John held his eight-year-old sister close, her cheek pressed against his chest.

"Your big brother is on deck helping your father. I need you to stay here, all right?"

"Where are you going, Mam?"

1

"I have to go help them for a bit. That's all."

Kaitlin's face crumpled into sobs. "What if the bad men get you?"

"Oh, love," Nora said as she embraced her children. "They're not going to hurt us. They're just robbers. When they have what they want, they'll be gone. But right now, I need you to be brave and stay here with your brother. I want you to mind Johnny and do as he says, okay?"

She exchanged a look with John. Her fifteen-year-old's eyes were hard and determined, but a crease in his brow betrayed his fear.

Kaitlin nodded, but the strain was too much. She started to bawl. "When are you coming back?"

On the deck above, there were shouts coming from the officers' wardroom. Axes chopped into bulkheads. Wood splintered and snapped. There were loud crashes. Pirates were sweeping through the ship.

"Soon, Katie," Nora soothed. "Here." Nora reached into the pocket of her trousers and produced a silver hunter-case watch. She held it out by its delicate chain. "Remember when we learned to tell time? I want you to count the ticks. When I come back, I'll ask how long it's been, and you'll see it was no time at all. Can you do that, love?"

Tears flooded Kaitlin's cheeks as she accepted the watch. She opened the case, revealing Roman numerals under stately black tines.

"All right," Nora said. "Johnny, you look after your sister, all right?"

"I'll keep her safe, Mam," John said. His eyes reddened as he fought back tears. Nora knew her son didn't want to hide, but Kaitlin needed him. "Be careful, Mam. Please."

"I will. Now, in you go, loves."

John and Kaitlin lay down in the tiny compartment. Kaitlin held the watch while John held her hand. Kaitlin's breath came quick and shallow.

"It's all right, Katie," John said softly. "I'm right here. Let's count while we wait."

Nora slid the loose deck planks over the hidden space. One board at a time, she sealed her children into darkness. Before the last plank snapped home, she could hear Kaitlin whispering.

"One, two, three…"

Part I

Wayward Hearts

Chapter 1

Five Years Later

Outside Philadelphia, Pennsylvania
Friday, June 24th, 1803

"Wake up, *alumno*. This is as far as we go."

John Hotspur Sullivan awoke in the corner of a wagon under a canvas tarpaulin. Stacks of crates hemmed in his legs. Bottles of rum jingled as the wheels came to a stop. *Comandante* Fernando Pavia jerked away the tarpaulin in one motion. John threw a hand up against the blinding noon sun.

"How you manage to sleep in such small places will always confound me," Pavia added as he jumped out of the box seat. He sauntered up close to his former student and drummed his fingers on the wagon rail.

Sensing the mercenary's impatience, John stretched his legs. "I took my first steps at sea—below the waterline," he said. "Can't sleep anywhere else." He jumped out of the wagon. His joints popped as he stretched.

"Are you certain you want to return?" asked Pavia. Words rolled off his tongue like musical notes. He might have looked aristocratic with his long-bow mustache and clean-cut features, but the scar tugging down on his left eyelid suggested otherwise. The *Comandante* hailed from Spain's Basque Country. Being the leader of Basque mercenaries and smugglers, Pavia preferred not to lodge in Philadelphia proper.

"No," replied John. "But it's not forever."

Borrego, one of Pavia's lieutenants, scoffed from the driver seat. He packed tobacco into a pipe while he waited. The wagon's two Andalusian horses grazed on grass between wheel tracks.

"Why take a chance?" Pavia asked. "It is a shame to lose you. I always have use for a skilled river pilot."

John rummaged through his worn leather satchel. His fingers brushed a change of socks, long johns, four pennies, a nearly empty powder horn, a compass, a pocket watch, and a tinderbox—until he found a buckskin pouch. The twenty-year-old Irish drifter fished out his last clump of tobacco. He pressed the shredded brown leaves against his gums and replied, "I'm not looking for work, *Comandante*. I'm looking to hire. Can your brother spare the men or not?"

"They are not sailors by trade. And they don't come cheap. Why not hire a few salts off the docks?"

"You know the kind of men I need. I'm going to free my family. For that I need soldiers. I need Basques." John and Pavia exchanged a smile at that. "As for seamanship—I'll show them how to tell sheets from stays."

"Ah, you will enjoy being *maestro* for a change, no? But despite your fine work and my boundless generosity, your earnings aren't nearly enough, I think."

"I'll get the money. Can you get me the men?"

"*Bien, alumno.* I can think of a few fine soldiers of

fortune who would be interested. When you have the money, find us at our usual camp. But if you come up short…"

"I won't."

Pavia smiled to himself. He handed John a coin purse. "Your share, *Señor* Sullivan." He slapped John on the back and climbed onto the wagon box seat. He pulled a bottle of duty-free *Isla Carillo* rum out of a crate and tossed it to John. "A bonus. To celebrate your success." He snapped the reins, and the horses reluctantly abandoned the grass. "And if your plan goes tits up—to commiserate." Pavia's mustache perked up as he smiled.

The horses clip-clopped into the western countryside. John watched them pass under the canopy of a willow, then disappear over a rise. The wind blew a white kerchief over John's boot. As he picked it up, he realized the crest marked it as Pavia's—a castle, two gold poleaxes crossing each other, and a field of red. He pocketed the kerchief and looked toward the Delaware River. The triangular sails of a schooner drifted on a reflection of white clouds, toward rows of docks and brick buildings. He chewed for a moment, spit a wad of tobacco in the dirt, and shouldered his satchel. He set off north toward the city.

An hour later, John approached Mrs. McClintock's Water Street Lodging. The boarding house sat across from a forest of masts and spars lining the wharf. It was two stories of uneven brown brick nestled between The Delaware Chandlers and Bricklebrack's Bread and Hardtack. The wooden shutters were gray from rot. A tattered awning flapped above the door. On the porch, a row of potted herbs and a sleeping dog soaked in the afternoon sun. The place looked just as it had fourteen months ago. Back then, John rued every new day he had to spend in Philadelphia. Now, it felt more like coming home than he dared admit.

Sensing the newcomer, the dog roused from his sleep.

"Godfried!" John beamed. A salt-and-pepper Irish wolfhound bounded towards him. The shaggy dog was tall enough to nearly bowl him over. John tousled Godfried's ears while the hound licked his face. "How are you, boy?"

Godfried gave an excited whine, then nearly knocked John over with a "*woof.*"

"I missed you too, boy."

The dog would prove more agreeable than his owner, Mrs. McClintock. But he'd offer to pay his back rent, let her pinch his cheeks, and get his little corner of the attic back. John looked back down the road. A few streets south and an alley or two east would take him to the Sawduster Tavern. To the doorstep of his first friend in Philadelphia. His first home. He imagined Ethan on the porch swing, playing the violin for his little brothers and sisters. Imagined the look on Ethan's face when he noticed John walking up. Would it be a smile? Or a frown? John shook his head. Too much had happened. Besides, Ethan was probably in the Navy. He likely wouldn't even be home. John stepped onto Mrs. McClintock's porch, Godfried in tow.

Chapter 2

The Cat and Queen Playhouse
Philadelphia, Pennsylvania
Friday, June 24th, 1803

Melisande Dufort pressed close against the skin of her lover. In her fingers, she twirled a long, red feather. She grinned when she decided on the most tempting target. She traced it along naked curves, up toward the underarm. A jolt. A gasp. Her lover awoke.

"Melly!"

A mouse-chewed pillow swatted Melisande in the face. She fell backwards laughing. A warm body rolled on top of her.

"I *hate* to be tickled," said Sarah. Her curly brown hair fell across Melisande's face as they kissed. Their lips teased and explored one another. Melisande caressed the small of Sarah's back.

"But you're so cute when you're cross," Melisande said between kisses.

"Am I?" Sarah leaned in, tracing her tongue under Melisande's lip.

Melisande squeezed Sarah's ass. "Less cute when you snore." She slipped a hand between her lover's legs.

"You're rotten," Sarah murmured. Her eyes slipped closed, and she rolled her hips forward.

"And randy as a beast with two backs. I ain't missing brag to watch you sleep, wench."

Sarah's eyes flew open in mock offense. "Oh?" She pinched Melisande's hip.

Melisande gasped. She pinched back.

Sarah shot upright. "Why you little villain…" She bumped her head on a ceiling beam and lost her balance. They tumbled off the bed, giggling.

Melisande looked up at a jagged shard of mirror hanging by the window. "Come here." She came to her feet, tugging Sarah up behind her. She looked at her own naked image through a spindle of cracks. Sarah circled her arms around her lover. Melisande admired the sight of her tan, muscular body nestled against Sarah's pale curves. She liked Sarah, but she longed to be home with her clan. Melisande might have been French by birth, but in her breast beat the heart of the Tuscarora and the People of the Longhouse. Not all of her kin approved of her choice in lover, but they loved her anyway. Here, in this crowded, noisy city, she had to hide in a stuffy attic. Melisande's sister, Dominique, insisted on living among the colonials.

"I wish I had this for a painting," said Melisande.

"If we could just find an artist willing to stare at two naked women," Sarah murmured. She planted the feather in Melisande's raven-black hair. "Pretty. Where did you get it?"

"My brother. Found it while hunting. Dropped by a red-tailed hawk." Melisande's eyes drifted out the window. A drunkard with stockings sagging on his ankles zig-zagged through the alley. A trio of filthy children in patchwork clothes played at marbles. Two boys and a girl taking a break from begging to play. Few of Philadelphia's respectable or affluent ever passed by these narrow, muddy streets.

The Cat and Queen Playhouse was an aging brick theater on the old western wharves near Front Street. A wooden sign portrayed a queen with an orange-striped cat on her lap. Among the poor, the drunks, and the unwanted, the odd theater provided a discreet haven for those not welcome elsewhere. Regulars simply called it "Kitty's." In this city, Melisande called it home.

"The stories you tell…" Sarah was saying, "will I ever see him?"

"Grey Feather doesn't like the city."

"To have an Indian for a brother…Take me with you to the country. I want to meet him."

"Oh, he'd love that. The wife of the Prune Street Warden poking at him like he's some curiosity. And right after I got out of the clink." A young man in a rain-spotted jerkin walked by. His rolled-up sleeves revealed slender arms, taut with muscles earned on the frontier. He didn't bother to tie back his shoulder-length hair, auburn as autumn leaves…

Wait! Melisande leaned forward, squinting her eyes. *Could it be?* A shaggy, gray hound trotted up beside the youth. As the man looked down at the dog, his face turned in Melisande's direction, though he didn't see her. "It's Sully!"

"What?" said Sarah.

Melisande squirmed free of her lover and dashed to a string of crumpled clothes. "He's back in town."

"Who?"

Melisande hopped on one leg, then the other, as she

pulled on her deerskin breeches.

"Where are *you* going?" Sarah wanted to know.

Melisande threw on her white shirt and buttoned up her black waistcoat. She hurried to give Sarah a kiss. "Gotta run, my lovely."

"Melisande," Sarah called after her lover. "Wait, the rules! We entered with a beau, we *leave* with a beau. I only just got you out of Prune Street prison—you want us in the pillory next?"

Melisande paused, bouncing with energy. She hated stopping once she'd started. She hated being nagged. And most of all, she hated rules. But these rules were important.

"Fine!" She went to the door across the hall.

She flung it open to find a naked Thomas pinning his lover Archie to the wall as they kissed. They were a bricklayer and a silversmith who took more of a liking to each other than was considered proper. They leaped like startled cats.

She put a hand to her mouth and giggled. "Oh, my. They were like little dogs sniffing noses."

"Melly!" griped Thomas.

"Don't you knock?" complained Archie.

"C'mon, boys," trumpeted Melisande. "You've had your fun. Put 'em away so one of you can escort me out."

She folded her arms as they collected their underclothes. They moved with all the enthusiasm of drunks sent home from the tavern.

John stood on the highest yardarm of the *Morrigan* looking west over Philadelphia. Gables and turrets bit into the setting sun. The early evening light refracted off the neat rows of red brick. The westerly streets became golden spokes radiating through the buildings. The steeple of Independence Hall rose above all at the center. His right hand gripped the prickly halyard. He watched the bustle of the city winding down along the docks below.

The proprietor of Horace's Fine Breads carefully unhooked the brass bell from his door and brought it inside. John remembered being a starving fifteen-year-old orphan and breaking in to eat the sweepings. The baker had screamed until beet red and chased the Irish vagrant out with a cane.

Mr. Samuelson of the Society of Friends watched eagerly at the door of Gilbert's Tavern. Every drunken sailor, dock worker, or builder choosing that hour to leave was treated to the same sermon. "Have you heard the Lord's message of salvation?" the Quaker began. John couldn't make out the lewd quip by two men stumbling arm-in-arm, but their mocking laughter failed to daunt Mr. Samuelson.

Mrs. O'Malley ambled by. Her husband was long dead, her children grown, and her hair gray. She strolled along Water Street in her Parisian jacket and plumed hat, determined as ever to be a model for Philadelphia's young ladies. John still remembered her tip of an extra penny whenever he would run mail to her—and the sting of her fan when she heard him swearing.

It was an odd feeling, John decided, to discover the city he had so long wanted to escape became the place that won his heart. He held up a delicate silver chain over the Philadelphia skyline. His mother's watch shimmered above the horizon like a rising moon.

"Go on then, love," his mother says. "Wind it up."

The lantern flickers on ribbons of sienna hair. The brass cylinder housing the marine chronometer gleams from inside the oak box. John holds up the silver watch, carefully turning the crown. He strains his eyes in the dark of the Wandering Hart's *hold, patiently cranking until the hour hand agrees with the chronometer.*

Her nose scrunches when she smiles. "Very good, John. And the minute?"

"Five past, of course," says the boy of ten. He winds the second hand.

"Fancy a look then?" Nora observes her son's work.

"Is it right?" He's hopping in anticipation.

"Spot on. You don't need me to check anymore."

"I know."

"Run along then, love. Your father will need the time."

The boy dashes off. He takes the ladder two rungs at a time.

Looking to starboard, a few berths down, John marveled at the polished black hull and towering masts of USS *Philadelphia*. The yellow stripe on her gun deck brandished a dozen long guns like a wasp flashing a stinger. Her eighteen-pounders were probably run out for drills, John decided. Or perhaps to inspire the pride of her namesake city. Oh, the reckoning John could bring to bear on his family's captors were she under his command. He could tear down the whole of Tunis to free his mother and sister with a mighty frigate like that—and repay the bey's injustice in the bargain. But alas, the little sloop on which he stood would have to serve. The rickety ship on which he now stood represented his last chance to rescue them—that is, if he could raise the last thousand dollars he needed for the journey.

John closed his eyes. In his mind, he took command of *Morrigan* and felt the thrill as the ocean spread across the horizon. He imagined the ship cutting through the swells with him riding the bowsprit. For the first time in five years, he would be home again on the open sea. Wind, water, sky, and the racing of his heart would become all that existed in the world.

With a flick of the wrist, John wound the chain around his hand. "Mother, Kaitlin," he whispered, "I will find you. I will see you free. I will bring you home. This I swear.

"And for what they did to us…" John's fist closed on the watch. "I will be revenged."

An unmistakable voice on the deck below shattered the peace of the evening. "Sully, you ole mick!"

John looked down at the deck and recognized a dark-haired woman of twenty-five staring up at him. She wore deerskin breeches and a black waistcoat. A walnut Iroquois war club in the shape of a raven's head hung at her belt. The antler hilt of a seven-inch hunting knife poked out of her boot. He smiled wide as he recognized Melisande Dufort. He jumped onto the shroud and started the climb down.

"You're going across the ocean…in *that*?" Melisande Dufort wrinkled her nose as if carrying out the chamber pot. Her mouth hung open. She stood next to Sully on the wharf, trying to imagine how this floating piece of junk could help him rescue his family. A wad of tobacco stewed under her lip.

The boat—or "fifty-nine-foot schooner" as Sullivan had described it—creaked more loudly than the other ships. Sullivan proudly explained her name was *Morrigan*.

With most of her yards stowed, her single mast looked as lifeless as a winter birch. The black band, red trim, and gold highlights had chipped and faded into large patches of exposed wooden hull. The figurehead was once a black winged maiden but had worn down into a withered crone. Melisande felt sorry for the poor old bag. She was clearly miserable in the evening heat.

"Well…" Sullivan said, "she isn't properly fitted out yet. She'll be a much fairer sight under a full press of sail. That is, once I've raised the money for a crew brazen enough to sail to the Barbary Coast."

"Ugh. The thought of being on that hunk of wood gives me the creeps."

"Christ, Melly. You can traipse through a mountain blizzard with a smile, but a day on calm seas and you're whining like a puppy."

"It isn't natural! We're meant to have dirt under our feet. You must be out of your head to travel months with nothing but water as far as you can see. And *that* thing's a scrap-pile!"

"She's seaworthy."

Melisande cocked an eyebrow. "She's a hag."

Sullivan sighed. "Aye. She's a hag. But she's my hag."

Melisande snickered. "Heard *that* before."

"We can't all have such adoring lovers as yours."

Melisande chuckled and tousled John's hair. "I missed you, Sully."

Sullivan looked askance at her, smirking. His hazel eyes turned gold in the afternoon sun. He didn't have to say it. Melisande was used to him feigning temperance just before joining her in another piece of mischief. She knew her rash actions often got him in trouble. She knew her preference for women bewildered him. She knew he had the charm and smarts to pass himself off as a poufy-shirted gentleman. But Sully always watched her back. Saw the real her. And she saw the real him. He had an honest heart. Most of all, she knew that after a year away in Florida, he missed her like flies missed dung.

Melisande pointed to the ship. "But you were kicked by a horse if you think you're getting across the Atlantic in that."

"The *Morrigan* has had three years of repairs. She'll hold together for one more voyage—and that's all I need."

"Is that really a bet you want to make?"

Sullivan looked at her seriously. "You know I have to."

Melisande looked away, remembering to chew her tobacco.

They silently gazed at the old ship.

An aged woman's voice came from behind them. "Shameful!"

Melisande and Sullivan turned around to find a pair of stuffy, overdressed older ladies carrying their baskets of goods home from market. They both scowled at Melisande and the stream of spit juice at her feet. "Her poor mother…" said the other.

"Both of my mothers are buried on the frontier, you old shrews!"

The first woman said, "You ought to find Christ!" She shook a loaf of bread in her plump fingers.

The other stiffened her skeletal figure, scowling at Sullivan. "And you ought to find a proper lady to court, young man."

Sully smiled. "What fun would that be?"

In unison, Melisande and Sullivan spit murky globs

into the street. The appalled women shuffled away, muttering to one another. Melisande and her favorite Irishman snickered like adolescents in the farthest church pew.

"Come on, Sully!" said Melisande. She reached for Sullivan's shoulder, which was a head higher than hers. "This courtship is going so well, I've decided to let you buy me an ale."

"I'd love to Melly, but I can't. I need to win a few checks at the card tables tonight."

Melisande slapped Sullivan's back. "Right! Brag! Even better. The Duke and the Duchess—back together. Then ale."

"No, I'm not out rooking."

"Who said anything about a scam?" Melisande raised her hand to her forehead as if to swoon. "I'm a silly girl playing with my beau's checks because I'm *so in love* and could *never* be apart from my handsome Duke!" She dropped her romantic pretense. "I pluck 'em right out of the stream. We split the take."

"It took half a year for my shoulder wound to heal, Melly. And another half-year working for Pavia in the festering swamp to earn what money I have. And it's still not enough to outfit the *Morrigan* and hire a crew. The Piping Plover's Independence Day game is the highest stakes in the city. It's my last chance."

"Bullshit. Those puffed up old goats would never let you in the door. Probably chase you out with a broom."

"Not if the owner's wife put in a word for me."

"My sister? She won't even talk to *me*. Why would she—?"

"It took some convincing, but Dominique got Richard Aubert to give me a seat. If there's even a whiff of cheating on me, I *will* get the broom. I need the money at that table, Melly. I can't risk it."

Melly grunted. She hated it when Sully got all stubborn and serious. It made him seem like all the rest of these fancy city people. Boring. Hearing the mention of her sister's name only further soured her mood. Dominique had no business marrying that prancing little bastard Aubert. Now *she* was fancy like him. Disgusting. Of course, Melisande imagined the only alternative would be Dominique marrying Sullivan. She supposed that's how things ought to be—true love and all that. But then Sully wouldn't have time for drinking and cards if he was busy making babies.

"Yeah, yeah, fine," Melisande said. "Kitty's later?"

"Melly…"

"Oh bugger it, Sully! You leave me for a year, and you're barely back a day before it's off again to drown in some leaky raft."

Sullivan sighed and rubbed his temples. Melisande could read the fatigue on his face. She was wearing him down.

She puffed out her lips. "Not so much as a farewell drink with your best chum."

John rolled his eyes.

"Who saved your life at least twice," she added.

"And endangered it once."

"Which puts the balance in my favor."

"*Fine.* Kitty's. After…"

Melisande beamed.

"…For *one* drink."

She tempered her smile. "Of course. Fair is fair."

Sullivan smirked and nodded down the docks. She suppressed her grin until his back was turned. Godfried was sniffing a horse tether a hundred paces away. The hound barked and came bounding after them.

Sullivan glanced back at the *Morrigan*. "One more voyage, old girl. One more."

The hideous old boat wheezed as its weight shifted in the river.

Chapter 3

Mrs. McClintock's Water Street Lodging
Philadelphia, Pennsylvania
Friday, June 24th, 1803

"Is that the last of it?"

"Yup." Melisande dragged a sleeve across her mouth. It came away yellow with undigested dumpling. Squinting, she shoved off the alley wall of Bricklebrack's Bread and Hardtack. She wobbled a moment, then lost her balance.

John caught her and pulled her arm over his shoulder. "Almost there," he slurred.

"No…" Melisande mumbled, her eyes drooping. She squirmed out of his grasp, about to make a bed of her own vomit. "I'm-a-go to sleep now."

John pulled her back to her feet. "No, Melly, not in the street."

Godfried trotted out of the open kitchen door and began lapping up the remains of Melisande's last tavern stew.

She feebly slapped at John's hands as he carried her across the alley to Mrs. McClintock's.

He picked her up in a cradle position. Mercifully, she was nearly passed out and gave in.

John nudged through the door into Mrs. McClintock's kitchen. The scent of broth and onion filled him with nostalgia. Firelight slipped through the cracked parlor door. He tugged it open with the tip of his foot. Godfried panted by, into the empty sitting room, and plopped down in front of the fireplace. The only light came from embers in the hearth. The plush armchairs on either side cast long shadows towards the dining tables where the tenants would sit down to breakfast in a few hours. John lay Melisande—already snoring—on the sofa. She mumbled something he couldn't make out and curled into a fetal position. He tugged a knitted pillow under her head and drew a plaid quilt over her.

He gratefully settled into the adjacent armchair. The room spun the moment he came to rest. He and Melisande began the night with an ale-guzzling contest at the Cat and Queen, continued by joining a group of dockside sailors in song, and ended with rowdy dancing at a tippling house on the edge of town. Godfried had followed them all night, begging for ale and scraps. Melisande loved drinking companions, no matter their number of legs. She had frequently tipped her cup in the direction of the dog's slobbering jowls.

John still felt the sting of Tabitha's mysterious punch recipe in the back of his throat. He chuckled. "Goddamnit, Melisande." When he closed his eyes, he heard footsteps on the stairs.

"I'll pay her lodging for the night, Mrs. McClintock," said John. "Kitty's was too far to go."

A familiar voice replied in an Irish accent. "Your speech—it's different since my last visit. You sound like a yank."

Peter, John sneered to himself. His uncle and the last

man he wanted to see. *What's he want this time?*

A man with red hair combed back and a pair of bushy mutton chops stepped in front of the other chair. Peter Sullivan dressed much finer than his last visit two years ago—a green silk waistcoat, silver buttons, and black corduroy trousers. His belly was getting portly.

"What are you doing here?" John snorted.

Gesturing to the empty seat, Peter asked, "Do you mind?"

"I do. You won't be staying."

Peter sighed. He sat down anyway. "I've been waiting here for hours, Johnny. The least you can do is hear what I have to say."

"The name is 'John.'"

Peter looked over at Melisande, raising an eyebrow. "Is this your…lass?"

"A friend."

"That's a blessed relief."

"Tell me what you want, Peter. The faster you do, the faster you can fuck off."

"I understand you're angry, son, but I'm not your enemy. Whether you believe it or not, I'm trying to help."

"Really? Then you've brought Ma and Katie home like you promised?"

Peter sat back in the chair, rubbing his sideburns. "You know how badly I wished it all turned out better. I went to the Barbary Coast with a king's ransom—all the worldly wealth my brother and I ever had. I was ready to offer it all to the Bey of Tunis. Declan died in the quarries. Nora and Kaitlin went to the markets at Constantinople. There's no amount of money that could bring them back. I did all I could."

John shot his uncle a glare. "Did you sail for

Constantinople? Did you even try?"

"We've been through this. You know as well as I: once a slave passes through that place, they never come back. I'm sorry, truly I am. But they're gone, Johnny, and that's that."

"They're not gone!" hissed John. "They're *slaves!*" He shouted the last word, causing Godfried to whine in his sleep.

"You've been through a terrible ordeal, son. But this suicide you're planning…you have to let it go."

The younger man bounced his knee, brooding.

"Mrs. McClintock is as worried about you as I. She says you've been smuggling, gambling, dueling. That you want to hire a band of Spanish sell-swords. To sail a ship your father planned to break apart for scrap right into the jaws of the Barbary Pirates. John, can you hear how mad that sounds?"

John looked at Peter with a cold smile. "I'd rather be mad than a coward."

"We have to live in the real world. A terrible thing happened to our family. We've no choice but to move on. I've come with important news to help you do just that. Hear me out, at least."

John considered driving Peter out—at the point of a fire poker if necessary. Peter had convinced John, the sole heir to his father's half of The Brothers Sullivan Shipping and Consignment, to sell his inheritance. Two remaining ships, a warehouse on the Belfast docks, a handful of cargo and salvage. John kept only Declan's first ship, the *Morrigan*, which had been rotting at anchor. Peter had taken the money to the Barbary Coast and promised to return with John's family. Instead, he returned with defeat.

Still, as much as John reviled his uncle, the man's presence brought a curious feeling of comfort. Perhaps Peter's familiar smell of shoe polish and pipe smoke reminded John of childhood. Summers learning knots with Da on the wharf. Falls pestering Isaac to take him fishing. Winters watching Mam stir the Christmas pudding over the fire. The spring he met his sister for the first time, a swollen-eyed infant sleeping in Mam's arms. Or perhaps John knew Peter was right. His uncle was the last of his kin, and better selfish kin than none at all. Whatever the reason for John's nostalgia, he nodded for Peter to continue.

Peter produced a leather-bound sheaf of papers from his jacket. He laid it open on the table. "Your Grandfather O'Regan has passed away, I'm sorry to say. But, he left an inheritance to your mother. Not much, but enough to start a young man off well. Your grandfather's last wish was that your mother's wealth pass to you."

"An inheritance? It's mine?"

"Aye, it will be. All I need is your signature, and the money is yours." Peter pushed the papers toward John. "It simply acknowledges that you are your mother's heir, allowing you to take possession."

"And how much will be left after our business debts are paid?"

"Not much," admitted Peter. "But signing would show me you're ready to take responsibility as a man. In return, I'd help you get established in Belfast. At least read it, son."

The firelight flickered over elegant cursive letters. *...whereupon Declan and Nora Sullivan have been declared lost at sea...undersigned having assumed legal ownership of all* *assets…with the aforementioned amount earmarked for funeral expenses…*

"It's the responsible choice, son." Peter set a quill and inkpot beside the document.

John's eyes roamed across the page. *…Wandering Hart lost with all hands…John Sullivan, sole living heir…on condition of return to Ireland…*

Grief welled up in John. The will required him to go back to Ireland. To make the death of his family official. "What the hell is this?"

"Nuthin'!" muttered Melisande, still dreaming. She must have overheard the conversation in her drunken dreams. Now she was contributing nonsense. "Pigs in…red shoes…*Va te faire foutre!*"

The two men looked askance at the woman drooling on her own hair. She smacked her lips and returned to snoring.

Peter continued, "This is your future, Johnny. What's rightfully yours."

"You want me to seal their fate."

"I want you to grieve. To come home to Ireland. And to move on."

John flipped the leather cover closed. "My mother is alive."

"Try to be sensible, lad." Peter's tone sharpened. "Your father didn't just leave us his business. He also left us his debts. You and I have responsibilities in Belfast. You're a man now, and it's time to act like one. Sign it, take the money, and start your life."

John grunted, shaking his head. "You don't care about my future. I was a slave—fighting rats away from maggoty bread while my father begged you in letter after letter for ransom money. Mother warned us you would ignore those letters, and my fool father wouldn't see it. He defended you while we slept in chains."

"Your mother and I never got along, but Declan was my brother, and I loved him. That you could think I'd betray my own kin—it's a stake through my heart."

John stood. He walked up to the hearth. He pulled a poker off of its wrought iron rack and prodded the embers. "Just get out."

"John, don't throw your life away."

"I listened to you once. Not again. I will go to the Barbary Coast. I will succeed where you failed. I will bring my mother and sister back. And God have mercy on any man in my way, *Uncle*."

Peter stormed to the door. He paused to look over his shoulder. "Fine then. Join these godless traitors. Run with mongrels and whores. Sail to a watery grave for all I care. Turn your back on your home."

John stared into the blistering coals. "I don't have a home."

Peter shook his head. "Just as stubborn as Declan."

John looked at Peter. "You're wrong about that."

"Am I, now?"

"I'm far more stubborn than my father."

Peter grunted. He stepped into the street and slammed the door.

John heard a low *woof* at his feet. Godfried craned his neck towards the door. Melisande mumbled a few vulgarities in French.

"It's all right, boy," John whispered to Godfried.

The hound peered up at John beneath shaggy brows, then returned to his dreams.

Chapter 4

The Merchant Schooner *Wandering Hart*
The Mediterranean Sea
Tuesday, June 12th, 1798

"Four, five, six…"

On the lower deck of the *Wandering Hart*, stuffed into a tiny space under the boards, John listened to Kaitlin count. A stampede of boots flooded through the stacks of cargo. Sharp, foreign words came with them. The men celebrated and bickered as they chopped open every box, chest, cabinet, and barrel. They stomped over the boards concealing John and Kaitlin, raining dust through the cracks. John resisted the urge to sneeze. His heart pounded. His sister squeezed his hand so hard, he lost feeling.

When they found a crewmember, they would spit a flurry of threats and demands. Every now and then, John caught a word he recognized. "Yield, dog!" "Christian filth." "Open that. Give it here!" They beat anyone that resisted.

"Come out, you fat old blighter!" shouted one of the invaders not far away.

The terrified cook begged for his life. His pleading

voice faded as the pirates dragged him above decks.

"Johnny," whispered Kaitlin, "what if they find us?"

"It's going to be okay, Rabbit," whispered John. He looked into her eyes, glinting under a shaft of light. "Be very quiet. Mother will be back soon."

John marveled at the calm in his voice. It was an act. He was so afraid, he felt as if his throat might close and suffocate him. But he had to be strong for Kaitlin.

How can this be happening? Wasn't I on the weather deck a moment ago? The sea calm? The Hart *safe?*

John had been standing at the bow with Kaitlin. Their family's second merchant ship, *Dolorous Fénnid*, had been on the way to help them repair their broken mast. His parents, Declan and Nora had been sipping their coffee. His oldest brother Isaac, the first mate, had command of the watch. The storm had frightened Kaitlin, but she was so delighted when John gave her the *Islanded Lion*—to him a common silver coin but to her, a magic talisman. Then a pirate flag appeared on the *Fénnid,* and minutes later, armed raiders were swarming over the ship.

"No, please," came a distant plea. John recognized the voice of Patrick, the boatswain's thirteen-year-old son. John had been shortening the fore topsail with him just hours ago.

"I'm not armed," Patrick cried. There were curses and shouts as the pirates dragged the boy away.

Mam and Da were having their coffee. Isaac had the deck. Katie was smiling again. How can this be happening?

As the pirates tore apart his home, terrorized his family, and beat his friends, John felt a madness stirring in him. It scratched under his skin like an animal trying to claw its way out. He imagined finding a weapon—a shard of glass, a cooking knife, a carpenter's axe. He imagined seeking out the nearest pirate and plunging the weapon into his chest. He wanted to see the look in the dying villain's eyes. He wanted blood.

A terrible scream came from above decks. The pirates were hurting someone, demanding answers. The cries grew more pained and more desperate. It was Patrick, the boatswain's boy, pleading for mercy.

And all at once, silence fell again.

Then a tremor of boots pounded down the hatchways. At least half a dozen men were coming towards them. He could see their shapes through the cracks.

They found us.

"*Huna! Huna!*" cried one of the foreign voices.

The pirates tore off the boards. Hands were all over John. Their grips bit like jaws. John squirmed and reached for his sister.

"Katie!" John yelled. "Katie, no. Don't touch her!"

"Johnny," Kaitlin cried. "I want Mama!"

"Fucking beasts! Let go of her."

A fist struck John's temple and the world became a blur.

When John came to, he was on the weather deck of the *Wandering Hart*, surrounded by foreign attackers. There were at least forty or fifty, packed shoulder to shoulder on the gratings, between the starboard boats, perched on coils of rope—everywhere. They were of every height, shade of skin, and age he could imagine. Those not bare-chested wore billowing trousers, sashes, and turbans, in bright colors of every kind. The hate in their glaring eyes terrified John more than their strange, curved swords.

In this clearing among the pirates, John's family and the twelve hired crew of the *Wandering Hart* huddled together, kneeling. The men were naked to a man. Patrick lay in the arms of his father, his eyes swollen shut. To John's right, Declan and Isaac kneeled, stripped of their clothes. Nora kneeled nearby. The pirates had stripped her of her jewelry, shirt, and trousers. They allowed her to keep her shift. John held back tears as he beheld his mother's humiliation. Her eyes reached for him, like a doe separated from a fawn.

The pirates dropped Kaitlin near her parents, and she ran into Nora's arms. "Mam!" she cried.

"Katie," Nora said. Mother and daughter held each other tightly, tears blazing paths through the dirt on their faces.

John felt a strange delirium fogging his mind. As if none of this were real and he was only an actor in a play. Three pirates tore off his clothes. One of them inspected the copper buttons on John's shirt, smiling with yellow teeth. John watched with detached curiosity as the pirates stripped him. *Not to humiliate*, he realized with fascination, *but to steal.* Shirt, belt, breeches, stockings, boots, buckles—they took it all in a race to claim each article and add it to their spoils. John cupped his groin. In his state of shock, he felt more rude than embarrassed. As if he was to blame for his immodestly. It felt as if somewhere, a stagehand was lowering the chandelier above John, but he couldn't remember his lines.

"We found our little rats," boomed a strange voice with a Turk accent. The crowd parted for the most ornate pirate of all, decked in green and yellow brocade. He looked first at Kaitlin, then John.

"The old man wouldn't talk, *Re'is* Raakaan," said a younger pirate with long hair and handsome features. His English was much better than his captain's. He nodded toward Patrick. "Until Hamit whipped this boy like a goat."

Declan looked up at the pirate captain with pleading eyes. "Please, sir. We surrendered peacefully. We have means to pay a ransom. There's no need to involve the children."

"Truly?" said Raakaan. He cocked his head and nodded with great interest.

"Yes, sir. I swear it. I can see you are a prudent man. I am as well. I wouldn't sail your waters unless able to honor you with tribute."

A smile spread across the pirate captain's face. "*You* are a filthy Christian dog. Your ship, its contents, and its crew belong to me. Your wife belongs to me. Your children belong to me. You belong to me. Your only hope is to beg Hammuda Bey of Tunis for mercy." The *Re'is* backhanded Declan, knocking him down.

"Naim," said *Re'is* Raakaan to the handsome young officer, "load the slaves." He looked down at Kaitlin. Raakaan ran a hand down his beard. "Bring the girl to my cabin."

"No," Nora said, clinging to Kaitlin. "Take me instead. I'll go with you to your cabin. Please, take me."

Raakaan's eyes glinted with interest. "A fine idea! I'll take you both."

"No, you can't," commanded Isaac like a judge pronouncing a sentence. "You cannot."

Raakaan froze, his eyes narrowing at Isaac. He scoffed and said to Naim, "Three hundred bastinados for that one." Raakaan seized Kaitlin's arm.

The animal under John's skin writhed and flailed. It clawed and spit. But John couldn't move. He couldn't even speak. Terror froze him in place.

Isaac launched. He spiraled a fist into the bare gut of his nearest captor. He yanked a curved dagger from the pirate's belt and sprinted the two strides to Raakaan. The corsair captain dropped Kaitlin's arm, whirling to face the charging youth. Isaac thrust the dagger. Raakaan stiffened, choked on a breath. The *re'is* teetered, his face frozen in surprise, and fell backwards. He landed with a single, booming thud. Blood spread through layers of colorful silk. The dead captain was gazing straight into the sun. John looked at Isaac.

"Isaac," Declan cried. "Son?"

Isaac stood frozen, blood trickling from his parted lips. A towering pirate loomed behind him—the one they had called "Hamit." Under the man's ornate silk jacket, his muscles rippled like hills. Isaac's eyes drifted to his stomach where a thick blade had chopped a path from his side to his navel. Where the sword should have had a point, gore dripped from a scythe-like crescent. With a wet, ripping sound, Hamit slid the sword free of Isaac's trunk.

Nora let go a wail of horror. Isaac's eyes grew distant and he sank in a heap. "Isaac. My boy," Nora bawled, clawing toward his corpse.

The pirates exploded into a frenzy. Blades rang out of sheaths. Gun hammers clicked into place. They shouted hateful epithets. The naked sailors cowered as pirates vented their anger with fists. Naim shouted orders in the Barbary language and brought the crew to some semblance of order.

At the young man's command, the pirates prodded captives toward the gangway one by one. They seized John's arms. The ocean breeze raised goosebumps on his naked skin. He looked back and saw Isaac's body face down in a pool of blood. John stumbled over a loose cable on the deck, tears chilling his face. A foot kicked his ribs. All at once, John felt the horror of his nakedness. At the thought of being beaten in this state, he scrambled to his feet.

The next few minutes became a haze of sound and fear. The pirates herded John onto the *Dolorous Fénnid*—once his father's ship, now the enemy's. They prodded him down into the hold. John knew the stale smell of bilge water, but this exceeded all notions of foul air. When he landed in the viscous water, his throat opened and pumped jets of vomit.

A hand pushed John away. "Watch it, 'ere," muttered a voice in English.

John blinked. He heard coughs in the darkness, shifting bodies. To John's horror, he realized they were the crew of the *Fénnid*. One of the pirates came down with a lantern. Flickering light poured across dozens of faces. Naked, bony bodies lined either side of the hold. *They've taken others!* thought John. How many days had the pirates been slaving with Declan's merchant ship?

The pirates shoved John against the hull and locked an iron ring around his ankle. A one-foot length of chain bolted him to the floor. The cold iron hung like a marble block. They chained Declan directly across from him. One by one, the men of the *Wandering Hart* were packed in. John read such shame in his father's eyes, he was relieved when the lantern passed by and left them in darkness. A moment later, Hamit came down with Kaitlin slung over his shoulder. He shackled her beside John and left without a word.

"Rabbit!" John said. "Are you all right?"

The hatch shut the prisoners in and the last rays of

light disappeared. Kaitlin didn't reply at first. She spat something into her hand, then whispered, "It's ok, Johnny. I did just like you said—I never let go of it."

John was astonished. He could still hear the tears in her voice, but she didn't sound afraid. She sounded almost...*hopeful*. "You did?" he asked dumbly.

He felt her press a coin, wet with saliva, into his palm. The silver piece of eight he had given her that morning. They called it "The Islanded Lion."

"It's all right, Johnny," she said. "Don't be afraid."

John looked in the direction of her voice, unable to see her in the darkness.

"I've got him, Johnny. The Lion. He'll keep us safe."

Kaitlin placed her hand in his, the silver piece pressed between their palms. In the darkness, John wept.

Chapter 5

The Piping Plover Inn
Philadelphia, Pennsylvania
Friday, July 1ˢᵗ, 1803

One big hand. That was all John needed to reverse his fortunes in this brutal Independence Day brag tournament. He failed to win a single hand in the hour since he sat down at the Piping Plover Inn. At last, he had the hand he needed. The ace of clubs, a king of hearts, and a queen of clubs. The fourth—a worthless deuce—went to the discard pile. It was a "run"—the best hand from Boston to Charleston.

"'Now stop tearing apart my goddamn rigging and go secure the cargo!'" Lieutenant Richard Aubert said as he leaned into the red velvet back of his chair. He had short curly black hair, a thick mustache, and a neat goatee. Just over thirty, the young captain of the sloop-of-war USS *Allegheny* was fit, smart, and confident. That, and the fact his wealthy French family owned the inn, made him the preening center of attention. He had been entertaining the half-dozen men at the table with a story from his years at sea.

"Those are lads flirting with a flogging," said

Commandant Pritchett of Philadelphia's Southwark Naval Yard, whom Aubert had been working tirelessly to impress. Pritchett's authority would allow the *Allegheny* to sail to war against Tripoli rather than patrol the coast for smugglers.

"So I said, 'I want all of you damn idiots out of my sight,'" Aubert continued. "They all scatter, but the powder monkey, who spotted the shifting cargo in the first place, just stands there. I ask, 'are you disobeying my order, boy?' The lad says, 'No, sir. I thought the order was for the idiots.'"

Everyone erupted in laughter. Aubert dropped a few eagles into the pot, the gold epaulets of his uniform gleaming in the light of the chandelier. His boasting turned John's stomach.

"What a shame our Lieutenant Aubert isn't out thrashing those Barbary savages," said Captain Forester. The retired hero of the Revolutionary War had spent most of his time losing money, drinking, and heaping praise on Aubert.

"At least it affords me a little time for the finer things," Aubert smiled. He swirled a glass of ten-year-old brandy under his nose, then took a sip. Dropping a stack of checks into the pot, he looked across the table at John. "Raise to twenty-five. What about it, lad?"

John sat up straight. Aubert usually bet aggressively against weak plays, often with nothing, but only stayed in a hand this long if he was strong. The lieutenant wasn't bluffing. John had to be careful.

The *Allegheny* commander must have read the hesitation on John's face. He added, "You might have made a fine midshipman on my vessel before your...unfortunate choices. But then, a merchant's son isn't a naval officer, and a dockside rogue is no brag player." A smug grin spread across Aubert's face.

John's upper lip twitched with anger. He yanked the entire wad of bills from his pocket and slammed it on the table. Sixty-four dollars. All he had left in the world.

"Mr. Sullivan, are you sure?" said Samuel Humphreys, the man to John's right. He was the twenty-five-year-old son of famous shipbuilder Joshua Humphreys, and the only gentleman at the table to show John any warmth. "There is no shame in stepping away with what you have left."

"Call," said John.

"What have you, then?" Aubert cocked his head. "A flush? A run I think." He exposed his best three cards: A king of diamonds. A king of clubs. A king of spades. "Will a prial do?"

John felt sick. A prial—three of a kind. The most rare and powerful hand in brag.

Aubert pulled the massive pile of checks, coins, and bills into an unruly heap. With all the mirth of a man bidding his friend farewell, Aubert said, "I'm glad my wife offered you a seat, Sullivan. You've been sporting company."

John stared at the pile, unable to move. His ace, king, and queen sprawled across the felt like corpses on a battlefield.

"Would you stay on as a spectator," said Aubert, "or have you something to barter for more checks?"

John reached into his pocket. He ran his thumb over his silver watch. "No." Barely above a whisper, he said, "Goodnight, gentleman." He stormed out of the gaming parlor.

###

John hurled his fist into a tree behind the Plover. Then again. And again. The fifth time, it left a bloodstain on the bark. Sparrows chirped and chickens clucked in the evening quiet. "Goddamnit," he breathed.

"Richard doesn't like to lose," said an urbane voice. "He also fails to realize he can."

The voice came from Dominique Dufort—or rather, Dominique *Aubert*—Melisande's sister. As she approached, John felt heat in his muscles. She walked with the confidence of a captain and the delicacy of an actress. In the year since they parted, she had traded center-laced jackets, leather breeches, and Iroquois moccasins for a dandelion dress, gold earrings, and a big diamond ring. He gawked at her slender curves.

"I know it isn't much comfort," Dominique added as she came alongside John, "but he went to great pains to defeat you in front of his friends."

She reached a hand towards John's battered knuckles. "Let me see."

John looked away. "Forget it."

"Don't be a child. Let me see." Her words carried wisdom beyond her twenty-eight years. As if she were a traveler on the Silk Road, resting at a tavern and trading stories. He did as she said. She felt along the finger bones and said, "Nothing fractured, I think. Don't know how you plan to swing swords and shoot muskets breaking yourself against trees."

"You didn't hear what it called me."

"Might have been the wind."

They shared a smile.

"Five years, Dominique. Five years at this one cause.

Every gamble, every hardship, every sacrifice to free what's left of my family. And it's all come to nothing." John looked at her. A few blonde strands escaped her ponytail and blew across her cheek. Her eyes were as blue as the bottom of the ocean. Desire flashed through him as he remembered the feeling of her skin against his. How he longed to hold her again. "It's cost me everything."

"I'm sorry, Sully," Dominique said, looking at him sincerely.

"No need to be sorry. I gambled. I lost. Nothing so fair as that."

"You've done more than anyone could have expected. Maybe some odds are just too long."

"I'm the one that escaped," insisted John. "Their freedom depended on me, and I failed them."

"I know what Melly would say to that. 'Quit mewling and have a chew.'"

John snickered. "Aye, she would."

"And for once I agree with my sister. Self-pity doesn't suit you."

John pulled the watch from his pocket. He flipped open the case and read the inscription. A few tranquil words from his mother's favorite play. They were John's daily call to arms. No matter how weary he got, how desperate to lay down his burdens, they always gave him the strength for one more step. One more fight.

Dominique reached for the timepiece, and John allowed the watch chain to slide out of his grasp.

"Still keeping your mother's watch," Dominique said. "Perhaps it's time to let it go."

"It's all I have left of her."

"Maybe that's why you lost."

"What?" John shook his head. "No. I got sloppy and

made a mistake."

"Your mistake is that you keep coming back to this city. You keep struggling. You keep planning. You keep holding on to the past. You never leave it all behind."

"You really want me gone that badly, huh?"

"Yes," she replied.

"I guess we parted on worse terms than I thought."

"'Draw for the ace, win with the deuce.' Isn't that what you like to say?"

"That's just gambler's nonsense," John snorted.

She flipped open the watchcase, read the inscription, and closed it again. "You've still got a deuce, Sully."

The two fell silent. A breeze whispered in the pine branches overhead. They were alone in the field of grass behind the Piping Plover and its neighbors on Market Street. The workers had trimmed the gardens, stabled the horses, and carried in the yield of ale from the brewhouse.

"Melly tells me you married," John said.

"Aye. The first day of spring."

"I meant to congratulate you. I'm happy for you."

Her eyes roamed his face. "You are?"

"Of course," John lied.

Another gust of wind rustled the tree leaves.

"How have you been finding, uh…marriage?" John asked.

"Well."

"Ah, good. That, uh…is good."

"It is."

"And Aubert?"

"Yes, he's my husband."

"Right. I mean—he treats you well?"

"Looking for a dragon to slay in my name, Sully?"

"I just meant—does he make you happy?"

"He loves me," sighed Dominique. "I know my past still bothers him, but I'm doing my best."

"There's nothing wrong with your past."

"Everything is wrong with my past."

John looked into her eyes. Behind her soft, petite features, he could see the ferocious resolve Aubert would never appreciate. "He doesn't know you. Not like I do."

"Unlike you, he was here."

John looked away.

"I had to make a choice, Sully," said Dominique. She handed the watch back to John, and he took it. "Now, so do you."

She gave him a faint smile, then headed back into the tavern.

John held up the watch. He stared at the silver, gleaming in the dusk.

John walked toward the Piping Plover with renewed purpose. A few moments later, he strode into the gaming parlor, the watch in hand. The men at the table stopped their conversations and looked at John. He pulled off his weathered jacket, slung it over a chair, and sat down.

"Mr. Sullivan," Aubert said in a regal voice. "Forget something?"

"As a matter of fact, I did." John tossed the watch onto the table. "Perhaps one of you gentlemen would be so kind as to credit me a few checks for good silver?"

Aubert smiled, blinking. He set his drink down. "I think we can oblige." Aubert dropped ten dollars of checks into a stack. He slid it smartly across the table to John.

John smiled. "My thanks, Lieutenant. Might I jump in now, or shall I wait for the deal?"

Aubert's smile became strained. "By all means. Forester, deal the lad in."

The old war hero shrugged his shoulders and began the deal.

"A delight to have you back, Mr. Sullivan," said Samuel Humphreys. "Good luck to you."

"Thank you, sir," John said. He took a slow deep breath. His hands trembled. He peered down at his cards.

"Now what could you mean by a bet like that?" said Lieutenant Richard Aubert. John privately celebrated his opponent's frustration.

Hours of attrition left circles under Aubert's eyes. Every time he failed to defeat John in a hand, the naval commander loosened another gold button on his navy coat. He burned through his pipe until he was packing new leaves on sooty resin. "Well, Sullivan, I suppose raising blind is a better strategy than another failed bluff. Unfortunately for you, I raise again." He picked up a stack of bills from the rail and said, "Your five…" Then, thumbing each crisp note into the pot, "…and ten more."

A few askance glances fell on John. Since his return, he had won every hand he chose to play. Sure, a few lucky draws helped. But his reads were exact, his bluffs believed, his traps unsuspected. Now, the son of a merchant—a dockside rogue—sat before the largest heap of money. Only Aubert still had a stack big enough to threaten. The lieutenant pursued victory as aggressively at the card table as at sea. John opened the current hand by betting without looking at his cards—"playing blind"—to throw his rival off balance. In theory, Aubert would likely have an average hand and be forced to fold to John's bets. The strategy would be repeated again and again, driving Aubert mad. Instead, John's dogged opponent raised, suggesting strong cards.

John wore a mask of indifference. But as he waited for each man to act, he privately cursed his bad luck. The point was to *appear* reckless, not to actually *be* reckless.

"We might as well play faro!" said Tappling, the owner of a small merchant fleet. He threw his cards away in disgust. One flipped over, exposing a six of diamonds to the room.

"Watch it there, Tappling!" Complained Captain Forester. The first big pot went to John the last time Tappling flashed an ace. Forester loomed over Aubert's left shoulder as he attempted to coach the younger man back to victory. With each passing glass of brandy, a few more white strands came loose from the captain's wig.

The action moved left to Commandant Pritchett. "I think it's good sport." He dropped a waterfall of coins into the pot.

"Good sport?" said Forester. "He plays like a child."

"I don't know," said Samuel Humphreys, leaning forward in his chair with both hands clasped under his chin. "Mr. Sullivan has played very well so far." John couldn't have chosen an admirer with more prestige. It was Samuel's father, Joshua Humphreys, who had built the United States Navy's six new frigates, including Philadelphia's own USS *United States*. Samuel Humphreys had himself designed USS *Philadelphia*. Despite John's private awe for the brilliant builder and his father, he bankrupted him all the same.

"His luck is out, and Lieutenant Aubert has him on the retreat," said the pudgy trader Martin Jameson, who had long since busted. The wealthy merchant moonlighted as Philadelphia's most prolific fence for smugglers, pirates, and thieves. But John could no more divulge Jameson's secrets than his own. Jameson sniffed. "This is what happens when you let a penny-stakes player from the docks into a *gentlemen's* game. If you'll excuse me, I've had my fill." On his way out of the parlor, he leaned close to John's ear. "Let's hope your luck holds, boy." With that, the sycophant left, and John considered it good riddance.

All eyes fell on John, awaiting his action. His heartbeat rose. He had bested Forester, Jameson, and the affable Humphreys. Tappling was still in but always folded easily. Pritchett threw money away cheerfully. But Aubert had enough skill and money to turn John's victory into defeat. Aubert chewed his pipe the way he always did when holding a powerful hand. John reached for his cards, ready to fold.

"Richard, *mon trésor.*" Dominique's voice rang like silver tapping crystal. Her floral perfume cut through the haze of smoke. Her dress rippled like a waterfall of gold. She circled the table to Aubert and slid a white-gloved arm across his shoulder. "How long must I lose my husband to this boring game?" she quipped.

The men replied with charmed laughter.

Captain Forester tried to smooth a strand of his wig and failed. "Forgive our boorishness, *madame.* The complexities of the game would escape you but suffice to say, your husband rules the table like Charlemagne reborn!"

"Your radiance is a welcome distraction," added Humphreys.

Dominique pretended to pout. "All this fuss over

faces painted on paper?"

Another laugh of delight.

Only Aubert appeared annoyed. "I shall come to you soon, *mon chaton*. In the meantime, I would ask you not to disturb our game." The lieutenant took up her hand and planted a kiss on her ring finger.

Eyes shifted awkwardly. Dominique's smile weakened a little. "Of course, darling," she said and pecked Aubert's cheek. With her lips on her husband, Dominique's eyes flashed to John for a heartbeat. Then she sauntered out of the room. Necks craned after her.

"Make the bet one hundred," said John.

Forester choked on a gulp of whiskey.

Humphreys shifted uncomfortably.

Tappling snorted.

"Well, I'm far too curious to fold *now*," said Commandant Pritchett. He gleefully paid the bet—more than a sailor earned in three months.

Aubert's teeth clenched on his pipe "As you wish, Sullivan. I raise." Aubert matched John's bet of one hundred from his bills on the table. For his raise, he reached into his pocket. He produced the silver watch and tossed it into the pot. "The value of this quaint little woman's watch. I was saving it for a special occasion."

The room chuckled.

"Go on then, love. Wind it up." Nora's words returning to John, from many years ago. He wanted to climb over the table and belt Aubert. Instead, he stamped on his own foot, focusing on the pain. His mother's last possession had bought him back into the game. He had looked for every chance to win it back, but Aubert never offered one. Now, Aubert's largesse was demeaning. When he looked at his cards, and in all likelihood found them

wanting, John would have to endure the loss of the watch all over again.

Aubert spoke through clenched teeth. "Well if you're not sure whether to bet, perhaps a peek at your cards…"

There was no choice now. John cupped his hands over his cards. He revealed each one-by-one. A three of spades. A jack of hearts. A two of spades. John's stomach tightened. *A draw for either a run or a flush.* He looked at the last card. One beautiful ace of spades.

And just like that, a running flush. The second most powerful hand in brag. Aubert could only beat John now with another prial, and it would require the hand of fate to duplicate such a miracle. But how to set the trap? How to appear to be a fool overplaying a bad hand?

"You don't seem happy with your draw," said Aubert. "Quaint watch. Shame to lose it."

John had him. Aubert knew what the watch meant to John, which meant John knew which tell would lure in Aubert. "Make the bet three hundred."

Tappling sighed and folded his arms. Humphreys leaned forward with a smile. Forester shook his head as he poured another whiskey. Pritchett paid the last of his money into a side pot.

"Clever fucking devil," Forester grumbled. "He's priced you out of seeing his cards. You either fold or cover the bet and show."

John smiled. "If Captain Aubert wants to borrow a few checks for his bet, I can spare them." Time to fake the tell. A little "fear of loss" should do the trick. John allowed his eyes to flash toward the watch, then back to Aubert. John thought he saw the slightest tick in Aubert's brow, but he couldn't be sure.

"I might think you were bluffing if I thought you a

fool," said Aubert. He stood up, picked up the brandy decanter, and walked to the window. He stared into the summer night as he poured. As he sipped, only the smoke curling up from his pipe broke the stillness. Outside, a drizzle thickened into rain. Market Street dissolved into mud. Wind battered the tavern's bird-shaped sign. The lieutenant returned to his seat and tapped his pipe on the rail.

"All right Sullivan," said Aubert. "Everything I've got, and I'll borrow what I owe to cover the rest."

"No need," said Forester. "I'll cover your bet. You're about to win, after all." Forester unbuckled a short, sturdy rapier, still in its sheath, and laid it on the table. Spirals of silver formed the basketwork. A gold sun formed the pommel. He added a matching naval dirk with a fleur-de-lis pommel. "The sword, *Roi* and the dagger, *Soleil*," he said. "Named after the Sun King himself. Fitting they should restore order to this table."

Aubert protested, "Your prizes from the HMS *Ernie*? Captain Forester…"

"I'm not letting this failed midshipman win and disgrace our table," growled the drunken captain. "Or the Navy. Certainly not days before we celebrate our country's birth. The *men* at this table have fought too hard."

Aubert looked at John. He turned over his cards. A four, a five, and a Queen—all diamonds. A flush. "To think, Sullivan. That old beaten watch almost saved you."

All eyes in the room turned on the brash youth, eager for the reply.

John broke into a grin.

Chapter 6

The Piping Plover Inn
Philadelphia, Pennsylvania
Friday, July 1st, 1803

After a week of sleepless attrition at every card table in Philadelphia, John stepped out of the Piping Plover Inn with a bag of wealth. The satchel hidden under his coat held all the money he needed to fund his rescue mission, and then some. His heart warmed with pride. And relief. He couldn't resist reaching into his coat pocket to feel the cold silver of his mother's watch. Tomorrow morning, he would read the inscription as he did every day.

He heard muffled bickering through the window of the gaming parlor.

"It was a lucky draw."

"He grifted you, Aubert!" accused Captain Forester.

"Me? You're the old fucking sod that covered the bet."

"He's got you there, Forester. Always blathering advice after you've been nipping at the brandy…"

"Oh, piss off, Pritchett. You nursed his bankroll like a great Irish tit!"

And on it went. John chuckled to himself. He drew his

rapier *Roi* and dirk *Soleil* in a single motion. He posed as if to lunge, feeling their balance in each hand. He admired their double edges and deadly points. For a moment, he was a boy again, fencing bridge trolls with a wooden sword.

John swung the rapier upright. "But I think I'll call you…*Ace.*" Then he flipped the dagger and held it by the blade. "And *Spade.*" He named his weapons after the card that won him the game. Smiling, he sheathed them both and started down Market Street.

John had to be careful. Years on the streets of Philadelphia taught him every trap that could part him from his winnings. The poor boy who lost his way home—and would pick a Samaritan's pocket. The drunk tramp seducing a man into an alley—where a man waited with a club. Or that eager night watchman who didn't mind extorting a tax from vagrants or other "undesirables." He carefully studied his surroundings. Green fields and tall trees lined blocks of red brick houses. A courier galloped by. A drunken reveler nodded off in a coach. Otherwise, the streets of western Philadelphia were deserted.

John ducked into an alley for a while, patiently waiting for any would-be followers to reveal themselves. A dog howled in the distance. Horse hooves sloshed through mud. John looked up to see the North Star adrift in the heavens. It had been a long time since he measured the Pole Star's altitude on a sextant. Too long. But soon he would be on the deck of the *Morrigan* and back where he belonged—at sea. Satisfied he wasn't being followed, John resumed his route to the riverfront.

At last, he sighted the candlelight in Mrs. McClintock's window. As a year of living on adrenaline came to an end, exhaustion landed on John like an anchor hitting the ocean floor. Soon he would be in his tiny attic room, rocking to sleep in a hammock. In the morning, he would fill his belly with all the biscuits and bacon he could eat. He couldn't wait to see Mrs. McClintock's face when he paid his debt like he was tipping a coachman. Distracted by his relief, he didn't hear the footsteps.

A figure charged out of the darkness and slammed a fist into his jaw. John struck back, but he was already staggering off balance. It felt like punching underwater. His fist hit nothing. Sensing men surrounding him, he reached for his rapier.

"John, please," a man cooed in a French-creole drawl. John recognized the French privateer, smuggler, and occasional pirate, Pierre Laffite. "That is not wise."

A taller, more muscular man grabbed John's sword arm. The attacker overpowered him and twisted his wrist behind his back. *Ace* fell harmlessly to the ground. A short, bony man held John by the other arm. The smaller assailant wore the deep lines of a man aged by the sea.

"Men are always most careless a few feet from their door. Don't you find that?" Laffite puffed on the long stem of a churchwarden pipe. The glow flickered over a black goatee and dark eyes. His coat, breeches, and tall hat were jet black. His cravat added a splash of bright red.

A third man approached with a lantern. John recognized the portly merchant from the brag game, Martin Jameson.

"Jameson. You fucking boot-licker." John clenched his teeth.

"Yes, our little man of the hour," Jameson crowed. He pulled *Spade* from its sheath and handed it to Laffite. "You really think a filthy orphan was going to waltz away with the wealth of his betters? Not a chance." He yanked John's satchel free and handed it to his employer.

"*Merci, Monsieur* Jameson. I see you two are already acquainted." Looking at the muscular man, Laffite said to John, "I don't think you've met Samson." Laffite nodded towards the bony one. "…And Renaud. They're quite unpleasant but well suited for this kind of work."

Laffite jingled the bag with a grin, the pipe pinched between his teeth. "Shall we take account?" He rummaged through the bills and coins. "Hmm. I see. Now then, John. Why did I first hear of this from Jameson's courier?"

"I didn't know you'd slithered out of your swamp."

"Such boorishness, *mon ami*. And after all my generosity?"

"That's half again whatever I cost you. Take your share, Laffite, and call us even."

"Ah, my friend, but interest accrues. I fear you haven't the head for business. Dallying on a debt has a cost. Particularly a debt of your kind. Our account is far from settled."

John slammed his head into the distracted Samson. His right arm loose, John sent his hardest hook straight into Renaud's nose. John felt the nose bone crunch under his knuckles. He scooped up *Ace* and tore off the sheath.

John froze where he crouched. The point of Laffite's sword hovered under his chin. A ray of lamplight refracted off the gold basket guard of the privateer's rapier. Laffite relaxed into his stance, his arm steady as a surgeon's. John's sword hovered a foot over the ground. Samson and Renaud rushed forward.

Laffite held up his hand, smoke curling off his pipe. The two men stopped short. Jameson skittered several feet beyond the range of John's lunge. Laffite said, *"Incroyable!* You kill one southern yokel in a pasture and think yourself a swordsman. How about it, John? If you think you're fast enough…" Laffite tapped John's chin with the flat of his blade.

The rain started again. John's legs burned as he crouched. His hair turned sodden and clung to his face. He relaxed his grip. He watched Laffite's eyes for a tick, a moment of distraction. He visualized how to attack: Swipe Laffite's sword aside, then side-step, and end with a lunge. He could do it. He was fast enough.

Like a mother coaxing a toddler to walk, Laffite said, "Come then." Another tap. Drops rang on Laffite's blade like a bell.

Kaitlin whispered in John's memory. *I've still got him, Johnny. The Lion. He'll keep us safe.*

John squeezed rage and despair into the hilt. With the slightest twitch of his arm, *Ace* sang through the air. But Laffite's sword darted away. *Ace* missed.

Laffite cuffed John's left cheek with the acorn-shaped pommel of his sword. John sprawled in the mud.

Samson moved in and kicked *Ace* away. Renaud kicked John hard in the small of his back. Samson kicked John's stomach again and again. Renaud threw punches at random. Laffite calmly sheathed his sword and sniffed. He cupped his hand over his pipe and blew on the damp tobacco, trying to relight it.

Laffite looked down at John. "That was not your finest effort, John. But what do you expect? Shit swordsmen, the Spanish. Should have chosen a Frenchman for your teacher."

Laffite pulled a red silk kerchief from his coat pocket. He dabbed at the blood near John's left eye. "Awe. Look at this. What a shameful state…easy, now John."

"You still have a play here," said Laffite as he concluded his ministrations. "Thanks to your feud with the Tindalls in Richmond, I've lost my business in the Chesapeake to Fernando Pavia. He's bad for business. You're going to make that right."

John coughed flecks of blood. Several inches away from his chest, he saw a silver glint. His mother's watch had fallen out of his pocket.

"The Basque's have attacked American riverboats, in addition to smuggling over the Florida border. I want the location of their ill-gotten goods."

"Pavia's no river pirate. You'd have to frame him."

Laffite patted John's shoulder. "You let *me* worry about the details, John. I just need a location."

"I don't…know where his cache is…" John rasped. It was half a lie. John knew every cove Pavia used on the Delaware. He could use Godfried's nose and the scent on Pavia's kerchief to find the exact one.

"Of course not. But you know Pavia. He is your old mentor, no? Use a little of your mick charm to get it out of him. Three days from tonight, I will look for you at Jameson's warehouse with the information I want. If I have to delay my departure for New Orleans and hunt you down, I will be terribly put out."

"Fuck off, Laffite. I won't help you get my friends hanged."

Laffite stood. He gestured to Renaud, who handed over a thin, finger-length stick—a spill—and opened the glass door of his lantern. Laffite calmly lit the spill, sheltering it from the rain with the brim of his hat. He lit the bowl of the churchwarden.

Taking a puff, Laffite said, "I hear Henry Tindall was

very fond of the brother you killed. I could hand you over to him tonight and earn a handsome reward. I admit it's tempting. But I have a forgiving heart. This is your last chance. I know you'll help me take back what's mine.

"Of course if you don't, you won't be the only one meeting an unpleasant end. I haven't forgotten the part of the Duforts in your betrayal. Aubert's good behavior has kept those pretty sisters safe for now—but that can change. *Merde,* who am I forgetting? Ah yes, your other friend—the black fellow. The Tindalls have a long memory. The bounty for all of you is sure to be high."

John coughed. Ropes of blood hung from his nose. He reached for the watch. Laffite snatched it up by the chain.

"Fond of this piece? I don't know why. Shit for taste, the bitch who bought it. Keep it." Laffite dropped the watch in the mud. John could hear its gentle ticking. "Three days, John." Laffite smiled and walked away, Renaud and Jameson in tow. Samson picked up *Ace* before joining the others.

John writhed onto his hands and knees. He crawled toward the watch. The lid of the hunter-case lay open. He closed his hand around it, touching the words etched in silver.

"Mr. Sullivan?" Cried Mabel McClintock. "*John!*"

John heard footfalls coming towards him. He blinked blood out of his eyes. Pain radiated from the pit of his stomach to his extremities. His mother's watch ticked softly as he slipped into darkness.

Chapter 7

The Port of Tunis, Barbary Coast
Monday, July 30th, 1798

For weeks, John and the other slaves slept, ate, and shit in the hold of the *Dolorous Fénnid*. All the while, tiny bugs crawled over his skin, through his hair, and into every crevice. He scratched the bites until they bled. Rats brushed against him in the pitch darkness. He could rarely sleep, and time was impossible to tell. But nothing was worse than the hunger.

Once a day, a crewman would bring down a bucket of rusk biscuits doused with water and vinegar. The man would silently hand out one piece to each slave, never talking to them, never looking at them. John always offered half of his biscuit to Kaitlin, but she always said no. When the hunger pangs didn't overpower him, he would insist. When they did, he would devour every crumb and weevil, hating himself for his weakness.

When *Re'is* Naim's crew finally dragged John and the other slaves out of the hold, John drank in the sun and sea air, thinking his prayers were answered. But then the pirates shackled a four-foot chain to each slave's ankle, which dragged like an anchor. Using the bilge pumps, they hosed the stench off their prisoners and loaded them onto a flat barge. They rowed them across a lake stinking of rotten eggs. John looked down at the rusty water and shuddered—if he went overboard, the chain would drag him straight to the bottom. The limestone buildings and minarets of Tunis rose from the harbor to the foothills. On the eastern shore, yellow pillars and arches crumbled in the desert—all that remained of ancient Carthage. A cormorant perched on a piling and spread its velvety black wings. It peered at John through a single ruby eye.

When the barges reached the docks, the crew herded the slaves up winding streets, through angry crowds hurling epithets and rotten food. The miles-long march in the hot sun ended in the throne room of the bey's palace. Three corsair captains stood before Bey Hammuda, ruler of Tunis, and presented a total of fifty-one captured slaves. They were mostly bedraggled men, with a handful of women, boys, and girls. All thirsty, sunburned, and exhausted.

Prussian blue tiles blanketed the marble walls of the palace. Elegant spiraling letters gleamed on the columns. The Janissary soldiers stood like pillars around the room, muskets propped on their shoulders, scimitars sheathed at their belts.

The bey gloated in the Turk language, smiling proudly from his plush couch. His silk cloak and turban were studded with jewels of every kind. He clutched his beard as he examined his shackled prizes. He exchanged a few words with *Re'is* Naim and the other captains.

"Yussef," said the bey to a lavishly dressed young man beside his throne. He uttered a few words John couldn't catch.

The young man said in English, "Hammuda Bey has

made his first selections." Yussef looked more like a trophy than a minister, dressed in iridescent gossamer, jeweled rings, and golden arm circlets. His slender muscles gleamed with oil. He walked the line of slaves, picking one of every six.

Those selected were immediately dragged away, among them Patrick, the boatswain's son. Any that resisted caught a blow from the Janissaries.

Hammuda looked at the *Wandering Hart* captives and asked a question.

Looking in Declan's direction, Yussef said in English, "Hammuda Bey asks which of you was the captain of the captured vessel."

Declan cleared his throat. He licked his peeling lips. "I—I was the captain of the captured ship."

Hammuda asked another question. Again, Yussef translated. "'The man you serve, is he of noble birth? How many ships does he own?'"

"No, Your Highness. I was the owner of the *Wandering Hart*, and four other vessels."

The bey spoke again, and laughter broke out among the pirates and soldiers.

Yussef translated, grinning with amusement. "'You own a fleet, yet you sail with your woman? Are you a fool?'"

Declan fumbled for words. He looked at Nora, and their eyes reached for each other as if from opposite sides of a chasm.

"'Do you hold noble title?'" the bey continued through his translator.

"No, I do not," admitted Declan.

"'Your family—how wealthy are they?'"

"They are…of modest means, but I can sell my ships

and my properties. My brother can send you tribute."

"'Why do you sail with your woman?'"

"I…We sailed as a family because the sea…" Declan's eyes settled on the floor, gazing into an abyss only he could see. "It was our dream."

The bey knit his brows at Yussef, waiting for the translation. When he heard it, his face lit up.

"'Perhaps you should have dreamt of gardening,'" said the bey.

Another round of laughter.

"'You, your urchin pup, and your woman'" the bey continued, "'I grant to my loyal re'is, Ilyas Naim for his glorious victory in the name of God.'"

"Thank you, Hammuda Bey!" said Naim with a bow. "You honor me."

Hammuda looked at Kaitlin. "'The girl I take for my seraglio. I will offer her at eight thousand piasters.'"

The soldiers moved towards Kaitlin.

"Wait," Nora pleaded. "Please, let me go with her. She doesn't understand…"

"Mama!" Kaitlin cried as the guards pulled her out of Nora's arms. "Mama! I want to stay with you. Da!"

John started forward, ready to strangle the soldiers with his own chain, but a hulking hand seized his shoulder. The point of a blade twisted against his back. He felt hot breath on his ear. It was Hamit, the pirate Janissary that had killed Isaac.

Hamit whispered, "Do it, boy. Give me a reason to kill you. You'll die faster than your brother."

John ground his teeth. He wanted to murder Hamit. He wanted to strangle Yussef. Bludgeon the garish, gloating bey—anything to protect his sister. But he was afraid. He was unable to act, unable to think. He watched

Kaitlin sob and plead as they took her away.

"A shame," said Hamit as he released John.

The bey dismissed the audience, and John could hear the distant cries of his sister echoing through the palace.

"Oi, she's a pretty wench!"

"Come here, cherry, darling!"

"She must have been lovely on her wedding night."

Soldiers led Declan, Nora, and John down a long corridor. Catcalls and unwashed bodies overwhelmed John's senses. Slaves taunted them in a dozen different languages. Pillars and iron bars divided the enclosures of the *bagno*—the Tunisian slave pens. Filthy hands reached for Nora, a finger occasionally managing to brush her arm.

They can't put her in with them! John panicked.

At the north end of the *bagno*, they came to a cell with solid walls and a wide, barred gate. The soldiers flung it open and thrust each of the Sullivans inside. When the gate screeched shut, John glanced around. Nothing but the same sand-colored brick walls and a bare floor.

After the three of them paced the dungeon room quietly for a moment, Declan spoke. "Are you all right, Nora?" He reached out to console his wife.

She stepped back, a hand over her mouth. "Don't you touch me. I don't want comfort. Not while our baby is in danger. I want a plan to save her, to escape."

"A plan?" Declan shook his head as if bewildered.

"To get our daughter out of that harem!" Nora snapped.

"I'll get word to my brother as soon as I can, and I'll

go to the English embassy. I'll seek help from the Trinitarians. Whatever it takes."

"Begging? Charity?" cried Nora. "Katie is a slave in a *harem*! My God, Declan, what are they doing to her? What is *he* doing to her? To our baby?" Nora's composure cracked, and she began to cry.

"I know!" shouted Declan. "God, don't you think I know? It's all I can fucking think about. For Christ's sake, Nora!"

John felt a surge of adrenalin. "Mam's right, Da. We can't abandon Katie. We need to fight."

Declan shot an index finger at them. "No! Don't even think it, and keep your bloody voices down. You think you're the first slaves to dream of escape? They'd *love* to beat a lesson into a troublemaker, and I won't give them a reason to hurt either of you."

"You should listen to your husband," said an aged voice.

John, Declan, and Nora turned around. A white-bearded African stood at the bars of their cell. He wore a long, sleeveless tunic. His skin was stretched thin over sinewy muscles. He unlocked the gate and stepped inside.

"The *bagno* is easy to escape," said the man. "But the Janissaries patrol the streets at night. Slaves are easy to spot. Even if you made it to the harbor, how would you steal a barge? And if a barge got you across the lake, what ship could you board? Any ships not going *al corso* have their spars and sails stored under lock and key. To say nothing of sneaking into a bey's seraglio to steal his prized possession. Not a good plan."

Nora fell to her knees. "Please, sir, it was a slip of the tongue. Please, we beg your forgiveness."

The man waved his hand. "Rise, rise. Do not kneel to

me. You may indulge in your little fantasy. I might care if it had the slightest chance of success."

"Who are you?" Declan asked.

"My name is Ibrahim. I am the guardian *bachi* of this *bagno*, a broker in the *bastedan,* and like you, a slave."

"Please," Nora implored. "Can you help my daughter?"

"Your daughter is in the safest place she could be, for the moment."

The Sullivans stared at Ibrahim, puzzled.

Ibrahim chuckled under his breath. "I see you have not been in Tunis long. Hammuda Bey has no interest in your daughter—or any daughter. His foreign minister, Yussef Sapatapa, is his lover."

"His lover?" echoed Nora.

"He's a…lover of…?" puzzled Declan.

"Men," Ibrahim added helpfully. "The bey wants to sell or ransom the girl. Your daughter's virtue is intact, for the moment."

Declan collapsed to the floor, head in hands. Nora sighed, her hand on her heart. John closed his eyes.

"'Our dream,'" said John, quoting Declan.

"What?" Declan said.

"'Our dream.' That's what you said to the bey, Da. 'The sea was our dream.' But it was never Katie's dream, was it? It was *your* dream. Kaitlin always hated the sea. It frightened her. Your dream killed Isaac, and it destroyed Katie's life." John's voice cracked with anger. Tears brimmed in his eyes.

Declan stared at John with hurt in his eyes, as if his son had stabbed him.

"John," Nora said, trying to calm him.

"It's your fault!" John shouted, the tears falling now.

"You lied. You gave up the ship, and you're giving up again. You've killed my brother. You've made my sister a slave!"

"John," Nora chided. "This isn't your father's fault."

"It is!" cried John. He took a step toward his father. "You should have fought."

"John, stop!" Nora gasped.

"Listen to me," said Ibrahim to all of them. "This will be the hardest night of your life. I have been where you are. I've known despair you can't imagine. It will get worse. Then, in time, it will get better. You will come to accept this fate." Ibrahim fetched a bundle outside the cell door and tossed it to Declan. "Blankets and provisions, but I will expect repayment. For now, lie down. Rest. Tomorrow, you begin earning your keep."

"Thank you," Declan said numbly.

After Ibrahim was gone, Nora took John's arm and led him to a corner of the cell. "Here, love," she said. "Sit down."

John obeyed, surrendering to his exhausted body. Nora sat with him, holding him close. John had not slept on his mother's shoulder in more years than he could remember. But feeling her warmth, her soft touch, her strength, he dropped all pretense of adulthood. He leaned against her, his eyes drooping.

"It's all right, my handsome man of the sea." She lay a hand on his head.

John couldn't understand where she found the strength. All around the prison, there were odd sounds—banging, thudding, and clattering. Occasionally, a voice would shout or cry out. Always John could hear the pitiful, quiet sobbing of a solitary voice. Whether man or a woman, child or adult, he didn't know. He was so afraid—for Katie, for Nora, for himself, for his brother's immortal soul. But in this moment, Nora shined on him like the beacon of a lighthouse.

"I'm the one," John murmured, another tear running off his chin.

"What, love?" Nora said.

"I told Katie the Lion would protect her."

Declan looked over at John. "The 'Lion?'"

"I told her everything would be all right." John's eyes slipped closed. "I'm the liar."

Chapter 8

Mrs. McClintock's Water Street Lodging
Philadelphia, Pennsylvania
Friday, July 1ˢᵗ, 1803

Dominique Aubert's left cheek throbbed. Her yellow dress was soaked and splashed with mud. Threads of hair clung to her face. She stood hugging herself on the porch of Mrs. McClintock's Water Street Lodging. The rain dribbled on her through the ragged awning.

Mrs. McClintock opened the door. She was a stout old woman with white curly hair. At the sight of Dominique, she touched her chest. She said in her Scottish accent, "Dominique, love. Are you all right?"

"Can I come in?"

"O' course, dearie." Mrs. McClintock gently took Dominique's arm and ushered her in. "You'll take ill, standing out in the rain like that."

The warmth of Mrs. McClintock's parlor poured over Dominique. A pair of older gentlemen sat by the fire, smoking their pipes. A trio of young men played a game of dice at the table. They all looked in Dominique's direction. She was used to carnal looks from men—that was nothing new—but recently, she noticed something different in their eyes.

Before Aubert, when she dressed like a frontiersman, it felt like swatting away dogs begging for scraps. Men looked at anything feminine with rabid hunger when they were weeks away from the nearest fort. After Aubert reconnected her with French culture, however, something changed. He filled her wardrobe with tailored dresses, corrected her lost accent, imported fine cosmetics from Marseille, and introduced her to ladies with impeccable etiquette. When the last frontier mud was gone, men continued to lust for her with one crucial difference. Now they tried to hide it.

Mrs. McClintock gently touched Dominque's left cheek. "Oh, what happened here?"

Dominique looked at her but didn't answer.

Realization came into Mrs. McClintock's eyes. "This way, love." She wrapped an arm around Dominique and showed her into the kitchen.

Dominique could smell the thyme, marjoram, and garlic Mrs. McClintock used in her roasted chicken supper. The cooking hearth cast flickering shadows. The five branches of a candelabrum lit up the bench in the center. Flour covered the table. A roll of biscuit dough sat next to a jar of honeysuckle jam. Dominique leaned on the edge. She didn't speak.

After a moment, Mabel asked, "You walked all the way here in the rain?"

Dominique nodded. It hadn't occurred to her how long of a walk it actually was. She felt carried through the streets like driftwood in a stream.

"What happened, love?"

"Nothing, I just…I just needed to see a friend."

Mrs. McClintock laid a hand on Dominique's. "You've

come to the right place."

Dominique smiled weakly. Rain pattered on the roof. The dying fire crackled.

"Well, then, let me find you some dry clothes. You can stay in my room tonight."

Before Mrs. McClintock could walk away, Dominique said, "Richard didn't take his loss well."

"Oh?"

"He had a bottle of brandy at brag. After the game, he had another."

"I see," said Mabel quietly.

"We…argued."

"What about?"

"It was my fault."

"What was?"

"John Sullivan. He wanted a seat at the brag game, and I talked Richard into letting him join. Serves me right. That's how it is with Sully—you always think he means it when he asks for 'one last favor.' He completely humiliated Richard in front of his friends. Richard thinks I conspired against him."

"Men and their bloody gambling—they can never leave their dicks off the card table."

Dominique chuckled, even though she was holding back tears. She wondered why she hadn't come to visit Mrs. McClintock in so long.

The boarding house proprietor caressed Dominique's cheek. "Dominique, did he do this?"

Dominique felt a jet of pain and shuddered. "I'm fine, Mabel. I'm not afraid of my husband. I've dealt with far worse on the frontier."

"This isn't the frontier. This is your home. This is the man who took an oath to care for you."

"And he does. In every way imaginable. He sacrifices his own reputation to protect Melisande and Grey Feather. If he went after the Laffites' smuggling enterprise, Pierre Laffite would retaliate against my brother and sister. He's given me back the life that was stolen from me. Reminded me where I come from. He didn't deserve what happened tonight." Dominique trailed off.

Mrs. McClintock gently squeezed Dominique's shoulder. "Dearie, you've nothing to feel ashamed of. He was beaten at cards, not pissed on in a pillory."

As they stood in silence, Dominique noticed the basin sitting on the table for the first time. Looking closely in the dim light, she realized the water was murky. A rag with red splotches lay next to a bloody stitching needle. "What's this? Was someone hurt?"

Mrs. McClintock sighed. "Aye. Come. Let's get you dry and into a nightgown."

Dominique followed Mrs. McClintock upstairs to her bedroom. Neither of them spoke as Dominique shed her dress and donned dry clothes. She sat at the vanity and let Mrs. McClintock clean her face with a damp cloth. The lady of the boarding house hummed an old Scottish lullaby as she brushed Dominique's hair.

Several minutes later, Dominique stood in the doorway of the small attic room where John Sullivan slept. He lay in a hammock strung between the beams of the A-frame roof. Rain drizzled down a small circular window above him. The space was more like a closet than a room. Barely enough room was left for John's coat, satchel, and a bottle of rum in the corner. Two candlestick nubs and a pewter cup sat on the floor below him.

John tossed in his sleep. "Katie...no... Katie..." he whimpered.

"I found him in the street," said Mrs. McClintock from behind Dominique. "Someone beat the shite out of him. Robbed him."

"No...Don't touch her..." John moaned.

Dominique walked over to him. His hair was matted with sweat. His right eye looked as red and swollen as a strawberry. Mabel had sewn three stitches into his left eyebrow. A clump of blood bubbled in his nostril. The blanket had slipped below his navel. Purple and green bruises marred his chest. The muscles of his waist convulsed in his delirium. "How long has he been like this?" Dominique asked.

"Hours. He keeps calling out that name. 'Katie.'"

"His little sister."

"Funny. I read the pamphlet many times. She was never mentioned in his ordeal. And he never talks about her."

"The Barbary Pirates took her as a slave with his family, but he left her out of the published account."

"Why?"

"I don't know. He was very drunk the night he told me. He rarely speaks of her."

Dominique ran a finger along his prickly stubble to the slight dimple below his lips. Sweat beaded on his muscular body. The memory of a summer night flashed in her mind. The two of them sitting on a rickety fisherman's jetty, dipping toes in the water. Fireflies over the pond. Whispering reeds. A symphony of singing frogs. The breeze cooling the mist on their faces. The taste of tobacco and blackberries as she kissed him. Their hearts beating against one another.

"I'll give you some time alone," Mrs. McClintock said.

Dominique pulled her hand away from John. "No, Mabel, that's all right. I'm feeling rather tired. I think I'd like to go to bed if that's all right."

"Of course. Go on. I'll look after him a while longer."

Dominique stood up and turned towards the door.

"Dom…" John murmured.

Dominique stopped and looked over her shoulder. For a moment, she thought he woke up, but his eyes were closed. He continued tossing and turning. Before she could leave the room, Mrs. McClintock took her hand.

"Sweet dreams, love."

Dominique hesitated. Like a sheet of ice on a frozen shore, the hurt within her broke loose. Her chin quivered. She tried to stop the tears, but they spilled out anyway. She submerged into Mrs. McClintock's arms.

"Oh, you're all right, dearie," Mrs. McClintock soothed. She stroked Dominique's back like a mother comforting a daughter. "It's going to be all right."

Chapter 9

Mrs. McClintock's Water Street Lodging
Philadelphia, Pennsylvania
Saturday, July 2nd, 1803

The scent awoke him. John pried his crusted eyes open. In the darkness, only the drops on the window announced the rain. A lightning strike of pain followed every movement of his ribs. How long had he slept? Horses clip-clopped in the street outside, suggesting early evening. But Laffite's attack had come near midnight. John realized he had slept through a whole night and the following day. After a few tender stretches, he half climbed, half fell out of his hammock. As he crawled to his feet, groaning in pain, he inhaled. It was *her* scent. Like orchids. Had Dominique been here? He shook his head. She had a life now and better things to do than call at a seedy boarding house.

A few minutes later, John limped off Mrs. McClintock's porch onto Water Street. In the summer heat, rain like bathwater came down in sheets. John turned south, clutching his side. After sloshing through the mud for half a mile, his muscles warmed up and he could walk upright. After another half-mile, he sensed someone watching him. Following. He spun around. An empty street. Rain steaming on the lampposts. Was that a shadow on Second Street? No. He decided it was the swaying of a poplar and limped on.

By the time John stood outside the door of the Sawduster Tavern, he was soaked. He approached the uneven glass window by the door. He looked in on the silhouettes rippling through the light. An Irishman was an unusual traveler here. Built entirely by Philadelphian Negroes, this public house provided members of their community a welcome place to find news, work opportunities, and leisure. The Sawduster's proximity to the waterfront made it a popular haunt for African sailors, shipbuilders, and dockworkers. A fiddle warbled a somber melody. The instrument was a Norwegian Hardanger fiddle—rare in the Americas. No one played it more beautifully than Ethan Auldon.

A fife joined the fiddle. Then a pair of hands patting a kettledrum. Ethan sang the melody:

Down yonder green valley, where streamlets meander,
When twilight is fading I pensively rove
Or at the bright noontide in solitude wander,
Amid the dark shades of the lonely ash grove;

There was a time when John couldn't fall asleep unless his mother sang *The Lonely Ash Grove* to him. As he got older, he stopped asking for her lullabies. On a lark, she would offer to sing, and he would say no. It didn't occur to him that she might lament her boy no longer needed her songs.

That changed on John's first night alone in Philadelphia. After his escape from Barbary slavery, he found himself soaked and shivering on a night much like tonight. Crouched under an alley doorway, he sang it to himself over and over. Even now, he would have given anything to hear his mother sing it again.

Down yonder green valley, where streamlets meander,
When twilight is fading I pensively rove
Or at the bright noontide in solitude wander,
Amid the dark shades of the lonely ash grove;

John entered the taproom, greeted by the aroma of spilled ale and buttered rum pudding. Sage and rosemary dried over a crackling hearth. Spreads of chicken and dumplings, fresh bread, and cabbage with onions covered the tables. Mothers fed toddlers on their knees, groups of children huddled over games, and young lovers courted on the dance floor. As John edged around the crowd for a view of the players, he ducked under low wooden beams.

There was a man on the drum, a man on the fife, and Ethan Auldon on the Hardanger fiddle. They played next to the red brick mantle in the northwest corner. Ethan's bow glided over the Norwegian instrument. Its unique resonating strings richened the sound, reminding John of the folk music he heard as a boy. A man of eighteen, Ethan had chiseled cheekbones and dark stubble around his chin. His brows knit fiercely over his eyes. His vocals filled every corner of the room. He had the attention of more than a few young women.

My lips smile no more, my heart loses its lightness;
No dream of the future my spirit can cheer.
I only can brood on the past and its brightness
The dear ones I long for again gather here.

A strange calm fell over the room. Children ceased their frolicking. Sailors forgot their drinks. The barmaid mopped the same spot over and over.

The ash grove, the ash grove, again is my home.

The fife fell quiet. The drumbeat stopped. The last draw of Ethan's bow faded. Ethan smiled with big cinnamon eyes. Applause roared through the room. John stared, still lost in the nostalgia of the song. The pain had subsided as John listened to the music, but now he felt it scraping again like a blade.

"Beautiful, lads," shouted a young man at the bar. "But let's have a jig!"

"Aye!" cried another. "Play *Jenny's Lucky Penny*!"

"*The Summer Step*!" said another.

The drummer and fife player smiled, drinking in the cheers. But Ethan walked towards the crowd and handed his Hardanger and bow to an older man.

John felt something strike his leg. He spun to find a little boy—eight or nine—had slapped him. The boy looked up at John, eyes wide, then darted off. There were more than a few curious glances in John's direction. He thought he caught a woman around his age staring at him—the barmaid—but when he looked over she busied herself with collecting a tray of cups.

John grew anxious. The Auldons had taken him in a long time ago, but that was the past. He might as well be interrupting a family at dinner to sell snake oil. He turned back for the door.

"John!" Ethan called out. "John Sullivan!"

Considering how they last parted, John thought about stealing away while he could. Instead, he turned around. Ethan pushed through the crowd towards him.

Ethan stopped short. He looked at John slack-jawed. "John. What happened?"

For some reason, John smiled sheepishly. "Ethan— oh. Just a little trouble on the road. Nothing I couldn't handle." He reached out for a handshake.

But to John's surprise, Ethan pulled him into an embrace, wet clothes and all. "On your feet again. I knew you would be. It's good to see you again, mate."

After so long on the frontier, so many years removed from his family, Ethan's arms felt like a brother's. Like a soothing balm. A moment longer and John feared he would break down. He drew away, grasping for composure. "Aye. I've missed you, mate. Playing as beautifully as ever. I knew you would be."

The two were drawing a few curious looks—it had been a while since John set foot in the Sawduster Tavern. Ethan said, "There, the table in the corner. Let's get you some food and get you dry."

Twenty minutes later, John sat near the hearth, both hands around a flagon of ale. The Sawduster's pudding bubbled in a pot. The warmth of the embers chased the last moisture from John's hair. He wore one of Ethan's cotton shirts and a pair of his breeches—both a bit long on him. The lateness of the evening cleared out most of the families. A few clusters of patrons drank ale or played cards.

"Here, dear," said the barmaid. She laid a gentle hand on his back and slid a heaping bowl of dumplings in front of him. A hunk of bread soaked in the gravy. "There's more where that came from."

It was more hospitality than John deserved after so long away, but his growling stomach disagreed. "Thank you, very kindly."

She handed him a poultice. The pungent scent of mint and lavender tingled in his nose. "This will help with the swelling. Hold it here." She pressed it to John's temple.

John flinched at the pain. The young woman looked familiar—probably a member of Ethan's church, St. Thomas. As he reached for the poultice, their hands met. It had been a long time since he felt the touch of a beautiful woman. Their eyes came together. He felt a flutter of mutual allure. They exchanged a tentative smile. The firelight set her amber eyes aglow. "Thank you. It helps."

"You're welcome, John." Her hand slipped away. She walked toward the bar before John could ask her name.

A small paper pouch landed on the table by John's bowl. "Compliments of the house," said Ethan as he sat down across from his friend. "But you ought to give up the stuff. Can't be good for the humors."

"You ought to give up hounding me," John teased. He unfolded the pouch and inhaled the tobacco's hickory scent. "Can't be good for your humor."

"Blackens the teeth. Puts off the ladies."

"Whiskey cleans them. And I prefer ladies who chew."

"And smoke. Smuggle. Steal. Swing war clubs." Ethan grinned.

John grinned back. He used his bread to scoop up a big mouthful of stew.

For a moment, Ethan watched him eat. "I was wondering when you'd come by." As if to answer the question in John's eyes, Ethan said, "Mother still has tea with Mrs. McClintock on Thursdays. No secret survives those meetings."

John's chewing slowed a moment. What could he say? That he thought Ethan would never forgive him for backing out of their plan to join the Navy? That if Ethan knew the whole truth about the Tindalls, he'd never forgive him? He bit off a large chunk of bread and shrugged his shoulders.

"You don't need to stay at Mrs. McClintock's," said Ethan. "You'll always have a home here."

"I might have come by sooner," John smacked around a mouthful of bread, "but I thought you'd be off fighting the Barbary Pirates by now."

"I could say the same of you."

John didn't answer. Instead, he sopped up the last bits in his bowl.

Ethan looked ruefully at the fire. "Dr. Cowdery of the *Philadelphia* was impressed by my medical knowledge. All those years of study with the Bartons and doctoring folks around here… I guess I picked up some skill. He offered me a berth as a surgeon's mate."

"Surgeon's mate?" John smiled. "Ethan, that's great."

Ethan snorted. "Yeah, grand. Until Captain Bainbridge said he'd never hear of a Negro apprenticing to a surgeon on his ship. Wasn't 'proper' he said."

"Ethan…I'm sorry. Bainbridge is a fool."

"I knew it was too much to hope. Dr. Cowdery's been slipping me books and teaching me what he can—at least until the *Philadelphia* leaves dry dock. He says he may get the captain to change his mind. It's a kind lie."

They drank in silence for a moment.

When he had a good wad of tobacco in his lip, John spoke again. "I came to say goodbye, Ethan."

"You walked a long way in the rain to say goodbye."

"Some things won't keep till morning."

"Where are you going?"

"Ireland. First thing tomorrow, I'll declare my mother lost at sea. Most of my inheritance will go to pay off a ruthless smuggler and pirate, and what's left will go to my corrupt uncle's political schemes. And I will never see these shores or my family again."

"It's not like you to give up so easily."

John spat a joyless laugh. "I don't dare imagine giving up with difficulty."

"Is there no other way?"

"I've lost everything, Ethan. Pierre Laffite has left me no choice. I either give my uncle what he wants, and pay Laffite off, or I betray *Comandante* Pavia just to keep a small inheritance. I can't do that to Pavia. Not after all he's done for me. And for you."

"Aye," Ethan agreed. "Can't say I like that idea. But either way, you don't have to leave Philadelphia. You can stay with the Auldons until you're back on your feet."

John shook his head. "Your family gave me a home, and I squandered it. I don't deserve your kindness."

"Bullshit. Of course you do. You took a bullet from Clyde Tindall. Saved me from Whitlock. I'll be buying you ales for a while. And anyway, kindness is ours to give."

"It was nothing you haven't done for me. You don't owe me anything."

"I owe you everything."

John felt a stab of guilt in his stomach. He wanted to come clean. Tell Ethan the rest of what happened. Instead, he drowned it in another gulp of ale.

"Tripoli is still at war with the United States," Ethan continued. "What the Barbary Pirates did to your family—it's been going on for centuries. We could enlist like we planned. Fight slavery side by side."

"Always the revolutionary, eh? Sorry, Ethan, but there's no fighting the way the world is. Men like Laffite, Whitlock, Tindall, Bey Hammuda—they'll always exist. Joining the Navy won't change that."

"You're wrong, John. My father lived to see the Gradual Abolition Act. The day is coming when there will be no slaves in the Commonwealth. The world is changing. We must carry the truth that 'all men are created equal' in our hearts. It's a truth we must all fight for."

"But you said Bainbridge wouldn't make you surgeon's mate. And I lost my midshipman's berth when I got wounded. What would we do?"

"Swab decks. Trim the mains'ls. Man the guns. *What we can*. Forget our old berths—call this a re-berth!"

John smiled in spite of himself. "It's a fine idea. And there's no man I'd rather swab decks with. But I never wanted to go to war. I wanted to save my family."

Ethan stared into his own tankard. "Yeah. 'A fine idea.' I suppose too much has changed."

The drummer stumbled out of the crowd and leaned on Ethan. "Come on, Auldon," he said, spitting and blustering. "One more song. A good one this time!"

Ethan laughed and shoved him away. "Christ, Bridges. Keep that breath away from candles. Go on, now. I'm visiting with an old friend."

John stood up. "I was about to leave. I don't want to keep you."

Bridges crowed with delight. "Good. I was tired of all that Irish wailing." He hurried off to his drum.

"I suppose there's no changing your mind." Ethan came around the table to meet John. "I shall miss you, my friend."

"And I you, mate." They shook hands. "Thank you. For everything."

It felt as though there was so much more to say. Ethan nodded and took his Hardanger from the next table. The fiddle came to life with a pleasant tune. John watched for a moment, then turned toward the fire. He pulled Pavia's kerchief out of his pocket. He examined the castle crest on a field of red. He could use it, with Godfried's nose, to find Pavia's secret cache. To betray a mentor and at least keep a little inheritance. John looked through waves of heat rising off coals. No. He wouldn't destroy a good man just to keep a forlorn hope alive. His hand hovered over the fire, ready to let it burn.

"My baby can't say no to you, can he?" said a woman's voice.

John pulled his hand back, startled. He looked to his left as Grace Auldon, Ethan's mother, came alongside him. She stood still and upright as a marble statue. She watched her son's performance with a serene smile. A few spots of gray dotted her hair, mostly covered by a shawl. She looked at John, her tea-colored eyes filled with firelight. While John fumbled for a polite response, Mrs. Auldon continued, "Something tells me you have that effect on a lot of people."

"Mrs. Auldon, I…I never meant to bring trouble on Ethan."

"What we mean is so rarely what we do."

They both looked at the fire. Ethan's bow see-sawed a flurry of graceful notes. The patrons clapped along.

"I overheard something about returning to Ireland?" asked Mrs. Auldon.

"Yes. I came to say my farewells."

"Good. Your mother would be relieved. She would want you to give up revenge. To be free."

"How do you know that?" asked John.

Mrs. Auldon looked into the hearth as if seeing the past in the flames. "My son was a slave to the Tindalls.

For three weeks. The longest three weeks of my life. I prayed every night. First, I asked for his safe return. Then I pleaded. Then begged. And then I bargained. 'Let my son be free, and let me take his place in hell.' That is a mother's love for her son. Something you can never know." She looked at John with a wry smile. "Of course, you brought Ethan back. For that, I owe you a debt."

John shook his head. "Mrs. Auldon, I know you and I have never seen eye to eye. But you took me in all the same. If anyone owes a debt, it's me. Perhaps the best way I can repay it is to leave before I cause any more trouble."

"Mr. Sullivan, I know there's more to Ethan's ordeal than you're telling, but I want you to know—it doesn't matter. Not to me."

A chill shuddered through John's aching ribs. "What?" But he knew damn well what she was talking about.

"Whatever wrong you may have done," she continued, "whatever guilt you're carrying, I release you. Go back to Ireland with a clear conscience. Marry some pretty Irish girl and have darling Irish babies. Live a long, happy, peaceful life. With family. And good friends. Forget you ever heard of the Barbary Pirates or Philadelphia." Mrs. Auldon looked at John with a haunted expression. Like a woman who had seen a ghost, but knew no one would believe her.

A cold bead of sweat slipped down John's temple. He felt his soul laid bare. As if he could hide no truth from her. "I aim to. Just as I told Ethan. What else would I do?"

"All the same, Mr. Sullivan, heed my advice: Go, and don't ever look back."

"Why?"

"Because if you do," she continued, her eyes fixed on his, "the past will draw you like a moth to a candle. Revenge will lure you into the fire."

The song came to an end. Mrs. Auldon's foreboding vanished behind a smile. She joined the uproar of applause and disappeared into the crowd. John stood there, speechless. It was a lot of nonsense of course. Damned if John believed a word. So why then, he wondered, were his hands shaking?

Chapter 10

The Streets of Philadelphia, Pennsylvania
Saturday, July 2nd, 1803

John tried to keep under eves as he edged along the street, but each time he passed under the sky, water penetrated his borrowed shirt like musket fire. He had gone a block from the Sawduster when he heard the footsteps. Since Laffite's ambush, John had resolved not to be taken unawares again. The stranger followed about ten paces behind—probably since the tavern, or before. John pretended not to notice. Without any weapons, he would need the advantage of surprise. He turned a corner into an alley.

As he crouched behind a barrel, he watched the stranger peer around the corner. A hunched figure in a patchwork slicker and oilskin hat eclipsed the flickering light of the streetlamp. Water ran off long snarls of gray beard. The man shuffled as if timid.

John sprang at him. He charged into the man and pinned him against the alley wall. He pressed his forearm against the man's throat. The smell of piss and stale whiskey stung his nose. He wound his free arm for a punch.

"Wait, John, please," rasped the man. One eye trembled with fear, the other was an empty socket.

John blinked, taken aback. He searched the man's face but didn't recognize him. "Who are you? Tell Laffite he'll get his money when—"

"I don't know this Laffite, I swear," he wheezed. "I have a…message… Please."

"Liar!" John pressed harder.

"I can…prove it."

John felt at the man's belt. Not finding any weapons, he pushed off him. "Who are you?"

"James Gilroy," said the man, coughing. "I mean you no harm. A message—that's all I have. A message for John Sullivan. You are he, are you not?"

"How do you know my name?"

"I've been looking for you in Philadelphia these six months. Asking after you everywhere I could. Like you, I was a slave on the Barbary Coast. I come with a message from your sister, Kaitlin Sullivan."

The animal stirred under John's skin. He took a step forward. "My sister? What game are you playing?"

Gilroy threw up his hands. "No, I swear. I was given proof." He retrieved something from his pocket and held his hand under the light of the street lamp. On his palm lay a silver piece. "I was told it meant something to you."

John's mouth fell open. The world surrounding the silver coin became muted, distant. As though he were peering through a keyhole. The coin was stamped with the seal of the Spanish throne. A crest stamped with a cross. In two opposing corners of the cross, there should have been two lions, and in the other two corners castles. But one lion was missing. Over the years, a crack had snaked around the lone lion, marooning him. "The

Islanded Lion."

John snatched the coin. "Where did you get this?"

"As I said, I was a slave. In Algiers. A renowned thief calling himself 'the Silver Hand' saw to my escape and freedom. In return, he asked of me an errand. He said to go to Pennsylvania, in America. To find a man of your description named John Sullivan. I was to relay to you a letter, on behalf of a Kaitlin Sullivan. He said the coin would prove the truth of my words."

John felt suddenly short of breath. As if the rain were drowning him. He had given this coin to his sister five years ago. He told her it was "magic." Only she would have known its significance. His voice broke as he said, "A letter?"

"Aye." Gilroy's one eye glistened like a muddy pool. There was anguish in it, an anguish that couldn't be faked. The anguish of one who has witnessed cruelty and changed forever as a result. He pulled a leather envelope from his coat and produced a folded paper. "He bade me deliver it safe to you. The price for my freedom. I gave my oath."

John reached out slowly as if afraid his touch might dissolve the paper. He took it from Gilroy's grasp and read.

My brother John,

Mam and I have been reunited on the Barbary Coast. We have learned of your escape to America. We think you must want to try for our rescue, and though we dream of freedom, we beg you: Never come back here, for the danger is too great.

We hope that you are happy and well in the Colonies. Mam bid me keep our location secret and bid me further to say: While we hope to meet you again on the shores of this life, know that our family shall be whole on the tranquil waters of the Eternal Sea.

All our love,
Your sister, Kaitlin, and mother, Nora.

John staggered back a step. He blinked back tears he hadn't even felt welling up. He folded the letter and stuffed it in his pocket. "When did you receive this message?"

"One year and six months ago."

"Where are they?"

"I don't know, I swear. The Silver Hand didn't tell me, and I never spoke to them. He said they feared you would return to the Barbary Coast. Attempt rescue. By the look of it, they were right."

The man started to walk away, but John darted into his path. "Wait! There must be *something*."

"It's a fool's errand, lad. I wouldn't want to be a woman in Barbary slavery."

"This Silver Hand," snapped John, causing Gilroy to shudder, "where can I find him?"

Gilroy's eyes searched crazily. "Wait, I know! Chester Ryland. A lieutenant on the frigate *George Washington*."

"What of him?"

"When the Silver Hand broke me out of the *bagno*, he brought me to Lieutenant Ryland. Ryland gave me a place on the *George Washington's* crew. That's how I got here. Ryland and the thief seemed to know each other. It looked as though Ryland were repaying a favor."

"Chester Ryland? Where can I find him?"

"I saw him in port last week. I overheard a

midshipman from the USS *Philadelphia* call him 'Lieutenant.' It must be his new posting. That's all I know. I swear that's all I know."

John thought about demanding more. But that damn eye. In that terrified gaze, John could see the despair of loss. The torment of the cane. A wound in the soul that could never heal. A look Gilroy might see in John's eyes at this very moment. He couldn't bear to wring any more out of the man, so he nodded.

Gilroy tottered past John. He stopped in the street. "Lad."

John looked over his shoulder at Gilroy. Lamplight quivered in the vagrant sailor's single eye.

"Don't go back." And with that, the stranger disappeared into the night.

Chapter 11

The City *Bastedan*
The Port of Tunis
Thursday, October 28th, 1798

Ibrahim swatted John with a cedar cane. "Again."

John glared at him, his calf smarting. Ibrahim waited, looking at John expectantly. The old slave broker mopped sweat from his forehead. Declan's letters home, petitions to the embassy, and pleas for charity had come to little. Uncle Peter hadn't replied, and they only had enough money to bribe Ibrahim for a better outcome at the slave market. John practiced hobbling again.

Swat! John recoiled from another strike.

"Show me again!" commanded Ibrahim. He spoke in Lingua Franca, the odd mix of Arabic, Italian, Spanish, and Portuguese used between masters and slaves in Tunis. Having visited ports all over Europe, John picked up the slave language quickly.

John continued rehearsing his limp in the shady corner of the *bastedan*. Behind rows of horseshoe-arches and marble columns, brokers could ready their property for display. John's eyes drifted out over the square. The ocher walls of slave pens, shops, and neighboring tenements surrounded the hub of commerce. Narrow alleys meandered between the buildings. Beyond the nearby rooftops, slender minarets with graceful pointed domes stabbed into the sky. A crier on a raised wooden dais solicited bids for kneeling captives. Heat shimmered over the white-pink pavement.

The s*wat-swat* of Ibrahim's cane brought John back to attention. This time, he resisted the reflex to jump. He gimped backwards.

"Good, Johnny," Declan said, relieved. "Good lad."

"He's ready," agreed Ibrahim. "Your son will appear crippled and look unappealing for hard labor. But I can't promise him a generous master."

"Thank you, Master Ibrahim," said Declan, "for what you're doing."

"Do not thank me. This is not charity—your piasters bought my help."

"You have my thanks all the same."

Ibrahim waved dismissively. He coughed and spat phlegm.

"Nora," said Declan. "You remember your story?"

In the back corner, Nora sat against the wall. Her arms encircled her knees. She stared vacantly at her own shadow.

Declan went to her side and dropped to one knee. He took her hand, looking at the pale stripe where her wedding ring had been. "Nora," he coaxed. "My love."

Nora didn't look at her husband.

"Please, dear. This is important. We haven't much time."

John had never seen his mother so despondent. Her spirit of adventure had always driven the family over the next horizon. Her wonder had always inspired them to explore. Since the bey had taken Kaitlin, that fire had cooled, smoldered, and suffocated. To make her appear older, Declan and Ibrahim had smeared dirt on her face, kept her hair tangled, and reduced her rations. But the emptiness in her eyes had done far more than their efforts.

"Mam, please," John said.

Nora looked at John for a moment. She murmured by rote, "I'm forty-nine. My child-bearing days ended two years ago. I am an excellent cook."

John hoped the buyers would believe the lie. His mother only turned thirty-six last April. Even gaunt and filthy, her skin was smooth, her sienna hair reflecting the sun. But they wouldn't see her radiant smile. They wouldn't hear her musical laugh. Desolation would hide her youth.

"Good," observed Ibrahim. "It's time."

Ibrahim led John, Declan, and Nora into the square. The three-foot, thirty-pound length of chain John had been dragging behind him for weeks felt heavier than ever. The iron quickly heated in the sun. The hard edges rubbed his right ankle raw. He marched with his mother, father, and dozens of other slaves in a melancholy parade. Auctioneers fanned themselves and occasionally lashed their offerings with canes or whips. In a row of curtained stalls in the southeast corner, customers gawked at the slave women in privacy. Merchant stalls sold cheap roughspun clothes, a dry grain called bulgur, and second-hand tools—provisions for slaves. They even peddled refreshments for the buyers: figs, dates, thick black coffee, and tobacco for pipes.

A few buyers looked over Ibrahim's slaves, asked questions, and moved on. A few showed interest in John.

They forced open his mouth and looked at his teeth. They ordered him to strip naked. They slapped his abdomen, thighs, and buttocks. It was a humiliating march, but the worst wasn't long in coming. Barely half an hour had passed when a tall, muscular soldier showed interest in Nora.

"Ibrahim," said the man. He was a Janissary judging by his saber and pistol, felt jacket, and gold spoon on his hat. "Where have you been hiding this lovely creature?"

John felt his rage uncoiling as he recognized the man grabbing Nora's chin. It was the Janissary commander that had killed Isaac on the *Wandering Hart*. Nora's eyes were downcast as Hamit scrutinized her face. John wanted to strangle the soldier with his ankle chain.

"Hamit," replied Ibrahim. "I am at your service. This one is barren, but a perfect house servant. Eleven hundred piasters. Your wife will love her."

The Janissary laughed. "This is another of your games, isn't it? You wouldn't be double dealing with your master's property, would you? Selling them low to lenient masters, then pocketing a bribe?"

Ibrahim's iron gaze didn't falter. "You wouldn't be questioning my honor as a businessman and loyal servant, would you? A shameful ploy to get a better price?"

"Never!" said Hamit, feigning outrage. "But I will pay the asking price and throw in a bonus for you personally—larger than any a slave could pay. *After* I've had a chance for inspection and *if* she is of the quality I suspect."

Ibrahim considered a moment. "Done."

"What?" cried Declan.

"No!" John shouted. He started forward, but Ibrahim swatted his legs out from under him. The slave merchant brought the cane down on John's back, knocking him to his stomach, and raised for it another strike.

Nora touched Ibrahim's arm. Her expression froze the old man in place. She eased the truncheon down and moved in front of John.

"Awake, John," Nora said softly. For a moment, a distant spark of that fire rekindled. She knelt and touched a hand to his face.

"Mother?" John said, the fight draining out of him. A tear ran down his cheek.

"My sweet boy," she said.

The Janissary Hamit closed a hand on her arm and led her away.

"Mother," John called after her, his eyes filling with tears. "I love you. I'll find a way to free you, I swear."

"Nora!" Declan said, his voice breaking up. "My love."

On her way to the private stalls, Nora stole one last look back. She smiled at John and Declan as though admiring a painting. "My handsome men of the sea."

They watched in powerless despair as Nora and the Janissary disappeared behind a curtain.

Hours later, the spires and minarets cast long afternoon shadows across the *bastedan*. Most of the slaves had been sold, including Declan. The buyer who purchased John's father needed skilled laborers for the shipyards, and Declan fetched a sizable price. Ibrahim allowed barely a moment for Declan to say his goodbyes.

"John, son, I…" Declan embraced John with tears in his eyes. "I…want you to know, son…"

John looked at Declan, but the words he had intended for his father stuck in his throat.

"That's enough," the portly buyer said, pulling Declan away by the chain.

"John," Declan said as his new master took him away. "I love you. Forgive me, John. Forgive me."

The auctions had come to a close and the sun nearly set when John finally met his own buyer. Ibrahim had been leading him around the square for hours. John had been trying not to think of water or food or the shade. Most of all, he tried not to think of Declan or Nora or Kaitlin.

"Sorry I'm late, Ibrahim," said a man in Lingua Franca. John recognized the pirate Ilyas Naim, the young man who took command after Isaac slew *Re'is* Raakaan.

"*Re'is* Naim," said Ibrahim deferentially. "I was beginning to lose patience."

"I was delayed on business." Naim looked at John. "He has not been sold?"

"I agreed to hold him as long as I could, and so I have."

John looked at them both, puzzled. What had they arranged? John had thought the purpose of his ruse was to avoid a brutal fate—not to be part of a secret deal.

"Good. Eight fifty then, as agreed."

"Done!" said Ibrahim. He accepted a purse of money from Naim, smiling as he felt its weight. "A pleasure doing business with you." Ibrahim bowed and walked out of the *bastedan* square, looking relieved to be done for the day.

Naim watched Ibrahim go, then regarded John for a moment. At length, he said, "I wish I could thank your brother—he rid me of a dangerous rival and made me a captain. Your ship, the *Wandering Hart,* is now my ship, the *Bosphorus Crescent.*"

"I wish Isaac were here too," said John, thinking to himself, *So he could kill every last one of you.*

"A shame," said Naim. "He fought bravely. He died a noble death."

John was surprised at Naim's condolences. *Does he admire* Isaac? John wondered. He said, "Thank you, *Re'is*."

"Ibrahim tells me your father taught you well. That you're an able navigator."

"I'm an excellent navigator."

"And not lacking for confidence," smiled Naim. "Good. You will come aboard my ship as a personal servant. In reality, you will be my teacher. You will tell no one of your real purpose, and your knowledge will swiftly make me a rich man."

I'll send you to hell! John screamed in his mind. But what he said was, "You're a *re'is*. What could I have to teach you?"

Naim considered a moment. "I will tell you this once, and then we will never speak of it again. It was Raakaan who navigated our course and planned our raids. He loved sailing and fighting but hated the men. So he left the leadership of the crew to me. They are happy I'm captain. Despite my popularity, it was only a few months ago that I went to sea."

"You're a good cutthroat—but a bad seaman. You better not let them find out."

For all his education and pleasant demeanor, Naim took a menacing step forward. "Listen very carefully, slave. Obey me and you will have a life of comfort unknown to most in your position. I'll even allow you a small share of the prizes and you may buy your freedom in time. But cross me, and you'll suffer. I will find your father, your mother, and your sister, and see them cast into a pit of despair. As you put it, I am a very 'good cutthroat.'"

John swallowed hard. "Yes, *Re'is.*"

"Now, will you serve me faithfully? And teach me all that I require?"

"Yes, *Re'is.*"

"Good," said Naim, slipping back into a pleasant tone. "Now, before we go, one more thing."

"Aye, *Re'is?*"

"I will hear you say it."

Sweat beaded on John's forehead. He felt nauseous. He knew exactly what Naim wanted, but he couldn't bear the thought. "What, *Re'is?*"

"What all slaves must say. I will hear it."

John looked across the square to the private stalls. The curtains were open, the buyers and human chattel gone. There was no sign of his mother. As he scanned the other slaves awaiting the next stage of their social death, he couldn't find his father. He looked back at Naim.

"Aye. Master."

Chapter 12

The Piping Plover Inn
Philadelphia, Pennsylvania
Sunday, July 3rd, 1803

Dew melted off daffodils in the morning sun. Leaves cast a patchwork of shadows. Behind the Piping Plover, a brown and white-dappled mare crunched a bushel of grass. She pricked her ears toward John, staring intently for a moment, then went back to grazing. A scarecrow wearing a tattered British redcoat stood watch over a garden of gourds, carrots, and potatoes. Sparrows sang in an ancient walnut tree. Other taverns, barns, and houses lined the square patch of land.

"John Sullivan." Captain Richard Aubert approached from the back door of the Plover.

"Captain Aubert," John replied.

"You've transgressed with my wife." His stride continued unbroken, directly towards John.

John's face flushed with heat. He and Dominique had parted ways well before her marriage to Aubert. There had been temptation, but no infidelity. Still, John felt as though Aubert could see through him, could see his desire for her. Sweat pooled under his arms. "I beg your pardon?"

Aubert walked past John to four white painted chairs and a table beneath the walnut tree. He took a seat and crossed his leg. "You enlisted her aid to interrupt my morning chess game. You've some goddamn bollocks to show your face here."

An African woman dressed in a cotton dress and apron approached. She set a candlestick and a saucer with a steaming cup on the table. "Your coffee, sir," she said.

Aubert took up the candle and puffed his pipe to life. He acknowledged the servant with a perfunctory grunt, and she returned to the tavern. "I told Dominique you could bugger yourself," continued the captain.

The knot in John's stomach tightened. His odds looked worse all the time. He took the seat to Aubert's left.

"But then she reminded me that it was an honest beat," Aubert went on. "She also reminded me that without you, she might never have given up crime in favor of our matrimony. So there it is, Sullivan. You have until I finish my coffee."

It might be wise to stroke Aubert's ego before launching into details. Or perhaps attribute Aubert's brag defeat to John's good luck and let an adversary save face. But Richard Aubert came from a noble French family— refugees from the revolutionary guillotine. In his eyes, John was a peasant. His compliments would irritate more than flatter.

"The *Allegheny*," said John, coming right to the point. "She belongs at sea, in the Mediterranean. You should be with the fleet, winning renown against the Barbary Pirates. Instead, you're chasing common smugglers up and down the coast."

"I'm fighting the enemies of our nation," Aubert said by rote. "There is no greater honor."

"And yet, I have your attention."

"Aren't you very clever," said Aubert with a wry smile. "For a callow Irish beggar."

"We have a common enemy, Captain. Pierre Laffite. He's bribed customs officials. Sold stolen goods in Philadelphia's shops. Taken over smuggling throughout the city. And to keep you cooperative, he's threatened retaliation against your wife, her sister, and her brother. A captain who finally puts an end to him will be the toast of the Navy. Such a captain would have the gratitude of Commandant Pritchett and his good friend, Navy Secretary Smith. Such a captain could have any posting he wants."

Aubert narrowed his eyes at John, chewing on his pipe. "A fine statement of the obvious. But Laffite could be moving his goods through any number of coves and inlets on the Delaware. I could patrol the river with a dozen ships and never find the one. You don't know where to find him, or you would've said as much."

"No. But if we work together, there's a way."

Aubert snorted and set down his cup. He stood and smoothed his spotless silk waistcoat. "Please. You and your friends are a perfidious rabble. There is nothing I require from such villainy." The exiled French noble emptied his pipe, ground the last embers of tobacco with his toe, and set off for the Plover.

John came to his feet. "Captain, this is a chance for both of us to get back to sea. Don't let it slip through your fingers."

"I don't want to see you at my door again," said Aubert, not looking back.

John's mind raced. If he lost Aubert, he lost his only play against Laffite. He lost his last chance to find his family. "I've known your wife."

Aubert spun around. His eyes narrowed to slits. "What the fuck did you just say?"

"For much longer than you."

Now Aubert was storming back towards John.

John didn't move. "She admires men that fight. She thinks she's happy now, but 'captain of the card table' won't satisfy her for long. She'll grow restless."

"You insolent rascal! I'll fetch my saber and cut you to bloody rags."

"Do it, if you think I'm wrong." John stood his ground as Aubert seethed. "But I know what you really want: to put Laffite in irons, set sail on the *Allegheny*, and prove you're worthy of her."

Aubert reached a hand up as if to seize John's neck, but instead curled it into a fist and let it drop. His eyes drifted as he considered. "How could it be done?"

"Martin Jameson. The merchant at your brag table—he's Laffite's fence. He sells stolen and smuggled goods throughout the city for Jean and Pierre Laffite. He also likes to gamble. He takes on debt with very dangerous creditors. His loss at your table on Friday was a large one. Seize his warehouse of illegal goods, and he'll be in a corner."

"Don't be obtuse. He'll just pay a fine and go about his business. Meanwhile, I'll have made an enemy of every official the Laffites have bribed."

"It won't matter—we're not after Jameson. As the only man allowed in Laffite's counting-house, he knows where the loot is stashed. A year ago, when I was working for them, I saw Jameson steal a stack of bills and alter the ledger so no one would notice. Seize Jameson's goods, and he'll have no choice but to steal from Laffite to pay his debt. A friend of mine will follow Jameson to Laffite's hideout, then report the location to you and your Marines."

"And I put an end to all of them."

John replied with a nod.

"And what's your part in this?"

"Laffite expects me to settle my debt to him tomorrow night, or else. I'll keep him distracted while you lead your Marines to his cache. Then you haul in the Creole scourge of Philadelphia, remove a parasite from the treasury, and set course for Tripoli with Secretary Smith's gratitude."

"That is if Laffite hasn't slit your throat."

"Ideally, yes."

The mare sputtered and pissed loudly in the dirt.

"What do you expect in return?" Aubert wanted to know.

"Not much. A small share of the prize money. A midshipman's berth on the *Philadelphia*. From what I hear, your good word would go a long way with Captain Bainbridge."

"I detest that man!"

"Aye, but he admires men of high station, and you'll have the commandant and the secretary behind you."

"Risking your life to purchase austerity at sea? Hardly sound business acumen."

"And yet, a bargain for you."

Aubert regarded John with a smirk. As if, for the first time, he recognized a competitor in the game of court intrigue. "Aye. A bargain that could go badly for me in any number of ways."

"Men like us have never been afraid to gamble."

Aubert offered the slightest tilt of his chin. "Perhaps not."

"One more thing. I have a friend. His name is Ethan Auldon. Bainbridge denied him a berth as surgeon's mate because he's black."

"So?"

"Convince Bainbridge to change his mind."

The captain curled his lip as if puzzling over a strange foreign custom. "Are you serious?"

John ground his teeth. "That is my price, Captain."

"I underestimated you, Sullivan. The revolutionary attitudes of this country suit you. Your facility for subterfuge far exceeds that of the *common* rabble." Aubert fastened a few loose buttons at his collar. "If a courier needed to find me, he might look at the Blue Anchor Tavern tomorrow night." Without another word, he walked away and disappeared into the Plover.

John let go a heavy sigh. The mare whinnied and scratched herself against a tree. He set off towards the street. As he passed the stack of firewood outside the kitchen, he noticed Dominique in the corner of his vision.

"You've 'known me?'" she said.

John pivoted. Dominique was leaning against the stack. A corncob pipe hung from the side of her mouth.

John shrugged. "I just needed to get his attention. Don't think too much of it."

"I don't."

The heat of the evening left a mist of perspiration on Dominique's cleavage. John's eyes traced up the curve of her waist. He wasn't used to seeing her in a corset. And there was that beautiful ponytail again. He felt his breath quicken. "How long were you listening?"

"Long enough to know you're going to pull Grey and Melisande into another dangerous game."

"I'll leave Melly out of it."

Dominique scoffed and rolled her eyes. She took a deep drag.

"Dom, this isn't a game. This isn't some selfish racket. The Laffite brothers have ruined our lives. I have a plan to fight back."

"You never learn, do you?"

John edged close to her, muttering under his breath, "And you do? Marrying this French stuffed-shirt? Just so you can play at being some aristocrat? It won't change who you are."

Dominique poked a finger in John's chest. "At least I'm trying to build a life. A future. Here you are again, doing what you always do. Scheming, smuggling, gambling, fighting—always for me, you say. Or my brother. Or Melly. Or Ethan. Or Katie. But it's for you— only for you—because you love the chaos. All you'll do is stir up more trouble, and we'll pay the price."

John growled in frustration, looking at his feet. He thought for a moment, and began again, "I know what this looks like, but it's different this time. I'm going to make things better for all of us. I promise."

"I know you believe that. You always do."

John edged even closer. He caught the sweet, acrid smell of tobacco on her breath. His heartbeat rose as he felt her body close to his. "You used to trust me."

"My mistake."

They fell quiet. John could see the pulse in her tender neck. A flush in her cheeks. He breathed in her scent. Like an orchid after the rain. He reached up and gently tugged the pipe out of her lips. "Your husband hates your smoking. I thought you promised to give it up."

He could see her breath quickening as she replied, "I only slip out for a pipe once in a while."

John moved closer. He studied the little mole above her lip. The tiny dimple in her chin. She didn't pull away. "Sounds like you're breaking a vow."

She lifted her face closer. "Some are harder to keep than others," she murmured.

John leaned in for a kiss. She closed her eyes. Before their lips could touch, she pulled away. John stood back and closed a hand over his mouth.

Avoiding his eyes, Dominique said, "Get going, Sully. Do what you're going to do. Then you can be done with this city and out of our lives."

John sighed. She wouldn't look at him. He offered a nod of resignation. "Aye. Goodbye, Dominique."

"Goodbye."

As he headed towards the street, he thought he heard her add, "…John."

Chapter 13

The Sawduster Tavern
Philadelphia, Pennsylvania
Monday, July 4th, 1803

"He said he'd be here, right?" Sullivan asked again. The next time he asked, Melisande worried she might pull her raven-head war club on him.

"He'll be here!" she groaned, sitting on a barrel in the Sawduster's brewhouse. A sludge of malted barley bubbled in a copper kettle at the center of the room. The bitter scent of hops mingled with maple-sweet steam. She loosened another shirt button in the heat. Humidity pooled under her arms. There was barely enough room for Sully to move among the casks of beer, but still he paced, often knocking his head on the hand-carved ladles hanging from the ceiling.

"I know what you need, ole Sully." Melisande rummaged through her black bandolier bag. It had been a gift from *Maman* Fawn, her Iroquois mother, years ago. *Maman* died of the pox years ago. When Melisande missed her the most, one look at the blue beadwork flowers and she would feel *Maman* Fawn's spirit close by. She pulled out a green onion-shaped bottle and yanked the cork with her teeth. It plucked free with a merry squeak. She took a long pull and offered the bottle to Sullivan.

Melisande's favorite Irish rogue looked doubtful.

"Don't be rude, now, Sully," said Melisande. "It's better than my old recipe."

Sullivan took a sip. He turned beet red as he swallowed, then exploded into a fit of coughing.

Melisande grinned. "That's the way, my lovely."

"Christ, Melly, what is this bilge?"

"Beggin' your pardon, m'lord, but nothin' you'd pour out of fancy crystal."

"A chamber pot, perhaps…" Sullivan touched the chipped rim of the bottle to his lips for a smaller sip.

Melisande shrugged. "I was in prison. Where else would I brew it?"

Sullivan paused. He looked down the bottleneck, then again at Melisande.

"Only a jest, Sully," Melisande said with a wink. "Drink it long enough, and there's no other kind you'll want."

Sullivan furrowed his brows as if arriving at an epiphany. "Not unlike you."

Melisande laughed and sprung off the barrel. She snatched the bottle for another swig. "I don't get it. How can you be so sure Jameson will steal from Laffite? And today?"

"Simple. Laffite sets sail for New Orleans tonight. First, he'll load cargo and collect the money in his counting-house. Jameson knows this, and he'll have to move fast."

Melisande punched Sullivan in the arm. "You clever fox. So while you're meeting the frog, I'll be keeping to the shadows and watching your back."

"No. I have to go alone. I'll give him a location for the Basques, and he'll set sail. If he were to spot you, it would be all over."

"But what if the frog kills you once he has what he wants?"

Sullivan took the bottle and forced down another eye-watering gulp. It looked to Melisande like buying time for an answer. "Laffite thinks of himself as a gentleman. If he believes me, he'll keep his end of the bargain. Besides, I can take care of myself."

"What aren't you telling me, Sully?"

His eyes darted away and he took another sip.

A hollow metal bang sounded from the back wall. To the casual observer, it would have appeared to be nothing more than the kettle expanding with heat. But to Melisande and Sully, it was a secret knock. Sullivan went to the columns of barrels stacked three high, end-on-end, near the source of the sound. He reached to the cask farthest back and lowest to the ground, then turned the metal tap near its bottom. There was a satisfying click, and four columns shifted. Sully tugged, and the barrels slid over the stone floor on hidden wheels. A false patch of wall came away with them, revealing a small passage between the brewhouse and the tavern.

Ethan Auldon stepped out, dirt smudges clinging to his sweat. He and Sully clasped hands.

"Ethan," smiled Sullivan. "Any trouble?"

"No trouble. No one saw him enter the city."

Sullivan let go a sigh of relief. "Thank you for doing this, mate. I know this isn't what your father had in mind. If there were another way…"

"My father built this tunnel to free families from

slavery," said Ethan, with more than a hint of pride. "If it helps you free yours, then I'd say it's just what he had in mind. Besides, I owed you one."

The young man that followed Ethan was a member of the Tuscarora Nation of the *Haudenosaunee*—the Iroquois, as settlers called them. Melisande's heart swelled with both affection and guilt at the sight of her brother, Grey Feather. He wore a twilight blue tunic and buckskin leggings with the intricate beadwork of a sachem's son. His head was shaved and painted black but for a feather-laced braid falling down his back. *Papa* Grey Fox's antler-hilted knife was sheathed on his chest. After four months in debtor's prison, Melisande wanted nothing more than to throw her arms around him. But she and Dominique were also the reason he lived in exile.

"Grey Feather," said Sullivan, extending his hand.

"John Sullivan." The Tuscarora warrior hesitated a moment, then shook hands.

"I can't thank you enough for helping me."

"I'm not helping you. I'm helping my sisters."

A tense silence passed between the two men.

"Grey, I don't think Sully likes our longhouse brew," Melisande said, pretending to be casual.

"He doesn't have a *Kautanohakau* stomach," said Grey Feather. He looked sternly at her. "White settlers should keep to their perfumed punch."

Melisande risked a smile. "I missed you, Grey."

For a moment, it looked as if her brother's frown might not break. That he might start a lecture. But then, amusement tugged at his eyes. "I missed you too, Little Crow."

Melisande felt tears welling. She'd have died before letting them fall. So she chuckled and threw an arm around his muscular shoulders. "You boys aren't smelling any prettier in this heat. Let's go in for a drink."

A few minutes later, Melisande, Sully, and Grey Feather stood around a table in the deserted taproom of the Sawduster. Chairs stood on tables. Cold ash dusted the hearth. Musical instruments hung on the wall over the stage. The doors were locked, the curtains drawn. There would be Independence Day festivities later, but for now, Ethan had the place closed. Sully outlined the last few details of his plan to bring down Laffite.

Ethan closed the valve on a beer cask behind the bar. He placed four flagons on a tray, foam running over the rims, and brought them to the table. "On the house," he said cheerfully.

"For me, Fiddles?" said Melisande. She was never one to turn down free booze. "I always liked you."

"Very kind of you to say, Melisande," said Ethan. He furrowed his brow seriously. "Tell me, do you know *anyone's* true name?"

Melisande batted her eyes. "My names are always true."

Ethan sighed in defeat.

"Thanks, mate," Sullivan said to Ethan after a long draught, a bit of suds on his upper lip. "Now then, we're agreed?"

Grey Feather ran an oiled cloth over the head of his tomahawk as he spoke. "In an hour, Dominique's husband will seize Martin Jameson's Third Street Warehouse. The fat trader will run to Laffite's hideout to steal from his counting-house. I will follow him there, then double back to the Blue Anchor Tavern and bring the white soldiers."

"While I distract our quarry," said Sullivan.

"Very fine, Sully, very fine," declared Melisande. She sat on the tabletop and crossed one leg over the other. She leaned back like a Siren sunning herself on a shoal. "And while Grey leads a bunch of noisy soldiers with muskets, I glide silently along behind them, keeping to the brush. Your finest plan yet."

"On any other day, you'd be right," said Sullivan. "But Laffite is having you followed, which is why I need you in the city, at the Cat and Queen. I need you to keep his thugs occupied and far from Grey."

"Wait at Kitty's? While you have all the fun? Sully, you'd waste my talents!"

"Sullivan is right," insisted Grey. "Stay at the cat tavern."

Now Melisande was pissed. Typical dumb boys. Always leaving the girls out so they could play Chief Prick Hero. "This was Dominique's doing. She made you promise, didn't she?"

Sully scratched the back of his head for a moment, then admitted, "She wanted you kept out of this."

"I knew it! My sister doesn't get to stick her prissy little nose in my business. Did she ever take *my* advice when she married that poncy asshole?"

"Melly, your sister is only looking after you. Pierre Laffite is dangerous, and he knows you're in the city. This isn't because I don't trust you—it's for the good of the plan."

"And what if you and Grey get into trouble? What if you need help? I don't need you looking after me. It's the other way around."

"Do this? For me?" Sully made his bright, wheat-colored eyes pout at her. Like he always did when he wanted something.

Melisande glared at wood shavings on the floor. She'd be damned if he got a smile out of her. "Fine," she muttered.

Sullivan nodded, grinning like an idiot. "Thank you."

"Yeah, sure. Hairy sheep-shagging…" Insults trailed off under her breath.

"Grey Feather," said Sullivan. "I don't know how I can repay you."

"Simple," replied Grey. "When it's done, repay me by leaving this city and my sisters' lives. For good."

"Aye. That's the best deal I'm getting these days."

Melisande snorted.

"Right, then," Sullivan said. "See you tonight."

"I'll walk you out," said Ethan.

Ethan unlocked the back door. Melisande watched him and Sully step outside. When the door closed, she said in Iroquois, "So when do we leave, Grey?"

It was a bold statement. She knew Grey Feather wanted her to stay. He could give the order, but they both knew she would follow him anyway. So it had been since Melisande was six years old. And while he was a better fighter, she was a better tracker. After a long sigh, he said in Iroquois, "Soon, Little Crow. Be ready."

Chapter 14

The *Bosphorus Crescent*, formerly the *Wandering Hart*
The Mediterranean Sea
Friday, January 4th, 1799

John poured vinegar into a slender bottle. He uncorked a cask of the ship's sour, stinking water and added some to the bottle. Next, he took a wedge of rusk from a pile on the table, poured a little of the mixture onto the biscuit, and added it to a wooden bucket. He worked in the quiet of what used to be the *Wandering Hart's* galley. Now, it was the place where he prepared slave rations. When he had the bucket filled with rusk, he started down to the lower deck as he did every night.

He passed the rows of hammocks filled with Turks, Jews, renegade Europeans, Janissaries, and enslaved crew snoring and farting. Some played dice or cards in the corners. No one spoke to him, and that's how he liked it.

John opened the hatch to the *Bosphorus Crescent's* hold. The fumes of sewage and vomit hit him like a hot belch. He lit a lantern and climbed down. There were sounds of coughing, groans, and occasional weeping. Twenty-four captives chained to the hull, looking up at him. He didn't look at them. He never did. He shuffled from prisoner to prisoner, handing one rusk biscuit to each.

"Thank you, lad," said an older man. The pirates had taken him off his fishing boat, a mile from a Sicilian village.

"Please, *signore*," said a middle-aged woman. She was taken with her daughter while gathering muscles on the shores of Malta. She didn't accept the ration. Instead, she tugged at his shirt. "*Dove?* My...Daniela, *dove*—where? I have not seen. Days. Not seen for days. *Per favore, signore.*"

Her daughter, an eleven-year-old girl, had been locked in the first mate's quarters since their capture. John didn't think about that. If he did, he might think about Kaitlin, and he never thought about Kaitlin. John pulled away from the woman's grasp. He thrust the biscuit into her hand. She failed to grip it and it fell into the murky water. He moved on.

"Please, *signore*," said the woman again. "*Mia* Daniela. Where?"

John ignored her and finished his rounds. Later, as John was putting away the bucket and vinegar, a crewman told him to report to the captain's cabin. The *re'is* wanted to see him. He did as ordered, and when he entered the cabin, he found Ilyas Naim dining alone at his table.

The pirate captain was cutting into baked chicken and sipping red wine. The dishes once belonged to Nora. John's eyes drifted towards the dark stern windows. In his mind, he saw Mother and Father's upholstered chairs looking out to sea. He saw them sitting there, watching the sunset, their hands joined. To their right, he saw Kaitlin digging for a doll in her cedar toy chest. Isaac was setting down his chart and compass and taking up his lute. John's grown brother struggled on a few chords, but it sounded beautiful anyway.

"You wanted to see me, *Re'is?*" said John.

"Sullivan," said Naim more cheerfully than usual. "Good."

The imagined sunlight faded from the windows. The ghost of John's family vanished. Isaac's musical notes soured and died away. John looked across the table at his master.

Naim dabbed a napkin across his thickening mustache and beard. "I have something for you." When John said nothing, his master slid a brass key across the table.

John looked at the key, frowned, then looked back at Naim. *Is he testing me?* John thought, panicking. *Have I forgotten a task he assigned me? My God, what can I tell him?* "Forgive me, *Re'is,* I don't understand."

Naim sighed impatiently. "Do you not remember?"

John's panic was only worsening. Hopefully his punishment would be *bastinadoes* on his feet, rather than lashes. "Please, forgive me, *Re'is,* I don't…"

"John," Naim sighed. "You asked for this. Two weeks ago."

"A key?"

"You asked me if I would consider removing your irons. I said no." Naim circled around the table. "But this voyage has been an incredible success. The crew is happy, the hold is full, and my investors will be pleased. I'm going to be a wealthy man, due in no small part to you. So, I have changed my mind. You no longer need to drag that chain with you everywhere you go."

John picked up the key. He turned it over in his hand.

"Well?" Naim said. "Are you going to stand there?"

Dreamily, John knelt down. He slid the key into the iron ring around his ankle. He turned it, felt a click, and saw the shackle come apart. His foot came free, feeling like a foreign object grafted onto his body. As though it was too light to be his own. With the manacle gone, the air cooled his tender skin. He took a few lopsided steps, trying to remember how to walk without it.

"Well, how do you feel?" Naim asked.

"I feel…It feels good. Thank you, *Re'is*."

"Don't thank me yet. There's more." Naim reached for a small wooden box on the table. He presented it to John. "Go on."

John began to wonder if this was some kind of trick. Such generosity didn't feel possible. He fumbled with the copper latch and opened the lid. He fought back tears.

His mother's silver watch. He touched it, not believing it was real. He flipped open the hunter case. He read the inscription inside. His hands trembled.

Naim broke into a warm smile. "I know how fond you were of her. And I know how much the inscription means to you. A fitting memento. I want you to have it."

John looked at Naim. "Thank you, *Re'is*. This is…I don't have the words."

"You are welcome, John." He stepped back to his chair. "And I told you before—when we're in private, call me Ilyas." As an afterthought, he pointed at John and said, "But *only* in private."

Naim took a sip of wine. "I've left word with the quartermaster to give you a full seaman's share of the spoils. Keep up this pace, and you might be free in a few years. Come, let's celebrate. I'll pour you some wine."

John felt a bittersweet nostalgia. He had never been thanked so directly by *Re'is* Naim. At the very edges of his being, he could feel the touch of personhood. As if he was at the bow of the *Wandering Hart* again, the day after the storm; when he was still Irish, still free, still a friend, a son, and a brother.

He wanted the feeling gone.

"Thank you, *Re'is*. Am I dismissed?"

Naim frowned. "If you like." He propped his elbows on the table. "I had hoped you might stay for a while, like you used to."

"Then I will, *Re'is*."

Naim's smile slipped away. He took a sip of wine. "No, that won't be necessary. You may go."

John went to the door. Before stepping out, he asked, "Would you like me to check our course before I retire?"

Naim shook his head. "You did an hour ago."

"Right."

"Is everything all right, John? You've been very quiet the last few days."

"Yes, I'm fine. Tired, that's all. It won't affect my duties."

"I wasn't worried about your duties. I was worried about you."

"I'm sorry to have worried you, *Re'is*." John almost left right then, but for some reason, he said, "*Re'is,* may I ask a question?"

"You may."

"When did I tell you about the inscription on the watch? I can't recall."

Naim's eyes searched his memory. "I don't recall either. It must have been over wine one night."

John smiled. "Of course, must have been."

Naim smiled back. "Sleep well, John. Peace be upon you."

"And upon you, peace, Ilyas."

John left the cabin and walked to the bow of the *Bosphorus Crescent*. He stood on the exact spot where he had been the day of the attack, with Kaitlin standing beside him. He looked down to where their noble red stag once reared over the sea. In its place was a figurehead of Sultan Mehmet Han II, conqueror of Constantinople. John held up his mother's watch like a moon above the starlit waves. He would never be free. He knew he would never see his mother, father, or sister again. John held the watch out over the waves, and he let the chain begin to slip from his grasp.

That's when John saw the breaker. His fist tightened on the watch chain. He leaned forward, squinting into the darkness. He saw surf shimmering in the moonlight. Waves were crashing against a reef, dead ahead.

John spun around to warn the officer of the watch. There might be time to alter course or heave-to before impact. He got two steps before he stopped. John looked around. The lookouts in the crosstrees were calm. A couple Janissaries walked the deck. None of them had seen the danger. An idea occurred to John.

He was moving again, but this time calmly. He headed below decks as casually as if he were delivering the rusk and vinegar. He lit a lantern and climbed down into the hold. The slaves all looked at him in surprise, no doubt confused why he would be visiting again so soon. John found Naim's key in his pocket and used it to unlock a prisoner's shackles.

"Listen carefully," John said to the captives. "Get yourselves free, then hide on the deck above. Wait for a few minutes, then get above decks as fast as you can. There won't be much time."

"But the pirates…"

"What's happening? What are you doing?"

"How long do we wait?"

John handed the key to the first freed captive, who in turn unlocked the next. "Just do it," John commanded. "You'll know when to move. This is the best chance I can give you." He ignored their hail of questions and climbed back up.

A moment later, John stood at the bow once again. He looked out over the water, squinting. At first, he didn't see anything. He felt a nervous panic at the thought he might have imagined the reef. But then a spray of foam caught the light. With the *Bosphorus Crescent*—no! With the *Wandering Hart* making seven knots, a reef that size would gut her from stem to stern. She would strike the rocks within ten minutes. Sink within five. He leaned on the rail, looking out to the horizon. A cold smile spread across John's face.

John Sullivan woke up coughing on water. His lungs burned as he gasped for air. Cool sand drained through his fingers. He heard the sound of chuckling surf and crying gulls. He pushed up on all fours. Water rushed around him. The wave tried to wash him backward, but he dug in.

"Are you all right, son?" A voice boomed above. The words were English, but in a hard, blunt accent.

John felt a shadow over him and looked up. A man in white trousers and worn boots towered against the noon sun. He had short, black hair and a long beard.

"I said, are you all right?" the man repeated.

John looked around. A beautiful beach snaked through craggy inland cliffs. Low growing scrub speckled the dunes. Broken bits of wood and scraps of rope danced in the breakers. "What happened? Where am I?"

"Shipwrecked, it would appear. You're in Sicily, near the town of Palermo. What's your name, son?"

"John. John Sullivan."

"I'm Captain Mooney of the *Calypso*. My crew spotted you here. You're the only survivor we found."

"Captain, you said?"

"Aye. Out of Philadelphia." The captain offered a hand.

John accepted Mooney's grip. The captain hauled John up like a toddler. "What city is that?" John asked.

Mooney scoffed. "Philadelphia, Pennsylvania," he proclaimed in a proud baritone. "Capital of the United States of America."

"United States?" John parroted. He recalled stories of the Yankee rebellion across the Atlantic. Beyond that, he knew little of the place.

"Aye. We're setting sail for home presently."

John cast another look around. There were a few scraps of wood littering the beach, but otherwise no sign of the *Wandering Hart*. John looked at Captain Mooney. "I'm a skilled hand at the mast. Might I trade work for passage?"

Mooney smiled. "We're not headed to Ireland, lad, but I could get you as far as Lisbon."

John realized the captain had recognized his accent. Until this moment, the thought of Ireland hadn't even entered his mind. "No. Philadelphia will be fine."

Mooney's eyes narrowed. "Are you sure? Wouldn't you rather go home, wherever that might be?"

John's eyes drifted out to sea. He imagined the wreck of the *Wandering Hart* on the ocean floor, resting in cold darkness.

"I don't have a home."

Chapter 15

Church Creek Mill
Outside Philadelphia, Pennsylvania
Monday, July 4th, 1803

The full moon hung low and orange, like a bruise in the night sky. Cicadas buzzed the counterpoint to a symphony of croaking frogs. Fifteen smugglers rowed a small boat against the lazy current of Church Creek. Fifteen men spitting tobacco over the side and scratching beards with filthy hands. A sleepy mist broke apart in their wake. All around them, silhouettes of ash and hickory leaves blotted out the landscape beyond.

As the boat came around a bend, the narrow Delaware tributary opened up into a large millpond. A twin of the moon brooded in the glassy surface. On the far side, a three-story mill rose out of the mist like an apparition. Light in its windows filtered through a ghostly shroud. The gabled roof appeared to drift against the stars. At the foot of the mill, below a fifteen-foot cliff, a dock extended into the water. A dozen men with torches lined its edges. At the end stood a dark figure in a tall hat, sipping a churchwarden pipe.

John sat near the bow, feeling the eyes of Laffite's

henchmen on his back. The moment John showed up at Martin Jameson's warehouse, they gave him no choice but to come along. There was nothing to do but sit and chew his tobacco. All was in motion. Triumph or fail, live or die, John's days in Philadelphia were done.

The rowers shouldered their oars as the boat coasted toward the dock. John caught the bow, stepped out, and tied it to the cleat. Pierre Laffite waited a few feet away, patiently rolling a coin down his knuckles. As the other smugglers disembarked, John turned and faced the French pirate. His men were sweating through shirts and kerchiefs in the summer heat. Martin Jameson stood a few paces behind his employer, mopping a soaked cravat across his forehead. Laffite, by contrast, looked like a courtier missing from a ball in his long black jacket and crimson waistcoat.

"It seems my men owe me a handsome little sum," said Laffite. "They all bet you would not show."

"I considered alternatives."

"Running? It's not like you, John." Laffite lit a spill from Jameson's lantern and touched the burning stick to his pipe. As he puffed the tobacco to life, he said, "I take it you have something for me?"

"Fernando Pavia keeps a small stash a few miles downriver. The site is owned by local Spaniards—friends of the family. They expect one more drop tomorrow. If you want to make your move, it has to be tonight."

"And how do I know this information is good?"

"Godfried."

"Come again?" Laffite said, the pipe pinched in his teeth.

"Godfried. My landlady's Irish sheepdog."

Laffite plucked the pipe from his mouth. "Your

landlady's sheepdog."

"Godfried has an exceptional nose." John pulled Fernando Pavia's kerchief—the one he'd found in the road—from his pocket. "All I needed was Pavia's scent. Godfried did the rest. Remarkable animals, dogs."

Laffite looked at the rag, then back at John. He broke into a grin. "Very good, John. I must say, I'm pleased. When my men finish loading the boats, we will board the *Penelope*. I expect you to guide us to the Basque's anchorage without incident; otherwise, it will go badly for you."

"And you won't get the location a moment before."

Laffite chuckled. "I like this side of you, John. Though I'm hurt you find me so untrustworthy."

"I don't trust any man wearing that much velvet." John spit tobacco juice on the dock.

"I think this country is having an un-civilizing influence on you, my friend. Of course, how civilized are the Irish to begin with?"

The group of smugglers laughed—Jameson the loudest.

"Very well," said Laffite. He swept a hand toward the mill like a gracious host welcoming a guest. "Come along then, John. We are in for a long night."

John stepped forward, and the two men started down the dock shoulder to shoulder. For a moment, they walked in silence.

Then Laffite said, "With your love of brag and whist, I imagine you would be fond of poque. Very popular with my countrymen in Bordeaux. Have you played?"

"Never heard of it."

"Really? I'm surprised, given your penchant. For my part, I never liked cards."

"Is that a fact?" John replied flatly.

"Backgammon—now there is a *real* game."

They reached the end of the dock where, on John's right, a hook dangled over a large platform. John's eyes wandered up to the rope's source high above. On the highest floor of the mill, an enclosed jetty projected over the creek like a castle turret. Through the open trap door in the bottom, he could make out the block and tackle used to haul up loads on the hook. The two men passed the platform by. They started up three flights of stairs zig-zagging to the top of the embankment.

"Never liked dice games," said John.

"Pity. They say it was played by the ancient Pharaohs of Egypt. I used to play in Cap Francais with a favorite business client of mine. A very wealthy planter, Monsieur Claude Gabauriau. As ruthless a player as he was a businessman. We would sip sherry and discuss philosophy under the shade of a lime tree in the square. A fine way to pass a hot day in the West Indies."

"How wonderful," John said, raising his voice over splashing water. Directly beside the stairs, the mill's wheel rotated forty feet in the air. Drops from the paddles alighted on his face.

"Oh, yes," Laffite agreed cheerfully. "He thought of his slaves as his wards and tried always to treat them with boundless generosity. I once asked him if he ever worried about his 'wards' joining the uprising. '*S'il vous plait, mon ami!*' he once told me. 'To call this a rebellion is so much melodrama! Dogs may escape a leash, but that hardly makes them conquerors.' His favorite house slave was standing right there when he said it—what was his name—Michel? Mathis?"

Laffite and John came to the top of the stairwell. John

could hear the creaking and clunking of the mill's machinery. Fog swirled through the lamplight of the ground-floor windows.

"'Look how finely dressed and well-mannered my Mathis is!' he'd say. 'But for the kindness of white men, he'd still be wearing rags and dancing around fires in the jungle.'" Laffite gesticulated dramatically. He quoted in a deep, pontificating voice. "'Once these rebels get a taste of life outside our care, they will tire of their tantrums and come running home.'"

Laffite chuckled to himself. He and John came to the large double doors on the east side of the mill. To their right, the conical roof of the grain silo pointed towards the North Star.

Laffite stopped short of entering. "The last day I was in Cap-Francais, I was ordering the crew of the *Penelope* to cast off while a mob of rebels overran the last soldiers. But Gabauriau—the fool would not board."

Curious in spite of himself, John asked, "What was he doing?"

"As the *Penelope* was drifting out to sea, Gabauriau was screaming at Mathis and the mob behind him. 'How dare you! After all I've done for you! Get back to the house at once!' He drew his sword and charged. The last thing I saw in Saint-Domingue was Mathis beating the brains out of my favorite backgammon player."

John dug through his tobacco pouch. He pressed a pinch of leaves under his lip. He looked at Laffite as he kneaded the tobacco with his tongue.

Laffite put his hand on the doorknob but didn't turn it. "You see, John, in the end, he couldn't accept his cause was lost."

John stared at Laffite a moment, forgetting to spit.

A smile crept into Laffite's eyes. "We could all learn a lesson from *Monsieur* Gabauriau."

Laffite gave a push, and the double doors swung inward. A clockwork of clicking gears, rotating shafts, and connecting sprockets crowded a factory floor. Dozens of sconces—the candles enclosed by glass so as not to ignite the grain dust—filled the space with light. John saw no sign of Captain Aubert and the Marines, but it was early yet.

"Samson, Renaud," Laffite nodded at the two men. "Get started, if you please."

Jameson fidgeted with his cufflinks. He paced erratically, beads of sweat forming on his face. "I trust all is in order then, Mr. Laffite? You received my shipment last night?"

"*Oui, Monsieur* Jameson." Laffite wrapped the words around his pipe stem. "All is accounted for, ready to be loaded."

"No trouble, then?"

"Trouble? Certainly not. The imports are sold, the exports ready to be loaded, the count whole. The Basques will soon be removed."

John felt a pit in his stomach. By now, Jameson had swiped the funds he needed from Laffite's counting-house. Grey had to be on the way with Aubert and the Marines. *But what's keeping them?* John worried to himself.

Laffite barked orders for his crew to start moving crates to the docks. John couldn't help searching the nooks and crannies for signs of a Marine ambush. On the south wall, the water wheel shaft cranked a series of cogs, connecting belts, and gears. A line of six millstones on the south side of the ground floor spun beneath hoppers. Crushed grain spilled down chutes into stone basins ten feet across. A narrow mezzanine ran along all four walls. A catwalk cut east to west across the middle of the room. Machinery, workbenches, and stacked barrels of grist cluttered the north side. Ropes and pulleys dangled from the third floor like vines in a jungle. There were no workers—probably dismissed by the band of criminals graciously renting the space.

"Where shall I start?" John said to Laffite, gesturing to the crates of illegal goods stashed throughout the building. Casks of liquor, clothing, tobacco. Ingots of copper and steel. Weapons of every kind. All free of tariffs and excise taxes. Ten paces away, John recognized two hilts sticking out of an open barrel. His weapons, *Ace* and *Spade*.

Laffite tilted his head. "*Au contraire.* Allow me to start by thanking you, John."

"Spare me, Laffite. I take no pleasure in betraying the Basques."

"No," Laffite smiled. "For this."

In a single motion, Laffite pulled his pistol, cocked the hammer, and raised it in John's direction. He fired.

Smoke exploded from the barrel with an ear-splitting crack. John looked to his right. A neat red button of blood oozed from Jameson's forehead. A jet of brain matter fanned out on the floor behind him. For one brief second, Jameson's corpse remained standing in wide-eyed surprise, then dropped.

As his crew pulled pistols on John, Laffite added, "I always wondered if he was shorting me. But you settled that matter, didn't you?"

"Laffite," John said. "What are you doing? We have a deal."

"No, John, we *had* a deal. And had you kept your end,

I would have been happy to let you go. But you conspired to double-cross me."

A cacophony rose from the granary door as it scraped open. John looked to the source of the sound. The bony sailor Renaud and his muscular counterpart Samson led two prisoners out of the silo: Melisande and Grey Feather. Ropes bound their hands behind their backs. Blood trickled from Melisande's swollen lip. Violet blotches darkened her jaw. Grey Feather's right eye had nearly swollen shut; blood crusted over the other. Melisande looked at her adversaries like an angry badger; Grey assessed them calmly. Blood drained from John's face.

"Come on, you buggers!" spat Renaud as he dragged Melisande. She jerked and kicked.

Two men seized John and pulled him to one of the columns supporting the catwalk. Wrenching his arms behind him, they bound his hands to the thick beam with cords of rope. Renaud and Samson tied Melisande and Grey Feather to adjacent columns.

"Your little plan almost worked," Laffite said, shaking his head. "My men weren't watching Jameson or the savage. And your little squaw easily lost my clumsy oafs." Laffite sneered askance at Francois. Then he sashayed toward Melisande, celebrating with a titter. "Ah, but you never saw my man Nichols blending into the crowd, slinking through the trees. He's half-Indian—or didn't you know, *Mam'selle* Dufort?"

"You're done, frog!" Melisande spat. "Sully's a bad enemy to have."

"Really, my dear?" replied Laffite. "Then why is he the one tied up?"

"You can still have the location of the Basques,

Laffite," said John. "Just let them go."

"It's too late for that, John. Captain Aubert won't be joining us tonight, but I'll keep his wife's pets hostage all the same."

Francois flashed a yellow grin at Melisande. "Before the night's done, I daresay we can teach this one to like the menfolk."

Melisande's eyes turned feral. "Before the night's done, I'll have your guts."

Francois took a step forward. "Is that right?"

"Careful," Grey Feather said. "She means it."

Francois glared at the Iroquois prisoner and drew his knife.

"Francois," interrupted Laffite. "Your boorishness is beneath the reputation of the Brothers Laffite. Now get to work."

"Mr. Laffite, sir," said a tan, skinny man with dark mutton-chops. He approached Laffite out of breath.

"Yes, Nichols," Laffite said, still leering at John.

"Whitlock's on his fastest horse. He should arrive with the bounty by dawn."

"Do you hear that, John?" Laffite nodded toward Grey Feather and Melisande. "Those two will give me Aubert. Aubert will give me the Basques. And the Tindalls will give me a small fortune for you." His eyes became distant as if he were slipping into a pleasant daydream. "This night could only improve if a Parisian courtesan tickled *mon cul.*"

John's face twisted into an expression somewhere between curiosity and disgust.

Laffite smiled and sauntered out of the mill. His men dispersed, quickly falling into a line of workers hauling crates, barrels, and sacks out to the dock.

"I never should have trusted you," Grey Feather said to John. "This is your fault."

"I made Melisande swear to keep out of this!" John spat back.

"You knew *damn well* she would follow. You used her."

"I am trying to help her. Help all of us."

Melisande slumped into a sigh. "All right, all right, you can stop whining like a *pair of nannies who spilled the governess' tea*," she said, slipping into a poor English accent. "This one's on me, ok? I didn't think Laffite was smart enough to hire a Seneca tracker."

"No, the fault is mine, Little Crow," said Grey Feather. "I should have known it was too easy to lose the others."

"We'll kick Laffite in the bullocks, yet. Sully's already got a new plan. Sully's always got a plan. Isn't that right, Sully?" She looked over at John, worry creeping into her voice. "Sully, what's the plan?"

"I'm sorry, Melly," John said. "Nothing yet."

For a moment, none of them spoke.

Then John added, "But we still have until dawn, and we're not giving up."

Melisande lit up. "Right! Let's try those ropes."

In silence, the three fumbled at their knots while Laffite's crew began their long night of work.

Chapter 16

Church Creek Mill
Outside Philadelphia, Pennsylvania
Monday, July 4th, 1803

Samson shoved John into a chair, hands bound. For hours, John, Melisande, and Grey Feather struggled at their bonds in vain. The ropes were tied well—certainly a testament to Samson's seamanship. Now, Laffite stood over John, puffing his pipe. Blood-stained floorboards drew John's eye. The image of Martin Jameson's pale corpse flashed through his mind, dead eyes locked in eternal surprise. The mill door scraped open, and the sound of heavy boots approached from behind.

Laffite looked in the direction of the newcomer. "Your cargo, delivered in promised condition."

Spurs rang with each footfall. A towering, grizzled man circled into view. His salt and pepper hair, beard, and mustache hid much of his weathered face. Sweat beaded below the wide brim of his hat. John could never forget Francis Whitlock. The grotesque slave-driver who once served Clyde Tindall, a wealthy Virginia planter. That is, until their attempt to enslave Ethan Auldon ended with John killing Clyde Tindall in a duel.

Whitlock stared at John with narrow eyes. "Good." He handed a heavy purse to Laffite. "All eagles."

Laffite opened the purse and ran his index finger through the coins. "Very good. Do convey my gratitude to *Monsieur* Henry Tindall…"

"Aye," Whitlock replied in a Virginia drawl. "Mr. Tindall regrets this unpleasant misunderstanding. He welcomes your renewed business in the Chesapeake."

In his most phlegmatic French accent, Laffite replied, "Of course. My best to *Monsieur* Tindall and his kin."

Whitlock stepped forward. He loomed above John like a cliff. "As I hoped. You look healthy. Vigorous."

"As I expected," John replied, "you smell like horse piss."

Whitlock's expression didn't change. He didn't reply. He brought his right hand to rest on John's left shoulder. His grip closed like a bear trap.

A deep bundle of scar tissue seized up. John felt the phantom bullet like a hot spike. The pain forced out a yelp. He flushed red as he resisted the urge to cry out again.

Whitlock released his grip. "I'll return directly." He strolled out of the mill.

Laffite sighed, shaking his head at John. "Don't be cross with me, John. I can hardly apologize for applying a firm hand in business."

John's eyelids drooped as he recovered from the jolt to his shoulder. "You're scum, Laffite, and so is your brother."

"This from a man who smuggled in my employ? Used his friends like pawns? Killed Clyde Tindall in cold blood?"

"Clyde Tindall profited from human misery—like you. He got what he deserved."

"*Mon Dieu,* there is your proof!" Laffite spread his hands like an attorney before a court. "You chose your own tiresome sanctimony over survival! I'm just a trader John. I can't help it if flesh is in demand. A man is only as good as the world allows him to be. There is an order to things that will never change."

An odd movement stirred in John's periphery. It came from somewhere up high, in the northwest corner of the mill behind Laffite. With Laffite's eyes on him, John couldn't risk a better look.

Ethan watched from his hiding place at the base of a rotating wooden column. Fernando Pavia carefully climbed onto the west end of the Church Creek Mill's catwalk. While Ethan waited for Pavia to get into position, he heard John Sullivan crying out in pain. Francis Whitlock was squeezing Sullivan's shoulder, tormenting an old wound. Ethan's hands had been shaking with anger ever since he saw Whitlock enter the mill. The scars crisscrossing his back began to itch. His breathing quickened. He felt cool beads of sweat pooling on his chest. Sullivan cried out again.

The rope cuts like piano wire.

"Ten!" Shouts Whitlock. The whip slices across Ethan's back.

Each new stroke sets his body on fire. Each is more painful than the last. His legs buckle under him. The twine rips deeper into his hands.

"You learnin' yet, boy?" Another stroke. "Eleven!"

Like a fishhook ripping his flesh. He feels urine running down his legs. He hangs from his hands, bound high on a post. Blood runs down his body.

"Twelve!"

Ethan forced the memory away. He slowed his breathing the way Pavia taught him. The fear could wait. The rage could wait. His friends needed him. He resolved to follow his Basque friend's lead.

Be with me Lord, in the watches of the night, he prayed.

Ethan threaded himself through the assemblage of machinery, grist barrels, and workbenches on the north side of the mill. The cranking shafts and squealing gears were so loud he hardly needed to quiet his footsteps. As he listened to Laffite and Sullivan talk, he crept behind the stacks of barrels until he reached a patch of open floor. Just ahead, Grey Feather and Melisande sat with hands tied to thick support beams. A series of turning shafts behind them would give him some cover, but he would need to cross the gap. Laffite and the four men with him were distracted by the conversation with John. Hopefully, they wouldn't see him in their periphery.

I cling to you; your right hand upholds me. His father's favorite prayer.

None of them were looking. Ethan struck out, crossed the gap, and came to a pair of bound hands. The beam was just wide enough to hide him. He gently tapped Melisande's forearm.

Melisande kept her eyes forward.

"Pavia and the Basques are here," he whispered. "Be ready."

Melisande gently squeezed Ethan's hand. She remained perfectly still as he cut through her bonds. When the rope parted, Melisande kept her hands against the sides of the beam. Ethan pressed the hilt of a copper dagger into her palm. She closed her grip around it. Ethan shuffled to the next column where Grey Feather waited.

"You're wrong, Laffite," John was saying. "The world is changing. You won't be able to sell slaves forever."

"I doubt it, but either way, I will be alive and well."

The movement in the corner came closer. Towards the back of the mill, a figure nimbly dropped from the railing of the catwalk onto one of the horizontal gears spinning ten feet above the floor. The man timed his landing with the loud *cuh-clunk* of a nearby sprocket.

"Whitlock doesn't have me yet," John replied.

"Always the gambler, eh John? I'm afraid that lucky card isn't coming this time."

Fernando Pavia came into view as he ran across the series of interconnected gears. He stopped on the last one, six feet behind Laffite. Two pistols were tucked into his gold sash. He wore a saber across his back, and a long, curved dagger on his hip—his favorite Sikh *kirpan*. Another dagger hilt poked out of his tall riding boots. He held a piece of slow-burning cord in his right hand, a grenade in his left. Making brief eye contact with John, he looked in the direction of a stack of grain nearby.

Laffite patted his prisoner on the cheek. "*Au revoir, mon ami.*" He turned to walk away.

Pavia crouched as the rotating gear brought him around. He lit the fuse.

"Don't you find, Pierre?" John said, causing Laffite to pause. "Men are always most careless a few feet from their door."

The smuggler frowned.

Pavia tossed the grenade. John dove onto the floor. A blinding flash as several sacks of grain ignited. A deafening concussion. Flaming grist filled the air. Renaud screamed as he landed on the ground, fire spreading over his jacket.

Pavia leaped off the gear and tumbled forward. "How about an easy surrender, eh *amigos?*"

Laffite, Samson, and Nichols, recovering from the blast, reached for pistols.

Pavia shrugged. "Worth a try." He charged, saber singing out of its sheath. He drove the blade between Samson's ribs, carried forward a step, and hooked the *kirpan* into Nichols's neck. Renaud slashed at the Basque's stomach with his cutlass, but Pavia turned it aside. Steel struck steel as the two traded blows.

Laffite had his pistol cocked and aimed at Pavia. John, hands still bound, charged headfirst into the pirate's stomach. The two men sprawled on the ground. Laffite's pistol slid away. Laffite thrust his right knee into John's side. Sitting atop Laffite, John head-butted the smuggler. A gash ripped open above Laffite's right eye. White light shot through John's vision with the impact. Before John could land a second blow, he caught sight of Francois running towards him, saber drawn.

John rolled beneath Francois's swing just in time. Now on his back, John looked up to see Francois pulling back for the killing thrust.

A copper dagger thudded into Francois' right side. He growled in pain and fumbled at the hilt. Melisande, following her throw, charged his flank. She swung the beak of her war club full force into his knee. The leg staved in with a wet snap. The pirate collapsed in a fit of wailing. Melisande piled onto his belly, plucked her dagger free, and reversed the grip.

She wore a gleeful smile. "I did promise, didn't I?"

Her knife plunged with the speed of a pouncing cat. She opened his belly from ribs to groin. The flesh parted so fast, there was no blood. Then it welled up like a spring.

"*Alumno!*" Pavia called as he pressed a boot into Renaud's corpse and pulled his saber free.

John saw Laffite reaching for his pistol. Following Pavia's cue, John dashed the few paces between them and turned his bound hands toward the sword-master. Pavia severed the ropes with a swift stroke.

"Move!" Pavia ordered. He, Melisande, and John dove behind a grouping of columns and gear shafts. Laffite fired. The ball bit the corner of a beam in front of John.

"Kill them!" Laffite shouted to a group of his men who had stormed into the mill.

The men hesitated at the door. Fire was spreading through the grist and machinery on the south wall. The air was choked with ash and burning kernels. They held out their hands against the heat. One managed to level a musket toward John. Before he could fire, a hail of shots poured into him. Several of Pavia's Basque mercenaries charged into the mill behind the smugglers, swords drawn.

Seeing his men outnumbered and engulfed in a losing melee, Laffite ran for a ladder onto the second-floor mezzanine.

"Where does he think he's going?" said Ethan, coming up beside John. Grey Feather crouched beside him.

"To a fiery death," said Melisande.

John clapped Ethan's arm. "Glad you could make it, mate." They exchanged a grin.

"How did you find us?" Grey Feather asked Pavia.

"We did as *Señor* Sullivan instructed," said Pavia, looking past the column for a clear path to the door. "We watched *Señorita* Melisande. When Laffite's man Nichols followed her, we followed him. *Facil.*"

"You *knew?*" Melisande punched John's arm.

John smiled. "I knew you'd be you."

That got her beaming.

Pavia's men had cleared Laffite's men out of the way, and the Basque signaled for his companions to make their exit.

"And you didn't tell us?" Grey Feather demanded as they broke cover.

"I couldn't tip my hand in front of Laffite, could I?" John winked. "Pavia, get them out of here." John hurdled over debris, shielding his face from the withering heat.

"Where are you going?" Melisande called.

"Laffite and I have business," John called back. Over his shoulder, he saw Pavia lead a charge into a few pirate stragglers. The mercenary's saber sliced through the first. Grey Feather buried his tomahawk in the chest of a second. Melisande clubbed a third.

From a barrel near the spreading fire, John snatched his rapier, *Ace*, and his dagger, *Spade*. The hilts were hot to the touch. He grimaced as he sheathed them in his belt and made for the ladder.

Smoke stung John's eyes when he made it onto the catwalk. Soot clogged the air, but he could make out movement in the northeast corner. He crossed over the rows of millstones and gears beneath, then wove his way through the clutter of crates on the mezzanine. He found a ladder thrust through a window, but no sign of anyone. He scanned in every direction. Flames licked up the walls from the first floor. The teeth of gears ground and snapped. Shafts and beams sheared apart. John heard footsteps behind him.

Spinning just in time, John deflected Laffite's thrust. The rail boxed in John's sword arm, so he fell back, dodging Laffite's slashes. He ducked a swing aimed at his throat, then zagged behind Laffite. The two enemies faced each other. Laffite held his sword high and level; John kept *Ace* low, close, and pointed at Laffite's chest.

"You see, John?" Laffite said. "You'd rather burn here with me than escape with your friends."

"I'm not here to burn, Laffite. I'm here to deliver one last piece of cargo—in promised condition."

"You forget how our last bout ended." Laffite lunged.

John's hand smarted as he blocked Laffite's strikes. Peals of clashing steel joined the crackle of the fire. Laffite sneered and launched into an ambitious lunge. The smuggler was angry. Giving up tells. Sloppy.

John let Laffite take ground. He kept his stance low, concentrated on turning away the precise strikes and staying clear of the wild ones. He watched for another sneer—his opening. Infuriated at the stalemate, Laffite fell back onto the catwalk. John pursued, forcing him back and back again.

Laffite's upper lip twitched. John saw the sneer and darted back, letting his opponent stumble with failed momentum. With a quick thrust, John opened a hole in Laffite's shoulder.

"Agh!" cried Laffite, backing off. "It's wasted effort, John. Poor *Papa* is feeding the buzzards by now. And *Maman*? Dead of whore's disease."

John relaxed his grip. Leveled his rapier. "You're bested, Pierre. Drop the sword."

A cloud of grain dust ignited and exploded. The shudder in the catwalk sent both combatants reeling. John felt like he was in a kiln. His white shirt clung to his skin, soaked with sweat. Black clouds of soot roiled overhead. He grabbed the rail to right himself.

Laffite looked around as if only now noticing the mill on fire and Church Creek swarming with Basques. He dropped his sword. "I guess you win, John. Savor this moment. Because I can promise you: the Laffite Brothers have a long memory."

The catwalk shuddered again. Then dropped five feet as the supporting column gave way. Boards parted under John's boots. He dove for the next supporting beam. The catwalk collapsed underfoot. His fingers barely caught the ledge. *Ace* clattered on the walkway above. Columns of fire rose from barrels and collapsing machinery nearby. Flames licked up towards his dangling feet. Over his shoulder, he saw Laffite fleeing along the opposite mezzanine.

The fire below crept higher. The soles of his boots heated like coals. John struggled to pull himself up, but he couldn't find purchase. The harder he tried, the more his fingers weakened.

He was slipping…Slipping…

"Sully!" Melisande appeared above him on the catwalk.

"Melly?" John looked up in astonishment. "Where did you…?"

"What? You thought I'd let you roast like a rabbit on a spit?" Melisande grabbed John's right forearm with both hands. She braced her feet and helped him up. When they were both sitting on the catwalk, panting, she smiled like a gambler gloating after a win. "That's *two* you owe me, ole mick!"

Choking on smoke, John scooted back from the ledge. "Laffite…"

"Forget the frog!" Melisande tugged John to his feet. He scooped up *Ace,* and the two ran for the mezzanine.

A chunk of the third floor came crashing down in the center of the mill. Fire crackled in every pile of crates. No path down, no path to the windows. "Melly, we need a way out."

"The way I came. Hurry!"

John followed Melisande up a ladder leading to the third floor. His lungs burned. His head swam, and his balance faltered. Melisande caught his arm when he tripped over a fallen plank. They staggered through the crumbling mill until they reached a door in the corner. Melisande threw it open, pulled John inside, and slammed it shut.

John realized he was inside the small jetty that extended over the creek. The large trap door in the floor looked down onto the docks below, where John and Laffite had walked only hours ago. A series of pulleys fed a thick rope through the opening, down to the cargo platform. A hook dangled at the bottom of the rope, inches above the dock. Firelight flickered in the inky surface of the creek. The rope was on fire, and a trail of flames was climbing towards them.

"Shit!" Melisande jumped onto the rope and quickly sawed through the piece inches below her feet. Just as the fire neared her toes, the burning length fell away.

John stared at the coil of cable, now burning on the dock some fifty feet down. "Shit."

Still wrapped around the rope, Melisande pointed to the cleat mounted on the wall. "Lower me down."

John untied the rope. When he gained a hold over

Melisande's weight, he doled out slack. He reached the end after twelve feet. Melisande still hung two stories above the platform. He tied off and said, "That's it."

"What do you mean 'that's it?'"

The timbers of the jetty groaned, threatening to collapse. John jumped onto the rope and slid down to Melisande's level. He entwined his feet with hers. Her eyes flickered like those of a wolf beyond a campfire.

"The creek," said John.

Melisande looked at the water below. She grinned. "I like it. You think it's deep enough?"

"One and a half—two fathoms. At least."

"Sully…"

"Well, we're about to find out."

She tightened her grip. "Towards the mill…Go!"

They kicked their feet in unison, first towards the building, then back towards the water. Steadily, they built momentum. After several swings, John managed to land a foot against the mill. He kicked off, and the two went hurdling. Then they kicked off again.

"Now?" Melly asked.

"No."

Another swing got them a foot past the platform.

"Now?!" she said.

"One more."

A final kick off the wall and they passed over the water.

"Jump!" cried John.

They dropped. John brought his feet together. Straightened his legs. The water hit his feet like the canes of his former captors. Cold swallowed his world. He landed in the soft mud of the creek bed. All motion ceased. He drifted in the depths, the heat of the fire driven out. At last, in this place, he could breathe.

John breached the surface and gulped in air. He found himself treading water beside Melisande. They stared at the spectacular blaze.

"You realize, Melisande," John said. "If we're being truthful, *you* are a frog."

Melisande pondered a moment. "And you're one lucky mick."

The pair snickered.

The mill's roof fell in, and they snickered a little louder. The walls collapsed next, and their snicker became a chuckle. The silo crumbled to kindling. They looked at each other for a moment, then back at the blaze. They reveled in the cold water, the fresh air, the joy of being alive.

They howled with laughter.

Chapter 17

Near Church Creek Mill
Outside Philadelphia, Pennsylvania
Monday, July 4th, 1803

Ethan Auldon ran as hard as he had ever run in his life. His heart pounded in his chest. He felt pure terror. He scrambled up an embankment with a pistol in his hand. He slipped in the soft earth, then grabbed a wet tuft of grass to regain his balance. He crashed through brush. Trampled stalks of teasel. Ignored the switch of stinging nettle ripping across his arm. He could hear footsteps nearby, crashing through reeds. He could hear gunfire and the roar of the burning mill far behind. He felt the fire of adrenaline in his muscles. He was closing in. About to catch his quarry. Ethan Auldon was terrified—of himself.

Ethan had no name for what drove him. But it pushed his legs past exhaustion, his senses past their limits, his mind past fear. The thick tangles of grass, weeds, and brush parted into a clearing. Ethan's momentum nearly sent him sprawling. He slid to a stop and looked around. He stood in a copse of tall pines. Blackberry brambles threaded between thick trunks. Treetops obscured the dying light of the moon. Without a lantern, Ethan could only see by starlight. The sounds of battle faded in the distance. Even the crickets sang softer, as if afraid to disturb the night. He heard no footsteps. He wanted to rush ahead, but his wits took over. He ducked behind a tree and waited.

Being still felt like standing on hot coals. To busy his mind, he checked his pistol. Half-cocked. When he saw the target, he would bring it to full-cock. He carefully watched the clearing. Concentrated on slowing his breathing. Deep breaths from the belly. One at a time.

He listened. A rustling of leaves. Shouts echoing in the distance.

And then: footsteps. Ethan tensed. He repositioned his grip on the pistol. His finger settled on the trigger guard. He waited.

Francis Whitlock peered into the clearing from behind a spruce. He calmly searched the woods. Satisfied, he stepped into the clearing. A well-worn trail cut north towards the city, and the slave-driver headed for it. When he had his first foot on the path, the unmistakable cocking of a pistol hit the night like a thunderclap. Whitlock froze, staring into the woods.

"Hmm," Whitlock scoffed. "I tried to out-skulk a nigro. Guess it serves me right."

"Fuck you," Ethan said, his pistol aimed straight at Whitlock's head. He stood ten paces away. The gun trembled in his grasp. "Turn around, you ugly shit!"

Whitlock turned a slow circle to face Ethan. He put his hands up. "We got to know each other pretty well on the Tindall Plantation, didn't we, boy?"

"Aye, and I've been dreaming of this moment ever since." Even as Ethan savored his revenge, he thought of his late father.

Another log pops as it catches fire. The light of the hearth illuminates Father's face. The Bible is the only book Seth Auldon can read, mostly because he's memorized the words. Mother sits on the couch holding Priscilla. Judith and Ansel lay on their stomachs on the floor, legs kicking in the air. Ethan prods at the fire, listening to his father recite the Gospel of Luke.

"Love your enemies, do good to them which hate you."'

"I don't think you got it in you," gloated Whitlock. "I think—"

The hammer struck. There was a pop. A flash lit up Whitlock's wide-eyed shock.

Whitlock grasped at his chest. He patted himself, swiveled his head both ways. But there was no wound. No holes in the tree behind.

Ethan's arm remained suspended in midair, a puff of smoke rising from the hammer. The pan had flashed, but the powder failed to ignite. A new feeling washed away the old one—a sickness. He stared at the man he had failed to murder. He couldn't move.

Whitlock gushed a sigh of relief. He shook his head, clucking his tongue. "Misfire. Damn shame. Don't worry—I reckon this will be a short fight." Whitlock's shoulders straightened. His hands balled into fists. He took a step forward.

A new voice came from the dark. "Shorter than you think, *señor.*"

Fernando Pavia burst out of the nearby brush and kicked Whitlock's legs. As Whitlock fell to his knees, Pavia followed with a palm strike to his face, then a jab to the ribs. Caught off guard and off balance, Whitlock didn't bother with fists. With speed that didn't seem possible, the larger man launched headlong into Pavia like a charging bull. He lifted the Basque in a crushing embrace, then slammed him to the ground.

Whitlock closed his hands around the mercenary's throat, ignoring three punches to his face.

Ethan's ramrod piped a sour note as it plunged down the barrel of his pistol. When the ball and wadding reached the bottom, he snatched the powder horn from his belt and started to pour. As badly as his hands were shaking, he spilled most of the black powder on his feet. How many times had he loaded a gun with ease and speed under Pavia's watchful gaze? But now that a man's life depended on it, he could hardly remember how. A howl of pain drew Ethan's attention.

Pavia had plunged his *kirpan* into Whitlock's beefy arm. He yanked the dagger, then wrapped his opponent in a leg hold. With the precision of a Greek wrestler, the Basque twisted his opponent to the ground and slipped free. On his feet, he sauntered around Whitlock, greasy ropes of blood hanging from the *kirpan*. Whitlock struggled to get up, but Pavia harried him with a slash to the thigh. Another cut to the triceps and the hefty overseer crumpled to the ground.

"'Bless them that curse you, and pray for them which despitefully use you.'"

While Whitlock sputtered on the ground, Pavia calmly cleaned his blade and sheathed it. Even from a quarter mile away, the burning mill cast the clearing in a dim glow. As Whitlock struggled to his knees, cradling his arm, Ethan felt like throwing up. Water gathered at the edges of his vision. He felt hate. Guilt. Fury. Despair. He longed for home. And he longed to sail to places unknown and never return.

Fernando Pavia came alongside Ethan, still panting

from his fight. He pulled a pistol from his belt. He traded it to Ethan for the half-loaded one.

"Go on then, *Señor* Auldon," said Pavia. He cocked an eyebrow at Whitlock. "Like I always say, practice is the key."

Whitlock half sneered, half smiled. "Well, how about that? It's your lucky day. Don't even have to break a sweat for your revenge! Just like your kind to let someone else do all the work."

To kill a man on his knees—it went against every lesson Ethan's father ever taught him. Christ died on the cross to save all—even men like Whitlock. To Him alone did vengeance belong. It was a fact. So why did Ethan find himself stepping forward? "It doesn't matter who kills you," said Ethan, the pistol in point-blank range of the slave-driver's forehead. "It's justice."

"Oh, let's not go fooling ourselves with all notions of civility, boy. Go on and murder a white man. You'll never get a better chance."

"Do what you must, *Señor* Auldon," said Pavia. "So long as you're prepared to live with your choice."

The cool metal of the trigger dug into Ethan's finger. Ethan wanted to squeeze it. At that moment, there was nothing he wanted more.

"'And unto him that smiteth thee on the one cheek, offer also the other.'"

"Three slaves go free," Whitlock said, "if you spare me."

Ethan's finger loosened. "You're lying."

"Ain't lying," Whitlock calmly argued. "I brought three house slaves with me for personal needs. They're on a farm with friends of the Tindalls. It's not far."

Ethan ground his teeth. He looked at Pavia.

The swordmaster shrugged his shoulders. "Up to you, *alumno*. But you should know, chances for retribution don't come often."

Ethan shifted his balance forward. He pressed the gun to Whitlock's skin.

"Go ahead," Whitlock crowed. He pressed closer to the gun barrel. "Hollow out my skull and send them slaves right back to the plantation."

Ethan's face twisted into a snarl, his nostrils flared, and he roared. He jerked the gun barrel to the right and fired into the dirt. Whitlock recoiled from the deafening shot. Pavia sighed and looked at the ground. Ethan felt his muscles go slack.

Ethan handed the pistol back to Pavia and murmured, "He'll tell you where they are. In exchange, he lives."

The mercenary tilted his head by way of a nod. He touched Ethan's shoulder, then drew his saber. "On your feet," Pavia commanded Whitlock.

Ethan turned back. He trudged through the brush, not bothering to avoid thorns or twigs. He felt numb. The glow of the smoldering mill poked through the forest. From the depths of the past, while he walked in the dark, it wasn't the words of the Savior whispering to him, but his father's.

"We can't choose the world we live in, but we can choose how we live in the world.

"When it's your time to choose, son, I'll be with you."

Hot tears ran down Ethan's face.

Chapter 18

Mrs. McClintock's Water Street Lodging
Philadelphia, Pennsylvania
Thursday, July 28th, 1803

In the parlor mirror of Mrs. McClintock's Water Street Lodging, John Sullivan inspected his navy uniform. The double-breasted coat was the perfect shade of dark blue. The trim was gold, though for the lapel buttons he had to settle for brass. His white stockings, breeches, waistcoat, and under-collar fit without a wrinkle. His black bicorne hat pointed forward and back, rather than side to side, in keeping with modern fashion. *Ace* and *Spade* were sheathed at his belt. His new shoes were polished to a perfect jet-black, his beard clean-shaven, and his hair tied back. Godfried sat behind him panting as if to share the moment. John thought he hadn't wanted an officer's commission, but now that he had it, he felt euphoric. For the first time in five years, he felt true freedom. John Sullivan was going back to sea.

"You look very handsome, Mr. Midshipman Sullivan," said Grace Auldon.

John hurried to remove his hat and tuck it under his arm. Mrs. Auldon came into the frame of the mirror and hung an arm on his shoulder. She admired the image, her cheeks dimpling as she smiled. If he didn't know better, he might have described her expression as one of pride.

"I suppose I do," John smiled.

"A bit lacking in humility though." She feigned a disapproving frown.

John awkwardly scratched his head and turned to face her. "I meant to say—thank you very kindly, Mrs. Auldon."

She cocked an eyebrow. "Better."

"Come for tea with Mrs. McClintock?"

"Not today. I came to say my farewells."

John looked around the otherwise empty room. "Ethan is coming here?"

"No, Mr. Sullivan. Ethan went aboard the *Philadelphia* yesterday. We've said our farewells."

"Then you've come to say farewell…to me?"

"You *are* departing for the Barbary Coast today, are you not?"

"Yes, ma'am, I am. I suppose I'm just a little surprised, given our differences over the years."

"You've grown on me. By small degrees."

"Well I…I don't know what to say."

"You usually don't. But you're young."

John smiled. He stared at his feet a moment. "I suppose I could say that…I'm grateful. That I will never forget your kindness. Or everything you and Mr. Auldon, and Ethan, did for me. I hope you can forgive me for the trouble I brought to your family."

"You misunderstand, Mr. Sullivan." She straightened John's upper collar. "You're part of the family now."

Taken aback, John replied, "I'm honored."

"Oh, don't get too excited just yet. Family means duty.

It means you can sail to the far side of the world, but you'll never be rid of us."

"Doesn't it follow that you'll never be rid of *me*?"

Mrs. Auldon frowned. "Yes, it had occurred to me. I did say 'by *small* degrees.'"

"I can't help it if I'm charming," John shrugged.

"There's a lot about yourself you can't help. Fortunately for me, I'm getting something out of it."

"And that is?"

"A promise. That you'll look after Ethan for me."

"Actually, he tends to do a lot of looking after me."

"I know. You don't have to tell me he's strong—I know he is. This is different."

John knit his brows, waiting for her to elaborate.

"You and I—we do what it takes. We survive. We fight for our own, and we let go of the rest. Not Ethan. He has so many passions. So many dreams. So much that he carries."

"Mrs. Auldon, I'm not sure I understand what you're asking me."

"You remember the story of Icarus?"

"One of my favorite fables. Icarus's father made him a set of wings with feathers and wax."

"And we know what happened next. You and I see a sun that could melt our wings. Ethan just sees the sun."

"You want me to keep him from soaring too high?"

"No. Be there to catch him if he falls."

"You never had to ask, Mrs. Auldon. I'll look after Ethan with my life."

"I know." Trying for a more chipper tone, she said, "Well, Midshipman? This is the chance you've wanted for a long time. Are you ready?"

"There's no going back now. I sold all that was left of

my father's business, as my uncle wanted. Then I signed over every penny of my proceeds to Fernando Pavia for his help against Pierre Laffite."

"You gave up your inheritance?"

"I wouldn't have seen a penny, what with Uncle Peter turning all his Belfast connections against me. But he'll think twice before cheating a band of battle-hardened mercenaries. Better they should have it. My small share of prize money went to naval books, a few personal effects, and this very handsome uniform."

"What if you reach the Barbary Coast and what you find isn't what you expected?"

"Mam and Katie are out there. They're alive, and they're waiting for my help. Their message proves it. I *will* bring them back."

"Well then, John. I wish you luck. And Godspeed."

John nodded. She embraced him warmly, if briefly. She looked at him a moment with the same haunted expression he had seen in the Sawduster. Without another word, she left the boarding house.

John felt a wooly shape nuzzling his hand. He looked down and saw Godfried begging to be petted. John tousled the hound's shaggy head.

"I shall miss you, boy."

Godfried gave a loud *woof.*

Midshipman John Sullivan stood on the pier, under the shadow of the U.S.S. *Philadelphia* gently rocking at anchor. He looked up at the figurehead of Hercules on her bow. The mythical Greek hero, carved into the same live oak that built the ship, wore only a loincloth and rippled with muscles. He carried a gnarled club in his right hand at the apogee of a swing. He strangled a snake in his left as it slithered up from underfoot. Above the sculpture, the bowsprit jutted forward over the Philadelphia wharf. The foremast teemed with sailors working in the rigging, some of them a hundred sixty feet above the water.

John walked the one-hundred-fifty-foot length of the vessel. Her copper plating shimmered below the waterline. Sailors hauled supplies over the side of her boot-polish black hull. A glossy yellow stripe of paint ran along her eighteen starboard gunports. Gone were the raised and segmented decks of British ships from his youth; the young American frigate's single, flush spar deck defied centuries of shipbuilding convention. His eyes landed on the stern where the flag of the United States fluttered from the ensign halyards. Eight red stripes, seven white stripes, and a constellation of fifteen stars. John felt suddenly astonished to stare at the colors of a country barely older than him.

"We almost left you, mate," said a familiar voice behind him.

John smiled and turned around. "Nah, mate. I'm a fast swimmer."

Ethan Auldon strolled up to John, smiling just as wide. His arms were tucked neatly behind his back, the tails of his double-breasted coat trailing in the breeze. He reached out, and the two friends clasped hands.

"Have a look at us," John said. In the corner of his eye, he caught a few sideways glances from sailors and dockworkers. No doubt they found this warm exchange strange between men of different races. In another time, he might have cared. A time before the Auldons gave him a home. Before Ethan stood with him against Pierre

Laffite. Before he lost everything to the Barbary Pirates. So John smiled the brighter. "I'd say Captain Aubert was as good as his word."

"So were you," Ethan said.

"I couldn't have done it without you, mate," John replied. "But I bet Laffite won't be long for prison. Not with all the men he's bribed and his brother's influence."

"At least he'll be choking on Whitlock's stink for a while. Never were cellmates more perfectly matched. And don't forget—the Navy got his ships. The Marines got his loot. And we both got a share. If a small one."

There was a ringing of spurs as another set of feet clunked toward them. "And you only had to burn down a mill with you inside," added Fernando Pavia, his arms spread with a dramatic flourish. He looked every inch the Spanish don with his mirror-polished breastplate and waxed mustache.

"I don't recall throwing the grenade," said John.

"True, *alumno,*" said Pavia. "Your approach, I think, would have been much less…ah, what is the word?"

"Subtle," said Ethan flatly.

Pavia shot an index finger at Ethan. "That one! Subtle. That is the word."

"We won, didn't we?" John grinned.

"Right," Ethan said, looking at John. "Do they have mills in Tripoli? Because I'd prefer not to fight outnumbered, outflanked, and surrounded by fire."

"Don't worry," John said. "Next time we'll have cannons."

"Very subtle," said Pavia.

"I feel better already," said Ethan.

"Avast, there!" cried a sailor.

They narrowly avoided collision with a crewman

pushing a wagon full of chicken cages. The hens trundled by in a flurry of clucking and flapping.

"I should get aboard," Ethan said. "Dr. Cowdery is expecting me." He touched a closed fist to his forehead by way of salute. John and Pavia touched their hats in kind, and Ethan hurried away.

After a moment, Pavia said, "That was a near thing, *alumno*. Not that I don't appreciate the generous gift of the Sullivan inheritance, but had we lost Nichols in the woods…"

"You didn't," said John, his eyes wandering over the black lacquer on *Philadelphia's* hull. "And here I thought you only came to bid me farewell."

Pavia's gaze followed John's as though they were two strangers happening to stand side by side. "Allow your old swordmaster to impart one final lesson before you set sail."

How often had John groaned at Pavia's lectures? His lessons had often consisted of arguments and shouting as often as swordplay and marksmanship. John had been impatient to learn, frustrated by Pavia's methodical attention to technique. He should have felt like protesting as he had always done before. But today, he found himself grateful for—even relishing—one last piece of advice from his mentor. He wouldn't dare admit it, so he listened.

"I've always told you where to find your sharpest weapon," said Pavia, and he pointed to John's forehead. "But never forget where to find your greatest strength." The Basque mercenary closed his fist and pressed it to his student's chest. "Stay true to the man you are, and others will continue to follow your lead. Let the enemy take that away, and you have lost."

John nodded and shook hands with his mentor. "Thank you for everything, *Comandante* Pavia."

"Good luck, *Señor* Sullivan," said Pavia. He tipped his hat and said in his Basque language, "*Nola bizi, hala hil.*"

John loitered on the dock a moment longer, watching Pavia go. Just as he decided to head to the gangway, a sailor sidled up to him and said, "What, no salute for me, sir?"

John frowned, puzzled. He looked at the short, skinny boy standing next to him. The boy was somewhere between twelve or fourteen. Judging by his white shirt, blue dungarees, and black neckerchief, he was among the lowest ranked crewmen.

Considering the impertinent way the young man had addressed one of the ship's officers-in-training, John felt magnanimous to reply, "I beg your pardon, Seaman?"

"What, all your other friends get a fancy salute, but not even a 'hello-how-are-you' for the lowly cabin boy?" The sailor looked up at John with a grin.

Sullivan went slack-jawed. He recognized the wolf-like blue eyes. With shock, the boy's identity dawned on him. "Melisande?" he said under his breath. "What are you—*Melly*?"

Her eyebrows wiggled with the delight of a prankster. "Had you fooled!"

John looked around. The sailors on the docks were far too busy with their own tasks to take notice of the exchange. Keeping his voice low, he said, "What the hell are you doing?"

Mimicking John's surreptitious tone, she leaned in with her hand cupped over her mouth. "What does it look like, sir? I'm setting sail. In the Navy. On a big boat."

"Melly, you can't. You—*can't.*"

"I know," cooed Melisande, tilting her chin like an opera singer basking in a rain of roses. "You're probably thinking, 'Our boys'll be so dazzled they'll run the old boat right into a reef.' Don't fret. If Melisande Dufort is the height of charm and radiance, *Michael* Dufort is the *sheer peak* of dull and ordinary." As if revealing the dramatic linchpin of a conspiracy, she whispered, "He's a boy."

"We're going to war."

"I'm good at war."

"What about Grey Feather? He must be up in arms about this."

Melisande poked her tongue at the tobacco in her lip. "Aye, he gave me a big earful of all that. I tried to talk him into enlisting with me, but he said me and Dom are stubborn fools and he's done coming to our rescue. I told him *how dare he* call me stubborn and there's no way he could change my mind."

"But—you hate the ocean."

"I thought I hated jumping out of burning buildings, but that turned out pretty fun."

"What about Dominique? You're going to leave her?"

"I'm not leaving her—I'm following her."

"What?"

Melisande scoffed. "You didn't know."

For a moment, John forgot he was a midshipman. Forgot about the docks, the sailors, the ship. "Didn't know what?"

"That poncy ass is taking her with him."

John absently stared across the river. He could barely see the rigging of the U.S.S. *Allegheny* above the masts of its neighbors. It was rare, but not unheard of, for a captain to take his wife to sea. But aboard a naval ship in a time of war—this was almost scandalous. "Aubert is taking Dominique to sea?"

"Oh, I get it. You thought she would be here at home, no husband around, pining for ole Sully. Sorry, but you had your chance. Aubert thinks he owns her now. He thinks he can hurt a Dufort and get away with it. I'll teach him different."

"But you won't even be aboard her ship."

"The *Allegheny* is sailing with the *Philadelphia*. That's close enough. I'll find a way to protect her."

John sighed. "Melly…"

"We always find a way, Sully. No matter what. 'Draw for the ace, win with the deuce.'" Melisande saluted with the wrong hand—her left. Her palm faced out—an insult to an officer. "See you aboard. Mr. Midshipman, sir." Then she trotted away.

John pulled off his hat. He thought for a moment as he smoothed a wrinkle out of the brim. "I suppose we'll have to work on that salute."

John put his hat back on. He turned around to take in the busy wharves, shops, and taverns of Philadelphia one more time. A boy, perhaps ten or twelve, dashed from door to door, delivering one of the many city newspapers. A tavern keep rolled a wheelbarrow full of flour sacks. Mrs. O'Malley sipped tea on a coffeehouse patio in her plumed hat. Bricklebrack was arguing with Horace over who baked better bread. John reached into his pocket.

He withdrew the piece of eight and held it on his open palm. John had called it "The Islanded Lion." He told Kaitlin it was magic. Somewhere on this ship, John would learn the clue he needed to find her. A clue he would get, one way or another, from a fourth lieutenant named

Chester Ryland.

"I'm coming, Katie. Just hold on."

John closed his fist around the coin. He turned away from the bustling riverfront. He tucked the Lion back into his pocket and boarded the USS *Philadelphia*.

Chapter 19

The Merchant Schooner *Wandering Hart*
The Mediterranean Sea
Tuesday, June 12th, 1798

"I don't feel good," Kaitlin mumbled.

"So I see, Rabbit," said John. He had found his eight-year-old sister standing near the bow of the *Wandering Hart*, heaving over the side. Her freckled face was pale. Tears ran from her cognac eyes. A few red curls had slipped her blue ribbon. A spot of vomit flecked her chin. "Look at you. Worse than dolly after her little tumble over the pier."

"You *threw* Cora!" snapped Kaitlin, sticking her tongue out.

"I'm teasing, Rabbit," laughed John. "I said sorry and fished her out of the Thames, didn't I? Why don't we get you below. I'll read *Tommy Gingerbread* if you like."

Kaitlin shook her head.

"What's the matter?"

"It's scary." She looked away bashfully.

"Nonsense. The goblins under the deck won't be hungry for at least a few hours."

Katlin's freckles screwed up in resentment. "I *know*

there's no goblins—Mam even said so."

"Well, there you have it, then."

"What if the ship sinks?"

"Nah, a little wind and rain won't sink our *Hart*."

"How do you know?"

John thought a moment. "Mother and Father, and Isaac and I, the crew—we look after the old girl, and she looks after us. Just like I look after you."

"What if another storm comes?"

"Don't forget who we are, Rabbit. We're Sullivans. We always find a way."

Another tear ran down Kaitlin's cheek. "I don't like it here. I want to go home."

John sighed. "This is our home."

Kaitlin buried her head in her arms, one eye scowling at John.

As her elder by seven years, John knew this was the time to be a caring brother. But how could he console her? The sea wasn't an adventure for Kaitlin—not like it was for John or the rest of the family. She had always been a girl that loved to run and jump. It was solid ground and wide spaces she wanted, not seasickness and damp.

Then John remembered something. A present his father gave him in Barcelona. He pulled the old silver coin from his pocket. Nearly a hundred years ago, it had been stamped with the seal of the Spanish throne. A crest stamped with a cross. In two opposing corners of the cross, there should have been two lions, and in the other two corners castles. But one lion was missing. Over the years, a crack had snaked around the lone lion, marooning him.

"Hmm. I suppose you're old enough to hear about…" John began but stopped short. He gave a severe frown. "…No, I couldn't possibly."

"What?" asked Kaitlin, curious in spite of herself. "I'm old enough!"

"All right," said John reluctantly. "But you can't tell anyone."

"I won't." John's little sister whispered as if they were discussing a map to buried treasure. "I promise."

"Open your hand."

Kaitlin did as he asked. John dropped the silver piece in her palm.

"What is it?" she asked, her face drawing close to her hand.

"*That* is The Islanded Lion," John said, marveling at his clever improvisation. "It's a magic piece of eight. You see, a long time ago, there was a wealthy, fearsome pirate named Samuel Bellamy. He was one of the cleverest pirates that ever lived. But his dear love, Maria, worried about the dangers of him being at sea."

"She was afraid of the ocean too?"

"Aye, she was. But, it so happened that an old fortune teller from the West Indies gave her an enchanted silver coin—a bit of Spanish treasure said to make any man's ship impossible to sink. So Maria gave Captain Bellamy the magic coin and made him promise to always keep it close."

"And did he?"

"For a while, he did. And for a while, the worst storm, the sharpest reef, even cannon fire—nothing could sink his ship. And he became one of the richest pirates ever. But old Captain Bellamy didn't believe in magic, you see. So one day, when he said goodbye to his love, he foolishly left the piece of eight behind. On his return voyage, his ship got caught in a terrible storm—much worse than anything we've ever seen. Without The Islanded Lion to protect him, the ship went down."

"He drowned?" She said, becoming distressed again.

"Uh…Well, yes…" *Clever indeed, John,* he cursed to himself.

"That's so sad," Kaitlin said, on the verge of fresh tears.

"Yes, it's very sad. *But* that will never happen to us…is my point. Because the coin you hold in your hand is the very magic coin that Maria gave to her love to protect him. If he had believed in the magic and kept this coin close to him, he would have come home to her safe and sound."

"This coin?" Kaitlin said.

"This coin."

"How did you get it?"

"Father gave it to me."

"Where did he get it?"

"Well, he got it…from his father…who got it from a friend who knew Maria's cousin, who had a…The point is, it'll keep you safe."

The silver reflected in Kaitlin's eyes as she stared transfixed. "Magic…" she murmured.

"Magic," John smiled.

Kaitlin smiled back.

"Will you keep the Lion safe for me, Katie?"

She nodded.

John feigned a stern tone. He wagged a finger for extra effect. "This is important now. The safety of everyone aboard the ship is in your hands. You mustn't let him out of your sight."

Kaitlin closed her hand on the coin. She nodded eagerly. Her tears had dried. Color had returned to her face. "Don't worry, Johnny, I won't. I'll keep the Lion safe. I promise."

She threw her arms around him.

"Whoa," John said, a bit taken aback. He returned her hug, chuckling. "Easy now. I haven't forgotten about you spilling ink on my *Navigatio Britannica.*"

"Thank you, Johnny," she said.

"You're welcome, Rabbit."

"Avast!" cried the lookout from his perch on the foremast. "Pirates to starboard! Pirates to starboard!"

There was a commotion aft. Sailors scrambled to the sides. Mother and Father were looking towards the *Dolorous Fénnid.* But something was wrong. Dozens of men lined the decks and clung to the rigging, shaking swords, shouting curses, firing pistols.

John watched as the pirates ran the Union Jack down the halyards. A flag striped in red, yellow, and green rose in its place.

Chapter 20

Aboard USS *Philadelphia*
The Atlantic Ocean
Monday, August 8th, 1803

John swayed over the briny depths of the sea. He held onto the bowsprit, one hand on a lanyard, one foot on a ratline. The bow of the *Philadelphia* cut through the waves, bathing the curly hair and beard of mighty Hercules in the surf. John looked over his shoulder. The last edges of the American shore were disappearing astern. Looking forward, the Atlantic Ocean spread as far as he could see. He closed his eyes, feeling the wind coursing over him. He listened to the seamen sounding off in the rigging behind. Felt the steady rise and fall of the bow. Filled his lungs with the smell of salt and sea life. His world became wind, water, sky, and the racing of his heart.

John reached into his pocket. He opened his mother's silver hunter-case watch and admired the engraving. The words were etched in his heart, but he wouldn't abandon his morning ritual. He ran his thumb over the letters and read, then snapped it closed. He smiled and looked to the horizon.

Awake, dear heart, awake. Thou hast slept well.

"Beautiful, isn't it?"

John looked over his shoulder to see one of the senior lieutenants edging his way along the bowsprit a few feet behind. His uniform had much more gold trim than John's, a pennant on the bicorne, and prominent epaulets. John realized he had not seen the officer before. In the breakneck hustle of his new duties among three hundred other crew, perhaps John had simply not made his acquaintance. He looked about twenty-five. A few tufts of his short, dirty blonde hair rustled in the wind. He had spirited hazel eyes, weathered at the edges, and a round, handsome face. There was a quick clip to his speech, typical of New Yorkers.

"Sir?" asked John.

"At ease, Midshipman," said the officer. "Mind some company while you're off watch?"

"Of course not, sir."

"I didn't think anyone else spent their leisure time here," said the affable lieutenant. He edged along the port side of the bowsprit until he was abreast of John. He inhaled a deep breath of sea air. He scanned the horizon with a smile. "Such a beautiful view."

"Like it's just you and the sea," John added.

"Exactly."

They exchanged a smile.

"I don't believe we've had a proper introduction," said the officer. "I only came aboard a few days ago, when the *Beagle* joined the squadron. Midshipman John Sullivan, isn't it?"

John was caught off guard. "Yes, sir. How did you—?"

"My brilliant gift for arithmetic—naturally," said the lieutenant, his eyebrows rippling with bravado. "I met the other ten midshipmen in the books. Your name was the only one missing a face."

"Your intellect truly towers," smiled John.

"Chester Ryland. Ship's fourth lieutenant. A pleasure."

John felt his pulse rising. A flood of adrenaline. The titillating thrill of both danger and opportunity. Like any good card player, he knew how to hide his tells. With his most sincere smile, he said, "The pleasure's all mine."

Part II

The Islanded Lion

Chapter 21

The USS *Philadelphia*
The Atlantic Ocean
Wednesday, August 17th, 1803

On a normal afternoon, the sun would flicker on the water like a longhouse fire. Melisande Dufort would close her eyes and feel the warmth on her skin. For a moment, she would hear the whispering pines. She would pretend the yardarm was a dogwood branch, the mast a treetop. She would be home. On a *normal* afternoon.

Today, clouds roiled across the sky. Gray twilight smothered the sun. The sea foamed and boiled. The wind roared in Melisande's ears as if she'd angered the Thunder Spirits. She endured a wave of nausea as the *Philadelphia* sledded down a roller. The yardarm, some hundred feet over the ocean, swooped low enough to almost touch the water. Melisande held on for her life as the yardarm soared upward again. A blue bolt sliced the clouds. She felt the thunderclap in her gut.

"Hrmm!" moaned the giant to Melisande's left. Seventeen-year-old Seaman Kelham snapped his eyes shut. He was tall as a horse and thick as an ox, but the seaman had always been a picture of docility. Not today. "Hrmm."

"Come on, Big Paw," Melisande yelled over the wind. Kelham had taken a liking to Melisande the moment she gave him the nickname. That didn't help her now. Kelham dropped his share of canvas, preventing the rest of the maintop men from reefing the sail. "You're ok, Big Paw. Just a little thunder. You gotta haul, now."

Further down the main topgallant yard, the leader of their crew yelled, "Hold, men! Hold." Able Seaman Meadows put a hand to his mouth and called to Kelham, "Take ahold of yourself, lad. Furl sail, or we'll lose the canvas!"

The sky spat a cascade of lightning. Kelham shook his head and gripped tighter.

"Ahoy," Meadows cried to the other side of the yardarm. "Ahoy there, lads. Hold."

Melisande looked to her right where half of the sail was lopsided. The men on the port side were still spooling the canvas. Seaman Prince, a bully the same age as Kelham, was ignoring the trouble to starboard. He and his mates were risking a tear.

"What's the matter, boy?" Prince yelled at Melisande. He turned his long face toward them, the rain pelting his grin. "Can't get your village dunce to work?"

Prince's mates tittered. Melisande boiled with anger. They were always teasing poor Big Paw—calling him slow or a dimwit.

"Just give him a minute!" shouted Melisande. "He's not himself, is all."

"What is he normally?" snickered Prince. "A walrus?"

Prince's friends broke into snotty laughter. Added to the thunder, their voices took on a hint of madness.

"You lads, hold, I say," Meadows shouted. But the wind kicked up and sound melted into the howl.

Melisande caught sight of Lieutenant Ryland and John Sullivan on deck, squinting up through the rain. Their lips moved, but their words were lost.

Melisande drew close to Kelham's ear. "You want to know why I call you 'Big Paw?' I mean, the real reason?"

Kelham's eyes were shut, puffy cheeks ashen.

"Don't take this the wrong way," said Melisande, trying to sound as if the wind *wasn't* about to fling them into the ocean. "It's 'cause you remind me of *Nyah-Gwaheh*—the Naked Bear."

One of Kelham's eyes crept open. One terrified pupil fixed on her.

"He was a hairless, man-eating beast," she went on. "The other children were terrified when Papa Fox told the story. But not me. I knew the others had it wrong— poor *Nyah-Gwaheh* just wanted a friend. After all, he was naked in the forest, without a longhouse fire. I wanted so badly to invite him in, give him some furs, and feed him. Then I would have a friend like no other. *Nyah-Gwaheh*— my own special protector."

Kelham's other eye opened. Melisande saw Meadows watching them intently.

"I used to go out looking for *Nyah-Gwaheh*," Melisande went on. "I tried to tempt him with berries, corn, even a rabbit leg—nothing worked. I was so sad. Until I met you, Big Paw. No one in the world's got a friend like you. Except me."

At this, Kelham's head lifted off the yardarm. He looked at Melisande, his brows relaxing. She snatched a look at the spar deck. Sullivan was still yelling, his words lost in the wind.

###

"Let fall!" shouted Midshipman John Sullivan. "I say again, let fall!"

"It's no use, Sullivan," said Fourth Lieutenant Chester Ryland. Water spilled from the brim of his bicorne hat. "They can't hear. Merrick!"

A skinny midshipman snapped to attention. "Sir?"

"Lay aloft and tell them to let fall and start again!"

"Aloft, sir?" stammered Merrick, shocks of brown hair lashing his face.

"The weather topgallant brace!" John cried, pointing to the lengths of rope running from the starboard end of the yard to the rail. The cable was waterlogged and shrunken. It vibrated under the tension. "Do you see it, sir? It's took up with the rain."

Ryland looked up through the driving rain. "Damn. It's liable to part. Sullivan—"

"Ahoy, men!" John yelled at a group of sailors. He had only moments—if the weather brace tore, the main topgallant yard would spin around the mast. The force might break the spar. Melisande and her mates could be thrown into the sea. "Let go the lee sheet! Let go the lee brace and halyards! Let go…"

A row of seamen jumped into a line near the port rail. They let out slack on each line as John gave commands. There was a pop and creaking of wood, and the weather topgallant brace broke away. The yard jolted and stopped. The deck crew had eased the strain just in time.

"Well spotted, Sullivan!" said Ryland. "Merrick, get the weather quarter lashed to the shroud."

"Aye, sir!" said Merrick, snapping a salute.

###

"Hrmm," cried Kelham.

The yardarm lurched, and Melisande felt her grip slip. There was a panicked moment when she had to dig in her fingernails. But the yard steadied, and her footing held. Her heart pounded as she watched Sullivan commanding the deck crew.

"Good ole Sully!" Melisande yelled. She turned back to Kelham. "All right, Big Paw. You're my *Nyah-Gwaheh*, aren't you? You're not scared of a little wind and rain!"

Like a turtle peeking out of his shell, Kelham looked up at her again. He shook his head.

"That's the way, my lovely!" smiled Melisande. "Now, let's furl this t'gallant!"

A smile tugged at Kelham's lips.

Half an hour later, as Melisande stepped off the shroud and onto the deck, she sighed with relief. Her trick with Kelham had worked. The big chap not only forgot his fear, he hauled up the canvas in record time. The repairs to the weather brace went fast. And finally, she could piss.

"Well done, lad!" cried Meadows, as he hopped off the shroud. He clapped Kelham on the back.

Kelham stood at his full six feet, smiling into the punishing rain. He might really have been the Naked Bear at that moment. "Thanks, Meadows."

"'Thanks Meadows!'" echoed Prince, mimicking the tone of a dunce. "Look, the ox did something right for a change."

"Belay that, Prince," said Meadows. "Get below before I tell the lieutenant you ignored my orders."

"But, sir…" Prince whined. "With all the wind, I couldn't—"

"Get you below! Now! And take your mates with you. We'll talk later."

Prince shot a scowl at Melisande and Kelham. "Come on, boys." Prince stalked off with his friends.

"Everything all right here, Meadows?" asked Sullivan as he approached.

"Just fine, sir," said Meadows with a chipper tone. "In fact, let's have three cheers for our Midshipman Sullivan and his quick thinking!"

"Meadows…" Sullivan objected, looking a bit sheepish.

"Hip-hip!" Meadows cried over the wind.

"Hooray!" replied Melisande and the others.

They repeated the cheer twice more, and Melisande threw her arm around her long-time buddy. "Sully's always got our back, doesn't he boys?"

Another whooping of approval. Meadows clapped Sullivan on the shoulder. Kelham followed suit, his unusual strength knocking the midshipman forward a step.

"All right, all right," Sullivan grinned. "Get below for some vittles and rest. You're all back on watch at eight bells."

"Aye, aye, sir!" said Meadows with a quick salute. "You heard him, lads. Off to our mess. Dufort, where are you going?"

Melisande stopped mid-step. "Just going for a piss, sir."

"Aye, all right. Careful you don't go overboard. And don't forget to bring the vittles. It's your turn."

"Aye, sir!" said Melisande, tapping her toe out of

anxiety. When meadows turned away, she beat a path forward.

There were no other sailors near the gangway—it was a perfect spot. She edged past the main hatch. Rain poured into the large rectangular opening in the spar deck. It ran off the ship's boats, stacked over the hatch in their cradles. The ship launched up under her feet. Seawater washed around her, reflecting columns of clouds. Forward of the main hatch, the steel chimney from the galley puffed smoke.

Melisande stepped up to a gap in the port side—the gangway—where wooden rungs on the hull formed a ladder. She reached into her pocket and pulled out a small goat horn, which served as a funnel. She held onto a wooden peg as the ship pitched and bucked. Just as she finished relieving herself, cold spray washed her backward.

"Dufort!" called a sailor dashing towards her. "You okay?"

Melisande coughed and spluttered saltwater. She scrambled to pull up her trousers. "Fine, fine." A beefy hand reached down.

It was Kelham. He said, "You've got to be careful."

"Yeah…right." Melisande took Kelham's hand, and he launched her onto her feet with ease. She looked around, but the goat horn was nowhere to be found. *Damn*, she thought. "All right, Big Paw. Let's go."

They went down the main hatch, just in front of the ship's boats. This took them to the gun deck, where long iron canons lined either side of the ship.

"Hold my place in line, would ya?" said Melisande, gesturing toward the galley.

"Okay, Dufort," said Kelham with a nod. He'd spoken

more in the last hour than he usually did all day. He lined up with other shivering and wet sailors near a brick-enclosed stove. Beans and stewed salt pork bubbled on cast iron burners. The cook ladled a portion into each man's mess bowl, along with a few hardtack biscuits.

Melisande walked the long continuous deck. The wooden beams between each iron cannon looked like the ribs of an enormous whale. She reached hers—gun number five—named "Liberty and Death." In battle, if her mates weren't assigned to the foretop, they would form the five-man crew for this gun. Melisande had begged for the job of firing the massive artillery piece, but Meadows made her the "spongeman." She had the boring job of cleaning the bore and ramming in the shot. Ten strides aft, a Marine stood guard near the door of the captain's cabin. Melisande took the quarterdeck hatch down to the crew deck.

She wove through the warren of wooden partitions, past the quarters of the warrant officers and midshipmen. The door to Dr. Cowdery's tiny little office was open. She stuck her nose inside and found Ethan Auldon studying by candlelight.

"Fiddles!" smiled Melisande.

"Dufort." Ethan looked up from the little chair at Cowdery's desk, nestled between two of the ship's ribs. Even sitting down, Ethan's head almost touched the planks. A cabinet of tonics and potions rattled above his head. He closed the book on his thumb. "Cowdery has gone to his hammock. Are you seasick?"

"Not a bit." Melisande batted her eyes. "Why?"

"Oh, I don't know," said Ethan, tapping his chin with a quill. "Because you filled three buckets with sick your first day?"

"Pish!" said Melisande, swatting the air. "You got me over that, and now I'm aces."

"And it only took three weeks." Ethan opened his book again. "So, what then? I'm way behind in my studies."

"I need a goat horn," Melisande whispered.

"You lost another one? That was the steward's last goat."

"Come on, Fiddles. You're smart. You gotta figure something out."

Ethan sighed. "I'll…fashion you a funnel out of something. Just use the head for now."

"*No one* goes all the way to the head to piss!"

"I'll see to it," groaned Ethan, pressing the door closed.

Melisande forced her nose through the closing gap. "Hey, when are you going to play for us again? I'm writing a dance number. It's a duet."

"*Goodnight*, Dufort," said Ethan. The door snapped shut.

Melisande bent close to the keyhole. "Books are making you grumpy."

There was no reply.

After a quick stop by the galley stove to pick up her messmates' dinner, Melisande headed down the forward ladder to the crew deck. The notes of a fife mingled with hundreds of voices. The ship groaned as it pitched and tossed in the storm. Hammocks rocked like cradles, dangling from hooks in the beams. Where there weren't partitions, sailors sat in groups, eating with their messmates. Boards hung from ropes, serving as tables. Sea chests served as chairs. Melisande could feel the heat of their bodies—and smell the odors of sweat and salt water.

"It's about time!" said Meadows when Melisande reached their berth. "I'm starving." The old sailor passed out the wooden trays. His curly gray hair was dry, and he wore a fresh striped shirt and neckerchief.

A sight to make Melisande jealous. She itched the gauze under her shirt. Every day, she carefully bound her womanly figure. Loose sailor's shirts and peacoats completed her disguise. The men aboard simply attributed her comely face and higher-pitched voice to boyish youth. They thought she was fifteen-year-old Michael Dufort from Philadelphia. Just to be sure, she often dusted her face with a little coal soot from the galley. A shameful waste of beauty, if you asked Melisande.

"Now don't lose your place, lad," said Meadows as he slopped beans onto William Butler's tray. "What was her name again?"

"Lucy, from Charleston," said Butler, a seaman in his early twenties.

"Lucy!" said Meadows. "A fine name, that."

"By the third pint, she was sitting on my lap," Butler continued as he told another story of dockside conquest. "She gave me a view right down her bodice."

Melisande's attention wandered, and her eyes drifted to the starboard side of the deck. Across the way, Prince sat with his mates under their hammocks. The snotty adolescent puffed out his cheeks and widened his eyes. He flopped his head back and forth to parody Big Paw Kelham.

"…Then she says, 'Don't stop!'" crowed Butler behind her. "So, then I really lay into her, biting those beautiful bosoms…"

Melisande tuned out the lurid story, fixing her gaze on Prince. The brat flashed her a taunting grin as he picked his teeth with a pork bone. She gave him a dark look as she gnawed a stale biscuit. At that moment, Melisande wanted two things most in the world—to beat the tar out of the bully Prince and a hunk of warm maize. If she couldn't have one, she'd settle for the other. She stood and balled her fists.

"Dufort!" said Meadows.

Melisande snapped her attention back to the table. "Huh? I didn't do nothing!"

"Not yet," Meadows admonished. He was always carping at her like a mother hen. As bad as Grey Feather. "Now are you going to answer or not?"

"Answer what?"

"About your first sweetheart. That is, if you've had one."

"What?" Melisande asked. She hadn't been listening to the conversation. "Oh, I've had lots."

Her messmates broke into laughter.

Butler pointed at her. "You're at least seven years my junior. 'Had lots' my eye!"

Melisande folded her arms. "Look, Bill, when Lucy called you the best she ever had, she was being kind."

"Bullshit," said James Dixon, the youngest at their table. "Nobody knows more about women than Butler."

"Really?" Melisande cocked her head. "Then why does he think 'don't stop' means 'bite my teat like a donkey?'"

Meadows coughed stewed potatoes all over the table. A fork fell out of Dixon's frozen hand. Sawyer, Kelham, and Butler were slack-jawed.

"Don't get me wrong, Bill," said Melisande, patting her messmate on the shoulder. "You're comely and all, but you lack practice."

"Now, boys," Melisande said, planting her hands on the table as though plotting revolution. "If you want a lass to beg for you like a cat for cream, here's what you do."

All five men leaned forward.

Curtains of rain hung over the sea. The clouds formed strange, mountainous shapes. They looked heavy enough to fall. Something about this storm unsettled John Sullivan, and he couldn't stop running his thumb over the edge of the Islanded Lion. He turned the silver coin over and over in his pocket. Sky and sea twisted like the landscape of a nightmare.

"Well done today, Midshipman," said Lieutenant Chester Ryland, flashing John a rakish smile. "Time for supper and a tot of rum. Or two."

"Thank you, sir," said John, yelling over a crashing wave. His friendship with the jocular lieutenant began as a ruse, but over the last three weeks, it had become something real. Soon, John would need to press Ryland for a clue to finding the Silver Hand. For now, it felt good to have a mentor. "I was only following your example."

"Finally," Ryland quipped. "Someone to appreciate my talents. And while I have you studying at my feet, I should mention something else. I've noticed you're very friendly with the seamen in your division."

John smiled proudly. "I hope the men think of me as a friend."

"You shouldn't. Seamen aren't your peers."

"Sir?"

Ryland cupped a hand over his mouth, raising his voice over a gust. "You're an officer, Mr. Sullivan. Those under your command must remain at a distance."

"But shouldn't a good officer inspire loyalty?"

"Aye. By becoming the example they follow—not their drinking chum. One day, when they're looking death in the eye, they won't want a friend. They'll want a leader."

John looked at Ryland, letting the advice sink in. "Aye, sir."

"Come," said Ryland, starting toward the quarterdeck hatch.

Before John could follow, a violet arc snaked through the heavens. A shape at the edge of the world caught John's eye. He dashed to the starboard rail, pulled out his spyglass, and strained for a look.

Vines of light crackled across the horizon. Through the drops on the lens, John could make out the shape of sails...two masts...a hull. Far in the distance, a brig-of-war drifted like a ghostly shadow. Unlike a typical brig, this one had a third mast set very close to the main. John remembered seeing the sleek, graceful curve of her hull four years ago—when she launched from the Philadelphia shipyards. A ship built by Samuel Humphreys—the pleasant young shipwright at Aubert's brag game. A work of art given as tribute to the bey of Tunis.

"What's keeping you, Sullivan?" complained Ryland as he came alongside John.

"Sir!" said John, pointing south. "A ship in the

distance. A snow brig—the one given to Bey Hammuda."

"How can you tell in this soup?" Ryland took the spyglass and searched the horizon. After a moment, he handed it back. "Nothing out there, Sullivan."

"It's right there, sir, it's…" John trailed off. Another flash lit up the sky, but the snow brig was gone. "It was…right there. She must have slipped below the horizon. I think we're being followed."

"Unlikely," said Ryland. He headed below, and John reluctantly followed. As they stepped into the shelter of the gun deck, Ryland shook the water from his coat. "Even if the bey of Tunis were at war with us, he wouldn't send the pride of his fleet out so far. He calls her the *Wolf of Tunis*. She's his finest warship. Wolf or not, she's no match for *Philadelphia*. I'm sure it was a trick of the light."

"How could we give that beautiful American frigate to a tyrant?"

"Every year, the Barbary princes demand more for the safe passage of our sailors," Ryland lamented as he led the way to the wardroom. "The more one prince gets, the more the next one wants. I'm sure the gift of a frigate to Bey Hammuda was on Pasha Yusuf's mind when he declared war. Still, if we hadn't given Hammuda the *Wolf of Tunis*, we'd be fighting *two* Barbary states instead of one. It's a sad thing, but that's the price of peace."

"More like the price of surrender," groused John.

Ryland slapped John's back. "Don't be glum. Join me in the wardroom for a drink. We'll commiserate over the poor girl's fate."

John nodded absently, still haunted by the phantom ship. "I'll be along."

Ryland nodded and headed down the next hatch.

A minute later, John ducked into the corridor by the warrant officers' quarters. He knocked on the surgeon's door.

"What *now*, Dufort?" came Ethan's annoyed voice.

"It's me, John."

Ethan snapped the door open. "Oh. Sorry, mate. I've had a devil of a time finding peace and quiet."

"I won't keep you, then," said John. He dropped his voice to a whisper. "Do you have what I asked for?"

Ethan rubbed his temples as if massaging a headache. "Ah, yes. That."

"I wouldn't ask if it weren't important," John said. "I've nearly got Ryland where I want him. I can feel it. Winning him over might be my family's only chance."

"Of course," Ethan sighed. He pulled open a drawer in the mahogany desk, then produced a key. "Just...bring it back as soon as you can, all right?"

John snatched it from Ethan's outstretched hand. "Thank you, mate. You won't regret it. I owe you one."

As John headed off to the wardroom, he heard Ethan say, "More than one."

Chapter 22

Dock Street
Philadelphia, Pennsylvania
Four Years Ago

Ethan crouched near the retaining wall, peeking through the rod-iron fence. He rubbed his hands for warmth. His breath fogged in the cold February morning. A bitter day to deliver newspapers on Dock Street. He scanned the frozen yard. Nothing but barren birches. An empty rocking chair on the porch. No sign of Grover.

There was no sign of Mr. Dunlap either. Perhaps the old man had slept in. As Ethan crouched back down, the cold biting through his wool coat, he considered throwing the paper. But what if he missed? Braving the yard with Grover's whereabouts unknown was out of the question.

There were other customers waiting, Ethan decided. He resumed his route, hoping Dunlap wouldn't miss one edition of the *Gazette*. By the time Ethan noticed Dunlap's gate was open, it was too late. An ear-splitting bark echoed across the yard. The muscular hound came bounding around the house. Ethan tore off at a sprint, hoping his head start would be enough. By the time he reached the nearest alley, he could hear Grover's feet scratching the flagstones behind. The farrier had left a mess of crates stacked against his building. Ethan flung himself onto the stack and scrambled up the shed. Grover's jaws snapped just below his heel. Ethan skittered back onto the roof, watching the frustrated dog jump at the crates, unable to gain purchase. *Damn dog,* Ethan cursed.

A few minutes later, as Ethan climbed atop the farrier's house, he thanked the heights of Philadelphia for saving him again. He sat against a chimney to catch his breath. A family of pigeons cooed in the eves. Grover eventually gave up, and his barks died away. That's when Ethan heard the tune. A song echoing between the buildings. Ethan climbed down to the opposite ledge and peered into the alley. Huddled in a pile of wet straw, shivering in the cold, a boy was singing in an Irish accent.

My lips smile no more, my heart loses its lightness;
No dream of the future my spirit can cheer.
I only can brood on the past and its brightness
The dear ones I long for again gather here.

Such a beautiful tune, but so sad. Ethan felt wrong to spy, but he couldn't tear himself away. As he listened to the next verse, a tear ran down his face.

From ev'ry dark nook they press forward to meet me;
I lift up my eyes to the broad leafy dome,
And others are there, looking downward to greet me
The ash grove, the ash grove, again is my home.

Ethan saw plenty of beggars in Philadelphia. Plenty of orphans. Some of them ran in gangs he knew to avoid. Most were taken in by churches or orphanages. Something was different about this one. Ethan had never seen anyone so alone in the world. Ethan somehow knew he'd suffered a terrible loss.

The boy started another round of the song but trailed off in the first phrase. Ethan ducked beneath the parapet, thinking he'd been spotted. When he heard voices at the end of the alley, he looked down again. At the alley entrance, three older boys were milling about, chatting and laughing with one another. The orphan looked at them the way Ethan looked at Dunlap's vicious dog. The others chattered and shoved each other, and finally moved on. The boy breathed a sigh of relief. He pulled a beautiful silver watch from his pocket, settled back into his nook, and gazed at the timepiece until he nodded off.

For the next couple of days, Ethan repeated that detour. After Mr. Dunlap's estate, he would find his way back to the farrier's, climb the stacked crates, and listen to the boy's songs. When the boy wasn't looking, Ethan would drop a bundle of food onto a bail of straw. A little bread, jam, and cheese from the larder of St. Thomas Church. Each day, the previous bundle would be gone.

On the eighth day of this routine, with snow falling in heavy flakes, Ethan was about to climb the farrier's crates when he heard voices. The snow on the roof would be treacherous anyway, so Ethan went to the alley entrance. As he peered around the corner, he saw the same three boys, all in their early teens, crowding around the Irish orphan.

"You're lying, Maggoty John!" an Irish voice gloated. "I can always tell when you're lying."

"Give 'im the glass, Fin!" said a pudgy boy, tallest of the three. His beard belied his youth.

Backed against the wall, John said, "I haven't got anything left to steal. Eamon would have sniffed out any food."

Eamon swung a fist into John's stomach. John gasped

and doubled over.

Fin, the shortest and skinniest of them, took a step forward. "I think Eamon's got a point." Fin pulled a broken bottle-neck from his pocket. He waved the jagged edge under John's chin. "You've still got that pretty face."

"You have any idea how long we searched, maggot?" squeaked the third boy. He had a curly nest of red hair and ghost-white skin. "Glass him, Fin!"

"Not yet, Sean," snapped Fin. "I'm feeling merciful. I want to give Maggoty John a choice." He took another menacing step. "What do you say, Captain Maggot? Give me that bobble in your pocket, or I give you the glass."

"I pawned it," insisted John. "For food."

"No you didn't, maggot. Hand over the watch." He pressed the bottleneck closer.

With the wall at his back, John was cornered. "Please, Fin. I'm sorry. I'll sleep somewhere else. Leave the city. Whatever you want."

"What I want, Maggoty John is for you to hand over the watch. Then, you're going to lick my boot."

Ethan's heart thumped. Freezing sweat beaded on his skin. He wanted to help John. He knew he had to. It was the right thing to do. The Christian thing to do. But there were three of them.

John snarled and bared his teeth, despite shedding tears. He muttered something Ethan couldn't hear.

Fin's voice turned deadly. "What did you say, maggot?"

John balled his fists. "I said fuck you!"

Ethan's heart pounded. His mind raced.

"Oh, you're the one who's fucked, maggot!" Fin seethed. "I'm going to turn your face to sheep guts."

"Let him be!" Ethan cried. It sounded like someone

else's voice. The blood froze in his veins.

Sean, Eamon, and Fin turned their gazes on him. "What's this?" said Fin. "A darkie with a death wish!"

John stared at Ethan in disbelief.

Now Ethan could see the jagged scar on Fin's face. A circle of mangled flesh cut across his right cheek, close to his nose and mouth. Ethan was terrified, but he stood his ground. "That the best you got, dimwit?"

Fin's mouth fell open. His face flushed red. "You're dead, darkie!" he screamed.

"I would be," taunted Ethan, "if ugly could kill."

"Get him!" ordered Fin. The three bullies charged after Ethan.

Before Eamon could make two steps, John kicked out a foot. The lumbering adolescent toppled to the ground. John shot past Fin and Sean.

"This way!" Ethan said, waving to John. He took off down Third Street.

Ethan and John sprinted for all they were worth. Fin trailed close behind, his face full of murder. Sean wheezed a few paces back.

Ethan rounded the corner onto Dock Street. He knew exactly what to do. And knew it might be the most insane thing he'd ever done.

"He's gaining," panted John.

"Keep going," encouraged Ethan. Chancing a look over his shoulder, he saw the brown bottleneck glinting in Fin's hand. He pushed his legs harder.

"He's still gaining!" shouted John.

Just as Ethan felt fatigue setting in, he saw the iron bars of Mr. Dunlap's yard. "Come on," he waved to John. He put on one last burst of speed, then skidded to a halt in front of the gate.

John nearly tumbled into Ethan. "What are you doing?"

"You'll pay for this, Maggoty John!" rasped Fin as he came around the corner.

"Trust me," Ethan said to John. Then he yelled to Fin, "Well? What are you waiting for, dimwit?"

Fin ran straight for them. Sean came around the corner next, then Eamon.

Ethan heard the scratch of paws. Saw a brown mass of canine muscle in the corner of his eye. Fin was two strides away when Ethan popped the latch and opened the gate. Fin stopped short, blinking. Grover leaped out of the yard. The dog froze, baying indiscriminately, unsure who to bite first.

Fin pointed his bottle-neck at the mutt. "Shut it, dog!"

Grover raised a mane of hair. Fin took a step back. Grover paced forward. Fin's scowl melted into fear, and he took off running. The mutt gave chase.

"Let's go!" Ethan cried.

He and John ran several more blocks before stopping to rest.

"Thanks, mate." John panted. He hunched over, hands on knees, fighting to catch his breath. "How did you...know the dog would...chase Fin and not us?"

"I didn't," Ethan huffed. "But I figured...creatures that mean deserve each other."

John and Ethan exchanged a look. They broke into laughter.

"You're right about that," John said. He extended a hand, and Ethan accepted. "John Sullivan."

"Ethan Auldon."

"I owe you, Ethan."

"You're welcome. John." Ethan noticed a silver chain

dangling from John's right fist. "Is that what they wanted?" Ethan asked, pointing.

John looked down at his hand. He opened his fingers to reveal the silver pocket watch. "Aye."

Ethan wanted to ask why it meant so much, but sensed it was a sore subject. "Well, I'm glad we deprived them of it."

John's eyes lingered on Ethan a moment. He nodded and slid the watch into his pocket. He started back toward the street, holding his bruised stomach.

Ethan watched him go for a moment, then said, "John, wait."

John looked back.

"Do you have anywhere to go?"

John looked toward the steeple of the Presbyterian Church. "I'll be all right."

"It's freezing. And Fin is still out there. Come home with me. We can give you a place to stay."

John's eyes searched Ethan as if reluctant. Or perhaps distrusting?

Ethan hurried to add, "Just until you find somewhere of your own."

"But..." said John, breathing clouds of steam. "Don't people keep to their own kind?"

Ethan shrugged. "Would that be the guy with the glass?"

"Aye, it would," said John, scratching his head.

The two of them shared a grin.

"I don't know," said John. "It wouldn't be right to burden your family."

"You wouldn't be a burden. My father owns a small tavern, and he volunteers with the Free African Society. He can always use another pair of hands. You would be trading work for room and board."

John considered a moment, then nodded. "In that case, Ethan Auldon, I gratefully accept your offer of work."

Ethan's eyes lit up. "It's settled then."

John smiled.

Chapter 23

The USS *Philadelphia*
The Atlantic Ocean
Thursday, August 18th, 1803

"I suppose playing blind is better than another bad call," said Chester Ryland. The fourth lieutenant sat directly opposite John. "Nothing else has worked for you tonight, Sullivan, but I do hope you'll keep at it." The leader of *Philadelphia's* outcasts chuckled into the rim of his bourbon bottle.

"It's worked for me before," said John. "And against better players." He sat on an overturned bucket at a surgical table. A single lamp swayed with the ship, dimmed by a cloud of pipe smoke. Dingy light washed over the four faces awaiting his action. John studied his poor hand of cards. With any luck, Ryland would believe a bluff. "I raise two pence."

"I doubt you've met a better player," said Ryland, smothering the last word in a drink of expensive whiskey.

The others scoffed. They were playing brag in the surgeon's cockpit, a dank room on the lowest level of the ship—the orlop deck. The low ceiling required a doctor to kneel when performing surgery, hence the low table. It was a young ship, and the oily smell of new paint cut through the odor of tobacco and rum. A wooden scent still clung to the new timbers. The notched table snagged John's calloused fingers as he added his bet to the mess of cards, coins, and cups.

"Is it true you won a blind hand against Captain Aubert?" asked Quartermaster Wilson, a blonde and muscular pleasure seeker. He smiled like a drunk asking for his favorite joke. "And won the whole game to boot?"

"I played blind until the showdown, anyway," John said. "Long enough to lure him in. Spring the trap."

"Damn," said Wilson. "I wish I'd seen the look on that boot-licker's face!"

"Aye, hear hear," agreed Midshipman Merrick, risking a smile. At twenty-four, he was old for a midshipman—his commission was the last hope for a destitute father. He lacked any skill at cards, so he passed the time by losing money and laughing on cue. "I fold," he said.

Sailing Master Knight brooded over his cards, pinching his bushy eyebrows. "Richard Aubert is rated the best brag player in the service," he said, folding. "You got lucky, Sullivan."

"No victory comes without a *little* luck," said John. He scratched his neck when he felt another of Merrick's awkward, fawning smiles. For some reason, he had the admiration of the awkward junior officer.

"You'll need a lot of luck tonight, Sullivan," said Ryland. His finger traced down his blonde stubble.

And there it was again. Ryland's tell. An unconscious gesture when pondering a decision. Ryland looked confident, but then he always did. Only this time, like only a few times before, the cocky lieutenant touched his beard. It either meant truth or deception. But which? John said, "Then place your bet, Lieutenant, if you're so sure."

Ryland smirked and took another drink. He pounded the bottle down on the table. "Very well, Sullivan. A dollar it is!" He thumbed a coin into the air. It pinged off the iron bottom of the lantern and skittered across the table.

"Horse's ass," griped Wilson. He flashed a pair of sevens before throwing them into the muck. "You cost me my lucky pair."

"Your *only* lucky pair," Ryland said. He reached as if to touch Wilson's cheek, and the quartermaster jerked away. "I think I can still see the handprint from that barmaid in Newport."

The room erupted in laughter.

"Aye, very funny," said Wilson. He never took offense to teasing when it came from Ryland. "At least I tried for her affection. I don't recall you leaving with any barmaids."

"I always leave the homely ones to you," said Ryland.

"No wonder you're so lonely on shore leave," said John, winning a few laughs of his own. He feigned a friendly, if competitive interest in the game, but Ryland was the sole focus of his mind. He couldn't win this hand—even a weak hand would beat him. But he was playing for something far more valuable than money. Information. "Make the bet a dollar, and I'll see your cards."

Ryland's snickering trailed off. "Damn. I admit, I didn't think you had me, Sullivan. A pair. Threes." He turned over his cards and fanned them across the pile of coins.

"You bluffing bastard!" groused Wilson, only contributing to Ryland's glee.

Deception, then, thought John before mucking his hand. "Threes will do."

"Really?" crowed Ryland as he collected his winnings. "Don't tell me you paid-to-see with an ace, Sullivan. You almost had my respect."

"Sometimes, an ace is all you need," said John.

Ryland chuckled. "Not today, Midshipman."

Let him gloat, John thought. *I have what I need.*

A series of chimes filtered down from three decks above. The *Philadelphia's* newly minted brass bell was tapping out the hour. *Ting-ting, ting-ting, ting-ting…ting.*

"Seven bells, sir," said Merrick to Ryland. "Morning watch starts soon."

"Yes, yes, Mr. Merrick," fussed Ryland. "I can tell time. One more hand. Come, men. Can't be I've emptied all your pockets."

"Merrick's right, Lieutenant," said Knight. "You insisted we adjourn at half-past three. We can't be crawling out of the hold when the watch changes."

"Aye, so I did," Ryland admitted ruefully. "Very well. A toast to Mr. Sullivan, for finding us this very fine venue."

"Mr. Sullivan," replied the others, and raised their bottles and pewter cups to John.

John clinked his pewter against theirs. He sipped the same small ration of grog he'd been nursing all night.

"Yes, a fine venue indeed," said Merrick. He wrinkled his nose as he looked around the room. The ceiling was painted white, as in most of the ship, but the boards underfoot were bright red. "Although, the floor could do with a more pleasant color."

"Wait till you see the surgery in battle, lad," said Ryland.

Merrick chuckled. He looked at his only friends on the ship, grasping for approval. "What do you mean?"

Wilson leaned close to Merrick as if telling a ghost story. "When 18-pound balls are smashing through bulkheads, you'll agree—red is *just* the color."

Merrick's beardless face went pale. The five men exchanged a sober look. The *Philadelphia's* ribs murmured in the silence.

The sun spilled its rays over the horizon. Pools of golden light settled across the placid sea. *Philadelphia* tacked across the wind, her port side basking in the warmth of dawn. As John passed the foremast, he found Chester Ryland near the bow, watching the sunrise.

The lieutenant had a leather-bound book of paper in his left hand, a shard of charcoal in his right. Ryland braced the sketchbook against the rail as he brushed small arcs of black across the page. He studied the horizon as he drew, eyes creased with concentration. As John came alongside Ryland, he watched the charcoal strokes turn white space into clouds on the water. Gulls in a flock. Bursts of sun.

"You have a gift, Lieutenant," said John, feeling the breeze wash through his hair.

Ryland smiled to himself and drew another wave crest. He blew a mote of soot off the page and said, "The images live in my head. Sometimes for days. Drawing them is the only way I can get them out." He smiled at John and nodded toward the sea. "No, Sullivan, the gift isn't in me. It's out there."

Inhaling the scent of surf, John said, "I think if you saw my ill-fated attempt to draw the queen of spades, you'd beg to differ."

Ryland gave John a sympathetic pat on the back. "Take heart, Sullivan. Mother Nature can inspire in other ways." Ryland looked over his shoulder for eavesdroppers. Just a few foretopmen laying out on the yard and some idlers holystoning the gangway. A crew, further aft, replacing the parted topgallant brace. No one in earshot. "Do pass my thanks to your friend Auldon. The surgeon's cockpit proved ideal during the midwatch. It's been ages since I played a game of brag."

Guilt niggled at John. The key to the surgery had been a lot to ask of Ethan, but what other choice was there? Despite his jovial nature, Ryland kept his peers at a distance. John couldn't ask for the truth until he knew the man. As it happened, Captain Bainbridge forbade gambling aboard ship, and Ryland pined for a game of cards. A perfect opportunity. "It was nothing. Ethan and I have always looked out for each other."

"A friendship like that is a rare thing."

John felt a chill as he recalled sleepless nights on wet straw. "Aye. But for Ethan Auldon, I would have starved in the streets—or worse."

"Good for us that he found you," Ryland smiled. The wind tugged a few blonde strands from his hat. "I do hope we'll have another game soon. That is, if a midshipman's pay can cover your losses."

"I went easy on a superior officer."

"Ah, just a little boot-licking for good measure? Shrewd, Sullivan. Shrewd."

"Just the once. Next time, I'll have your epaulets."

They shared a chuckle and another moment of silence.

After three weeks of manipulating Ryland—befriending him, earning his trust, learning his tells—John's moment had come. But it was harder than he expected. He hadn't counted on actually coming to like Ryland. "Mr. Ryland, I must thank you for your mentorship. Growing up on my father's ships, I thought I learned everything. But a Navy officer has to know more than braces and bobstays."

"Quite right, Mr. Sullivan. It's no easy thing to lead men into battle. And it's a rare few that put in the hard work. Keep this up, and one day you'll have your own command."

"Me?" said John. His eyes drifted dreamily toward the sunrise. He'd been so consumed with his personal mission, he hadn't considered the idea of commanding his own ship. "A captain?"

"I see a leader in you, Sullivan. *If* you can learn discipline. It doesn't hurt that you already know seamanship."

John feels the cool oak of the wheel. The warm touch of his father's hands. Captain or not, Declan still loves to stand on the crosstrees. "Feel that, John? A ship will always tell a good captain what she needs, if he knows to listen."

John hadn't thought about Declan for some time. He cleared a lump in his throat. "Aye. My Da taught me well."

"That will come in handy when we fight the Barbary Pirates."

A swell of heat rose in John's chest. He closed a fist around the Islanded Lion, squeezing until the coin felt like a knife. "When that day comes, I'll do a lot more than fight."

Ryland's brows drew together. He went to back to scribbling.

It was all John could do not to walk away. He wanted to be alone with his thoughts—and his anger. "Mr. Ryland, can I rely on your confidence?"

A smile tugged at Ryland's cheek. "Of course."

John folded his arms on the rail. He leaned over, far enough to see a few steely fish racing near the waterline. "I told you of my family and our ordeal, but not the whole story. A few weeks before we set sail, a man named James Gilroy came to me in the night. He carried word from my mother and sister, still captive in Tunis. Proof they live."

"That's extraordinary. Are you certain this Gilroy spoke the truth?"

John held up the silver piece between thumb and forefinger. "He had proof."

Ryland accepted the coin from John and tilted it toward sunlight. "An old piece of eight."

"I call it the Islanded Lion."

"Come again?" Ryland blinked as he handed it back.

"A silly child's story, really. My sister Kaitlin was always frightened of the sea. So, I spun a story about a magic piece of eight that could protect her. She held onto it, even after the pirates took us. I called it the Islanded Lion."

"Wait, you don't mean...*this* coin?"

"Aye. Kaitlin sent the Lion back to me as proof her message was genuine. Only she and I knew what it meant."

"Your sister must be very clever."

John smiled as he recalled six-year-old Kaitlin, tip-toeing over a log in a creek, arms carefully balanced.

"Clever. And nimble. I called her Rabbit." John's thumb dug against the edge of the coin.

"I'm so sorry for what you've lost, Mr. Sullivan. If there's anything I can do to help—"

"Actually, there is," said John. He watched Ryland carefully as he spoke. "Gilroy didn't know where to find them, but he did know someone who could help. A thief called 'The Silver Hand,' who helped him escape slavery in Algiers. He claimed he'd seen the Silver Hand talking to an American naval officer on the day of his escape. He overheard their conversation and the name of the officer."

Ryland's charcoal fell still. The lieutenant's gaze lifted from the page. "He did?"

"It was you, Mr. Ryland. He said the two of you looked to be friends."

"Me?" said Ryland, looking at John with an awkward smile. "Friends with a thief?"

"I'm not interested in your associations, Mr. Ryland. I need to find the Silver Hand. I need your help."

"Of course. I'll help in any way I can." Ryland traced a finger along his stubble—just as he had during the brag game. It was his tell. "But I don't know any man calling himself the Silver Hand, nor any other thief. Your Mr. Gilroy was mistaken."

Deception, thought John. He felt a stab of anger. And sorrow. Having a new friend on a ship of strangers—a senior officer no less—had felt good. And that friend had just lied to him. *Why?*

John wanted to scream, *You fucking liar!* But losing Ryland's trust would gain him nothing. "I see. I suppose it was a forlorn hope."

"Don't lose heart, Mr. Sullivan. We'll make Gibraltar

within the week, and then it's on to Tripoli. I'll offer whatever help I can to find your family."

"Thank you, Mr. Ryland," said John. "Your help is most welcome." He walked off before Ryland could reply, afraid his disgust might overwhelm him.

As John reached the steps of the main hatch, he raked his thumb over the Islanded Lion harder and harder. He thought his anger would boil over. He wanted to throw the holystoning crew's bucket. He wanted to take an ax to the mainmast. He wanted to…

A white smudge on the horizon caught his eye. The only sight, in that very moment, that could have calmed him. He walked over to the starboard rail. The sails of the *Allegheny* drifted on the sea like puffs of smoke. This far away, the black hull looked like a lump of coal. *She's aboard that ship right now,* thought John. He imagined Dominique walking along the *Allegheny's* gangway, looking west toward a tiny *Philadelphia.* He pictured her hair tied back, a few golden tassels tickling her nose. Her blue eyes narrow in the sunlight. A defiant smirk as she smoked her corncob pipe. John wondered if, at this very moment, Dominique was looking at him.

Chapter 24

The USS *Allegheny*
The Atlantic Ocean
Thursday, August 18th, 1803

God, Dominique needed a smoke. She stared at a soft-boiled egg on a crystal pedestal, yolk gleaming like melting wax. A night in the cabin retching did little for her appetite, but the embarrassment of eating in front of the crew did even less. Buttery brioche, fresh cream, orange meringue, and coffee with a lump of chocolate—all spread across a table draped in linen. Frigate quarterdeck turned sidewalk café—just for her. The sailors forward of the wheel, who lived on stale bread and leathery pork, could only drool with envy. It felt cruel to flaunt such extravagance above decks, but Aubert insisted their lifestyle was no concern of subordinates. She sighed, the wind blowing threads of hair across her face, and raked her fork over whipped meringue.

"Is something not to your liking, *Madame* Aubert?" asked Chef Jean-Christophe in a courtly accent. Aubert had searched the Americas for a French chef of the highest skill. What he found was a portly gourmand cooking for ungrateful fur trappers. "Perhaps I could bring something else?"

"It's fine, Jean-Christophe," said Dominique, dabbing her chin with a napkin. She looked past the empty chair across from her, allowing her eyes to drift with the peaceful waters of the Atlantic. The snapping of the fore-and-aft sail overhead lulled her into a trance. "My stomach's still a bit off."

"'Fine,' she says," muttered the chef, thick white mustache twitching. "Try the meringue. I used an infusion of syrup, in the Italian style." His shadow loomed over her as he pushed the confection closer. "Very gentle on the stomach."

"Lieutenant," said Dominique to the gangly twenty-two-year-old standing near the taffrail. "Where is Richard?"

"Ma'am?" stuttered the *Allegheny's* First Lieutenant Kimble. His polite Georgia drawl made him sound like a pious altar boy. "Uh, the captain wanted to join you but said you ought to go ahead. On account of his work—charts, logs, and such."

"*Madame*," fussed Jean-Christophe. He picked up her coffee. "The *chocolat* has just melted to perfection. Won't you take a sip?"

"Thank you, Chef, but I'm finished," said Dominique. She stood and smoothed her dress. "Will he be in his cabin all day?" she asked Kimble.

Jean-Christophe muttered to himself as he began stacking the plates. "That was my last Seville orange..."

"Captain Aubert asked not to be disturbed, ma'am," replied Kimble, hands fidgeting behind his back. "On account of—"

"His work," griped Dominique. "Too sensitive for the prying eyes of his wife."

"I…uh…"

"Mr. Kimble, I'm holding up your day."

"I beg your pardon?" Kimble replied.

Dominique looked out along the deck of the small, three-masted warship. Her gaze chased away several askance looks. The sailors on deck or in the rigging acted as though too busy to notice her presence. But she knew better. The men of the fleet called her "The Duchess"—as if she were an aloof heiress on a pleasure yacht. God, one pipe. Surely Aubert could forgive her that.

"You must have more important duties than attending to me," Dominique said to Kimble. A snapping sound and the yelp of a sailor drew her eyes forward. The *Allegheny's* bosun, a middle-aged man with thick sideburns and a short top hat, was yelling curses. He swatted at a group of seamen with a segmented cane. "Why is that man whipping the others?"

Kimble stood beside Dominique. "Mr. Toule, ma'am? He's the bosun, you see, and it's his duty to keep the crew from idleness. Captain Aubert expects our torn mains'l repaired before eight bells."

"Get up that shroud you lazy puppy!" shouted Toule. Thick brows and weathered lines gave the man a permanent scowl. He whipped a teenage seaman, and the boy scrambled to climb the rope latticework. "Slothful wretches, the lot of you!"

"The captain wants *Allegheny* ready for sail before *Philadelphia*," explained Kimble.

Dominique looked north, a mile or so to starboard, toward the flagship. The black and gold hull of USS *Philadelphia* shimmered in the sun. Like the *Allegheny* and the other three U.S. ships, she was hove-to—half her sails faced backward to the wind, preventing her from making headway. Bainbridge wanted the squadron to hold position for repairs. And Aubert was beating his men like dogs just to best Bainbridge. So typical. "Is it necessary to whip them so?"

"Uh...you see, ma'am," stuttered Kimble. "Naval discipline may offend feminine sensibilities, but a captain must be stern. If he were to indulge indolence or ill-discipline, the men could become mutinous. Better a few taps of the cane than a dozen from the cat."

"Indolence?" said Dominique. "They haven't had a moment's rest since the storm." The unpleasant sight of a man's back cut to bloody ribbons ran through Dominique's mind. She remembered the terrible snap of that nine-tailed whip, each stroke tearing off flesh. Aubert had already ordered several floggings. Yet another arena in which he seemed determined to outstrip the squadron commander. The most recent unfortunate had touched Dominique's arm. She had slipped on a puddle of sea spray, and the sailor moved to catch her. Try as she might, she couldn't convince Aubert of the man's innocent intentions. After that, the crew hated "the Duchess" more than ever.

"*Chocolat* at ten pence an ounce," muttered Jean-Christophe as he walked by with a stack of dishes, "only to feed the fish. What do I care?"

"Captain Aubert's orders were clear," added Kimble. "If the men fail in their repairs before noon, each division is to name their slowest man, who shall have a dozen lashes. You see, ma'am, in the Navy—"

"Jean-Christophe," said Dominique, holding up her skirts as she followed the chef down the steps of the quarterdeck. "Have you supplies for more brioche?"

The chef lit up. "Why, *madame,* fear not! I could serve

fine bread to you, your husband, and his senior officers thrice a day from here to Gibraltar. Shall I bake a fresh loaf?"

"Yes. In fact, I want you to bake all that you have."

Jean-Christophe gave a churlish laugh. "*Madame* must have found a large appetite indeed!"

"Not for me," said Dominique. "For the crew. I want fresh brioche for every man aboard. And butter and coffee—from our private reserves."

"But *Madame* Aubert," whined the chef. His stack of plates began to wobble. "Those reserves are for the captain and the lady of the ship. I couldn't possibly…"

"Right. I *am* the lady of the ship, am I not?"

"Well, of course, but I—"

"Then your lady is giving you an order." Her voice carried over the deck, and she felt more than a few curious glances. "The men preserved us through a terrible storm, and they've earned a good breakfast. Now snap to it."

"But—" Jean-Christophe's mustache started to tick. He sighed, shoulders slumping. "As you wish, *madame*." And he trudged below.

"Mr. Toule," said Dominique, steering the bosun's scowl in her direction. "Please pass word to the men. I wish to—"

"Mrs. Aubert," Kimble whispered to her. He shifted from foot to foot as though trying to hold his water. "I'm not sure it's entirely proper. The captain's orders were clear. The men aren't to bother you, and they've important work…"

"Very well." Dominique pivoted toward the captain's cabin. "I'll just take the matter up with Aubert."

"Erm…" stammered Kimble, skipping in front of

Dominique. "No need to bother the captain." The young officer cleared his throat. "Ahoy, there, Bosun. The lady of the ship has a request."

"As I was saying, Mr. Toule," Dominique went on, "pass word to the men. When repairs are done, the captain and I shall treat them to breakfast as thanks for their fine work. Along with the usual rations, they shall have fresh buttered bread and coffee."

Toule's eyes slid to Kimble. Kimble nodded sheepishly. Toule's eyes slid back to Dominique. "Aye, madam."

Before the grumpy bosun could turn away, Dominique added, "And inform each division: If their repairs are done before eight bells, I shall thank their fastest worker with a kiss."

Bosun Toule curled his lip. "Madam?"

"You heard me. Pass the word."

With a suspicious look at Kimble, Toule replied. "Aye, madam."

Over the next few minutes, Dominique smiled as she watched the word reach each sailor. The most common expression was disbelief, followed by a curious look at her, and finally a silly grin. The crew sparked to life. Within an hour, the doldrums vanished, replaced by vigorous action. Soon, the broken spars were replaced, new canvas raised, and parted deck planks resealed, all by seven bells. A flurry of industry inspired by a few words. For Dominique, it was a new kind of thrill.

As she walked from man to man along the spar deck, holding a tray of steaming brioche, it was hard to decide what gave her more pleasure. Each man smiling and tipping his hat as she handed him a roll. Or Jean-Christophe's chagrin as he poured them coffee. For the first time in a month, the crew didn't look at Dominique like a black cat crossing their path.

When she came to a middle-aged sailor with a long, craggy face, the man touched his forehead in salute. "Thank you, miss," he said as he accepted his share of brioche.

"How are you, Mr?" said Dominique.

"Able Seaman Avery, miss," replied the sailor. "And I'm just fine, thank you kindly. And this here…" Avery pulled a timid young man forward, laying a hand on each of his shoulders. "…Is Mr. Chauncey."

"Ah, and he's your fastest worker?" she smiled. Chauncey flushed and stared at his feet. His mates, all older than him, were smiling or chuckling.

"Never seen him tie a stopper so fast," said Avery, laughing with the others. "You'll have to pardon his shy nature."

Dominique smiled, raising his chin with her finger. "Very impressive, Mr. Chauncey."

Chauncey smiled back. "Th-thank you, miss."

The lad's eyes went wide as Dominique leaned forward. Her lips lightly brushed his cheek. She handed the rigid sailor a piece of bread.

Avery slapped Chauncey's back. "I think he's liable to faint, boys."

The rest of Chauncey's division broke into chuckling. A few of them clapped his shoulder. One tousled the grinning sailor's hair.

When all the men had been fed, Dominique slipped off to a quiet spot near the bow. The gunner generously provided her a slow-burning match for her pipe. She puffed on the tobacco as she looked out across the water. She could hear faint voices carrying over from

Philadelphia. She watched the tiny figures climbing the rigging.

Aubert's voice cut through the high-spirited chatter of the *Allegheny* crew. "Lieutenant Kimble, your report."

Kimble was too far away for Dominique to make out his reply to the captain, but she could hear the tension in his voice. She took one more drag, then spilled the tobacco into the ocean. She hid the pipe behind her back.

"And who gave that order?" Aubert was demanding.

Dominique faced toward her husband. On the other end of the ship, Aubert stood outside of his cabin, frowning in her direction. She tried her most charming smile, hoping to diffuse his irritation. Aubert looked around at his crew, all trying to appear busy. His frown deepened, and he marched back into his cabin.

A pit sank in Dominique's stomach. It had been a gamble either way. Either Aubert would be pleased with the crew's improved work ethic or incensed by her meddling. No luck today.

Before she dragged herself back to the cabin to smooth things over, she stole another glance at the flagship. *He's over there right now,* thought Dominique. She pictured Sully in his handsome midshipman's uniform, his face clean shaven again. That ridiculous brash smile as he stood on the rail, a hand on a halyard. His confident, determined eyes, never flinching from what he desired. Dominique wondered if, at this very moment, John was looking at her.

Chapter 25

The USS *Philadelphia*
The Atlantic Ocean
Thursday, August 18th, 1803

"Eight bells and all's well, sir!" said Eric Long. The ten-year-old had just tapped out the time on a brass bell engraved "USS Philadelphia, 1799." He looked up at John, his grin revealing a broken front tooth. Add his unruly black curls and snub nose, and his pride couldn't be more endearing. Had John ever been so young?

"Very good, lad. Hourglass turned?" John asked like a captain demanding a report.

"Aye, aye, Midshipman Sullivan."

"Then we stand relieved," said John. Another boy a little younger than Long took up the post at the ship's bell. For the *Philadelphia's* youngest, duties usually consisted of swabbing, fetching, and stowing. Only a lucky few had the honor of keeping time. "Off to the mess with you for some breakfast."

Long saluted and dashed off. John smiled to himself as he walked aft. The officers of the forenoon watch had already taken over, and he was looking forward to some time in his hammock. Especially after sacrificing his last four hours of sleep for brag. He only made it two steps down the main hatch when a voice stopped him.

"Midshipman Sullivan."

It was First Lieutenant Stephen Porter strolling along the starboard rail, hands clasped behind his back. A tall man of twenty-seven, he always spoke with a calm disinterest—as though too deep in philosophical thought to be bothered with duty.

"Sir?" replied John.

"Captain Bainbridge's compliments and he will see you in his cabin."

"Aye, sir." John saluted. Porter passed by and rubbed at a smudge on the bell.

John descended the main hatch steps into a cloud of steam. The galley fires filled the gun deck with the smell of leaven and wood smoke. A line of sailors waited for their share of pork, peas, and hardtack. He started down the hundred feet stretching toward the captain's cabin. His eyes roamed over the rows of black iron guns, each heavier than a horse-drawn carriage. Spare shot, horns of primer, and a barrel swab hung beside each. He stepped around rows of idlers scrubbing the deck, cleaning the cannons, or plugging a seam with oakum. Judging by the chatter filling the room, the men were in high spirits. He nodded to the Marine outside the cabin and knocked on the door.

"Come in," came the reply.

It was the second time John had entered the cabin. The skylight overhead and the row of stern windows filled the room with sun. Bainbridge sat on the port side, writing in his log. A candelabrum with long beards of wax occupied one corner of his desk. A sculpture of a skull— a prop from *Hamlet*—sat on the other. A mannequin between the cabin's two long guns wore Othello's kaftan, complete with a blunted scimitar. Playbills decorated the bulkheads, mostly from Shakespeare. The billing for *Richard III* at Philadelphia's Chestnut Street Theater adorned the beam over Bainbridge's head. The captain never tired of telling how Thomas Abthorpe Cooper, his favorite actor, had autographed it over dinner.

"You sent for me, Captain?" said John.

"Yes," said Bainbridge, still writing. "I wanted to commend your quick thinking in the squall. Easing the lee rigging to save the mast—spot on. I expect no less of a young officer."

It was an unexpected compliment. Bainbridge had been cool, if even-handed, toward John since he joined the crew. Given Aubert and Pritchett's application of pressure, John wouldn't have been surprised if Bainbridge took affront to the new midshipman. John's mission was to save his family, not impress his betters, but he couldn't deny his pride. The commanding officer of a forty-four was paying him a compliment.

"Thank you, Captain," said John. "I was only doing my duty."

"As do we all." Bainbridge dropped his quill and clasped his hands over his waist. The twenty-nine-year-old captain had a meticulous appearance. Gold buttons polished, collar starched till adamantine, curly hair shining like obsidian. "In honor of your heroics, I wondered if you might join me for breakfast."

"Of course, Captain," John said, embarrassed to hear his voice crack. "It would be my honor."

"Excellent." Bainbridge sprang from his chair. There were three domed trays and two place settings on the captain's long table. Neat rows of silverware flanked the plates. The captain gestured to a chair on his left. "Please."

John sat and watched Bainbridge pull the domes. Steam rose in plumes. There were glazed ham steaks, poached eggs, and fluffy biscuits. These would have come from the captain's private stores—luxuries not to be frittered away. As Bainbridge served each dish, John's eyes wandered over a compact piano between the guns on the starboard side. Above it, there were sheets of music instead of playbills. One read "*Sonata Number 3 in G Minor*" and was signed "J.S. Bach."

"Do you like them?" asked Bainbridge, nodding to his framed music.

"Yes, very impressive."

"I collect signatures of all the greats," said the captain, settling into his chair. He poured coffee for John and himself. "Music and theater are the finest achievements of Man. I keep them as a reminder—of what we fight to preserve." Bainbridge gestured to John's plate. "Please."

John dug into the ham, relishing a break from the ship's stale fare.

"Try the plum sauce," said Bainbridge, pouring a dollop on John's plate.

The first bite was exquisite. John chewed with his eyes closed, the ham melting on his tongue. The sauce added a tang, then turned sweet in the finish. "Delicious, sir."

Bainbridge smiled. "My steward's been with me for years. No man better." The captain looked thoughtful as he sliced off a strip of ham and drew little circles in the sauce. He plucked it off the fork, chewing loudly. "You and Lieutenant Ryland seem to be fast friends."

It was no secret that Bainbridge and his other senior officers disliked Ryland. Among the lower ranks, however, Ryland enjoyed wide popularity. Even John couldn't deny Chester Ryland had a certain charm. Like a champion drunk on victory, but always gracious to his admirers. Depending on the man, the fourth lieutenant was either loved or despised.

"I'm not new to the sea, Captain," said John, "but I am new to the Navy. I'm eager to become the best officer I can be, and Mr. Ryland has been a mentor."

"Naturally," Bainbridge said, daubing his chin. He sat back, jaw working on a morsel. "And how do you find our Lieutenant Ryland? Your impression of the man. His character."

John chewed on his biscuit, stalling for time. Finally, he said, "I wouldn't feel right to speak on a man behind his back."

"A captain is responsible for the conduct of all under his command. You would do well to remember that, Midshipman. I mean for my junior officers to learn from the best example. Come man, out with it."

"Mr. Ryland seems an honorable sort," said John. "He shows a competent hand at seamanship. The men respect him. I admit, his sense of humor is sometimes…indelicate."

"Crass, more like," snapped Bainbridge.

"But in the short time I've been aboard, he's shown himself to be an honorable man."

"Has he?" muttered the captain.

John still didn't know why Ryland had lied to him. He took the chance to gain some insight. "I prefer to judge a man by his actions, but I've heard rumors about him."

"Word travels fast on our little wooden world. What manner of rumors?"

"That the lieutenant is given to excessive drink.

Gambling." John's ears turned hot as he thought of the secret brag game he had organized below decks. "I also heard mention of an embarrassing incident in Algiers."

Bainbridge looked sharply at John. "Embarrassment? What embarrassment?" Something in the captain's tone suggested personal affront—as if he were being accused of something. John couldn't imagine why.

"Concerning Mr. Ryland," John hurried to say. "Something about his possibly being involved in a theft?"

"Ah, of course," said Bainbridge, his tone softening. "The Silver Hand incident."

John felt his pulse rise. "Silver Hand, you say?"

"Three years ago, I had the ignominious task of delivering tribute to the dey of Algiers. I was assigned command of the USS *George Washington*. Mr. Ryland served as my fourth lieutenant, then as he does now. It was a matter of great diplomatic delicacy. I tasked Mr. Ryland with transporting several chests of gifts from the docks to the dey's palace. On his watch, a chest containing a good deal of silver and jewels went missing. The dey was furious. He accused the United States of breaking her word to Algiers—we could have gone to war right then."

"A difficult position for any captain."

"Most difficult," agreed Bainbridge. "But a good captain doesn't lose his wits. I investigated the scene and discovered a handprint inside an empty cash box. It was in a curious color of paint, as though a man dipped his hand in silver and pressed it to the box. I showed Dey Muhammad the handprint, and he agreed it was the work of the Silver Hand. Apparently, this thief has irritated the Barbary princes for many years."

"Fortunate for us you were there to represent our

country," said John. A little flattery never hurt.

"Yes, fortunate indeed," agreed Bainbridge. "A lesser leader might have panicked. Still, Mr. Ryland was alone with the stolen boxes for nearly two hours—ample opportunity to assist in a theft and collect a share of the take. And the man's had a smug look in his eye every day since."

"Why would Ryland help a thief steal from his own ship?"

"I am loathe to speculate," Bainbridge said, straightening his coat. "But if I'm to be candid, it's obvious Ryland is jealous of his senior officers. Especially me. Some men are without honor. I believe Chester Ryland arranged the theft to subvert my command."

"That is…serious, Captain."

"Quite serious, Midshipman. It is, however, a charge without proof. So, Mr. Ryland remains an officer in good standing for the time being. But beware his charms—and his associations. Any of his mates might have been complicit. Especially that sailor friend of his—Mr. Sawyer. The pair of them are thick as thieves indeed."

John drowned his discomfort in a gulp of coffee.

"You come to us with something of an unusual background, don't you, Mr. Sullivan?" said Bainbridge. "There are more rumors circling you as well. Rumors of smuggling. Dueling…Gambling."

"Captain, I assure you—"

Bainbridge put up a hand. "Please, Midshipman. You are not under interrogation. Every man has something questionable in his past. On land, you've been a man of questionable character. But at sea, you can prove yourself a gentleman. I believe every man should have a chance to start anew. I see great potential in you, Mr. Sullivan. The question is, will you rise to the challenge?"

As much as John liked Ryland, he'd be lying if he didn't relish the chance to win the captain's respect. "I certainly will, Captain."

"I am a stern leader, but a fair one. Show me honor, and I will show you the same. Should you come across any evidence of dishonorable conduct on the part of Mr. Ryland, I trust you'll do the right thing."

"You can count on me, Captain."

"Good man. Now then, how was your meal?"

"Exceptional, Captain. The plum sauce—I've never had anything like it."

"Indeed. A Bainbridge secret family recipe. Now, if you'll excuse me, I must return to my duties."

John stood. "Of course, Captain. Thank you for your hospitality, sir."

"You're welcome, Midshipman. Dismissed."

John saluted and started for the door.

"And Mr. Sullivan…"

John looked back at Bainbridge.

"I can forgive a discreet bit of cards after a long journey, but I better not hear of gambling in my surgery again."

John swallowed, biting back his surprise. He raised a salute. "Aye, aye, sir."

Chapter 26

The USS *Philadelphia*
The Atlantic Ocean
Tuesday, August 23rd, 1803

One ratline at a time.

Gabriel Sawyer closed his eyes. His heart whirred in his ears. Sweat slickened his palms. *So far down.* It didn't matter that his eyes were closed. Sawyer knew exactly how high on the shroud he was. He knew exactly how far below him lay the deck. How much farther still, the ocean surface. *So very far down.*

Just one ratline at a time. He could do it.

But he couldn't. In his mind, he imagined every horrifying second of the fall. It would start with a slip of his sweaty hand. Then, this once, his other hand would falter. Now he would plunge through space, the final seconds of his life reduced to a jumble of flailing and screaming. What would he think about on the way down? His poor mother in Cardiff who would never know his fate. How sad that he never tasted roast duck. The beautiful despair on Chester's face. A plea to God for his immortal—*Crack!* And that would be that.

"One ratlin' at a time, son," said a fatherly voice.

Sawyer opened his eyes. He stared through the rope latticework of the shroud, halfway up to the maintop. Nothing but white billowing mainsail, the trunk of the mast, and so much terrible empty space. His eyes traced up to the topsails, above them to the topgallants, and up to the red-white-and-blue pennant trailing above the royals. He looked down, watching the deck lurch back and forth. To his left, Able Seaman Matthew Meadows perched on the shroud as easily as a sparrow on a branch.

"Meadows…I can't," stammered Sawyer.

"Come now, lad," Meadows coaxed, keeping his voice low. "We've been through this. A man taking his time to get aloft looks like laziness. What if the captain happened by? You don't want to end up at the grating."

A cold chill ran through Sawyer. Aside from the prospect of being flogged, he realized he needed to piss. *What if I piss myself in the rigging?* "I'm not…it's not," stammered Sawyer.

"Son, there's naught to do but climb. Keep your mind on the next ratlin', then the next. Like we've talked about. One hand for yourself, one for the ship. You'll be fine."

Sawyer closed his eyes. "I can't. The fear…what if it causes me to slip?"

"You won't. The fear makes sure of that." Meadows' voice became stern. "Come along, Sawyer. We'll make the climb together."

The young seaman took one last moment to gather his nerve.

"Come on up, Woodchuck!" cried Michael Dufort. Sawyer looked up to see the boyish grin of his messmate. Dufort straddled the maintop yard like a horse, his black hair poking beneath his hat brim. How could a man—half Sawyer's height, not a whisker on his chin, seasick his whole first week—scramble through rigging like a monkey in a tree? "What with all these ropes everywhere," Dufort added, "it's not even a real climb. You'd have to be a *swooning princess* to fall!"

Oh, God, realized Sawyer. *What if I swoon?*

"Mr. Sawyer," called a voice from the deck.

Sawyer looked down to see Midshipman Sullivan. "Yes, sir?"

"Come down for a moment," said Sullivan. "I need a word."

"Aye, aye, sir," Sawyer called back.

The moment Sawyer's feet touched solid planks, he felt his stomach caught in a tug of war. The relief of solid ground battling the fear of a beating.

"You all right, Sawyer?" Sullivan said. He looked the picture of confidence and authority in his officer's coat. The forward point of his bicorne hat cast a shadow over his face like the hand of a sundial.

Sawyer straightened his posture and faced the leader of his division with as much poise as he could fake. "Aye, Mr. Sullivan. Fine, sir." The knot in Sawyer's stomach tightened as he awaited his inevitable punishment.

Sullivan clasped his hands behind his back and started walking. "Lay forward, with me, will you?"

The two walked toward the bow. They passed Seaman Prince sleeping between two guns near the galley smokestack. How Sawyer envied the peaceful off-duty sailor. They came to the rail below the bowsprit. For a moment, Sullivan squinted across the rippling water. Pillow-like clouds drifted across the horizon.

"Still struggling with heights, I see," said Sullivan.

"Aye, sir," Sawyer said nervously. "Sorry, sir. I'll do better. I promise."

"At ease, Seaman," said John. "You're not in trouble. A lot of men struggle with it at first. I did myself, as a lad on my father's merchant ship. I can let this incident go, but the other officers won't be as lenient. You can't keep on like this."

"I know, sir, and thank you, sir." Sawyer felt a drop of sweat run into his eye. He was on the verge of despair. "What do I do?"

"I wish I could tell you," Sullivan replied. "Some fears are near impossible to conquer. But I may have another solution."

"What, sir?"

"What would you say to idler duties, with the other landsmen? It's not glamorous work, but—"

"Idler work! Why that would be...!" Sawyer could barely contain his excitement. "That is, deck duty would be fine by me, sir."

Sullivan smiled. "Good. Report aft to Midshipman Merrick on your next watch. It took some convincing, but Captain Bainbridge came around."

"It's already done, sir? Really?"

"It's done," Sullivan replied.

"Thank you! Oh, really, Mr. Sullivan, thank you very much indeed."

"You're welcome," said Sullivan, adjusting the angle of his hat. "Now that's done with, I thought we might have a chat. Not as officer and seaman, but as men."

"Of course, sir. What about?"

Gabriel looked into Sullivan's eyes. They turned gold in the afternoon light. There had always been something inspiring about the *Philadelphia's* mysterious newcomer. An infectious energy and confidence. Add this rescue from the rigging, and Gabriel wanted to bask in Sullivan's warmth all day. He made himself look away.

"Twenty years old is a late start for a midshipman," said Sullivan. "My father taught me seamanship, but there's so much more I have to learn. Chester Ryland has helped me a great deal, and it's meant the world."

Sawyer had seen Ryland and Sullivan chatting and laughing together many times. Their budding friendship was obvious. Despite his relief at escaping the rigging, Sawyer couldn't help feeling a little jealous. "Chester—er, I mean Mr. Ryland, is a good officer. I suppose you'd know better than me."

"Really?" said Sullivan. "I'd heard you and Ryland are good friends."

"I…suppose we used to have an occasional chat." Gabriel looked up at the spritsails, white as the clouds. He didn't want Sullivan to see the regret in his eyes. "But he's a senior officer, and I'm only a seaman. I wouldn't call us friends, exactly."

"Mr. Sawyer, I understand your misgivings about discussing Ryland, but I'm coming to you out of concern. I had breakfast with the captain yesterday, and he's convinced that Lieutenant Ryland participated in a serious crime. He doesn't have proof, but he's looking for it. He asked me to spy on him."

"He did?" Sawyer said, hearing the worry in his voice too late.

"It's all right," John said quietly. "I don't aim to, but you understand my concern. Chester Ryland is my friend, and if I'm to look after him, I'll need your help."

"Me? What could I do?"

"The thing is," Sullivan continued, "I've noticed Ryland drinking expensive spirits. Betting big at cards. Flaunting wealth he shouldn't have on an officer's salary.

There's nothing I hate more than America paying tribute to the Barbary Pirates, so if Ryland stole the dey's treasure, all to the good. But if someone loyal to Bainbridge finds the Silver Hand's loot in his possession, he'll hang. I said as much to Ryland, but he denied everything."

"And you…don't believe him?"

"I don't. I think he's underestimated Bainbridge. Mr. Sawyer, if I'm right, you know him better than anyone. You've got to find that evidence before the captain does."

Sawyer wanted to trust Sullivan. Only now that he considered confiding his secrets did he truly feel their weight. But he had to be careful. The midshipman could indeed be spying for the captain—or greedy for gold. "If you found such loot in Chester's possession, what would you do?"

"Send it straight to the bottom, of course."

Sawyer considered a moment. Movement tugged at the corner of his eye. He saw Michael Dufort creeping towards the sleeping bully Prince with a bucket of water. Dufort and Prince's rivalry was about to escalate, but Sawyer had his own problems. "I…if there was any treasure, Ryland wouldn't have told me. I'm afraid I can't help."

"Sawyer, listen to me. Bainbridge won't rest until Ryland hangs from a yardarm. If you care about him at all, you have to help me. Or find the evidence yourself. We have to save him from himself."

Sawyer sighed, watching a gray-feathered tern dive for a fish. Sullivan wouldn't find any treasure—that much Sawyer knew. But he *would* find something worse. Something Chester was a damn fool to keep. But how could he trust Sullivan? He had promised Chester. They could never tell a soul. "I'm sorry, Mr. Sullivan. I know of no evidence. I wish I could help. I really do." *Please believe it and go away.*

There was a splash and a flurry of curses. Aft of them, Dufort had tossed the bucket of water on Prince. Dufort laughed hysterically as Prince jumped to his feet. It might have come to blows, but Sullivan said, "Dufort, Prince— that's enough! Get back to work."

Dufort and Prince looked at Sullivan, then exchanged one last glare. They grudgingly went separate ways.

Sullivan sighed and looked back at Sawyer. "I understand, Mr. Sawyer. It was worth a try."

Sawyer released a sigh.

"Mr. Sawyer," said Sullivan. "One other thing."

"Sir?"

"You're relieved for the remainder of this watch, but don't be late for idler duties. Best to make a good impression."

"Of course, sir," said Sawyer with a salute. "I won't let you down."

"I know you won't," Sullivan said with a warm smile. He returned the salute and started aft.

Sawyer closed his eyes. He took in a deep breath. "Wait."

Sullivan turned around.

"I might know something that could help you."

"One more," Ethan Auldon soothed. He hooked the last suture through his patient's sliced palm. "You're doing great."

Matthew Meadows mopped a rag over his curly white

hair. "Christ. A little needle and I'm liable to faint like a girl."

The fifty-eight-year-old able seaman had been on deck supervising the effort to hoist a spar. When a block broke, and the crew lost their grip, Meadows caught the rope and held it for a full five seconds. The sailors were able to get out of the way just before it fell. Meadows was a tough old salt, but like all men, he had at least one private fear. Needles.

"I don't know about that," said Ethan, as he tied off the thread. "I happen to know one very tough girl."

Meadows winced as much as chuckled. "Haven't you got a bloody wit."

"Done," smiled Ethan.

"That's it?" said Meadows, looking at the bruised track of stitches across his palm.

"Aye. Unless I sewed your thumb to your forefinger!"

"I wouldn't tell if you did," laughed Meadows. He worked his wounded hand opened and closed for a moment. "Thank you, Mr. Auldon…for keeping this discreet."

"Fear of needles is common, Mr. Meadows. Nothing to be ashamed of."

Meadows patted Ethan on the shoulder. "All the same, you're a good lad." The moment the veteran sailor got to his feet, he started to wobble.

Ethan threw an arm around Meadows to steady him. "Easy, now."

"I suppose the laudanum left me a mite groggy. It's all right, son. I'll be fine from here."

"Off to the hammock, with you," said Ethan. "Get some rest."

"Aye," nodded Meadows with drooping eyelids. "I

think I'll go above decks and take the air first."

"A fine idea, Mr. Meadows," agreed Ethan.

Meadows hobbled off, and Ethan couldn't resist feeling a little pride. To put his medical talents to use, and spare a man's dignity in the bargain, made for a bright day. He had just begun to clean his tools when the sick berth door snapped open.

"Look alive, mate!" John Sullivan sauntered in and clapped Ethan on the back. "Saw any bones? Dispense any leeches?"

"Nah," said Ethan. "Not even a little bloodletting. Just a few boring stitches."

"Good!" John straddled the bench Meadows had been laying on. He bounced his legs like a nervous boy. On deck, he walked with the stiff posture of an officer. When it was just him and Ethan, the real John shone through. A man brimming with energy. Always in need of a hill to climb, a game to win, a clock to race. "I need your talents."

"I see. Lie down and I'll get my saw."

"*Musical* talents," John corrected, jumping up. "How would you like to play Bach for a full house?"

Ethan's smile fell away. "John, what did you do?"

"Don't look so worried, mate. This is a great opportunity."

The knot twisted tighter in Ethan's stomach. He turned away from John and busied himself putting away tools. "*What* opportunity?"

"I had breakfast with Captain Bainbridge last Thursday, and wouldn't you know it? He's a music lover. Bach. We had breakfast again this morning, and I may have mentioned your skill with the violin. Wouldn't you know it? The captain's yearning for a good concerto. He wants you to play for the officers, in his cabin, tomorrow night!"

"You didn't!" said Ethan, scowling at John.

"I thought you'd be pleased," John said, his smile falling away.

"And you didn't bother to ask me first? I don't want to play concertos for the captain or anyone else."

"Why not?"

"Forget it." Ethan turned his back again. He went back to running a cloth over each medical instrument. "It won't matter, because next, you're going to tell me it's part of your plan."

"I'm so close, Ethan," said John. "Sawyer told me where to find the evidence. I need to swipe Ryland's sketchbook, and he'll talk. Problem is, he carries it everywhere."

"And a concert is the perfect distraction."

"Bainbridge and Ryland can't stand being in the same room," confirmed John. "Ryland will be alone."

"And then what?" Ethan sighed. "You'll rap him on the head?"

"I'm hoping it won't come to that."

"Good God, John," said Ethan. "Are you mad? Striking an officer is a hanging offense. Besides, a blow to the head could render him deaf or insensible—or dead."

"You have a better idea?"

"No, but…" Ethan folded his arms. "There's got to be a better way, John. Let me at least think it over."

"There's no time, Ethan. We're a day from Gibraltar. I've made arrangements with Pavia's contacts there. Ryland's got to tell me how to find the Silver Hand before we make land. I'll take the risk."

"Of course. For Kaitlin."

"Yes, for Kaitlin. Why else?"

An inhuman cry fills the night. Ethan launches out of bed, panting. His heart pounds as he searches the darkness. The howling creature isn't outside. It's in the bed across the room.

John Sullivan twists and writhes in his sleep. His muscles are taut, his fingers gnarled. He's an animal held under the brand.

John never remembered having those terrible dreams. Never remembered the things he whispered in the night. On so many mornings, watching John slurp down porridge and coffee, Ethan would almost tell him of what he became in his sleep. But then Judith and Ansel would hear John's impression of a clurichaun, or some other mythical Irish character. His little brother and sister would be giggling too hard to breathe, and Ethan would feel better. Everyone had nightmares, after all.

"John," said Ethan, "I watched you chase Pierre Laffite through a burning building."

"We came out all right, didn't we?"

"I saw the look in your eyes with Clyde Tindall."

"Oh, not this again." John paced between a pair of sick hammocks. He hooked his hand on a beam overhead.

"Look what you're about to do to Chester Ryland. A man you admire."

John stared at the bulkhead.

"Others may not see it," Ethan continued, "but anger is consuming you. Every time you betray your conscience in Kaitlin's name, you lose another piece of your soul. You think only of the day Katie and Nora are rescued, but what of the day after? What will be left of John Sullivan?"

"I've made sacrifices to save my family," whispered John. "And there'll be more to come. If my soul is the price for their freedom, tell me where to sign. That's a bargain I can live with."

"Really?" Ethan pointed at John's right hand. "Then why are you bleeding?"

John looked down. He puzzled at what he saw. His sister's coin, the Islanded Lion, was pressed between his fingers. He'd been rubbing the jagged edge so hard, blood was swelling on his thumb and falling in fat drops. They added to a red jot on the planks.

Ethan picked up his surgical bag and started out of the sick berth. He stopped at the door. "Part of saving your family is saving yourself."

Ethan stepped out, leaving John to empty hammocks and the smell of old wounds.

Chapter 27

The Barton Estate
Philadelphia, Pennsylvania
Three years ago

"*Bien, Señor* Auldon," said the mustachioed Basque. "Again."

The snap of wooden swords echoed off marble. Near the fountain of Saint Marina, Ethan Auldon fenced with his instructor, Fernando Pavia. Rows of poplars, hedges, and columns enclosed the courtyard. The three stories of the Barton estate loomed all around them. Ethan's feet slid over the flagstones as he lunged. He landed his riposte on Pavia's shoulder for a third time, just as he'd been instructed.

"Good, good!" smiled Pavia. "You're improving. Time for a break." He offered Ethan a canteen.

Ethan drank greedily. He plopped down on the edge of the fountain next to John Sullivan. After Ethan's father nursed the Bartons' son back to health during the Yellow Fever of 1793, they'd offered to assist Ethan's education. Ethan had spent years tending to the wealthy Bartons and their sickly son, and in return, they offered another reward—the services of their cousin, Fernando Pavia. It was Pavia's job to teach Ethan to fight and help him enlist in the Navy. The truth was, Ethan wanted to join the Navy, but not alone. So, he shared his lessons with John.

"Can you believe it?" said Ethan, still panting. "We're really doing it. We're crossing swords with a veteran mercenary."

"We're crossing wooden wasters, anyway," smiled John.

"It's only been a few months, mate. We'll know the real thing soon enough. The Navy always has a choice berth for a skilled fighter."

John was tapping his foot. He drummed his waster on his knee. "Aye, our choice of berth. Sure."

Ethan offered the canteen, but John shook his head. "You still want to enlist with me, right?"

There was a distance in John's eyes. He didn't reply.

"Sullivan," said Pavia. "In your fighting stance." The Basque mercenary pointed with his waster.

A few minutes later, Ethan watched in amazement as John sparred with Pavia. Ethan's marksmanship had come along well, but he was still working on basic forms with a sword. John fought like a senior student. Spit flew from his mouth as he lunged. His nostrils flared as he dove under Pavia's swing. After weeks of training, taut muscles had appeared on his arms. John fought with the fury of a fox cornered by hounds.

Ethan caught movement in the corner of his eye. He glanced up at the manor's tall windows. A pale face peeked through the curtains on the third floor. Sixteen-year-old Diego Barton was watching from his bedroom, and Ethan felt guilty. Javier Barton's sickly son had always longed for athletic ability, but it was not to be. The face withdrew, and the curtains closed again.

"*Bien, otra vez!*"

John snarled. His waster launched at Pavia's stomach, trying to get below the parry. Except Pavia didn't parry—he stepped left. John fumbled to recover balance, but it was too late. Pavia's waster slapped John's from his hand, then delivered a chop to the back. John flopped on the ground, gasping.

"You're good, *alumno*," said Pavia, resting his waster across his shoulders. "But those weren't the forms I asked for."

"This is a waste of time!" John roared. He slammed the hilt of his wooden sword into the stones.

Pavia stood stork-legged, unmoved by his pupil's tantrum. "Oh, I don't know about that. Knocking you in the dirt is great exercise."

John got to his feet and began pacing. Sweat bled through his cotton shirt. Dirt stained his breeches. "To hell with sparring. You made your point—I'm not good enough to beat you."

"*Bien.* Back to forms. Now, then—"

"It's time for sharps."

Pavia chuckled and smoothed his mustache. "*Sharps?* You're still shaking off dust from your last defeat. I think not."

"I know every stance. Every parry. Every riposte. You haven't taught me a new technique in weeks."

"Learning skill at arms is not the same as memorizing a fishermen's bend. There are no constellations to navigate the field of battle."

"I fight with everything I have!"

"*Sí,* you fight with your passions."

"And yet, I can't win."

"It wasn't a compliment, *alumno*. If anger is your master, it is your enemy's servant."

"I don't have time for games," John snapped.

"John," Ethan said, "A few months ago, you never held a sword in your life. Look at how far you've come! Give it time."

"Ah, there," said Pavia, sweeping his hand toward Ethan. "I couldn't have said it better myself."

John's eyes drifted to a bee, burrowing into a rose. "My family doesn't have time."

"I know," Ethan murmured.

"Pavia," said John, taking up his stance. "One more bout. If I beat you, you get the sharps."

Pavia scratched at his goatee, then shrugged. "Very well. I get paid either way." He raised his waster.

John charged, and the swords disappeared into a whirlwind of cuts and thrusts. John fought with even more fury than before, and Pavia gave ground quickly. As Ethan watched, he began to believe John might really land a blow this time. As John brought his hardest strike down over Pavia's head, Pavia's waster rose to block it. A dry snap echoed through archways. The blade of John's waster was reduced to a splinter. The point of Pavia's wooden sword hovered beneath John's chin.

"Damn it to hell!" John cursed, taking a step back. "I had you. I had you that time!"

Pavia shrugged. "Perhaps. Perhaps not. I'll fetch another waster."

Before Pavia could set off for the barn, John said, "That wasn't fair. One more."

"I've never met a pupil so eager to be stabbed."

"I'm done playing with toys, Pavia."

"*Nola bizi, hala hil,*" said Pavia in his Basque language.

237

"What does that mean?" demanded John.

"A saying in my company of sell-swords. 'How you live is how you die.'" Pavia circled in front of John, gracefully twirling his waster into a fighting posture. "Trust me, *alumno*. You want to fight, so I will train you to fight."

John raised a shout across the whole courtyard. "Don't teach me to fight, goddamnit! Teach me to *kill*!"

Chapter 28

The USS *Philadelphia*
Near the British Imperial Colony of Gibraltar
Tuesday, August 23rd, 1803

Melisande had never seen such an ugly pile of rocks and scrub. Several miles off, a great mountain rose from the sapphire water. It was their destination, as Sullivan had told her, called "The Rock of Gibraltar." One side sloped gently, the other fell precipitously. The Rock's shape reminded her of a wolf, snout in the air and howling at the moon. Squat brush covered the slope and surrounding flatlands. There were no towering pines or leafy maples—just weeds and drab cliffs.

An odd buzzing drew Melisande's attention. She looked about her, expecting to see some strange bug beating its wings. She broke into an amused smile when she found the source. A few paces forward, Matthew Meadows was curled up between two canons, fast asleep and snoring. She envied the peaceful old sailor.

Melisande hated the dank bowels of the ship. It was nothing like an open camp, with the smell of pine and wood smoke, and good old-fashioned dirt. Or the longhouse, amid the scent of herbs and cornmeal. Being whipped about in a hammock couldn't compare with waking up beside kith and kin. Falling asleep with a lover. Life on this boat was like drifting across the ocean in a rotten barrel. Three hundred unwashed men—working, eating, farting. A smell like sour eggs blowing up from the hold. Chickens and pigs shitting in pens. Tar, gunpowder, bails of oakum, and the sweaty foot odor of damp. It redefined misery.

Another sound drew her attention. A snickering brat up to no good. Melisande recognized the blonde cork-screw curls of Robert Cowan, a twelve-year-old midshipman, creeping towards Meadows with a bucket. His childlike nose wrinkled with concentration as he raised it over the sleeping sailor. Before Melisande could open her mouth to warn Meadows, Cowan tossed the bucket. A gallon of deck-scrubbing water broke over the old seaman's face.

"Bleedin' Christ!" shouted Meadows as he jolted awake.

Cowan squealed with laughter. A few paces behind him, Midshipman Philip Grove joined in Cowan's hysterics. Grove was four years older, but no less puerile. The two of them were always prowling the deck, berating the seamen or threatening them with the cat. They were bullies with the authority of rank.

"Prince, you shit!" growled Meadows as he rubbed his eyes. "You'll have my boot in your ass! You'll…" Meadows trailed off. He paled when he saw Cowan staring down in slack-jawed shock. "S-sir, I…" Meadows stammered.

"Did you hear how he spoke to me?" Cowan shouted. He looked around the deck as if expecting to see a mob taking up arms in support. Crewmen working nearby didn't dare say a word, lest they draw Cowan's fury on themselves. "Did you *hear* how he *spoke* to me?" repeated Cowan.

"I heard it!" snapped Grove, nostrils flaring. "I heard what he said!"

Cowan glowered at Meadows. "How dare you. How dare you speak to me in such a way!"

"Midshipman Cowan," pleaded Meadows. "I apologize, sir. I didn't realize it was you. I'm sorry…"

"You will be, old goat!"

Melisande flushed with heat. She gripped the starboard rail so hard her hand hurt. It was Cowan that owed an apology, not Meadows. That little prick needed a punch in the nose, and she was about to give it to him.

"I apologize, Mr. Cowan," said Meadows, his back pressed up against the gun carriage. "I didn't think one of the gentlemen would be tossing buckets of water."

Before Melisande could take a step, another officer stomped past her. Captain Bainbridge swooped in like a hawk diving for prey. *That's more like it,* thought Melisande, directing a smug grin at Cowan. *An earful from ole Bluster-Britches ought to teach the little snot.*

But Bainbridge walked right past the two midshipmen. He yelled so furiously at Meadows, spit landed on the sailor's cheek. "You tell an officer he is no gentleman?!"

Meadows gaped at the red-faced captain.

"I'll cut you into ounce pieces, you scoundrel!" shouted Bainbridge. "On your feet this instant."

"Aye, sir." Meadows scrambled to get to his feet, tripping in the cables. "I'm sorry, Captain. I didn't mean to say…"

"Shut your mouth, brigand. I'll not be contradicted on my own ship."

Melisande gawked at the scene. She couldn't understand a thing so backward. If a Tuscarora boy threw water on an elder, he'd feel the scorn of his entire clan. The boy would be lucky not to die of shame.

"Marine!" snapped Bainbridge.

Private William Ray stepped forward. "Sir."

"I want this man taken below and placed in irons."

Ray closed his eyes for a heartbeat, then replied, "Aye, sir." He nodded to another Marine nearby, Private Burling. They each took one of Meadows' arms and escorted him to the main hatch.

This wasn't right at all! Melisande wouldn't have it. Bainbridge had to be told what a mistake—what an injustice—this was. A look from Meadows stopped her.

The veteran sailor held Melisande's eyes. Her resolve withered as if *Papa* Grey Fox had returned from the dead. Meadows gave the smallest shake of his head, a command only she could hear. She let go her aching fists. Against every fiber of her being, she held her silence.

"Disrespect a gentleman on my ship, will you?" sneered Bainbridge. He followed the Marines as they prodded Meadows down the hatch. "You'll learn discipline after a spell at the grating, I'll warrant. A mistake you'll not make again…" The captain's ranting disappeared below decks.

Melisande looked around, expecting to find shock and outrage among the crew. But they were already going back to their duties.

"I do believe I detect a note of disquiet, my lad," said Dr. Cowdery, thrusting an arm into a coat sleeve.

Ethan stood in the doorway of the surgeon's berth, staring at the medicine cabinet above Cowdery's desk. The door banged open and closed with the rolling of the ship. "Fiddling for the officers wasn't my idea."

"Ah," clucked Cowdery, threading his brass watch chain through a buttonhole. He stooped before a mirror on the bulkhead and tied back his hair. "That would be the hand of Midshipmen Sullivan at work."

By now, Ethan was used to Cowdery's quick insight. He couldn't reveal John's plans, but nor could he hide his frustration. He frowned at the colorful row of medicine phials.

"You could have said no," suggested Cowdery.

"You don't know John Sullivan. It's never that easy. Always there's a reason. Always there's a cause. Somehow, his friends always wind up saying yes."

Cowdery smirked. "From all you've told me of Sullivan, I'd say he speaks the language of the heart. Men like that inspire great feats—or provoke disaster. I suspect you've always known that about him. Yet, no matter how audacious his request, you offer him your gifts."

"Of course. Because he's my friend."

"Aye. And in the hope his gifts will serve *you*."

"You think *I'm* using *John*?"

For a moment, Cowdery fussed with a ribbon around his neck. When he had the shape of a bow started, he said, "I'll never forget the longest night of my life. I was only nine. Hotter than usual for Boston, even in July. So humid I kept sweating through my sheets. I couldn't sleep. My father and his friends were talking over wine in the parlor. There was such an energy in the air—like the night before a holiday. Every time father caught me creeping down the stairs to listen, I thought I'd be whipped. But he kept shooing me back to bed. I think he knew I sensed the importance of that night."

"Nine years old..." Ethan mused. "That would have been during the war."

"Aye. There was a newspaper due in the morning, you see. A paper that would answer the question: would Massachusetts and the other colonies have a king or a republic? Imagine our joy when father read the decision of the Continental Congress: Independence."

Ethan smiled. The Revolution was nearly won by the time he was born. He'd long wondered what those days had been like. "My mother was manumitted that day. My father won his freedom fighting for General Washington. When I was young, Father once said, 'Ethan, one day there'll be no more slaves, and no more kings.'"

Cowdery quoted, "'Of more worth is one honest man in the sight of God than all the crowned ruffians that ever lived.'"

"Thomas Paine," smiled Ethan, remembering the line from *Common Sense*.

"Very good, Mr. Auldon. Like your father, I dreamt of a better world. When I was a boy. But I grew up. Healing the sick and sailing the sea left me content. It isn't the fiery oratory and banner-waving I envisaged as a boy, but it's my own small contribution. The causes of the Revolution must fall to better men. I made you surgeon's mate not just for your medical skill, but for your passion. If I help you ascend, maybe that boy can still have his hero."

Ethan scoffed. "So, I'm to fight in your stead?"

Cowdery smirked. "Shameless calculation on my part, it's true. But our ideals never found purchase in a truer heart."

Ethan shook his head. "You're so sure I'm using John. But if my gift is championing the cause, what's his?"

"Simple. Beating the odds."

"I don't believe that. John is my friend, not some pawn in a game."

"Perhaps," said Cowdery with a shrug. He closed the last button of his coat and swept a few loose waves of hair to the side. He walked over and placed his hands on Ethan's shoulders. "You have an opportunity tonight, Ethan. Lecture an ignorant man, preach to a sinner, argue with a bigot—words get you nowhere. But music—ah, now music is a truth that cannot be denied. It isn't reason or sentiment. It's neither fact nor fiction. It simply is. Use this gift God has given you. When you play tonight, play from the bottom of your heart. Show them your very soul. Show them truth."

A part of Ethan wanted to smile and promise he would. But the knot in his stomach reminded him of his dread. He gave a faint nod.

"Good luck, my lad," Cowdery said with an encouraging smile. "Lock up the cabinet, would you? I almost forgot." He stepped past Ethan and headed for the cabin.

When the doctor was gone, Ethan looked at the medicine cabinet. The door banged open again. His eyes landed on a blue phial. Before locking up, Ethan reached for the shelf of potions.

Chapter 29

The City Tavern
Philadelphia, Pennsylvania
Two Years Ago

The moment the last string fell silent, Ethan knew it was the solo of his life. The last note of Bach's *Violin Concerto in A Minor* died away. For one heartbeat, silence held lease. Then the crowd of Philadelphia social elites exploded with applause. The grand hall of City Tavern sparkled with fine jewelry, silver wigs, and colorful apparel. Ethan bowed low, holding up his fiddle. He closed his eyes, breathing in the applause. A member of the Free African Society, standing in the beating heart of Philadelphia, performing for a packed room. It was like a dream.

A moment later, Ethan wove his way through the press of guests, greeting the gentlemen and ladies. He came to his benefactors, Theodore and Sarah Vansant. Mr. Vansant edited the *Gazette* he once delivered. She often held lavish balls for various charities. Tonight, the proceeds would go to the local abolition movement. After Ethan played for one of Mrs. Vansant's private dinners, she asked him to be the star of her City Tavern event.

"Why, Mr. Auldon," cooed Mrs. Vansant. "That was exquisite!"

"So kind of you to say, madam," Ethan smiled. He took up her hand and planted a kiss. "It was my honor to play for you."

"Oh," giggled Mrs. Vansant. She wagged her fan. "Isn't he charming, Theodore?" she said to her husband.

A smile tugged the corners of Mr. Vansant's mouth. "Mm, yes, indeed. I believe you were right about our Mr. Auldon."

"I'm just glad to do my part," Ethan said.

"That was brilliant, mate!" said the voice of John Sullivan.

Ethan beamed as John emerged from the crowd. Ethan wished his mother could have seen his moment, but his father's death had left her with too many burdens at home. Having John here took some of the sting out of their absence. And of course, it was amusing to see John try to fit in with high society. Seth Auldon's old coat and breeches were a bit loose on John. "Thanks mate," Ethan said. "You really thought so?"

"Best you ever played," said John, fidgeting with the buttons on his waistcoat.

"Ahem," said Mrs. Vansant.

"Oh, where are my manners?" said Ethan. "This is my friend, John Sullivan."

"Right," stuttered John. "John Sullivan. From Irish. I mean I'm Irish. That is, from Ireland." When Mrs. Vansant offered her hand for a kiss, John shook it instead. Realizing his mistake, he hurried to shake Mr. Vansant's but accidentally seized his fingers.

"I can see this one's still learning," chuckled Mrs.

Vansant. She nudged up next to Ethan. "Do help him, dear."

"I try," said Ethan, throwing John a teasing grin.

"Your instrument is very fine!" said Mr. Vansant. "Who gave it to you?"

Ethan scratched his head. "Actually, I found a trader selling it at a discount. It was broken, you see. I had to deliver a great many *Gazettes* to afford it. And then spend a great many hours learning how to repair it."

"Oh, yes, isn't it wonderful?" said Mrs. Vansant. "As a young lad, Mr. Auldon delivered our very own paper."

"A perspicacious hire on our part," added Mr. Vansant.

Mrs. Vansant leaned in close, speaking past her fan. "I don't like counting chickens before they've hatched, but judging by the applause, I think we've raised a small fortune."

"Thank you for helping our cause, Madam Vansant," said Ethan. "It means a great deal to the Free Africans."

"Not at all, dear Mr. Auldon," Mrs. Vansant proclaimed. "Abolition is the woefully unfinished work of our Revolution. My son died at the hands of the redcoats. Every day the dreadful institution of slavery remains, his memory is tarnished."

"Wherever did you learn to play?" asked Mr. Vansant.

"I mostly learned by ear at my father's tavern," said Ethan. "My mother taught me to read, and I taught myself to read music. The Bartons helped with my classical training."

"Remarkable!" said a portly reveler. He and his wife had been leaning toward their conversation, and now decided to join.

"Why, Mr. Stewart, did you hear that?" said the

newcomer's wife. "Classically trained!"

"Why yes, Miriam," said Mrs. Vansant. "Our Mr. Auldon is a true marvel. I had to show the nay-sayers how beautifully one can play."

Ethan's bow slipped out of his hand. Mrs. Vansant started when it landed at her feet. Ethan hurried to pick it up.

"Oops, oh dear," said Mrs. Vansant.

"Apologies," Ethan said. He had a sinking feeling in his gut. "What—what did you mean by 'how beautifully one can play?'"

"Oh, well I…" Mrs. Vansant wagged her fan.

"I should think it's perfectly obvious," shrugged Mr. Vansant. "Our purpose here is to help the cause of abolition by showing Negroes are possessed of many fine talents."

"And look how you've proven it, dear!" said Mrs. Vansant.

Ethan's eyes stung. Sweat beaded on his temple. Here he'd thought his musical talents were the toast of the town. Was he here as a mere object of curiosity? He felt sick to his stomach.

"You all right, mate?" John whispered.

"I do believe I owe my tailor an eagle," said Mr. Stewart, chuckling over his champagne flute. "I never thought I'd see a Negro play Bach."

"Mr. Stewart," gasped Mrs. Vansant. "I hardly think that's polite—"

"What did you say?" snapped John. His look struck the smiles from their faces.

Ethan tugged at John's elbow. "John, let's go," he whispered.

Mr. Stewart narrowed his eyes at the adolescent in

their midst. "I wagered my tailor one dollar that a Negro could never play Bach. Mr. Auldon proved an exception."

John's look turned menacing. "That is an insulting remark, sir. I demand you apologize to my friend."

"There is no insult," bristled Stewart. "I conceded my error."

"Gentlemen, gentlemen," said Mr. Vansant. "We're all friends here. United in common cause."

"You will apologize to Ethan," John persisted. "Or I will demand satisfaction."

"The *impertinence*!" Stewart retorted.

"Thank you for a lovely evening, Mrs. Vansant," said Ethan as if he hadn't a care in the world. He clasped her hand, then Mr. Vansant's, and nodded to the other guests. "It's meant a great deal to me. But the hour is late, and I must be off."

Ethan turned a hard look on John. "We're *leaving*."

John flashed another glare at Stewart, then reluctantly followed Ethan toward the stairs.

"I don't *believe* this," Ethan seethed. He was beating a path down Second Street, John barely keeping pace. A steady flow of carriages and riders trotted by. "You wanted a duel with that man."

"A man insults you, and you're angry I stood in your defense?" John argued, dodging passersby.

"You just won't give it up, will you? You'll find any excuse to issue a challenge."

John snorted. "It's always 'turn the other cheek' with you. I've had my fill of surrender. I'm for fighting back."

Ethan rounded and planted a hand on a hitching post.

"You mean *murder* a man for words? No, John, no. That is not justice. It's sin."

"It's *honor.*"

Ethan stormed off again. "It's an excuse! And you broke your promise. You just got your commission as a midshipman. You want to get yourself kicked out of the Navy?"

"You know what?" said John, his voice several paces behind.

Ethan stopped and looked back.

"I'm tired of your constant mothering. The Navy was your idea. Not mine." John started in the opposite direction.

"Wait, what do you mean?"

"I'll find my own way home!" John called back.

For a moment, Ethan considered following, not wanting to part in anger. Then his gaze hardened. His fist closed tight around the handle of his violin case. A walk on the wharf would do him good. He turned toward a winding alley nearby—a shortcut he used to take on his paper route.

He had gone about half the distance to Front Street when he heard the footsteps. He looked back—just brick walls blotting out the moon. A cat picking through rubbish. A pile of horse dung. A pair of cellar doors. No one. He started again and quickened his pace. A moment later, he heard more footsteps. Closer this time. He looked over his shoulder to find a tall shape moving through the darkness. The figure was only a few strides behind. Ethan broke into a run.

Just as Ethan reached the end of the alley, another figure stepped in front of him. The flicker of a street lamp illuminated the man's face.

"Well if it isn't the maggot's darkie friend," said a familiar Irish voice.

Ethan's blood ran cold. "Fin?" he breathed.

The other pursuer caught up. Eamon's pudgy hands closed on Ethan's arms.

Fin smiled, twirling a broken bottleneck. "Let's go for a stroll."

Chapter 30

The USS *Philadelphia*
Near the British Imperial Colony of Gibraltar
Tuesday, August 23rd, 1803

The row of cabin windows framed the dusk like a painting. As the last sliver of sun melted into the water, a blush of color radiated across the sky, cooling from crimson to violet. Twenty officers in formal dress filled three rows of chairs. The dying light of day gave the room a melancholy glow. A breeze through the open panes carried a whiff of distant trees and earth. All eyes were on Ethan Auldon.

"It's been a long time since I heard a Bach concerto," said Captain Bainbridge from the front row. Lieutenants Porter and Dalton sat on either side of him. "Midshipman Sullivan speaks very highly of your skills. A shame he's not in attendance."

Ethan cleared his throat. "Mr. Sullivan felt ill. I sent him to his hammock to rest."

"I'm sure he regrets his absence," said Dr. Cowdery, sitting with the warrant officers. "As do we."

"Yes, Doctor," stammered Ethan. "I'm sure he does."

Midshipman Grove rolled his eyes in the back row,

legs stretched out. Cowan sat next to him, arms crossed, smirking. Many of the officers looked equally bored.

"How did you learn to play?" asked Quartermaster John Wilson. Judging by the monotone of his voice, he did not mean, *Where did you study?* Or, *Who was the greatest influence on your style?* No. He had the look of a man trying to decipher a magic trick. What he wanted to ask was, *How does a Negro play Bach?*

"I learned by ear at my father's tavern," said Ethan. "I taught myself to read music. A generous Philadelphia family saw to my classical training."

"Hmm," sniffed Wilson. "Training, you say?"

Ethan boiled with anger. These men would never know what music meant to him. They couldn't understand years of painstaking work, for the simple joy of crafting something beautiful. They didn't deserve to hear him play. But there was no getting out of it. So, Ethan decided to spite them. They were about to hear the best concerto of their lives.

"Aye, sir," said Ethan. "I manage to get by."

"Excellent!" piped Bainbridge. He crossed his legs. "We're all in suspense, Mr. Auldon." With a wave, he said, "Please."

Five weeks of reading behind closed doors. Five weeks of hiding his vocabulary. Five weeks without a voice. All so his learning wouldn't draw attention—and threaten the more bigoted members of the crew.

Ethan nestled the Hardanger fiddle under his chin. He brought the bow to rest. Felt it catch on the strings. Let the anticipation build in the silence.

Tonight, Ethan would roar.

###

It wasn't the kind of music she could dance to, but Melisande had to admit: Ethan's violin filled the boat with beauty. It wasn't like a good tavern tune—thumping and pounding. It didn't put her in mind of dancing bodies pressed close, hot with exertion. Instead, Ethan's melody whispered and beckoned. It gave Melisande an ache for home. She yearned to see the first snow falling on pines. To see that first spark of desire from a pretty lass. She thought of the moment after lovemaking when she would lie quiet, feeling another's heartbeat.

Melisande looked across the berth deck. Groups of sailors sat with their messmates, lay in their hammocks, or leaned on the ship's ribs. They chatted amongst themselves, darned their clothes, played cards, or just listened. They were so quiet, so peaceful. She rounded the corner, passed the sick berth, and found the aft hatch she was looking for. She climbed down into a cramped compartment on the orlop deck, her head almost banging into a beam.

"That's far enough," said Private William Ray, standing guard before a narrow hall lit by a single lantern. She could barely see the balding Marine in the half-light. He was frowning. "You're not allowed down here, Dufort."

"I figured you'd be on watch, Soggy," said Melisande. "Soggy" was a nickname of course—an entirely playful reference to Ray's aborted decision to drown himself. Ray had chosen to join the Marines instead, and Melisande got the feeling he might still prefer the alternative. She did her best to keep him smiling, lest he change his mind. She pulled a flask from her pocket. "I just wanted to see

Meadows. Worth a rum ration to you?"

Ray eyed the flask, considering. "I've a better idea. You stop calling me 'Soggy.'"

"Sure. If you swear off self-drowning."

Ray sighed and grabbed the flask. "Rum it is. Just a few minutes now."

Melisande winked and started down the hall. The light crawled and recoiled along the corridor with the tilting of the ship. She looked through the bars of each door. The cells of the brig had only enough room for a hammock and a chamber pot.

"Meadows?" she whispered.

A white-bearded face peered through bars at the end of the hall. "Dufort? What are you doing down here?"

"I thought I'd offer to break you out," Melisande whispered, coming face to face with Meadows. "I'm sure I can work something out with Soggy."

"You'll do no such thing."

"How about a drink, then?" Melisande held up her deerskin canteen.

"I can live with that," said Meadows. Melisande handed the skin through the bars and took a long draught. He wiped his lips on his sleeve. "Thank you, lad. You're a true friend."

Melisande sat down, her back to the door. "It ain't right. You weren't hurting anyone, sleeping on deck like you were. It's that little brat that needs flogging."

Meadows joined her in sitting, his back against the opposite side. "You mustn't fret over that. It's not my first flogging. Doubt it will be my last. The sea's made of me a tough old salt. I'll stand it well enough."

"But…at least let me say something. I'm a witness. I can tell the captain—"

"Listen, Dufort, I'm moved by your kindness, really I am. But when all the crew is assembled, and I'm trussed up at the grating, and every man quiet and watching, you'll do just likewise. You won't say a word. And I'll take my punishment, they'll take me down, and that'll be the end of it. Got that?"

"But I can't bear to watch you—"

"You can, and you will. I mean it. Do this—for me?"

Melisande crossed her arms. "Fine. For you, old man."

"Good. Glad that's settled."

"I wish I could be as damn calm as you. I'm just so…*angry*."

"You think I'm not angry?" said Meadows. He took another pull on the deerskin. "I'm angry as hell. But sometimes, things are just unfair. I'll take a few new scars. And I'll still have coin in my pocket, food in my belly, and the free state of New Hampshire to call home. A man could be in worse straights."

"How can you give up so easily? Not even fight?"

"I ain't giving up!" snapped Meadows. He fell quiet for a moment. Ethan's song sped up now, frolicking through the silence. Finally, Meadows said, "When the English marched their soldiers into our homes and started taking whatever they wanted, I went to sea in a rickety ship, outgunned and outmanned. Looking back, it was the maddest idea I ever had. Beats me how I survived."

Meadows looked through the bars again. He wore a deep frown on his weather-beaten face. "There's something you need to learn lad: Every now and then, there's a time to stand, no matter the odds. But a body's only got so many fights in him. Choose yours wisely."

Ethan's fiddle sent a merry waltz dancing through the warrant officers' quarters. John Sullivan came to the wardroom door and knocked. Chester Ryland bade him enter. John opened the door to find the lanterns and candelabra burning bright. Ryland sat at the officers' table sketching. Other drawings were strewn over navigational charts and log books. The place was a mess—stockings, peacoats, and shirts draped over chairs or piled on the floor. A tin replica of a knight's helmet sat on the end of the table. A garish tabard was draped over a chair. Porter must have been practicing his King Arthur play again. There were no officers in the small compartments on either side—the hammocks were empty.

Ryland caught his glass of wine as it started to slide off the table. "I'm surprised you're not in the captain's cabin."

John took the chair adjacent to Ryland. He raised a bottle of brown liquor. "Care for something stronger?"

"Of course," said Ryland with a conspiratorial grin. He finished his wine and offered his glass. "What have we here?"

"The last of my *Isla Carillo* rum. A gift from my old swordmaster." Ethan's song became more anxious, frenzied. The rum glugged into Ryland's glass, pouring its sweet aroma into the air. "Ethan and I...aren't on the best of terms at the moment." John raised the bottle to his lips. "It's my fault the captain conscripted him to perform."

"Ah," Ryland said, raising his eyebrows. He drained his cup and let out a satisfied sigh. He held it out for a refill. "Bainbridge and his performing arts. Better stay that loose tongue. He and Porter are always looking for a new Juliet."

"That might not be so bad," said John as he filled Ryland's cup. "I'm rather fetching in a corset."

The two men broke into laughter, careful to keep their voices low.

"I don't blame Auldon for being angry," said Ryland. He finished another draught. "If I wind up the wet nurse to your Juliet, our friendship is damn well over!"

"Damn well worth it, to see you in a bonnet."

They laughed again, trailing off as Ethan's bow stirred up a wave of notes. Bach's concerto crashed and fell like the ocean against a reef. So loud for a moment, the two officers might have been in the front row. Then it settled again, the notes lapping at walls of timber.

"I must admit," said Ryland, licking rum from his lip. "I was surprised—flattered really—that you confided in me the other day. What befell your family—it can't be easy to talk about."

Interesting, thought John. So, it was on Ryland's mind. But why was he bringing it up? Perhaps he wanted a read on John. Perhaps he felt guilty for lying. Whatever the reason, John played along. "I've come to trust you a great deal, Mr. Ryland. It felt good to unburden myself."

Ryland's eyes drooped tiredly. "I regret that I could not help you find your mother and sister. Truly, I do. I've...known loss in my life."

"Haven't we all." John held the bottle to his lips again, his eyes drifting over the long shadows of the past. "I play that terrible day over and over in my mind. I imagine the day of my retribution. Dark thoughts are always calling. Sometimes I relent. Sometimes I resist."

"Have you, erm..." Ryland massaged the bags under

his eyes. "Have you thought about the next step in your search?"

The fiddle trembled with vibrato. "Actually, I've been thinking about that a great deal."

Ethan's song roamed from cell to cell, like the ghost of a woman looking for her lost love. Melisande felt the mood shift between her and Meadows. They sat quietly for a while.

After another drink of rum, Meadows said, "So tell me, lad. What the hell are you doing out here?"

"Out here?" asked Melisande.

"At sea. On the *Philadelphia*. You puked up your guts the whole first week. I thought you'd die of starvation. Half the time, you're as miserable as Private Soggy over there."

Melisande chuckled, but quickly put a hand over her mouth. She heard far too much feminine in that laugh. She cleared her throat and reasserted a baritone. "My sister...erm...lives in Gibraltar. With her bastard of a husband. I need to look in on her."

"You joined the Navy you hate, crossed the dreaded Atlantic, and endured a month of seasickness—to look in on your sister?"

Melisande shrugged. "Family's important to me."

The old sailor snickered. Such a pleasant sound, like gravel crunching in the road. Meadows said, "The few times I've joined my own sister's family for dinner, we barely went a minute without fighting. She's educated and cultured, and I'm a stubborn old salt."

"She sounds like mine," groaned Melisande. Meadows

handed the skin through the bars, and she took a good pull. "She's the most fussy, self-absorbed, prissy little cuss I know."

"Prissy, eh?"

"And stuck up," Melisande said, her voice cracking. "I mean, she stares at herself in the mirror all day. Always fretting over her reputation. She traded trousers for big poufy dresses. She prances around in dainty little slippers and makes fun of my boots."

Meadows sounded puzzled. "I wouldn't call dresses and slippers…unusual for a lady."

"She's even taken to wearing a corset! And she doesn't spit or smoke anymore."

"A vain creature!" Meadows agreed, sounding suspiciously insincere.

Melisande poked her nose through the bars. "And she thinks she'd be happier if she were some fancy boot-licking duchess. She married this pompous dandy just because he's French."

"Poor footing for a marriage."

"He hits her. I know it."

"Hits her?" Meadows frowned. "Where is he? I'll help you give him a drubbing."

"Aye, a damn hard drubbing! That's why I'm here."

"No better way to spend shore leave," smiled Meadows. "Unless you're wrong. Are you certain he strikes her? And have you supposed your sister might really be in love?"

"Not a chance. She didn't marry for love. I know it like I know every mile of the Little Bear hunting grounds."

"How can you be sure?"

A quilt flattens the tall grass. Two voices, giggling in duet. A ray of moonlight falls on bare skin. Melisande sees two lovers entwined through the stalks of rye. It's Sully and Dominique.

Melisande ducks behind a tree. She covers her mouth to stifle a chuckle. Sully and Dom? *she thinks.* They spent the whole week fighting like stray cats! *It doesn't seem possible. She risks another peek.*

Dominique squeals. Sully scoops her up, and she playfully slaps at him. "Unhand me, you brigand!" *she says.*

"Nay, wench. I shall abscond with you across the sea."

"Oh no! Will you ravish *me in your cabin?" Her voice is low. Intense.*

"What else is a dashing rogue to do?"

Their eyes lock, full of hunger. Their smiles fade. His lips devour hers.

Dom and Sully? *Melisande repeats to herself. She's delighted! What a perfect match! But then, another feeling nags at her. One she can't put her finger on…*

"Because," answered Melisande. "I know who she really loves."

"The more I think about what I have to do to save my family," John continued, "the more I think about something my father did."

"You've rarely mentioned your father," said Ryland. He leaned against the table, head propped on his knuckles.

"Why should I?" John said, glowering. "A fool that failed to protect his family."

"You're judging him a mite harshly, don't you think?"

"We had a chance to fight, and he gave it up. Five years and every time I see his face, I see Isaac on his knees. The look in my brother's eyes in his final moments. Lately though, I keep thinking about this near brush we had when I was twelve. Ever hear of *'Gaspar el Gallardo?'* 'Gaspar the Gallant?'"

"It has a familiar ring to it…"

"It was the summer of 1795. The *Wandering Hart* and the *Dolorous Fénnid*, our two biggest ships, were heading to London with a cargo of spices, fabrics, and wine. Four days out of Madrid, a pirate schooner gave chase. Our cargo made us too slow. Mother wanted to dump it and take the loss. Isaac and I wanted to fight—never mind our crew was outnumbered three to one."

Ryland smiled, the rim of his glass pressed against his temple. "Ah, the invincib-b-bility of youth." Ryland furrowed his brows. Drunkenness had set in. "What did your father do?"

"He ordered the *Dolorous Fénnid* to flee, and the *Wandering Hart* to surrender."

"A gambit, then," exclaimed Ryland far too loudly. "If you can't save all the goods, save half."

"I was furious, but Da said, 'That's the flag of *Gaspar el Gallardo*. He's famous for his code of honor.' The flag was definitely his—a Spanish rapier through a crowned skull. Da had the steward prepare a feast in Gaspar's honor."

"Why on Earth would he do that?" slurred Ryland.

"My thoughts exactly. I sat at my father's table in my Sunday finest, listening to this gaudy pirate in his feathered hat tell story after story. Father poured him more wine, laughed at his jokes, passed more bread. Gaspar was delighted. I was furious! But at the end of the night, Gaspar decided to spare our ship. He agreed to only steal the cargo—which Da had insured against theft.

By the time Gaspar left the *Wandering Hart,* he'd charmed the whole crew. One of our sailors even joined him."

"Clever! Your father flattered an enemy and made him a friend."

"I was disgusted," John snorted. "Night after night, I would lie awake in my hammock dreaming of a bloody revenge on Gaspar. I swore to grow up a pirate hunter."

"Ah! And here you are, on the hunt for the Bar-bur-bee Pirates!" slurred Ryland.

"A few months later," John continued, "we stopped in Madrid. I'll never forget it. Gaspar was hanging in a gibbet over the wharf. His corpse stuffed into a cage of iron bars. Torn flesh where the birds had been at him. And those empty eye sockets… A dashing rogue one day. Rotting meat the next. I threw up at the sight."

"A sad fate for any man, really."

"The boy who saw Gaspar hanging in a gibbet learned a lesson that day. He couldn't do all those terrible things he dreamt. He didn't have the stomach for revenge. But that boy's dead. Killed, by the Barbary Pirates. And someone else has taken his place…" John turned the bottle over in his hand. The rum hadn't lowered a drop. He'd only been pretending to drink. He continued, "The man I've become—he *can* do those terrible things. He *has.*"

The violin spun into a whirlwind now, an ever madder crescendo. John looked into Ryland's eyes.

Ryland broke into a nervous smile. "Easy Sullivan. I think the rum is putting you in a black mood."

"I told my uncle. I told Ethan. I've told God in the darkness of night. No man will ever have my surrender. Not Ilyas Naim. Not Clyde Tindall. Not Pierre Laffite. Certainly not you."

"Sullivan, if I've given offense I…" Ryland's head lolled to one side. He put a hand to his forehead as if dizzy. "There's no need for hard words…whatever you're thinking of doing…"

"You misunderstand. I've already done it. A little sedative in the bottom of your cup."

Ryland strained to keep his eyes open. "You—what did you—"

The violin spun into a cyclone. A fury of notes spilling through every hatch. Ryland slid from his chair. His arms floundered for balance, sending charts fluttering. Gravity dragged the lieutenant down. Ryland's eyelids slipped closed. His body went limp.

John knelt beside Ryland and reached into his coat. He withdrew the leather-bound sketchbook. After gathering up the other drawings on the table, he slipped out of the wardroom, leaving Ryland to slumber.

Ethan no longer moved his fingers. No longer read the notes from memory or listened for pitch. The music had taken over. His bow capered over the strings as if on its own. The song flowed through his soul, driving the beating of his heart. The beauty of Creation already extant, tapped like ore from a vein. Ethan was merely the vessel.

"What are you holding out for, boy?" says Francis Whitlock. "You put up a good fight."

Ethan's arm flew over the strings, no longer under his power. He held a long, high pitch. His hands began to tremble, threatening to falter. Was there no joy those terrible weeks couldn't poison? And yet, these beautiful songs had preserved him. Playing them now set him free. No man could take his music. Not Clyde Tindall. Not Francis Whitlock. Not this room of officers. Music belonged to all mankind. It was universal. Intangible. Unconquerable.

"Just one little answer. That's all I need."

The notes were coming so fast now. Ethan burned with fatigue, but he wouldn't stop. He couldn't. The tempo lulled. Like a sprinter fighting momentum, he resisted the urge to rush. He drew the bow in gentle strokes through the final refrain. Tears ran down his cheeks as he brought the piece to a close. The last whispers of the melody died a peaceful death.

"How long, Mr. Ethan, have you been here? On the Tindall Plantation?"

A storm of clapping shook the room. Ethan opened his eyes as if waking from a spell. Bainbridge rose to his feet, applauding furiously. Cowdery and Merrick followed close behind, then the rest of the officers. Their faces were filled with delight. Their applause deafening. Only Wilson, Cowan, and Grove were slow to clap. But even then, Ethan could see the grudging amazement in their eyes. Ethan was relieved it was over.

The applause died away, and Bainbridge said, "Bravo, Mr. Auldon. Why, aren't you a pleasant surprise." He swept the officers with a look of pride. "Did I tell you, gentlemen? Worth your time, indeed."

"Aye, sir," said Porter coolly. "Quite the surprise. I'm rather moved."

"Look at him," said Bainbridge, pointing at Ethan. "Shedding tears!"

Ethan raised a trembling hand to dry his eyes. How

could he let his emotions get the better of him? To be their curiosity for the evening was bad enough, but to weep? And the worst part was, he wanted to believe their applause. A voice in his mind wanted to take credit—to boast with pride. But were they applauding because of Bainbridge, or in spite of themselves? Ethan bowed, looking forward to his hammock.

Captain Bainbridge settled back into his seat, crossed his legs, and clasped his hands. "Let's have that last movement again."

The chairs groaned as the officers sat down. Ethan rose upright, blinking. He felt a pang of nausea. "Sir?"

"You heard me," grinned Bainbridge. He thrust up his hand. "Encore!"

Chapter 31

The Tindall Plantation
Outside Richmond, Virginia
Two Years Ago

Ethan watched a fly mine a pile of dung. His face rested in the mud. His bound hands and feet had stopped aching. Now they were numb. Flies picked along the wounds on his back. He could still feel the burn of the whip. His mind drifted through a fog, and sometimes he could catch glimpses of his family at dinner. He would see Mother setting down the stew. Priscilla banging utensils. Father leading the blessing. Ansel and Judith bowing their heads. Ethan would imagine himself spooning potatoes and mutton into a bowl, but he could never take a bite. The fantasy would shatter when a hog sniffed at his face.

"Now aren't you a sorry sight," said Francis Whitlock. Boots squished through the mud as he approached. Two thick legs came into view. "There really is no need for these accommodations. I made my point. You made your point. Frankly, I'm impressed."

Once Ethan's anger had been a blaze, dulling the pain.

Then it faded to a flicker, helping him endure the hunger. Now it smoldered under desolation.

Whitlock sighed. He sat down on a milking stool. "I ain't never seen a slave hold out longer. But it's time to come on home."

Whitlock dropped a tin plate near Ethan. He unwrapped a bundle of parchment and revealed a square of cornbread, a hunk of roast beef, and an apple.

Before Ethan lay a king's feast. His stomach growled. His mouth watered. But he refused to move.

"Who is your master?"

Whitlock had asked the question every day. The first day, Ethan replied, "All men are created equal." After a few more days of beatings, he managed to say, "no man." Today, he answered with silence.

"Tell you what," Whitlock continued, his voice soft as a pigeon cooing in a nest. "I'm feeling uncommonly generous today. It ain't often I cut a slave a break, but I admire your spirit. I'm going to ask you an easier question. Correct or not, give me an answer and this beautiful bounty is yours. I'll let you take the air with the others. Hell, you can sit under the maple tree if you like. All I need is one little answer."

Ethan couldn't let Whitlock see his temptation. In his mind, he leafed through sheet music. He thumbed to a piece so beautiful, it would overwhelm hunger or fear. It was Bach's *Violin Concerto in A Minor*.

"All right." Whitlock smacked his palms together. "Here it is: How long, Mr. Ethan, have you been here? On the Tindall Plantation?"

In Ethan's mind, he took up the fiddle. Touched the bow to strings. Felt the frets under his fingers. He spun notes like threads of silk.

"Come on, now, boy. I ain't got all day. How long have you been here?"

The race for an answer drowned out the music. Three months? Four? No. It had to be longer. But why hadn't the seasons changed? Ethan settled on two months.

"I ain't asking for much. Just a guess, really. It doesn't even have to be right."

Ethan stared at the cornbread. He could smell its buttery aroma. He could see the peppercorns seared into the roast. The red apple shined like a mirror. He wanted to answer. He *knew* the answer. He didn't want to be hungry anymore. He wanted to feel his arms and legs again. He wanted to feel the sun.

He clenched his teeth. Forced his eyes away from the food. A single tear ran off his nose.

The barn door creaked open. The voice of a younger man shouted, "What the hell are you doing, Frank?" It was Henry Tindall, the younger of the Tindall brothers. "I told you to fetch him, not feed him."

Whitlock leaned closer to Ethan. "Quick now, boy. The answer. You really going to choose the whip over home-cooked vittles? Last chance!"

Ethan fought back panic. He wanted to give in.

"Frank!" shouted Henry. "Sullivan is here, damn you! Quit fucking around and bring him out!"

John? Ethan's eyes widened. His heart pounded. *He's here. He's found me!*

Whitlock leaned down to cut Ethan's ropes. He whispered, "We shall continue this discussion. That I promise you."

Ethan felt a renewed vigor. Like Job of the Old Testament, he'd kept his faith, and his torment hadn't been in vain. God was about to give him justice. Ethan replied to Whitlock with a glare.

"Gentlemen, you have both agreed to the terms of this duel," said Merrill, a short man in a white wig, serving as officiator. "I shall count out eight paces."

Ethan's feet crunched on frozen grass as he watched John Sullivan and Clyde Tindall load their pistols. His breath fogged in the cold, gray morning. A ridge of barren trees wreathed the empty field. Clyde Tindall looked relaxed and limber, with his slick hair and fine waistcoat. He pulled back the hammer of his gun and examined the pan. His much younger brother, Henry, helped him pull off his long-tailed jacket. Several friends of the Tindalls stood nearby in wigs and tricorne hats. John looked drab in his threadbare shirt and breeches. Fernando Pavia stood as John's second. A pair of carriages bookended the battlefield.

"When you've paced the full distance," continued Merrill, "I shall give the order to face and take aim. Do not fire until I give the order. If neither combatant is defeated after the first shot, you will engage with swords until one of you is defeated or concedes."

The call of a raven cut through the still winter air.

"One last time, gentlemen," said Merrill. "Cannot you be reconciled?"

"We will be," said Clyde. He tugged his black gloves snug. "After I teach this dumb mick his place."

"It's all right, Ethan," said John, unsheathing a few inches of his sword. His thumb tested the sharpness. "You're going home."

Clyde scoffed, nodding at his brother. "Good God.

Look at him, Henry. I don't know who's worse. The abolitionists, or these dirt-eating yokels floating off the Isles. I worry for my generation."

"Gentlemen, take your marks," ordered Merrill.

John and Clyde stood back to back, pistols aimed at the air. A stillness settled on the field. The raven called again from somewhere unknown.

"You had only to make restitution," murmured Clyde to his opponent. "And show a little respect. Remember that, when you're bleeding in the dirt."

John's eyes stared hard at the horizon. "I'm going to kill you, Clyde Tindall."

Ethan felt Whitlock's hand on his shoulder. "I wouldn't get your hopes up," said Whitlock. "Clyde is an expert shot."

"You don't know John Sullivan," said Ethan, grinding his teeth.

"One," counted Merrill.

Each man took a step forward.

"Two."

One count at a time, the Virginia planter, and the Irish orphan marched toward opposite horizons.

"Face."

Clyde spun around. John wheeled. A breeze stirred, too light to disturb the silence.

"Take aim."

The two pistols leveled. Clyde tucked his free arm behind his back, his legs straight and still. John's left arm hung at his side, balled into a fist.

The breeze rustled the lifeless woods. Ethan felt hot coals in his stomach. Despite his confidence in John, he knew that in the next few seconds, he might watch his friend die. And with him, any hope of freedom. The phantom raven crowed.

"Fire."

Crack—Pop.

Smoke burst from each gun. A ball hit home with a snap. John jerked back. Clyde dropped his gun and clapped a hand over his face.

John teetered and landed on hands and knees. He wobbled, crawled forward, then collapsed onto his stomach.

"John!" cried Ethan. He started forward, only to feel Whitlock's cruel grip hold him back.

Pavia kneeled at John's side. "*Alumno?*"

"Brother?" cried Henry, coming to Clyde's side.

Clyde waved him off. "It's over. He's dead." His left hand came away from his bloody face. A ragged gash cut across his cheek. John's bullet had only grazed him.

"*Alumno?*" Pavia said again.

John jolted. He pushed off the ground. "I'm fine. I'm fine." He struggled to his feet, his hand pressed over his left shoulder. He leaned on Pavia for balance and faced the Tindalls. Ribbons of blood soaked his white sleeve.

Clyde's mouth opened in shock. "What?"

Pavia tore a gold sash from his belt. He tied it around John's shoulder. "You did well, *alumno*. You named me as second. I'll handle the rest."

"No!" John tugged his bandaged shoulder away from Pavia. "*I* finish this. Tindall, draw your sword."

Clyde wiped his hand on his dark trousers. He drew his cavalry saber. John stomped across the field of fire, gaining momentum. Clyde squared his posture, waiting for his opponent.

John sprinted the last meter. He stabbed with the speed of a snapping dog. Clyde turned away the thrust, racing to meet each new blow. John's steel tore at Clyde's. Each metal clang went galloping over the field. John matched every slash, driving Clyde back.

Ethan's heart leaped. He saw grit in John's eyes. Fear in Clyde's. Only a matter of time. John would win.

Clyde's feet chased each other backward. John dogged him with lightening thrusts, each one landing a little closer to Clyde's chest. The planter tripped on a clump of earth. His parry faltered. John slapped the saber away and thrust at Clyde's gut.

But the rapier went wide. John's face had gone pale, and he stumbled to his knees. Ethan recognized the vertigo of blood loss.

Clyde realized his advantage and fetched his saber from the dirt. He brought it down over John's head. John barely caught the blow with his own sword. The edges were locked together as each man resisted the other. Clyde snarled and forced John's arm down. All was silent, but for the scraping of blades. Sweat beaded on Clyde's brow. Blood dripped from John's sleeve. The saber closed in on John's neck, inch by inch. The two men stared into each other's eyes, hovering at the threshold of life and death. The saber kissed John's jugular.

John snarled, bared teeth—and chomped. Clyde Tindall shrieked as John's bite tore into his sword hand. John chewed harder, and Clyde's grip loosened. John tore out a chunk of flesh, and Clyde's saber fell to the ground.

John launched onto his feet and stabbed.

Clyde's shriek turned into a gasp. He looked down at his stomach. A thin blade pierced him above the navel. It slid free, and he dropped to his knees.

John loomed over Clyde Tindall, knees bent, sword pointed at the planter's throat. He looked feral. Vicious.

"Wait!" cried Henry Tindall. "It's over."

John's sword lowered a degree. The corded muscles in his shoulders relaxed, and for a moment, there was doubt in his expression.

"You hear that, mick?" spat Clyde. "It's over. Take your nigro and—"

John split the air with a primal roar. His sword shot into Tindall's chest, then out again. John thrust as fast as his arm could move. In the space of a blink, John cut half a dozen holes in his enemy. He pulled his sword free, droplets falling from the point.

A cloud of blood spread across Clyde's waistcoat. The life drifted out of his eyes, and he fell over dead.

Merrill drew his pistol and cocked it. "Murderer!" he shouted. He leveled the gun at John.

A shot ripped through the air. Merrill's weapon fell from his grasp. He put a hand over the hole in his chest, but he was already falling to the ground.

Pavia dropped his spent pistol and drew another. He pointed a gun from each hand, one at Henry Tindall, the other at Whitlock. "Easy now, *amigos!*"

"You..." Henry said to John. "You murdered my brother."

"You're fucking dead!" said Whitlock.

"You are, my friend, if I fire this pistol," said Pavia. "Now release *Señor* Auldon, and we'll be on our way."

Whitlock squeezed Ethan's shoulder, then reluctantly let go.

"*Señor* Auldon, come along now."

Ethan ran to John, who was still staring at the man he had killed. "Let's go," said Ethan.

John stared blankly.

"How far do you think you'll get?" said Whitlock.

Pavia pursed his lips. "Far enough to escape your stench, I hope."

Ethan put his hands on John's shoulders. "John, we're in trouble. We have to move. Now."

"It's no trouble, mate…" John's eyes rolled back in his head, and he collapsed.

Ethan caught his friend and threw him across his shoulders. He carried him to the carriage, feeling every lash on his back throb. When they were in the carriage, he heard the reins snap, and they were off. The carriage sped along the country road so fast, the wheels nearly shook themselves off the axels. The coach quaked and shuddered. The horses whinnied under the whip. John lay on Pavia's lap, barely conscious.

"More pressure, Pavia," Ethan said, pressing the Basque's hand into John's wound.

John cried out, then fainted from the pain.

"*Tranquillo, Señor* Auldon," said Pavia. "This is not the first wound I have seen. I will take care of Sullivan. Rest now."

Ethan hesitated a moment. He nodded and sat on the bench opposite.

"*Maestro,*" said Ethan.

"*Sí?*" Pavia didn't look up from the makeshift bandage, which was already soaked red.

"How long since Fin abducted me?"

Pavia looked up through his eyebrows. "Perhaps, three weeks."

Ethan felt as if punched in the gut. "Three *weeks?*"

"*Sí.* Why?"

Ethan looked through the curtains on the window. He watched the bleak winter landscape blur past, hoping Pavia wouldn't see his tears.

Chapter 32

The USS *Philadelphia*
Near the British Imperial Colony of Gibraltar
Tuesday, August 23rd, 1803

A strange quiet had fallen over the ship. The sea lazed under a light breeze. Ethan's bow sobbed its melody. Below decks, men talked softly, snoozed in their hammocks, or just listened. John took a few steps down into the hold, the warbling of the violin growing faint. He peered down into the cable tier, finding nothing but coils of rope. No one to disturb him. Bach's *Violin Concerto in A Minor* soared into a pleading timbre, then fell again.

John climbed down into the orlop deck. The ceiling here forced him to crouch as he stepped over the hoops of spare cable. Like a bird in a nest, he settled into a ring of hawsers. He opened his lantern. A few scrapes of his striker, and the candle guttered to life. John laid the sketchbook before him. He felt a pang of guilt as he remembered his promise to Sawyer.

"I have your word then?" Sawyer implores. "Straight to the bottom without a look?"

"That's good enough for me," John replies. He's curious why Sawyer doesn't want him to at least check for the evidence. "I won't

look in the case. The book goes into a sack with grapeshot, then straight to the bottom."

Sawyer sighs with relief. "Good. Thank you for what you're doing, Mr. Sullivan. I'm forever in your debt."

John listened to the jaunty scraping of Ethan's concerto as he unclasped the sketchbook. A sheaf of white pages spread out before him, Ryland's beautiful sunrise at the top. Charcoal and pencils lined the cover in neat rows. The pockets were rubbed coarse. John ran fingers under each flap, traced each worn edge. No jewels. No silver. No paper notes. His hand trembled with the violin's rapid beats.

Where is it? John cursed. There had to be *something*. He flipped the stack of pages over and searched the back pockets. Just a few brushes. Some vials of watercolor. *Damn it to hell!*

Hidden among the drawings perhaps? The violin sparked into a lively finale. The pages crackled as John flipped through each sketch.

A group of messmates laughing and drinking. A beautiful actress serenading her audience. The fiddle was beating faster now. John was paging more urgently. A ship's dog poking his nose through a gunport. Eric Long and his mates playing knucklebones. John paged more urgently still. Sailors laying on the yard. Sailors sleeping in hammocks. Sailors climbing the shrouds.

Ethan's bow scraped a dizzying flurry. John tore past each image, starting to panic. *Where is it? Where the hell is…*

The bow trilled a single, clarion pitch. Time came to a stop. As if some magic in the song turned *Philadelphia* into a bottled ship—her crew into wax figurines. John gaped at the drawing, hand hovering at the edge. It was…

A nude man. Feathery black strokes shaded the man's

cheekbones, the muscles of his waist, the crevices between his toes. He lay sideways on a luxurious couch in a lush garden. His eyes were closed as if in a dreamless sleep. It was…Gabriel Sawyer.

The last few notes of Bach settled like flakes of snow. John turned the next page. He felt his breath catch. Ryland and Sawyer. Together on the couch. Ryland draping an arm across Sawyer's chest as their lips met. There was an inscription in the corner.

To my sweet Gabriel,

Where the pen fails, let charcoal convey my unalterable love. For in your tender arms have I found paradise.

Eternally yours, Chester.

The music fell quiet at last. John slumped back against the hawser cable, staring at the flickering shadows. No jewels. No silver. No paper notes. No evidence of theft. Only the deepest secret imaginable, for the eyes of a lover. From the captain's cabin, John could hear the officers' ovation.

The sound of clapping muttered through the hatch.

Part III

Bloody Sully

Chapter 33

The USS *Philadelphia*
Off the Coast of Morocco
Friday, August 26th, 1803

The first sound Ryland heard was silence. His eyes opened to darkness. Then, a ringing rose in his ears. Faint at first, like a finger tracing around the edge of a wine glass. It grew steadily louder. He felt heat on his face. Tinny voices echoing around him, as if heard from underwater. The air stung Ryland's lungs. Shapes moved around him in a blur. The echoes became voices. His tongue tasted of brimstone, and he realized he was choking on smoke. Slowly his senses returned, and he could see legs flashing through a black fog.

"I want to go home," sobbed the voice of a young man. "I want to go home. I want to go home…"

Where am I? wondered Ryland. The gun deck. Near the bow. So difficult to think. *What happened?* Ryland had been running toward the bow chaser guns. An enemy ship dead ahead—he needed to man the forward cannon. He was about to order, "fire!" There was an explosion then—darkness. He could see a few dirty smudges of lantern light along his left, a gunport on his right. Four sailors dashed by carrying a hose. Water spluttered from the nozzle. Ryland crawled to the nearest gun, grabbed the iron knob, and pulled himself up. The moans of wounded rose above the din.

"I'm not supposed to be here. I want to go home." The young man's miserable cries had a familiar southern accent.

The *Philadelphia's* fourth lieutenant trudged forward, hand held out like a blind man. A dash of movement. Ryland shuffled behind a powder barrel just in time to avoid a line of men with buckets running straight at him. *Damn this climate,* he thought, tugging the kerchief off his neck. Then he remembered, it wasn't the Mediterranean heat—it was the burning galley stove.

"I want to go home," whimpered the southern sailor, closer now.

Ryland's foot stopped against a body. Seaman Dixon lay at his feet. Ryland dropped beside the boy and landed in something wet. A scarlet puddle spreading away from the sailor. Where the seaman's left calf should have been, there were only bloody ropes of sinew.

"I'm not supposed to be here..." cried Dixon, pleading to a judge no one else could see.

"Steady, lad, steady now," soothed Ryland, propping up the boy's head. "We'll...we'll find the surgeon. Steady now..." Ryland's mind was still foggy, and he looked around for help. But it was no use. Towards the bow, the crew were busy putting out the galley fire. He could barely see anything in the brume. He'd have to carry Dixon on his own. "Up you go, lad. Give me your arm..."

The boy's head lolled backward. Dixon's eyes went placid, lifeless as pebbles in the sand. Dixon was dead.

For some reason, Ryland thought of Sawyer. An image of the young Welshman's face flashed in his mind. Sawyer's fiery shock of hair wet with blood. His skin waxy. His eyes gone cold. It was the most selfish thing Ryland could imagine. A man dead in his arms and Ryland could only think of Gabriel. But there it was.

Two ear-splitting reports. A shower of splintered wood. Cannonballs ripped past, chewing through gun carriages, biting chunks out of pilings, shattering barrels. A seaman carrying a bucket disappeared in a mist of blood, only for his disemboweled remains to land six feet aft. Ryland felt a jet of air near his arm. The bite of a jagged tooth in his shoulder blade. He stumbled to his hands and knees. He pulled out the sharp object and examined the results. A reddened five-inch splinter. Ryland tossed it away.

Their broadside is to our bow, Ryland realized. *The enemy can gut us from stem to stern.* Dirty light filtered down from the main hatch. The smoke billowed up between the boat cradles. Men darted by on the deck above, their shadows flitting through the film. Ryland stumbled forward, following the light. A brawny sailor shoulder-checked him, and he caught himself on a piling.

"Sorry, sir," said the wild-eyed seaman, sweat cutting pale lines down his grimy face. He continued on and vanished into the smoke.

The wound from the splinter throbbed. Ryland's head still buzzed from the explosion. Finding the steps up the main hatch, he climbed into the light of day. He pitched onto the spar deck, lungs gulping for fresh air. His hands found the belfry, and he hauled himself onto his feet. The fourth lieutenant found himself at the center of a maelstrom. His head whirled from one scene of frenzy to the next.

Sailors and Marines swarmed toward the bow. The occasional curse or shout in Arabic or Lingua Franca floated up from the enemy ship beyond. Dead ahead, a two-masted schooner lay across *Philadelphia's* bow in perfect perpendicular. The American frigate dwarfed her Barbary opponent, and her bowsprit pierced the schooner's rigging. The jib sails of Philadelphia crumpled uselessly against the enemy's gaffsail. A tangle of ropes hung from *Philadelphia's* forward spars.

His lungs no longer suffocating, Ryland felt his mind rising from its stupor. The enemy ship was the *Mirborka*, Ryland dimly recalled. Twenty-four guns. One hundred crew. Against the *Philadelphia*, she was outgunned two to one. Outmanned three to one. The Barbary Pirate ship should have been no match for the powerful American frigate, but she had the bow of the larger vessel pinned. Ryland could make out the points of curved swords stabbing the air around *Philadelphia's* bow, nipping at mighty Hercules like the teeth of the Hydra.

A half mile to port, a stretch of blinding white sand snaked along the Moroccan shore, parallel with the ship. Dusty hills were covered in short palms, poplars, and cypress. Russet cliffs rippled in the Mediterranean heat. A reef and a long ridge enclosed the bay. The water slipped into darker shades of aquamarine with distance from land. In the shallows, one could see the rumor of coral below the surface.

"Move your asses, men!" yelled an officer.

Ryland spun to see First Lieutenant Stephen Porter stabbing a finger down the main hatch. Several seamen paid a hose down the ladder.

"Get that fire out," Porter shouted. "Or we'll have the whole ship ablaze. Marines, lay forward! Lay forward, I say."

Musket-wielding Marines tramped toward the bow in their white-feathered caps. After they passed by, Ryland approached the first officer.

"Lieutenant Porter," said Ryland. The other didn't look up, still preoccupied with the efforts of the hose crew. "The fire's mostly out. We need to lay on our broadside."

Porter scowled at Ryland as if interrupted by a pestering child. "No, Ryland, I thought we'd throw rocks. Of course we should lay on our broadside! Can't you see we're dead in the water? Our rudder doesn't answer the helm."

"Then…a boat with a tow cable. We could—"

"Damn it, Ryland, I haven't time for your nattering." Porter brushed past Ryland. "Lieutenant Gordon!" He stormed off after the commander of the ship's Marines.

There was a series of snaps, like branches shearing apart in a storm. Then a boom. Ryland looked overhead, towards the stern, to see several mizzen stays break. A clew line broke away, followed by a shroud, and the lower corner of a mizzen sail. The shots were coming from behind the ship. Ryland ran for the stern. He staggered to a stop on the quarterdeck, stunned by what he saw.

Dead astern, three gunboats, each with a triangular sail, sped towards the *Philadelphia*. A single 38-pound long gun and two small swivels pointed from each prow. Their wide, open decks swarmed with the rich colors of Barbary Pirate crews. The small vessels were less than a hundred yards off. When they arrived, they would add at least another fifty fighters to the battle.

"Mr. Ryland, why the hell are you dawdling?" Captain Bainbridge shouted from behind the ship's wheel. "What of my bow chasers?"

"Uh, I uh…" It was a simple enough question to answer, but the shock of the situation left Ryland stammering.

"Your report at once, sir!"

"Right, the bow chasers. Sir, there was an explosion forward. The galley stove, I think. The fire is under control, but the crews can't reach the guns."

"Are you daft? It can't have been the galley. A gun must have burst."

It did sound odd, Ryland realized. The cook's stove was hardly the most explosive object on the ship. But Ryland's memory was slowly returning. He could faintly recall the metal chimney splitting open at the moment of ignition. "I don't believe so, Captain. I saw the galley stove explode. I'm sure of it."

Bainbridge's upper lip twitched. He squeezed the hilt of his sheathed saber. "More sabotage, then."

"Sir?"

"The rudder, Mr. Ryland. The cables came apart. They must have been cut."

"Captain, if we can bring our broadsides to bear, we've won. Permission to launch a boat with a tow cable."

The captain narrowed his eyes at Ryland, considering. He might have preferred to hurl insults, but it was clear from his expression that he was considering the proposal's merit.

"Ahoy!" came a cry from the mizzen crosstrees above. "Ship on the starboard quarter. Ship on the starboard quarter."

Both Ryland and Bainbridge looked northwest, in the

direction given by the lookout. Ryland grabbed the spyglass from his belt and aimed it north. Another ship was rounding the long ridge to the west. A sleek, black and red hull with nine guns to a side. Two tall masts and a short mizzen. A snow brig. She could only be one ship: *The Wolf of Tunis*. A brig of American design, given to the Bey of Tunis in exchange for peace. Ryland almost chuckled at the irony. Her twenty-two guns and crew of a hundred forty would swing the battle decisively for the pirates. Could John Sullivan have been right? Had the brig been there in the storm, following the *Philadelphia*?

The spyglass slowly dropped from Ryland's eye. *So this is how it ends,* he thought. All these years of running. Of hiding. Of lies. Lies he told himself. He was a fool to believe a man like him could ever find love. Or peace. Chester Ryland was a liar, an imposter, and a coward. He deserved to end this day a slave—or dead. He had it coming, and that was a fact. But why did he have to bring Sawyer into this life? Because he was too weak be alone. And the damned irony of it was, most of the time he treated the man he loved like a perfect stranger. *To escape slavery, only to wind up in chains all over again.* Like the first man foolish enough to love Ryland, Sawyer would pay the price.

"Well, man?" demanded Bainbridge.

"Enemy—enemy ship, sir," said Ryland, his voice coming out in a croak. "It's the *Wolf of Tunis*. Gunports open."

The captain's hand slid off his sword. He stared at the small fleet closing in. "My God. We've lost the ship."

Chapter 34

The USS *Philadelphia*
The Port of Gibraltar, British Imperial Colony
Two Days Before the Attack

John drummed his foot. He opened Nora's watch and checked the time. *Where is he?* The ship was eerily quiet, especially down here in the surgeon's cockpit. With half the ship's crew away on leave, there was no bustle of feet on the decks above. No shouts or laughter or snoring. Only the muffled activity on the docks of Gibraltar. The ship barely moved in the calm harbor waters. A single lantern illuminated the table where they'd played brag a week ago. Darkness filled the spaces between hammocks with ghosts.

The door swung open. Fourth Lieutenant Chester Ryland stepped into the surgery. Gone was the cocky bravado, the serene contemplation, the affable advice. He looked at John like a stranger, studying him with disbelieving eyes. His voice was barely above a whisper. "It's rare to meet a man more duplicitous than our captain."

The Islanded Lion in John's pocket chewed at his thumb. He turned away from Ryland, rubbing the coin as he watched a flame lick the lantern glass. "You left me no choice. I did what I had to do."

Ryland swooped under a low beam. He slammed the door shut. "You poisoned an officer. An act so mutinous, even Bainbridge could set aside his hatred for me. He'd have you flogged through the fleet."

"He would," agreed John. "Right after he hung you for sharing another man's hammock."

Yelling echoed from the docks—as if from a mishap moving cargo. Ryland's brows pinched with fear. "What do you intend to do?"

"That depends on your answers," said John. "I've seen the drawings. *All of them*."

"Where are they?"

"A safe place." John walked the edge of the shadows. "You will tell me everything you know about the Silver Hand. Or I will ruin you."

The fourth lieutenant's posture withered. His eyes turned listless. "Ask your questions."

"James Gilroy came to me in Philadelphia with a message from my sister, delivered on her behalf by the Silver Hand. The thief wouldn't tell him where to find her, but Gilroy claimed he saw you and the Silver Hand together. In Algiers. Was that true?"

"Yes. The Silver Hand needed my help finding Gilroy passage to America. I owed the thief a favor."

"In return for the *George Washington* theft."

"Aye." Ryland looked up at the beams. He closed his eyes and let out a sigh. "But I didn't do it for gold—I never took a penny. I helped the Silver Hand steal a chest from the dey's tribute because it's what Bainbridge deserved. It was foolish."

"Why would you do such a thing?"

"He had Sawyer flogged!" Ryland snapped. "The charge was fabricated—Bainbridge was jealous of my popularity on the *George Washington*. He knew Sawyer was my friend, so he decided to send a message."

John couldn't deny his disgust at the captain's abuse— if Ryland's side of the story could be believed. But John had other problems. "Who is this Silver Hand? How did you come to know him in the first place?"

"The Silver Hand isn't one man," Ryland explained. "It's an order of sorts. A society of thieves—some of them free, some of them slaves. The one I knew went by the name 'Rune.' He was just a boy when I met him in Tunis. The last time I saw him, he must've been sixteen, seventeen perhaps. A slave from India, I think."

"And you met this 'Rune' in Tunis?"

Ryland nodded. "When the *Washington* was delivering tribute to Bey Hammuda, the bey invited Bainbridge and his officers to his palace for a diplomatic dinner. That night, I saw the guards chasing down a corridor. They asked me if I'd seen a thief hiding anywhere. As it happened, the boy they were looking for was clinging to a beam above their heads. But I said 'no' and sent them down another hall. Rune was grateful for my help and said if I should ever need a favor from the Silver Hand, I should light a candle in the highest window of a certain tavern. Then he stole out the window. Scaled the palace like a damn cat."

"Why did you help him?"

"I don't know," the fourth lieutenant groaned. "I suppose, in all that opulence, stealing a few bobbles seemed a poor reason to hang a man. Especially one so young. As it happens, I lit that candle the next night. You see, I had just met Sawyer." Ryland trailed off. His gaze looked a hundred miles away.

John tilted his head as realization dawned. "Sawyer once told me he'd been shipwrecked on the Barbary Coast. That's when he enlisted and joined the *George Washington.*"

"Aye," admitted Ryland. "Sawyer did shipwreck on the Barbary Coast, as I told Bainbridge when I got him entered in the ship's books. But I left out the time Sawyer spent as a slave in Bey Hammuda's palace. It's hardly a secret in Tunis that the bey prefers men—and keeps them in his seraglio."

"So I saw," said John, remembering the bey's foreign minister—and lover. "As a slave in Tunis."

"Ah," said Ryland, scratching at his temple. "Of course. Well, Sawyer happened upon me as I wandered alone in the bey's garden. It was a…singular moment." Ryland's voice ground to a whisper as if his throat had gone dry. He stared at his feet, a tremor in his brow. As if the memory brought him joy and sorrow in equal measure. "I enlisted Rune and the Silver Hand to secure Sawyer's escape. A few days later, they blindfolded me and whisked me away in a boat. When they took off the blindfold, I found myself in the courtyard of a beautiful estate."

"Where?"

"I have no idea. Some remote stretch of coast, perhaps. It was a mansion with fountains, rows of trees, flowers of every kind. I thought I'd stepped into the hanging gardens of Babylon. The walls were mostly red sandstone. They looked old—ancient, even. There were children, servants, men and their wives… Thieves drawn from the Barbary slaves, from every corner of the world. True to their word, there was Sawyer. That was the origin of the…" Ryland tugged on his neckerchief. "…drawings you saw."

"Did you meet their leader?" John demanded.

"No. I wasn't allowed to wander. The next night Rune smuggled us back to the docks. Again, blindfolded. In the morning, I left with Sawyer aboard the *Washington*. The rest, you know."

"So that's it then," suggested John. "I can light a candle, as you did."

Ryland shook his head. "They change the signal all the time. They're very cautious that way. Besides, in the year and a half since, I've heard rumors the Silver Hand were wiped out by agents of the sultan."

"No, that can't be. Katie's message suggested she wanted to escape. The Silver Hand must have been helping. I have to find these thieves."

"Rune told me we'd never see one another again. If I knew a way, Sullivan, I swear I would tell you."

John sighed. "What about this estate? What else can you remember?"

"There…was a girl," said Ryland. "I've always had a good memory for faces. She was young. Perhaps ten. I saw her in a window of the house. A small glimpse, mind."

"What did she look like?"

"She had long curly hair. Red. Freckles on her face."

"Katie…"

"Possibly. If so, maybe they kept her safe."

"I need more," pressed John. "Some clue to find that estate."

"No, Sullivan. You don't understand. I saw nothing on the route outside the compound. I could hear the ocean in the distance, see an ancient sycamore tree just over the wall, but nothing else. Nothing that could tell me where I was. I'm sorry."

"Fuck sorry!" snarled John, swatting a dark lantern. The metal frame banged off the beams. "This can't be all there is."

"Mr. Sullivan," began Chester, pressing his hands together. "I have no reason to keep anything from you. Whatever secrets I had, you know them. Whatever leverage you wanted, you've got it. I'm telling you the truth."

John snorted. "I really have no way of knowing, do I? Every day of your life is a lie."

"That isn't fair!" Ryland snapped. "I wanted to help you, Sullivan. Truly, I did. But how could I tell you about helping Rune steal? About Sawyer? And what could I have told you?" Ryland's voice shifted into a higher pitch. "That I might have seen a girl I don't know? In a place *I could never find?*"

"I guess you're useless, aren't you?" John growled. The moment he said it, he felt awful. He could be angry at Ryland all he liked, but facts were facts. Joining the *Philadelphia*, leaning on Ethan for favors, beguiling rival officers—it had all been pointless. Ryland didn't know anything. And he could hardly be blamed for wanting to conceal his nocturnal life.

A long silence passed. They heard the laughter of a few dockside drunks. Ship's bells tolled the hour.

Barely above a whisper, Ryland asked, "What do you intend to do with my drawings? Will you show them to the captain?"

John studied Ryland's haunted face. The face of a prisoner awaiting judgment. The drawings had extorted the truth. They could still give him leverage over Ryland, but to what end? And if he gave the drawings to Bainbridge, the captain would claim victory and hang two men. Suddenly, after all this wasted effort, every gut-wrenching favor, a month of deceit—all for nothing—the answer was oddly clear.

John stepped forward and reached into his coat. He withdrew the leather book of drawings and handed it to Ryland. "Take them."

Ryland stared at the book, then at John, as if suspecting a trick. He reached out with a trembling hand and took the drawings back. "Thank you," he croaked.

John paused at the surgery door. "Sawyer wanted those dropped in the sea. If I were you, I'd honor his wish."

Ryland shook his head. He looked at the drawings again, then at John. "Sullivan…why?"

For a moment, John considered answering. Instead, he stormed away through the hold.

Chapter 35

The USS *Philadelphia*
Off the Coast of Gibraltar
Two Days Before the Attack

"What the hell do you mean 'nothing to report?'" blustered Captain Bainbridge.

John stood at straight attention before the captain, hands clasped behind his back. Charts, logbooks, and theater artifacts littered Bainbridge's desk. The wide blue ocean filled the cabin with light. *Philadelphia* jogged over the waves, reveling in a fair wind. The Rock of Gibraltar was already sinking below the horizon, along with John's plan to rescue his family. He swallowed and said, "I've spent weeks observing Lieutenant Ryland. I have no evidence he took part in any theft."

"And he's spoken to you in confidence?"

"Aye, Captain. Many times."

"And in all those conversations," said Bainbridge, narrowing his eyes, "not *once* has he said anything suspicious?"

John tightened his knuckles. He'd decided not to tell Bainbridge about Ryland's indiscretions, but it looked like a simple omission wouldn't be enough. He would have to lie. "No, Captain. If Ryland did help the Silver Hand, I have no way of knowing."

Bainbridge pounded a fist on his desk. The skull from Hamlet nearly jumped onto the floor. "You know what, Sullivan? I don't believe you."

John felt a cold shiver. Bainbridge saw through him. "Captain, you would question my honor?"

The captain grunted. "Honor? Why, that must be a rare quality indeed among smugglers. Or in a seedy playhouse. Or among card sharps." Bainbridge leaned forward. "How remarkable to find a man of your virtue amidst all three."

The captain had a point. Before the Barbary Pirates, John had never taken up a weapon. Never stolen. Never told a lie—not a malicious one, anyway. Who had he become? "Captain, I…I'm telling the truth."

"The hell you are! Ryland is a sinking ship, and you're going down with him, Sullivan."

John's eyes fell upon Yorick's grinning skull, a pitiless witness to his fall from grace.

"I'm going to ask you one more time, Mr. Sullivan," continued Bainbridge, "and I want you to consider very carefully before you answer. You argued for leniency for Seaman Meadows. And I know of your desire to search for your family in the Barbary states."

John was stunned. He didn't realize Bainbridge had learned so much about him.

"I could show Meadows leniency," Bainbridge said. "And I could grant you extended furlough. The *Philadelphia* might even pass by Tunis, where you could disembark. *If* you were an officer I could trust. So, I ask again: have you uncovered evidence of Chester Ryland's corruption?"

And a pair of invisible scales counted up the bill. Balanced on one side, reprieve for Meadows and permission to search for Nora and Kaitlin—though John had no leads on their whereabouts. On the other, the lives of Ryland and Sawyer. John need only let two men hang for buggery and collect an alliance with Captain Bainbridge.

"You think only of the day Katie and Nora are rescued," Ethan says, "but what of the day after? What will be left of John Sullivan?"

"Well, man?" pressed Bainbridge.

Water welled behind John's eyes. "I regret I have nothing to report, Captain. I'm sorry if I've let you down."

Bainbridge looked away in disgust. "Dismissed. Get out of my sight."

John offered a meek salute and turned to leave.

"And Midshipman," said Bainbridge.

John stopped at the cabin door and looked back.

"Tonight, I'll make sure Bosun Clements braids his cat o' nine double thick."

Chapter 36

The USS *Philadelphia*
Under Attack off the Coast of Morocco
Friday, August 26th, 1803

The stern windows exploded. Shattered glass blew through the captain's cabin. Iron balls gouged fist-sized holes in the ceiling. Chips of wood and white paint rained down on Chester Ryland's head. Shrieks erupted from the crew fighting off boarders. A shard of bone pinged off a chandelier, and blood spattered the beams. A jet of red wrote over Bach's signature on *Sonata Number 3*.

"Get down!" Ryland shouted, diving for the floor.

The sailors defending the stern ducked under the windows. One of the gunboats blasted another shot through a quarter gallery, showering the room with splinters from the captain's privy.

Screams of pain followed. A shirtless sailor clutched his stomach, blood boiling out from under his hands. He collapsed wheezing, then went limp. Another touched a sliver of glass stuck in his cheek, his blonde sideburn soaked red. One young man stood in shock, examining the exposed bone of his forearm as a naturalist might study a beetle.

"Pass the word for the surgeon!" Ryland shouted over his shoulder. The walls of the captain's quarters had been removed before the battle, opening the space to the rest of the gun deck. All of Bainbridge's furniture had been carried off and stowed. One day the venue for a Bach recital, today a slaughterhouse.

Metal clanged on the floor. Ryland saw a four-pointed grappling hook a few feet away. The attached rope snaked through the broken panes. It scored the planks as the pirates hauled on the other end. The iron points found purchase on the sill, and four more grappling hooks flew into the cabin. Ryland scrambled up, drew his cutlass, and chopped through the first. He looked out, catching sight of the three gunboats pressing against the *Philadelphia's* stern.

The gunboats were built for swarming enemy vessels. They had wide decks with rails no higher than a boot, two swivel guns and one long canon on their bow, and a shallow hull. They were more maneuverable in bays and estuaries than large ships like the *Philadelphia*. Dozens of men in loose tunics and pantaloons crowded their open decks, with plenty of space to move and fight. The Moroccan pirates had lashed the three boats together and dropped anchors, positioned where *Philadelphia* had no cannons. With grappling hooks attached, some seventy hostiles were now piling onto the middle boat and preparing to storm the American frigate. The anchored gunboats would keep the *Philadelphia* pinned until the *Wolf of Tunis* arrived.

"Men, stand to," shouted Ryland, even as another volley of grapples came flying through. A row of men and boys lined up on either side of him. Some loaded pistols. Others aimed muskets. One lad shouted and brought his cutlass down on a grapple rope. Shots echoed from the taffrail on the spar deck. Months of monotony at sea, but when the moment came, the men showed courage. Ryland's heart swelled with pride.

Below the gold-painted trim of *Philadephia's* windows, a mass of hard eyes and dark beards glared at their prize. The Moroccans had the bronze complexion typical of Turks, but like many Barbary Pirate crews, Ryland could pick out faces of every shade. There were at least a dozen Africans, and more than a few Europeans. It was easy to forget how many Christian slaves converted and joined their former captives—or simply left home for the pirate's life. Several attackers climbed the ropes, the muscles of their arms flexed tautly. They didn't have far to go—barely the height of a man.

"*Luta!*" roared a voice. The word echoed over the water as though blown through an ox horn. "*Luta, cani!*"

Is that…Portuguese? And *Italian?* wondered Ryland. It must have been bits of Lingua Franca, the language used among slaves and masters on the Barbary Coast. If translated correctly, those words meant, "Fight, dogs!" Ryland looked for the source of the voice.

A muscular pirate whipped the press of bodies forward. He wore extravagant robes with ornate embroidery, marking him as the captain—or "*re'is.*" The other pirates cowered under his lash. The long-bearded captain sneered and barked orders, and even brandished his scimitar when one of their youngest took a step back. Could it be that simple? Not the barbarian horde of legend. Some looked like desperate souls fighting for a living. Conscripts trying to live another day under a tyrant. Ryland wondered, *In another life, would I be so different?*

The barrel of a pistol thrust through the window. On instinct, Ryland dropped his saber and grabbed it with both hands. The pirate held the aim on Ryland's forehead for a frightening heartbeat. Ryland wrenched the muzzle upward. Both men struggled to gain control, locked in a battle of raw strength. The fourth lieutenant looked into the snarling eyes of the man trying to kill him, bloodshot with murder. The gun inched back down.

If Ryland couldn't take the gun, he could at least spend the shot. He pressed the trigger, and the pistol fired into an oak beam. His ears rang from the report, his eyes stung from the gun smoke. Ryland threw a sharp punch and sent the pirate splashing into the pearlescent water.

Glass crunched underfoot as Ryland snatched up his saber. He shuffled a few steps back, his heart racing from the near miss.

"Clear a space," cried another voice. Surgeon's Mate Ethan Auldon brushed by Ryland, his white apron covered in red blotches. He knelt beside one of the wounded and went to work, though his pallor looked a little green. "You're all right, mate," he soothed over the patient's wailing.

"I passed the carpenter," Ethan told Ryland over his shoulder.

"The rudder?" Ryland asked.

"Hours. At least. And we can't rig rudder chains with pirates attacking astern."

Ryland looked forward along the gun deck. He shook his head at what he saw. Dozens of gun crews still manning their cannons, even though they could only aim at empty water. By having the *Mirborka* attack the bow, and the gunboats attack the stern, the corsairs had found the perfect blind spots. The *Philadelphia* needed every man aboard to take the fight to the pirates, hand to hand, but Bainbridge was too afraid to leave the guns unmanned. Ryland needed to get to the captain and explain their predicament. They couldn't maneuver the ship into broadside range, so they would have to win by boarding before the *Wolf of Tunis* joined the fray. He looked back at the mob of corsairs trying to hack and claw their way through the stern windows. He ordered a midshipman to take charge of repelling the boarders, then hurried toward the quarterdeck hatch.

"Ryley!" shouted the boyish voice of Michael Dufort. "I mean—Lieutenant Ryland."

Ryland stopped at the hatch steps and found Dufort following him. *The poor lad.* He didn't have a single whisker on his chin, was still short for his age, and had a boyish, piping voice. How he didn't get picked on by his mates, Ryland would never know. "Not now, Seaman. Back to your post."

"You need Sully!" Dufort cried.

"Sully—what?"

"Bluster-Br—I mean, Captain Bainbridge is going to get us all killed. Or worse. You need help. Get Sully out of the clink. He'll know what to do."

"Midshipman Sullivan is under arrest. Now, off with you!" Ryland didn't get a half step before he felt a hand on his arm. Dufort might have been short, but he certainly had a strong grip. Ryland found himself transfixed by Dufort's intense, pale eyes.

"We're going to lose," Dufort insisted. "Sawyer will die a slave."

"What?" Ryland breathed. He was nonplused. How did Dufort know the one name that could render him powerless?

Tolling each word like a bell, Dufort said, "Go get Sully."

As if pulled by a current, Ryland slipped from Dufort's grasp. As he climbed the steps, Dufort's warning haunted his thoughts. A few moments later, Ryland found Bainbridge at the bowsprit, shouting orders. *Philadelphia* sailors were climbing up the most forward spar, using hatchets to chop away the tangled enemy rigging. The *Mirborka's* crew crawled through their rigging, trading potshots. Below, Moroccans were climbing over the forward railing, driving into the Marines with swords and bayonets.

Blood ran in candy-apple streams across Ryland's path. Dr. Cowdery was tightening a belt around the stump of a seaman's severed lower leg. The patient gibbered with vacant eyes, his cheeks sunken and blue. An arterial spurt stained a swatch of Cowdery's stocking. The doctor pulled the ligature tight. The sailor screamed and fainted.

"Captain," Ryland said, but Bainbridge didn't look back at him.

The captain was fixated on the attempt to separate the two ships. A man up on the bowsprit yelped as a gunshot took him in the stomach. The ax slipped from his grasp, and he fell after it into the shallow bay. The man behind him on the yardarm shouted to Bainbridge, "There's too many, Captain."

"Climb, damn you," Bainbridge bellowed back. "I won't lose my ship to your cowardice."

"Captain!" Ryland repeated.

"Yes, yes," Bainbridge said, rounding on Ryland. "What the devil is it?"

"We're about to be overrun at the stern. I need the gun crews for a boarding action."

"What? No. They're needed at their posts. Can you hold your ground against the gunboats?"

"Captain," Ryland began, "we can take all these devils by boarding *if* we go on the offensive."

"Bugger your offensive!" Bainbridge shouted. "I'll not have our guns unmanned when the *Wolf of Tunis* comes into range. I didn't ask for your harebrained opinion, Mr. Ryland, I asked if you can hold off the damn gunboats!"

Ryland cast a glance over his shoulder. The *Wolf of Tunis* leaned gracefully on the starboard tack. With the tide bringing her in, it would be a matter of minutes before she could fire her 18-pounder long guns.

"Yes," Ryland admitted with a sigh. "I can hold them off. But the rudder's beyond repair. At least grant me a boat with Marines and a tow cable."

"And give the pirates a target to blow to splinters? Out of the question."

Pain squeezed Ryland's eyes. His forehead still throbbed from the galley explosion. The pressure built until words burst out of him. "Captain, I know it is a risk, but we cannot continue to sit here like a great *hog in the road*!"

Bainbridge's face turned beet red. "Mr. Ryland," he hissed, "use that tone with me again and I'll have you shot for mutiny."

Ryland nodded, quickly sobering. "Aye, sir."

"If the rudder can't be repaired, take what gun crews you need."

"Thank you, Captain—"

"—And point cannons at the *Philadelphia's* bottom. If we're forced to surrender, we'll sink the ship."

"Scuttle the *Philadelphia*, Captain?"

"I didn't say scuttle her *now*, you simpleton. Now get

going." The captain drew his sword and headed toward the boarding party massing at the bow. His shouts disappeared into the din of gunfire.

"Aye, aye, Captain," Ryland muttered. What could he do? William Bainbridge was master and commander of USS *Philadelphia*. His word was law. Ryland headed aft to prepare the self-destruction of the ship.

"Sawyer will die a slave." The words of Michael Dufort echoing in his mind.

Nothing for it be damned, thought Ryland. He stopped and scanned the deck. Midshipman Merrick was shifting from foot to foot near the main shrouds, a cutlass wobbling in his hand.

"Mr. Merrick," said Ryland as he approached.

The jittery midshipman rounded and held out the unsteady point of his cutlass.

"You going to use that on me?" asked Ryland.

Merrick looked dumbly at the sword. He quickly lowered it. "Oh, no sir. Sorry, sir."

"Good. Now go below and fetch gun crews one through five. Arm them for boarding and prepare the cutter for launch." Ryland strode off to the main hatch.

"Aye, sir. Where are you going?"

"To get help."

Chapter 37

The USS *Philadelphia*
The Mediterranean Sea
One Day Before the Attack

The sun was beating a sour odor out of the three hundred sailors lined up on the *Philadelphia's* spar deck. Melisande Dufort could hardly claim to smell better—her clothes were just as stained with sweat, sea spray, and spilled grog. Even standing between Dixon and Big Paw Kelham, true friends if ever she had them, she longed for home—and freedom. Instead, she was about to watch another macabre ritual flogging.

Two sailors beat a drumroll from instruments slung across their chests. The bosun, Jonathan Clements, piped an ear-splitting tone. A quartet of Marines marched out of the quarterdeck hatch led by Private "Soggy" Ray. A shackled prisoner rattled up the steps. Old Man Meadows shrank from the bright morning light. The Marines marched the old sailor onto a grating and shackled his feet to the wooden latticework. The other Marines removed the manacles on Meadows' wrists, stripped off his shirt, and tied his hands to ropes hanging from the yard.

"Heave," said Boatswain Clements.

The ropes hissed through pulleys, hoisting up Meadows' arms. Melisande saw Sullivan across the deck with the other midshipmen, but he didn't look at her. There were deep circles under his eyes. His coat buttons were loose, and his stockings bunched at the shins. She'd never seen Sullivan so slovenly. When Meadows was bound and standing spread-eagled, the drummers fell silent.

"You men and boys of the *Philadelphia,*" trumpeted Bainbridge. He stood in front of the wheel, raising his voice over the brisk wind. "We are at this very moment nipping at the heels of our enemy. Two years ago, Tripoli demanded two hundred twenty-five thousand dollars for our right to travel the sea in peace. The journey has been long, but at last, we have joined the war."

A grumble muttered through the crew.

"The Barbary princes slapped away the hand of friendship and threatened our sailors with slavery."

A louder grumble.

"And they had the foolishness to chop down the flag of our embassy."

The assemblage of sailors broke into jeers.

"Will you men stand for it?"

"No!" replied dozens of men.

Bainbridge raised his voice to a bellow. "Do you have a mind to teach these Barbary dogs a lesson?"

"Aye!" cried hundreds in unison.

"And teach them you shall. We are ordered to capture the *Mirborka.* To liberate our merchant vessel, *Celia.* It is our duty to reclaim the freedom of our countrymen, and the honor of our states. Every man jack of you has the opportunity to win his share of prize money—and to show the world what an American tar is worth! How does that sound to you?"

The crew cheered, the bloody business about to unfold all but forgotten. Even Melisande relished the prospect of a good fight. But then she caught another glimpse of Meadows and felt sick.

"That is music to my ears," said Bainbridge. "However, we cannot win victory without discipline. We must confront the specter of dishonor in our midst. The man standing on the grating before you spoke curses to a midshipman and disrespected his lawful senior officer. Let there be no doubt: vulgarity, insubordination, and mutiny will not be tolerated aboard my ship.

"Bosun Clements, do your duty and show this man no leniency, or I'll have you triced up next. Any man looks away, he gets *two* dozen."

The boatswain reached into his burlap sack and withdrew his cat-o-nine-tails. It was a thick handle with nine braids of cord, about four hands long. A series of knots studded each braid. Clements stood side-on to Meadows, wound his arm back, and swung.

The evil ropes hissed through the air and made a sound like jaws snapping. Red stripes appeared on Meadows' back. The whip tore pocks in his flesh. Meadows grimaced, every muscle in his body going tense.

"One," announced Clements.

Another snap. Meadows made a stifled moan. Burgundy drops ran from the rips.

"Two," announced Clements.

By the fourth stroke, Meadows' back was covered in blood. After the sixth stroke, the old salt couldn't hold back his cries. On the eighth stroke, his knees gave out. He collapsed in a gasp of agony, dangling from his trussed arms. Bloody clumps ran like molasses. Melisande fought back her tears.

Clements looked at Bainbridge, his cat dripping. Among the midshipmen, Melisande was able to pick out the grinning face of Grove—clearly enjoying the sight of Meadows' agony. Her rising fury cooled when she saw Cowan. Far from his expression of triumph after throwing the water, the twelve-year-old boy looked sickened. His eyes were watery and bloodshot. He broke under the strain and looked at his feet. Sullivan touched the back of Cowan's neck, and the boy turned his gaze back to the flogging.

"Surgeon's mate," Captain Bainbridge said. "Has he fainted?"

Dr. Cowdery and Ethan Auldon stood nearby, tasked with seeing to the seaman's health. Ethan bent down for a look at Meadows. He shook his head. "No, Captain. He's conscious."

"The full dozen, Mr. Clements, if you please," commanded Bainbridge.

And they call the Iroquois "savages," thought Melisande. *Look at them all. Standing around in all their fancy clothes, beating a helpless old man.*

"Twelve," announced Clements after the last stroke.

Meadows whimpered softly. The Marines took him down, clots of flesh slithering down his back. Ethan and Cowdery carried Meadows below decks. For a moment, the crew stood in silence.

"Let this be a lesson well learned," boomed Bainbridge, raking the crew with a sharp look. "And let it be behind us."

Bainbridge gave his words a moment to sink in, then turned to his first officer. "Mr. Porter, before we go into battle, I want men with full bellies and high spirits. See that every man gets an extra ration of vittles during the dog watches. And an extra tot of rum!"

The men sent up a cheer.

"Aye, Captain," Lieutenant Porter replied.

"And a little music wouldn't go amiss," said the captain with a playful smile.

The men replied with another cheer and a smattering of laughter.

Bainbridge's rare moment of mirth faded. "Lieutenant, dismiss the crew if you please."

Porter stepped forward and shouted, "All hands! *Dis-*missed!"

"Here you are, old man," said Melisande. "Take a load off."

Melisande and Ethan gently helped Meadows into a hammock in the sick berth. Meadows winced and settled onto his stomach, arms dangling over the sides.

"Steady now," said Ethan. "I'm sorry about the pain, but the captain forbade the use of laudanum. Try to rest if you can."

Melisande kneeled and pulled something out of her boot. "Yeah, but Bluster-Britches never said anything about my stash of rum." She jangled the metal flask.

Meadows pulled a grimace into a smile. "Oh, there's a sight to cheer the heart."

"That's it, my lovely." Melisande pulled the stopper and angled the spout into Meadows' mouth. "Take your medicine."

Rum ran off the seaman's chin. His eyes drooped. "Bless you, lass."

Melisande and Ethan exchanged a look of alarm. With a nervous laugh, she said, "That was only one pull, old man. Call me 'lass' again, and you're cut off."

"I said what now?" Meadows mumbled. He lifted his groggy eyes. "Damn if I did…" His head settled back onto the hammock. "Well, there it is."

"There's what?" Melisande chuckled, trying to sound nonchalant. "We both know Thomas Prince would look better in a dress."

"It's all right, lass," said Meadows. "You think you're the first woman to slip aboard a man o' war?"

Melisande's heart began to race. If the crew found out, if she were locked up, she'd have no chance to get to Dominique. She felt a rising panic. When things went bad on land, she struck out into the wilderness. But trapped on this boat…

Meadows must have read the look in her eyes because he said, "Don't fret, Dufort. The lads have no idea. I've had a few more years to season than most, and it still took me awhile to catch on." His eyes crinkled as he smiled, reminding her of *Papa* Grey Fox. "There's nothing to fear."

Until this moment, Melisande hadn't been aware of her anxiety. Weeks of deepening her voice, wearing itchy gauze, pissing through a funnel—even sneaking above decks to toss her raggings into the sea. Melisande couldn't remember ever living in fear of being herself. She missed home. She missed her longhouse. She missed Grey Feather. A tear ran down her cheek.

"For this old man," said Meadows, giving her hand a reassuring squeeze, "your kindness has made a dark day brighter. I'll never tell a soul."

Melisande broke into a smile. She hurried to wipe away the tear.

"How you stand the smell, I'll never know," said Meadows, taking another swig.

Melisande laughed. "Tobacco and rum. Lots of it."

The old sailor laughed faintly, already dozing off.

"Well done," Ethan whispered. "I think he'll sleep now." He dabbed at a few patches of blood on Meadows' back.

"It isn't fair," Melisande said, staring at the old man's tattered skin.

"No," Ethan agreed. "Something you and I know plenty about."

"What's eating at you, Fiddles?"

"Hmm?" Ethan looked up at Melisande as if lost in thought. "Oh, nothing really."

"Don't go all pouty on me. What is it?"

"I'm worried about John."

Melisande recalled the listless look in Sullivan's eyes and his slovenly appearance. Though she agreed, she shrugged off her concern. "Sully gets like that sometimes. He's got a lot on his mind. He'll be fine."

Auldon dipped his hands in a basin, watching the cloud of blood spread through the water. "Ma always tried to tell me, but I refused to see it. But every year, he gets worse."

"Worse how?"

"Forget it." Ethan busied himself cleaning his instruments.

Meadows was already snoring.

"I know what you need, Fiddles," said Melisande, springing to her feet. "I know what we all need."

"What's that?" asked Ethan, eyeing her suspiciously.

Melisande slapped a hand on Ethan's back. She didn't feel like smiling, but she could always sense when her boys needed her. She mustered her most infectious grin. "For you to earn your nickname!"

Chapter 38

The USS *Philadelphia*
The Mediterranean Sea
The Night Before the Attack

"Midshipman Sullivan!" Ethan cried, rum wafting off his breath. "Come join us, mate."

"Yeah, Sully," slurred Melisande, teetering on her heels. "We've rewritten a Morris song. You might call it…"

"A rendition," offered Ethan helpfully.

"Yeah, an er-dition."

John Sullivan watched his two closest friends giggle like childhood playmates. Two people who had always been at odds. Something strange was in the air.

John frowned, lamenting they were both drunk. They'd been singing duets while the men and boys on the crew deck got rowdier. Dozens of sailors drinking, laughing, and dancing to the fiddle. Among them, Eric Long and several other ships boys sitting on barrels. Old Man Meadows lay on his stomach in a nearby hammock, smiling even with his back covered in blood-stained bandages. Seaman Sawyer and Private Ray shouted dueling song requests. The air stank of rum and pipe smoke. They'd been singing from Captain Charles Morris, an English bard known for his risqué lyrics. John had given the songbook to Ethan on his birthday—and sang every number with Melly at Kitty's. Decisions he now regretted.

"You're both *drunk,*" John said under his breath. "Porter heard you from the quarterdeck. Christ, Ethan, I never took *you* for reckless."

"Maybe I'm sick of prudence," Ethan proclaimed far too loudly.

"Oh, Sully," slurred Melisande. She pinched his chin as if talking to a precocious boy. "You're adorable when you're all in a lather. Stay, and I promise I'll keep the boys in line. Now, we're about to sing a…what's the word?"

"Round," said Ethan after a drink of rum. He ran his sleeve over his mouth.

"A round!" said Melisande. "We're going to sing a round."

"Mell—" John quickly cut himself off. Whispering or not, he couldn't be careless with her name. "Dufort, I'm very tired. I'm not in a patient mood." It was true. With Ryland a dead end, Bainbridge an avowed enemy, and Meadows the man who paid the price, John could have collapsed of exhaustion where he stood. He opened his mouth to disperse the party, but before he could speak, Melisande pressed a wad of tobacco under his lip.

She smiled at him like a Christmas reveler gorged on goose.

John blinked. Melisande blinked back. He thought to spit it out, but then the hickory notes seeped into his gums. He felt transported to a sunny day on the Philadelphia docks, watching the sloops sail along wooded shores, dangling his feet in the Delaware. His eyes drifted closed. "Mm. That is good."

"Mm-hmm," Melisande purred.

"Thank you," he said, opening his eyes. "But listen, Dufort, this isn't Kitty's. No more—"

Melisande put a canteen to John's mouth, stifling his protests. He had no choice but to drink, and beer bubbled down his throat. He tasted oats and hops, as soothing as cold water on a hot day. He tried to pull the deerskin away, but she tut-tutted and kept pouring.

"A little more," she said. "That's it, my lovely."

When the canteen fell away, John felt a heady euphoria. The ale warmed his belly. "Where did you find red Irish beer?"

"I have my ways," Melisande winked. She hung her arms on Ethan's shoulders.

The surgeon's mate slung his fiddle over his back like a woodcutter's ax. "What do you say, mate? One song?"

John stared at them in astonishment…and grinned.

There was a moment, half an hour later, when John got the vague idea he should do something about the noise. Private Ray danced between rows of clapping sailors, followed by Sawyer, and Big Paw Kelham, and finally the ship's boys. The doubling crowd and Mediterranean heat rendered the air humid. John's shirt was damp with sweat, his coat tossed aside. He smiled and clapped with the crowd as Eric Long and his mates danced a lively jig. Ethan sawed away at his fiddle, racing the speed of their feet. The music finally stopped, and a cheer went up. It was the perfect moment to send them back to their hammocks. The men were happy, not too drunk, and their gathering a shot to morale. But John was drunk on beer and self-pity.

"You men and boys!" boomed a false baritone.

Melisande stomped out of the crowd in John's coat and bicorner hat. She swaggered around in a circle, thumbs through her belt loops. "It's time you all learned a lesson."

The impression of Captain Bainbridge delighted the crowd. They chuckled and crowed, and John along with them.

"What's that?" groused the imposter captain. "You mean to laugh at me? Stop that at once, or I'll trice you up by the toes!"

The sensible part of John demanded he cringe in horror. The spiteful part had him laughing.

"I've a lesson for you all, and you'd best listen, or I'll cut you scoundrels into ounce pieces."

The crew laughed, and Ethan launched into a jaunty tavern tune. The melody swayed back and forth, perfect for a ballad. After a few beats, Melisande's caricature of Bainbridge broke into song.

"The captain of the Philly, cursed with a small wily,
Complained of a most miserable trip,
For in Algerine port, he sail't under a fort;
Where the prince commandeered his ship;
Still more he became angry, that the dey should bring ladies,
But to touch him the damsels were loath;
Bluster-Britches then learned, the reason he was spurned,
And to the admiral fiercely quothe:"

Melisande exaggerated a scowl and shook her finger, sending the crowd into fits of laughter.

"'In Constantinople, my poor wily so hopeful,
The dey sent his messenger to port, sir,
As he knew on those shores, what a woman adores,
He assigned one well hung for the sport, sir,

He searched the divan, till he found out a man,
Whose bollocks were heavy and hairy,
And he lately came o'er, with the Barbary rowers,
As the great emissary."'

Long and the ship's boys crowed with laughter, relieved to be far from their mothers. Sailors and Marines clanked cups. Even the timid giant Kelham laughed merrily.

Ethan giggled so hard, he hit a few wrong notes. Melisande, like a proper troubadour, only increased her outlandish character's outrage.

"'To Byzantine he came, with his cock in a flame,
And showed it to a lady on landing,
Who spread its renown thro' all parts of the town,
As a prick past all understanding;
When his name was announc'd, how the women all bounc'd,
And their blood rushed up to their faces;
His loins made them itch, from the nave to the britch,
And their bosoms burst out all their laces!"'

It was a scene of bedlam now. The kind of hilarity that came once in a year. The music dropped to a soft piano, and Melisande sang in a whisper.

"'So much there was said of its snout and its head,
That they called it the great janissary,

And now in a loud fit of pique,

"'And nary could I sleep, with naught but a sheep,
Because of that damned emissary!"'

They guffawed, and they wailed. They rolled and beat on the deck. Men and boys gasped for air, their faces streaming with tears. Ethan ended the song with a flourish and spread his arms wide. Melisande swept the crowd with bow after bow, abandoning all pretense of modesty. At that moment, John imagined there could be no better festival on Earth.

"What the hell is the meaning of all this?" In an instant, the merriment snuffed out. Midshipman Grove stomped out of the crowd.

"Like a carnival of inbreds!" cried Midshipman Cowan in his reedy voice, following close behind. As usual, the little sycophant couldn't be too far from the leader of his clique.

Most of the crewmen were quietly shuffling away to their hammocks. Ethan was putting away his fiddle. Melisande slid cups behind a barrel. John squared up to Grove and Cowan.

"Good God, Sullivan," sneered Grove. "You've been rutting in the muck right beside them."

John flashed a cold smile. "No more than Cowan's been rutting in your ass." There was no laughter at that—just a deadly silence.

"Why, you drooling mick," growled Grove.

"Drooling cock-robin!" sputtered Cowan.

"Get these men dispersed, Sullivan," ordered Grove. "And for God's sake—get cleaned up and at least *pretend* to be a gentleman."

The men needed no order—they were already filing aft.

"Stand fast, men," said John, causing a dozen or so to linger in confusion. "The captain gave us leave to celebrate and celebrate we shall."

Something in John's eyes must have made an impression because Grove took a step back. "Why, you…I gave an order, Sullivan!"

Anger coursed through John's veins, quickened by liquor. "I don't take orders from you," he said, glowering.

Ethan's hand settled on John's shoulder. "It's all right, mate. Time to call it a night."

"Aye, Sully," murmured Melisande. "We've had our fun. No need to ruin a good memory."

"You should listen to your miscreant friends," sneered Grove. "These orders come from Lieutenant Porter. Unless you want your bare ass flogged over a long gun."

"Yeah," said Cowan. "Listen to your miscreants."

John seethed. He shrugged away Ethan's hand. He leaned close to Grove and said, "I suggest you and your snotty pup lay aft before you're both drooling on the deck."

Grove snorted. "Word around the ship is, those Barbary Pirates beat you into a mad dog. Looks like the rumors are true."

Blood rushed in John's ears. His hands balled into fists.

Grove sneered. "Word is, you're not even a Navy man. Just a crook on the run, crying about some dead sister."

John's knuckles crunched into Grove's cheek. The shocked midshipman sprawled across the deck. Cowan skittered back, eyes full of fear. In the next second, John was straddling Grove, pounding his face again and again.

A pair of beefy arms encircled John's chest and dragged him off Grove. John kicked and spit, elbowed and clawed, but it was no use. Big Paw Kelham had him in an iron embrace.

"What's going on here?" demanded Lieutenant Ryland

as he approached.

"Sullivan struck me!" whined Grove, his hand covering his nose. Blood gushed between his fingers. "Sullivan struck me and disobeyed Lieutenant Porter's orders!"

"Calm yourself, Mr. Grove," commanded Ryland. "Mr. Auldon, help Mr. Grove to the sick berth and see to him."

"Aye, sir," said Ethan with a salute. He offered an arm to support Grove, but the midshipman waved it away.

"I want him in irons!" shouted Grove.

"That'll be all, Midshipman!" retorted Ryland. "Cowan, fetch Sergeant Gordon. Tell him to bring irons. The rest of you, get to your hammocks or duties this instant."

The rush of adrenalin was fading now, and John stopped resisting. Cowan was already off to fetch the sergeant of the Marines.

"Thank you, Mr. Kelham," said Ryland. He said to John under his breath, "what the hell's the matter with you, Sullivan? You'll be court-martialed for this!"

"At least I'm not a coward," sneered John.

"You're out of your head!"

A moment later, Cowan came bounding down the deck, Sergeant Gordon and a few Marines in tow.

"Sergeant Gordon," said Ryland. "Place Midshipman Sullivan in irons and lock him below."

"Aye, sir," said Gordon, snapping a salute.

As the manacles snapped shut on John's wrists, he met Ryland's eyes. Ryland's brows were drawn together as if out of pity. John wanted to resent him—even hate him. All the hope he'd invested in Ryland had come to naught. But some part of him knew it wasn't Ryland's fault.

"Come along, sir," said Gordon.

The Marines marched John aft. When they reached the hatch down to the orlop deck, the sound of banging drums pounded through the ship. A call relayed from crewman to crewman.

"Beat to quarters! Beat to quarters!"

The *Philadelphia* came to life. Sailors flew out of their hammocks and raced up to the gun deck. The ship's boys ran to the powder magazine for ammunition. Officers shouted orders to their divisions. *The enemy,* thought John. *The Barbary Pirates.* Energy reanimated his tired limbs. He was a revenant ready for the fight.

"Ray, Burling," said Gordon. "Secure Mr. Sullivan in the hold and assemble with your company."

"Wait," said John. "Sergeant, please. Let me fight."

"You know I can't release you, Sullivan."

"Please, sir, I give you my parole. I swear I'll come quietly when the action is over." The desperation in John's voice surprised even him. "But if we're going into battle, I *need* to do my part. Let me fight beside my shipmates."

Gordon hesitated for a moment. Judging by his frown, he had sympathy for a man eager to help his comrades. "Sorry, Sullivan. It's for the captain to decide." Gordon nodded to Ray and Burling. "Take him below."

Chapter 39

The USS *Philadelphia*
Under Attack off the Coast of Morocco
Friday, August 26th, 1803

"Ryland!" Sullivan cried, grabbing the bars of his cell. "What's happening? Are we boarded?"

"Yes," said Chester Ryland. He was still catching his breath from scrambling down to the brig. "The *Mirborka* has us pinned at our bow. Three gunboats have us pinned at our stern. Our broadsides are useless. And very shortly, the *Wolf of Tunis* will have us in range of their long guns."

Sullivan gaped. "The tribute vessel? Here?"

"Aye," panted Ryland, rubbing at a side ache. "You were right. In the storm. She was there. Following us."

"And we've fallen into a Barbary trap."

"Yes, and I need your help to get us free."

A fire ignited in Sullivan's eyes. "Then what are you waiting for? Open the door and let's get to work."

"First," said Ryland, pulling a key from his coat pocket, "I need to know why."

"This is hardly the time," Sullivan groaned.

"It's exactly the time. I need to know I can trust you if we're to save the ship. You could have told the captain about my…indiscretions. But you didn't. Why?"

"Lieutenant Ryland," said Sullivan, shutting his eyes. "For this fight, I am your man. Afterward, I'll answer questions, recount childhood memories, sing Irish ballads. Anything you want. *After* we've won."

Sullivan was right. The ship on the verge of capture and here was Ryland trying to satisfy his own curiosity. It was insane. And yet, he had to know. "You could have borne witness against me and gained the captain's favor. Continued your search. Why not do it?"

"I…I don't know. I didn't see a reason."

"Bullshit. Face a court-martial to save a pair of sodomites? No man would."

"Maybe *I* would."

Ryland pressed his face close to the cool iron bars. "*Why?*"

"Because," blurted Sullivan, practically climbing the door. "However unnatural it's said to be, your…affection, for Sawyer, seemed like a poor reason to hang a man."

All Ryland could do was blink. It was an impossible answer. Ryland would never think to try such an outlandish defense. And yet, it had the ring of simplicity. Of…truth.

"Ryland," said Sullivan.

"Hmm?"

"Kindly get the lock."

"Oh," Ryland said, remembering the key in his hand. "Of course."

The tines clattered in the tumblers. The door groaned open, and Sullivan sprang out. He stopped when he saw Ryland holding out two weapons. A short rapier with silver basketwork, and a matching naval dirk. "I fetched these from your dunnage," Ryland said.

Sullivan smiled. With a hint of an Irish accent, he said, "Thank you kindly, Lieutenant."

As the two men took off, hurrying under low beams, Ryland explained, "The *Philadelphia* is rudderless, so we'll need to kedge the ship. A boat will drop the anchor into position with a tow cable, then help the assault on the pirates." Ryland shuffled down an aisle of barrels, Sullivan right behind. "Meanwhile, I'll lead the effort to cut the grapple lines."

"And once the ship is free," said Sullivan, jogging up a ladder, "we use the kedge anchor to tow our broadside into range."

"And blow these pirates to splinters." Ryland dodged a group of crewmen carrying a wounded sailor. The man babbled deliriously as he went by, entrails poking through a slash in his belly.

"A good plan, sir," said Sullivan when they reached the next deck. Boots scraped on the planks above. The fighting had worsened. The din of battle resounded through every hatch. "I volunteer to join the boat crew."

"Sullivan…" said Ryland, coughing on smoke. "You're *leading* the boat crew. And their assault."

"Me?"

"I didn't break you out to plaster oakum, Midshipman." The lieutenant stopped at a hatch. With a foot on the steps, he faced Sullivan. "You up to it?"

"Aye, aye, sir," Sullivan declared. "You can count on me."

"Good."

As they continued on, Sullivan asked, "How did this happen, anyway?"

"Sabotage," answered Ryland. "*Mirborka* was on a collision course. The gunboats were on the beach as if under repairs. Next thing we knew, our rudder was gone, and the gunboats were launching from hidden sleds. I went below to fire bow chasers. Then everything went black. When I woke up, the galley was a flaming wreck, and the bow guns were disabled."

"Who could have helped the pirates?" said Sullivan as they reached the gun deck. He gaped at the smoldering remains of the galley.

They were at the aft hatch, forward of the captain's cabin. Ryland motioned to Sullivan. "The fire's out. Let's go."

But Sullivan's gaze swerved to the stern, towards gunshots and clashing steel. The melee in the captain's cabin had swelled. Half the gun crews had abandoned their posts to help their mates. Pirates were flowing aboard while feckless officers bickered. A mash of bodies hacking, clawing, and spitting.

Sullivan's grip tightened on his sword.

"On me, Sullivan," said Ryland. "They have their job. Hurry—there isn't much time."

Sullivan reluctantly followed.

They arrived on the quarterdeck to find pirates swarming over the forward half of the ship. Sailors, officers, and *Philadelphia's* full complement of Marines were locked in a brawl near the foremast. One corsair had a Marine pinned against the ship's bell, scimitar grinding against musket barrel. Bainbridge stood a few paces behind the action, barking orders. At the stern, sailors fired over the rail, trading shots with the gunboats. Several *Philadelphia* sailors lay dead at their feet.

Near the mizzenmast, Midshipman Cowan was yelling at his peer Merrick, his voice cracking. The cutter hung over the port side, with a crew of sailors ready to lower it down.

"Sullivan," said Ryland. "Get aboard the boat and take the tiller. Make ready while I deal with Cowan."

To Ryland, it looked like Sullivan had forgotten where he was. He was looking over the port side at one of the gunboats. Its deck had emptied of pirates—most of whom were likely aboard. Sullivan eyed the crimson Moroccan flag fluttering from the boat's mast.

"Sullivan!" snapped Ryland.

"Aye, sir," said Sullivan. He saluted and trotted toward the cutter.

Nearby, Merrick was scratching his head while his junior peer berated him. "But Mr. Ryland said—"

"Bugger Mr. Ryland," squeaked Cowan. "The *captain* said no boats are to launch!"

Michael Dufort, waiting with the rest of the boat crews, started to object. "You bratty little..." Old Man Meadows grabbed Dufort's arm, wisely pulling him back.

"Sully!" cried Dufort. "'Bout time!"

When the assembled boat crew saw Sullivan, they became a row of surprised faces. As they greeted him and clapped him on the back, they were like new men. For the first time in hours, they stood upright. They spoke with confidence.

"Midshipman Merrick," thundered Ryland as he approached. "Why isn't this boat launched?"

"Erm...Sir," stammered Merrick. "The captain's orders—"

"I've just come from the captain," Ryland lied. "Launch your boat immediately."

"The captain said no boats are to launch," shrieked the twelve-year-old Cowan.

Ryland rounded on Cowan, and the boy's eyes went wide. "You contradict me, Midshipman?"

"No, sir, but—"

"Then assist Mr. Merrick." Ryland could have left it at that, but Bainbridge had poisoned the officers against him, and enough was enough. He loomed over the petulant child, backing him off a step. "And if I ever hear you curse the name of a senior officer again, Midshipman, I'll have the bosun horse-whip your ass over a gun barrel. Am I understood?"

Cowan swallowed, head sinking into his shoulders. He nodded.

"Mr, Merrick," said Ryland. "Launch your boat."

"Right away, Lieutenant," Merrick snapped a salute and turned to the seamen manning the cables. "Haul away!"

"Sullivan, you're in command of..." Ryland trailed off. The tiller in the boat sat unmanned. Sullivan wasn't in the boat—or anywhere to be seen. "Where the hell's Sullivan?"

The boat crew returned blank stares. Merrick shook his head.

"There he is!" cried Dufort.

Ryland followed the seaman's pointing finger.

Midshipman John Sullivan, wearing nothing but his breeches, climbed atop the starboard rail. Life at sea had carved muscular lines across his body. He stood on the railing as if he were part of the ship—balance earned from years in the rigging. A thick belt ran from one shoulder to his other hip, strapping his sword to his back, his dagger to his waist. He cinched the buckle tight on his naked chest, his eyes lost in the crystalline water. The breeze washed auburn locks across his face.

"Sullivan!" called Ryland. But the word had no effect. In the fury of gunshots, cannon fire, and ringing swords, Sullivan stood with eerie calm.

Without a word, the shirtless midshipman sprang into a swan dive. Ryland strained over the bulwark for a look. Merrick's mouth hung open. Stunned sailors watched the descent. Dufort crowed and pumped a fist.

John Sullivan vanished beneath a cloud of bubbles.

Chapter 40

The USS *Philadelphia*
Under Attack off the Coast of Morocco
Friday, August 26ᵗʰ, 1803

John Sullivan glided through an oil-painted world. Five fathoms down, rust-colored seaweed papered over rock. A turquoise fish bolted by, racing against the current. The water felt like a bath gone cool. Bursts of sound were far away—the echoes of a dream. John peddled his feet, resisting the hunger of his lungs. As the last of his air bubbled toward the ocean surface, he grabbed onto a vertical shaft of rope. Hand over hand, he climbed.

The tranquil marine landscape vanished like a mirage. John breached the ocean surface into a world of roaring thunder and screaming men. He clung to the gunboat's anchor cable, gasping for air. Tucked up close to the rudder, there were no pirates to see him swimming at their water line. They would all be forward—near the fighting. As he had done with the last two cables, John slipped his dagger *Spade* from its sheath and started sawing through the cord. It was thick as a fist, but his edge was razor sharp. Threads came loose one after another. While he hacked through the rope, he cast a look over his shoulder.

The graceful enemy ship flitted over the waves less than two miles away, her sails carrying her like wings. The snow brig's black and red hull reflected the sun like satin. What a thing of beauty the young Samuel Humphreys had built. But her name was *Wolf of Tunis* now, and any minute the pirates would fire her guns at her former countrymen. She was yet another Barbary slave.

The rope parted, and the lower half of the anchor cable spiraled to the ocean floor. It was done. All three anchors were cut, and the pirates none the wiser— *Philadelphia's* stern was free. John pinched the blade between his teeth—a macho stunt Pavia disapproved of. John closed his eyes and took a deep breath, hanging from the remains of the severed rope. Aboard *Philadelphia,* he'd noticed this boat slip its moorings and start to drift. With the anchor gone, the tide was starting to carry it away. Now was John's chance. He felt guilty abandoning Ryland, but there wasn't time to explain.

John climbed. When he felt his hands on the boat's rail, he propped a foot on the rudder. He pushed up high enough to peek over the side. An empty deck, but for two pirates climbing aboard at the bow. One had a scar on his bald scalp, the other wore a bright red sash. The rest of the pirates were busy laying siege to *Philadelphia.* Scar and Red Sash walked in John's direction, no doubt to investigate the anchor. John slipped below the rail, patiently waiting.

With a hand on the boat and a foot dangling over the depths, John listened to the approaching footsteps. He had to let the enemy come to him. He reached over his shoulder and gripped the hilt of *Ace.* The steps were closer now. His heart raced as he felt the cool steel strapped to his back. Closer still. The rapier scraped a musical note as it slid free. He listened to the creaking of the deck boards as the enemy neared.

"Johnny," whispers Kaitlin. "What if they find us?"

A knee planted on the deck, and Scar's face appeared above John. Not a hair on the boy's chin—he was no more than seventeen. It took one interminable heartbeat for the pirate to recognize his foe. Could it truly be so easy? One thrust and a boy's world ends. Would John's hand really be his death?

"Mama!" Kaitlin cries as they drag her from Nora's arms. "Mama, I want to stay with you."

The shaft of metal flashed upward. A shudder of resistance as John pressed the point of *Ace* into Scar's chest, then it glided between the ribs like butter. Scar's eyes bulged in shock. Confusion. A soft gurgle aborted his scream. A glob of blood shot from his mouth and streaked John's face.

"Aleadui!" shouted Red Sash. It meant "enemy," as John remembered from his time in Tunis.

John seized Scar's hair and hauled on it like a rope. He used the corpse as a counterweight to launch himself onto the deck. The dead pirate plunked into the water. Red Sash pulled his pistol, cocked it—but it was too late. John sprang forward, *Ace's* length easily crossing the distance. Red Sash gasped as the sword sank into his gut. John snatched *Spade* from his own teeth and stuck the pirate's throat.

Sailors aboard *Philadelphia* raised a cheer.

John plucked his weapons free, leaving Red Sash to flop on the deck. A jet of air whistled by John's ear. Gunfire crackled. The corsairs on the next boat were firing and shouting in his direction. With the anchors cut, the boats were all drifting apart. He stooped low and scrambled for the bow. Musket balls snapped and chewed at his feet. He hit his knees behind the vessel's single 38-pound gun and snatched up the slow-burning cord nearby. The tide was carrying away the stern, and it was about to aim the gun at a dozen snarling pirates. John hid behind the carriage for a few seconds, until the cannon aligned. Then he stepped aside, plugged an ear, and lit the touchhole.

The report pounded John's body like a mallet. The gun carriage launched back. A group of the Moroccan attackers broke apart into severed limbs. Moans argued with screams. The smoke stung John's lungs. The carnage was shocking. He had expected the gun to carry a solid ball, but it must have been loaded with canister shot—a shell stuffed with some thirty pounds of shrapnel. It turned a patch of the enemy deck into a butcher's block.

"Hurrah!" came a round of cheers. John looked up to see his comrades gathering at the rails, fists in the air.

"Get 'em, Sully!" cried Melisande. The cutter had just gotten into the water and was rowing toward John. Melisande stood with one foot on the bow like a figurehead come to life. Her crazed cheers had the rest of the rowers laughing and hooting.

With the pirates momentarily off balance, John jumped up and sliced the last rope tethering the gunboat to its neighbor. The current carried the boat under *Philadelphia's* port guns.

"Ahoy, there!" called John to the sailors on the ship. He could pick out Ryland's face filing along behind them. "Catch this line." He tossed them a rope, which secured to a cleat on the gunboat.

Three sailors caught the cable, nearly dropping it in their fight to gain a hold.

If Lieutenant Ryland was angry with John, his astounded smile gave no sign. "Good show, Mr. Sullivan!"

John hailed the approaching cutter. "Dufort, Meadows, get aboard and tow our broadside into range."

"Aye, aye, sir," Meadows called back.

"Hang on, Sully!" called Melisande. "We'll pick you up."

But John's attention was already elsewhere. As he slid his blades back into their sheaths, he scanned the lead gunboat for the *re'is*. He found a long-bearded man snapping at his crew with a whip. From across the water, John and the pirate captain locked eyes. If hatred were explosive, the look they shared was a lit match.

John took a running dive into the water.

"Fire as you bear, Mr. Merrick," ordered Ryland.

"Fire as you bear!" roared Merrick at the assembled gun crews.

"Fire as you bear!" echoed the order from Midshipman Grove.

A staccato firestorm roared through the ship. The carronades fired their 32-pound slugs. The 18-pounders fired double-shots. Gun carriages ejected backward, straining at their ropes. Ryland felt the deck list to starboard with the mass recoil.

Through the square of the nearest gunport, Ryland watched the cannonballs rip into the *Mirborka's* hull, filling the air with smoke and woodchips.

When the last port gun fell silent, Ryland bellowed, "gun crews, to starboard."

With half the ship fighting the boarders, the gun deck had been shorthanded. Now the crew abandoned the spent cannons and raced to those on the other side. Each man took a station, as he'd been drilled to do a thousand times.

"Run 'em out!"

Pulleys wheezed as the sailors pulled the gun ropes. The cannons trundled through their ports.

Ryland looked over the shoulders of one of the gun crews. The name *"Deadcoat"* was chalked on the cannon barrel. Every man wore a slurry of sweat and soot, giving off a vinegar odor of exertion. Somehow, Ryland found it exhilarating. Through the portal, he saw the last gunboat still teaming with pirates. Their whip-wielding captain cursed and lashed them at random. But Ryland could deal with them later. His eyes were on the *Wolf of Tunis*, wearing around to the starboard tack.

Sullivan had done it. Cutting the gunboats' anchors, then using one of their own boats to tow the *Philadelphia* into position—inspired. And dangerous as hell. But Ryland could hardly argue with the results. Now they could lay their guns on all enemies at once.

Stepping back, Ryland ordered, "Long guns, fire!"

Another round of belching cannons. Geysers of white spray pocked the waves twenty yards short of the *Wolf of Tunis*. A few shots nipped a stay or chunk of hull. Ryland expected as much. He had intended to send a message. "Long guns, reload. Smashers, run out."

The crews were already sponging barrels or running out carronades when a call came from the quarterdeck hatch.

"Gun crews, cease fire," called Lieutenant Porter. "The enemy has struck. Cease fire."

They've struck, repeated Ryland to himself. A wave of cheers swept the deck. Men threw their kerchiefs in the air. Ryland started as a nearby sailor grabbed his forearm and shook vigorously.

The seaman quickly sobered his smile and said, "Erm, sorry, Mr. Ryland."

"Quite all right," smiled Ryland, touching his shoulder. "Well done, man."

A moment later, Ryland climbed onto the quarterdeck to find a spirit of celebration. Just as Porter had reported, the *Mirborka,* now floating alongside *Philadelphia,* had struck colors. The flag of Morocco had been run down.

"Look, sir," said a reedy, confident voice.

Ryland turned to find Gabriel Sawyer behind him. He wanted nothing so much as to kiss him right then and there. But enough men had died today. "Yes, Mr. Sawyer?"

Sawyer pointed to the *Wolf of Tunis,* already beating a path out of the bay. "Looks like the fight's gone out of them."

"Right you are!"

Sawyer gave a shy smile. Ryland loved that smile. For just a moment, they treated themselves to each other's eyes.

"How about it, then, scoundrels?" Bainbridge barked at the whip-wielding pirate. The enemy *re'is* had not surrendered his gunboat, and he scowled defiantly at the *Philadelphia's* captain. "Will you strike, or shall I shoot you to pieces?"

"If you do," said the enemy captain in broken English, "the one who betrays ship...you will not know him."

"Of all the insolent..." Bainbridge growled under his breath, flushing red. He yelled back, "name the saboteur, brigand, and perhaps we'll discuss terms."

"*Re'is* Harrak does not surrender. You let us go, we leave message with name."

"Unacceptable! I warn you, sir, I am a gentleman, but even a gentleman has his limits..."

Ryland's attention wandered as Bainbridge pontificated to *Re'is* Harrak. A little way down the deck, he noticed Ethan Auldon scanning the water, blood-stained hand shading his eyes.

"Mr. Auldon," murmured Ryland, sidling up to the surgeon's mate. "Where's Mr. Sullivan?"

"I was going to ask you, sir," Auldon frowned.

Ryland cast a look around, but there was no sign. A half-naked midshipman would've stood out. When Sullivan dove off the empty gunboat, Ryland assumed he'd climb aboard *Philadelphia*. "I haven't seen him. I'll send Merrick to..." Ryland trailed off as Auldon rushed to the starboard rail.

Ryland followed Auldon's gaze. There was a stir of movement on the gunboat, at the stern. An arm snaked up like a creature risen from the deep. A wet body slinked over the taffrail and onto the deck. The pirate crew were too busy watching Harrak argue with Bainbridge to notice the man creeping up behind them. The man left a dripping trail as he crept forward. He clawed his way atop the four-foot hatch awning. Ryland's mouth fell open.

John Sullivan perched on the enemy companionway like a panting beast.

Chapter 41

Barbary Pirate Gunboat
Off the Coast of Morocco
Friday, August 26th, 1803

For John Sullivan, it was an occasion to celebrate. Twenty thieving, slaving, murdering barbarians were scattered between him and the bow. Kaftans and sashes rippled in the wind. They clutched scimitars, daggers, and muskets. They had stolen gold and silver hooped through ears, beaded around necks, studded across knuckles. Just as they were that fateful day on the *Wandering Hart*. The canister shot had painted the decks in glittering ruby. Chunks of flesh were strewn like flower petals. Gunsmoke and butchery blew on the air. Maimed pirates whimpered below decks, their cries floating up from the hatch under his feet. The perfect scene for their joyous reunion.

Yes, thought John as he coiled his hands around his weapons. *It's been far too long.* Their first meeting had been tempestuous. Their time apart interminable. This chance encounter precious. In the rapture of the moment, a tear slipped John's eye. He slid his sword, *Ace,* and his dagger, *Spade,* from their sheaths. *Re'is* Harrak stopped braying at

Bainbridge. The *Philadelphia* crew were staring past Harrak, at John, and the pirates had taken notice. *Don't worry,* thought John, feeling a flush of heat. *We won't waste a second.*

John leaped off the companionway. *Re'is* Harrak and the rest of his mob turned around. For one eternal second, they gawked at the lone midshipman crouched on the deck. John was a scorpion poised to strike. He brandished *Spade* like a pincer and held *Ace* over his back like a stinger. Water slapped the hull. A gull cried. Weapons clicked and scraped.

John's feet pounded over the deck. His war cry was inhuman—the noise of a creature preying on its young.

His sword sank into the soft tissue of a stomach until the point landed on the hip bone. A broken-nosed pirate stared at John in shock, a cocked pistol fumbling from his grasp. Before it even hit the deck, John ripped the rapier free. He caught the next pirate's scimitar with his dagger, then brought *Ace* across another man's belly in a backhand arc. A bruised-face wretch flopped on his back, crying in panic as his innards slipped through his fingers.

"Bleed!" John hissed.

But John had spent the initial surprise, and the others were closing in. A stocky bull of a slaver rushed forward, crescent blade held high. *Ace* clanged off the scimitar, turning it aside. John pressed in and caught the next blow low on his sword as he fended off another pirate with his dagger. The bull slaver's sword locked with John's, their noses almost close enough to touch. John stuck his dagger in the Bull's neck, jabbing again and again like a pestle pounding a mortar. Velvet drops spurted from each cut, showering John's face with warm kisses. In the Bull's dying eyes, John saw himself wearing a smile.

Three of them came on now, circling John like a pack of craven dogs. He flitted away from a swing, tapped aside the next, darted back another stride. A scrawny boy, young in his teens, swung clumsily. An old man with long Viking hair prodded with his bayonet. A bold young man with a handsome cleft chin lunged forward. John parried their strikes and gave ground, leading them into the bottleneck between the companionway and the sea.

Viking's eyebrow twitched, and he jabbed. The bayonet might as well have been underwater. John darted past the musket and swiped with his dagger. Viking's jugular opened, and he slapped a palm to his neck, lifeblood gushing through his fingers. In the next beat, John cuffed Cleft Chin in the temple with his sword pommel, knocking him against the starboard rail. Scrawny raised his sword for a strike, but John kicked him in the gut. The boy staggered back.

In a daze from the pommel strike, Cleft Chin took a swing at John, but *Ace* slapped the weapon from his hand with a satisfying ring. Before John could make the killing thrust, he caught movement in the corner of his eye. He whirled just in time catch Scrawny's sword with his own.

"*La taqtal 'akhi!*" cried the scrawny boy.

On instinct, John thrust his dagger into Scrawny's stomach. John stared into the boy's mahogany eyes, pooling with tears. There was fear. Confusion.

What did you call me? wondered John. *'Christian dog?' 'Infidel?' 'Slave?'*

The boy slumped onto the deck. John spun around and sank his sword straight into Cleft Chin's heart. The young man's scimitar fell from his arm, raised for a strike that would never land. John withdrew his blade, and Cleft Chin fell backward, his body dumping into the sea. Now pirates were closing in on all sides.

And to think—the night is young. John wrote his delight in a row of teeth.

He barreled into the crowd and thrust his rapier through a burly pirate's thigh, cutting it free with a backhand stroke. Blood gushed from an artery, soaking through Burly's loose breeches. A gently curved scimitar swished toward John, and he parried with his dagger. *Ace* and *Spade* launched into a whirlwind, trilling soprano notes as they fought off multiple blows. Something swatted the meat of John's calf. It felt like a thorny branch. John found a crimson-robed pirate behind him. Crimson-Robe had spent his momentum on a harmless scratch, and his eyes went wide as *Ace* slashed open his gullet. John snipped a second pirate's hamstring with his dagger. His rapier severed the sword hand of a third. John rounded on a fourth—and froze.

A pirate with a thick goatee looked at John down the barrel of a pistol. The hammer struck. The barrel fired. John flinched. John's heart was racing—but he was still standing. The bullet missed.

John lunged and speared *Ace* right through Goatee's gaping mouth. He leaped back, a bayonet missing his side by inches. He spun *Ace* over his back just in time to catch a blow from behind. A kick swept his feet out from under him.

Sprawled on his back, half a dozen pirates glaring down at him, it was the end for John. Or would have been. *Ace* whispered cleanly through the mainsheet. The gunboat's triangular sail snapped taut as it filled with wind, and the boom whipped over John's head. The wooden beam swept through the pirates like a scythe reaping wheat. John scrambled to his feet.

A pirate with dark eyeliner and a jewel-encrusted saber slashed at John's belly. John parried and riposted, but Eyeliner flicked away the blow. The pirate gave an arrogant smile. John cut, Eyeliner parried, and John's right foot slipped in greasy viscera. A stroke of bad luck—the chain shot had left this patch of deck slick with blood. John landed on his side in the gory muck. Eyeliner brought his sword down like a butcher knife, but John caught it with his sword, the two blades grinding against one another. John held off the saber with both hands, Eyeliner forcing it down with brute strength. Spit flew from John's teeth. He pressed with all the mad fury in his chest, but the enemy blade was inching ever closer to his neck.

"Koo-*yiii*!" cried a voice as shrill as a hawk's. A wooden club, shaped like the beak of a raven, thudded on Eyeliner's head. A foot kicked the stunned attacker aside. As if stepping out of a dream, Melisande crouched over John, offering him a hand. "On your feet, Sully!"

There was a crackle of gunfire as Melisande pulled John up. Over his shoulder, he saw Marines firing at the pirates from *Philadelphia*. Several pirates dropped. Melisande wove through the enemy, war club crunching bones, copper dagger slicing tendons. John saw Eyeliner crawling for the port side, long hair soaked with blood, and he dashed after.

A pot-bellied pirate aimed a pistol at John, but Melisande's war club smashed it from his hand. Pot-belly threw his arms around Melisande to trap her. She kneed his bullocks, then jabbed him in the side with her dagger. She fell to the deck, her war club spinning to John's feet. Seeing Melisande disarmed, John slid *Ace* over to her. She snatched it up just in time to let a charging pirate fall on the point. John picked up Melisande's war club, grabbed Eyeliner, and turned him over on his back.

Eyeliner looked up in a daze. John pinned him against the bulwark, watching the horror creep into his eyes. The war club came down. Eyeliner's throat staved in, and he gulped for air like a beached flounder.

"Choke," John rasped.

A shadow fell over John. A boot hit his side. He tumbled, back landing against the rail. *Re'is* Harrak towered over him, blotting out the noon sun. The pirate captain raised his gold-trimmed scimitar high. John grasped for a weapon but found none. It was over.

A musket ball ripped out of the pirate captain's chest, the gun's report echoing a half-second later. The scimitar clattered to the deck. John scrambled out of the way as the enemy captain fell to his knees. From just off the starboard bow of the gunboat, Ethan Auldon stood in the cutter, his smoking musket aimed at Harrak. As John rose to his full height, he saw the remaining handful of pirates kneeling on the deck, hands raised in surrender. The *re'is* made a wet growl as he glared up at John, a hand clutching his bleeding chest.

Surrender? thought John. *Oh no. None of you get to surrender.* He snatched up the fallen scimitar, wrapping both hands around the hilt. He raised it high over *Re'is* Harrak's head.

"Die!" John bellowed.

And the scimitar went to its bloody work. The first blow glanced off Harrak's skull, taking a swatch of scalp. John swung again, and again. He thought of every time his Barbary masters caned his feet. Every tear he shed in the dark. Every nightmare that haunted his sleep. The anguish of five long years. He poured it all into every impact. Even when the *re'is* flopped down, head reduced to offal, John kept swinging. Until he lacked the strength. Until…

"John!" The word echoed across the bay like a church bell.

As if waking from a dream, John stopped. The gore-caked scimitar clattered to the deck. John looked at Ethan, panting with exertion.

Where there had been cacophony a moment ago, now there was only silence. Hundreds of *Philadelphia's* sailors, Marines, and pirate captives all looking in the same direction. All with the same shocked stare. They didn't so much as cough. Even the wind seemed to die. Chester Ryland blinked at the lone midshipman standing on the enemy gunboat. John Sullivan stared at the *Philadelphia* crew as if uncertain where he was. *Who* he was. His matted hair, his streaked face, his dripping chest, his stained breeches. Every inch of him. Sullivan was a nightmare glazed in blood.

"John," said Ethan Auldon. He was in the cutter, which had just rowed up to the gunboat. He stepped over the side, medical bag in hand. "It's all right, mate." Auldon moved slowly, as one might approach a wild horse about to bolt.

Sullivan stood there panting, eyes fixed on the surgeon's mate. Blood bubbled from a gunshot wound in his side. He didn't seem to notice the scimitar slash across his back. And with his right calf split open, Ryland couldn't fathom how the midshipman was still standing.

Auldon touched Sullivan's arm, his voice barely

audible. "It's all right, John. It's over."

Finally showing a sign of lucidity, Sullivan nodded. His breathing slowed. Officers and seamen looked on, silent and stock still.

"Let's hear it, lads," cried Michael Dufort. He jumped on the boom of the gunboat like a jolly tar. "Three cheers for Bloody Sully!"

There was the briefest second of doubt when Ryland wondered if the men would reply.

"Hip-hip," shouted Midshipman Merrick.

"Hooray!" thundered hundreds of sailors.

"Hip-hip…"

"Hooray!" cheered even more of the crew.

"Hip-hip…"

"Hooray!" Their fists were in the air now, and they broke into hollering and clapping.

Ryland exchanged an uneasy look with a few officers, but the rest joined in the applause. Slowly, the cheering resolved into something more synchronous. A word. A chant.

"Sull-y…Sull-y…Sull-y…"

Dufort chanted loudest of all.

In the midst of that deafening fanfare, John Sullivan squinted as if he'd crawled out of a cave in the earth. Then his eyes rolled back in his head, and he collapsed in Ethan Auldon's arms.

Chapter 42

The USS *Philadelphia*
The Mediterranean Sea
Sunday, August 28th, 1803

A breeze ruffled the sails. A wake bubbled away astern. *Philadelphia* had a northerly wind at her back, and the yards groaned with full canvas. At this speed, the ship would make Gibraltar within the day. Ethan Auldon thought it an oddly pleasant afternoon for such a grim ritual. Most of the crew stood at attention on the spar deck. A few were posted in the rigging. All two hundred and eighty-three men—and one woman in disguise—bowed heads with hats off. Twenty-two of their fallen brothers lay on boards along the port rail. Each of their bodies was wrapped in canvas, their feet propped on the railing, their heads supported by a two-man detail. Occasionally a gull cried, or a man coughed. The surf whooshed at the waterline. Otherwise, the ship was silent.

"We therefore commit their bodies to the deep," intoned Captain William Bainbridge, reading from the ship's prayer book, "to be turned into corruption, looking for the resurrection of the body, when the sea shall give up her dead…"

Ethan should have been joining in the prayer, thinking of the fallen. But he couldn't get the images out of his head. A seaman in the surgeon's cockpit screaming as Ethan sawed through his leg. One moment the man's eyes had been living windows to the soul, the next lifeless gelatin. He recalled John Sullivan covered in blood, a madman drunk on killing. But worst of all, he kept replaying the moment in his mind when he followed Dr. Cowdery aboard the captured pirate brig *Mirborka*. The moment when he entered *Re'is* Harrak's cabin. Three naked, bruised, emaciated women chained to bolts in the deck. All three with strikingly similar looks—young, with long brown hair and dark eyes. All three cowering in terror.

"...and the life of the world to come, through our Lord Jesus Christ..."

It had taken an hour to gain the trust of the enslaved women. To explain to them that they were free. One spoke Spanish, which the others appeared to understand. Luckily, Ethan had picked up enough from Pavia to communicate. Cowdery had been remarkable, talking calmly and compassionately. Meanwhile, Ethan had applied poultices to their wrists and ankles, worn raw by the shackles. There were other wounds—older wounds. Bundles of scar tissue. Lacerations scabbed over. Angry pink burns. But the worst wounds they wore within. Ethan recognized the look in their eyes. The fear, the shame...the resignation. He had seen that look before. On the Tindall Plantation.

"...who at his coming shall change our vile body, that it may be like his glorious body, according to the mighty working whereby he is able to subdue all things unto himself." Bainbridge snapped the book closed. "Amen."

"Amen," Ethan repeated with the crew, making the sign of the cross.

The boatswain blew his pipe. The silver whistle sang a somber note, went high, then low again. Each two-man team, going aft one-by-one, lifted their board. One by one, each shrouded corpse slid feet first over the side and plunged into the sea. And twenty-two men and boys began a journey to their final place of rest.

Lieutenant Porter dismissed the crew, and the assembled men began filing back to their duties. Ethan had a long day of rounds to make, so he headed for the main hatch. At least tending to wounds might take his mind off things. As he walked along the port gangway, the sound of shouting from below drew his eyes to the large square opening in the spar deck. Between the boats nested on their cradles, he could see through to the gun deck, where forty pirates kneeled or sat. Rows of five were daisy-chained together by the hands and feet, kept under heavy guard. The shouts came from a pair of Marines, beyond the patch of sunlight. They were cursing at one of the prisoners, who cowered at their feet. Ethan hurried to the steps.

"Fucking vermin!" said Private Williams.

"God, but he stinks!" added Private Burling, holding his kerchief over his nose.

As Ethan reached the deck, he found the prisoner on all fours, at the mercy of the two Marines. The captive's skin was drawn and deeply lined, probably by age and malnourishment. A tangled salt-and-pepper beard buried his face. One of his earlobes was barely more than a lump of flesh, as if it hand been torn off. Blood and spittle crusted around his mouth. Grime colored his patchwork robe like an old bandage. The man crawled forward, groping at Williams' boot, mumbling something.

"Don't touch me, scum!" said Williams, kicking the old man in the side. "Make slaves of us, will you?" The second kick was harder, and the old captive made a rattling gasp. The other pirates paid the scene little mind, content to be left out of the matter.

"Please," said the man, in a Turk accent. "I am not a pirate. I am a slave. I only ask for water."

"Is that right?" said Burling. "Your water's all over my boot." His fist thudded into the prisoner's back, knocking him down.

"Enough!" said Ethan. "This man is our prisoner."

The two Marines glared at Ethan. "Watch it, Auldon," said Williams, narrowing his eyes. "I don't like your tone."

"There's no need to beat a man for thirst."

"He pissed on my shoes," griped Burling. "A beating's the least he should get."

"You are men of honor," said Ethan. "Patriots, out here to defend American sailors—not beat unarmed prisoners. You're better men than this."

Williams scowled and took a step forward. "And just who do you think you are—"

Burling put a hand on Williams' shoulder. "Easy there. The old blighter's had his lesson. Gordon wants us astern anyway."

Williams looked like he might protest but then relented. "Yeah, all right." He followed the other private, but not before hawking spit at the prisoner.

Ethan breathed a sigh of relief. He offered a hand to the prisoner. "I apologize for your ill-treatment."

A pair of murky green eyes, verging on yellow at the center, looked up at Ethan. "Thank you," said the man.

Ethan helped the prisoner back into his row, chains rattling on the deck as he moved. When the old man was seated, Ethan said, "I will see that some water is brought to you and the others."

"You are very kind." For all the man's decrepitude, his eyes flickered with energy.

Ethan nodded and headed to the berth deck. He felt the man watching as he walked away. It was a relief when he reached Cowdery's quarters—away from the pirates. He filled his medicine bag with supplies, trying to forget the episode. Ethan's faith called him to treat captives with dignity—even slavers—but that didn't mean he enjoyed it. In truth, a part of him understood Burling and Williams. The same part that pulled the trigger on Whitlock. He snapped the medicine cabinet shut, as if to lock away his vengeful thoughts, and carried his medicine bag to the wardroom. He tapped on the door.

"*Como estas?*" asked a soft, feminine voice.

"It's the surgeon's mate, Ethan Auldon." Ethan cleared his throat and straightened his waistcoat. Since their rescue, the three women hadn't wanted to see anyone but him or Cowdery. He had somehow gained their trust, and he didn't aim to lose it. "I've come with fresh bandages. I can come back later."

"*Puede entrar.*"

The door to the officers' room swung open. Only a small candelabrum flickered on the table, wrapping most of the room in darkness. Chicken bones, wedges of cheese, and scraps of bread littered a few plates. Wine breathed in a trio of glasses. They were generous contributions from the officers' private supplies. A large wooden basin steamed with hot water on the far side. In the half-light, Ethan could make out the youngest of the women, Sofia, soaking in the bath. The pleasant aroma of lavender permeated the air—a gift from Melisande's bandolier bag. Still, the odor of sweaty stockings and damp peacoats wasn't easily banished. The bravest and eldest of the three liberated women, Esmeralda, gently lathered Sofia's hair. A door to one of the officer's compartments hung open, where a third woman slept in a hammock. The rhythm of the ship rocked her gently.

"I brought new bandages," said Ethan in Spanish, careful to avert his eyes. He had to speak slowly, translating the words in his mind. He couldn't believe they'd invited him in with Sofia in a bath. Perhaps they trusted him more than he realized. "Do you have all that you need?"

"*Sí, Gracias,*" Esmeralda replied. "Please, come." She beckoned him over.

Nervously, Ethan approached, trying to find anything but a naked woman to occupy his eyes. He knelt down and inspected the bandages on Esmeralda's wrist. "I can...help with these."

Esmeralda turned to Ethan with a faint smile, showing him the melted flesh that had closed her left eye forever. Ethan could only imagine what sadistic reason Harrak might have had to mutilate her so. His heart pounded. Long brunette hair fell across her cheeks, her eyes, her slender neck. Her scars didn't change the fact she was the most beautiful woman he'd ever met. She said, "thank you, *Señor* Ethan. You have a generous *alma.*"

"I'm sorry, I didn't catch that last word."

Sofia looked up from the bath. "Soul," she translated. In broken English, she said, "You have a generous soul."

Ethan met Sofia's eyes, his heart aching to see an old cut across her cheek. He replied in Spanish, "It's...the least I could do."

"*Veo en ti la luz de Dios.*" Esmeralda said. In English, it meant, "I see in you the light of God."

Meeting Esmeralda's gaze was like watching an aurora. Ethan never wanted to look away. But he busied himself with his medical bag. "Let me see to those bandages."

"*Re'is* Harrak…" said Esmeralda as she let Ethan unwrap her wrist. "He is dead?"

"*Muerto,*" confirmed Ethan.

"Do you know the man who killed him?"

The sight of John hacking the pirate captain's head into a wet pulp flashed through Ethan's mind. He shuddered, still able to hear John's screams—like the wails of a rabid animal. "Yes, I know him."

Esmeralda's expression hardened. The look of a woman who'd seen Harrak's death many times in her mind's eye. "Thank him. For me."

Chapter 43

The USS *Philadelphia*
The Port of Gibraltar, British Imperial Colony
Sunday, August 28th, 1803

John drifted through a world of pain and shadow. He felt as though he'd been dragged to the bottom of a lake. He would look up and see the moon reflected on the distant surface, but no matter how he swam, he could never reach the light. Ferocious creatures harried him from the murk, dragging him down. He could feel their barbed grip digging into his flesh. Brine stung his wounds. He swam, and swam, desperate to escape. In this terrible place, his dreams always twisted into nightmares. Memories always brought heartache. In the end, he would want to sink into those dark depths, where dwelt the monsters.

But then, he would see her.

Shadows flicker on the walls of the wigwam. Dominique sits by the fire, running an old wooden brush through her hair. She's humming a song John doesn't recognize. His eyes trace down her slender back, from the rumor of her ribs to the curve of her bum. John slips his arms around her, and she smiles. He feels the warmth as their naked bodies touch. They're both wearing a sheen of sweat, their muscles slack with euphoria.

"What's that tune?" John asks.

"Something my mother sang to me," Dominique murmurs. "When she brushed my hair."

"It's beautiful." John smiles and kisses her neck. "You're beautiful. I want to be with you, Dom. This night, and every night."

Dominique turns around, locks of golden hair falling over her breasts. Her skin has a rosy glow in the firelight. Embers dance in her eyes. "I'm not going anywhere, Sully."

She touches his face. He tastes her lips. For the first time in years, he feels peace.

Light scratched open John's eyes. He awoke in a hammock, to the creaking of a ship. A blinding glow above him dimmed into the form of a lantern. He smelled the stench of dried blood. Flies buzzed around his ears and crawled on the bandages wrapping his stomach. John lifted his arm to swat at them, only to abort the attempt in agony. The monsters had been a dream, but the pain of their claws was all too real. A talon dug a trench across his back. A tusk bored through his abdomen. Incisors chewed at the meat of his calf. He wanted to squirm and crawl away, but they would only follow.

Hello? Where am I? John meant to say. The words came out as a moan.

"You're awake," said a soft voice.

John turned his head and saw Ethan sitting beside his hammock, reading a book on anatomy. From that small movement, John felt heat and agony flash through every muscle. "Ergm," he gurgled, his voice scraping his throat like a blade. He tried again, managing to rasp, "Ethan?"

"Aye, mate," Ethan said. His russet eyes looked tired. "It's me."

"I'm alive?" John's voice came more evenly.

"You meet the definition, yes." Ethan snapped the book shut and leaned forward. "After I stitched you with enough thread to loom a quilt. Twenty-centimeter laceration across your back—nearly to the muscle. Your calf cleaved half to the bone. A musket ball through the flesh at your waist. At least you weren't wearing a shirt— Dr. Cowdery might have killed you trying to dig out a scrap of cotton. You bled your wounds clean, but almost to your demise. You've been out for a day. I didn't know if your eyes would ever open again."

"The pirates..." John said. The battle came crashing into his memory. The foreign words of a scrawny boy. The words were playing over and over in his mind, though he knew not their meaning.

"Yes, 'the pirates,'" Ethan griped. "What the hell were you thinking?"

"The ship was in danger."

"No, John. The ship was out of danger. *Before* you climbed aboard a boat full of the enemy and tried to take them on single-handed. You were almost killed. If your wounds fester, you might be yet."

"But...we won?"

"Yes, we won," said Ethan. He looked down at his book. For a moment he didn't speak, his brow trembling. "I almost lost you."

John saw the worry in his friend's eyes. He murmured, "I'm sorry, Ethan."

Ethan shook his head. "Nah, don't say that." He managed a brief smile. "Gave me a scare, is all."

"A quilt..." John rasped. "You don't loom it. You sew it."

Ethan chuckled. "Really? A quip about looming? Of

course that's what you say to me. And how would you know anyway?"

John chuckled to himself. He felt the pockets of his breeches, then the sides of the hammock. He broke into a panic, terrified his mother's watch had gone to the ocean floor. Then a silver object caught the light. Ethan dangled his mother's watch overhead.

"I kept it safe for you, mate," said Ethan. He dropped it into John's hand.

John breathed a deep sigh. "Thanks, mate."

"I have something else for you." Ethan pulled a paper from the pages of his book. As he unfolded it, he said, "Lieutenant Ryland drew this from memory. He hoped it might be helpful."

Ethan held up the sketch for John to study. A courtyard paved in red sandstone, enclosed by walls with elegant horseshoe windows. Rows of palm trees, grape vines climbing lattice, and flowering bushes growing on either side of a cobbled path. The path stretched toward a gated arch. The jagged edges of a ruined tower poked above the wall. Growing out of the tower, the limbs of a massive sycamore tree blotted out the sky.

"The lair of the Silver Hand," John whispered, taking the drawing. "Just as he described."

"Anything that can help you find them?"

John crumpled the drawing. "No."

Another long pause passed between them. Then Ethan said, "You talked a lot in your sleep. You were calling out Dominique's name."

"I was?" said John, playing dumb.

Ethan got a glint in his eye. "I get the feeling it was a pleasant dream."

John smirked. "Forget it, mate. A gentleman doesn't

tell. Whatever happened, you'll have to settle for your imagination."

Ethan shrugged. "Can't fault a man for trying."

They shared a quiet laugh.

"Well, she gave you something to fight for," Ethan added. "I'm glad."

John stared up at the deck beams. He wished he could tear those nights of bliss out of his memory. If only to spare himself the pain of losing her.

"There's something else I wanted you to know," Ethan went on. "That *re'is* you killed—Harrak—his slaves…In his cabin, we found…" Ethan's voice turned hoarse.

"Found what?"

"There were three women, kept as concubines. He hurt them. Bad." Ethan scratched at the binding of his book.

Anger surged through John's muscles, worsening the pain. He wanted to kill Harrak a second time.

Ethan went on, "Because of the *Philadelphia* and her crew, they're free. Because of you. We're caring for them in the wardroom. I thought you should know."

Not wanting to invoke more pain, John gave a nod.

"You saved the ship, John. The whole crew's taken to calling you Bloody Sully. You're a hero. Well, most of them think so. Grove wanted you court-martialed for punching him, but the men would have thrown him overboard if he tried."

"Really?" John said.

Ethan smiled. "Really. He even went to Bainbridge and withdrew his charge. You're free and clear. Lucky as always."

"I don't feel lucky," John said with a wince.

They shared a chuckle, causing John another bolt of pain. "Hero, eh?" said John. "What do you think, mate?"

Ethan looked as though he would answer, until they heard the sound of the ship's bell. A chorus of bells from other ships followed. "Oh," said Ethan. "We docked an hour ago. We're in Gibraltar. I've been offered shore leave, but I'll be staying aboard to look after you."

"Thanks, mate. But you should go. I'll be okay."

"It's all right. I've been looking forward to some peace and quiet on the ship anyway. Men will be going ashore, and they'll be moving the prisoners. Peace and quiet for me to study."

"Prisoners?"

"Aye, from the battle. Dozens of pirates from the *Mirborka* and the *Celia*."

John blinked. He pulled open the crumpled drawing and studied the palatial garden. The view of a gate and a tree told John nothing, but what if someone had seen this view from the other side? A native of the Barbary Coast perhaps? His eyes went wide. "Prisoners..." John closed his fist on the paper. He sat up, his stomach feeling like it might tear apart.

"John, what are you doing?" said Ethan rising to his feet. "Don't try to get up."

"I have to," growled John, his face twisted with agony. His muscles had warmed up a little now, and he managed to dump himself out of the hammock. The floor was only a couple feet below, but the deck hit him like a mallet. "Argh...Goddamnit all to hell..."

"Are you mad? You need bed rest. Where the Hell do you think you're going?"

John pushed himself to his feet, drawing clutched in his fist. He shambled like a hunchback. "Can't stay. Have to go." John lost his balance, but Ethan swooped in and caught him.

Ethan slung his patient's arm over his shoulders. "For God's sakes," said Ethan, "you're being held together by stitches. You lost a lot of blood. Without rest, you could take ill and die. This is serious, John!"

"Aye, it is, mate," John said, looking at Ethan. "I know how to find Katie."

Chapter 44

The USS *Constitution*
The Port of Gibraltar, British Imperial Colony
Monday, August 29th, 1803

The music of an orchestral quintet floated off the deck of the USS *Constitution*. Dominique Dufort walked along the dock with her husband, hand on his arm, admiring the mighty frigate. Lanterns lit the towering masts and spars, strung beneath furled sails. Red, white, and blue streamers adorned the black and white hull. The smell of sizzling beef wafted out of the galley. Well-dressed revelers mingled near the taffrail, above bright stern windows. Their laughter echoed across the water. Ships usually looked the same to Dominique, but the *Constitution* was notably larger than the *Philadelphia* and dwarfed the *Allegheny*. She couldn't deny a certain awe looking at the powerful United States flagship.

"Now remember," said Aubert. He tugged her elbow as they neared the ramp onto the *Constitution*. "I went to great lengths to get us at Commodore Preble's table. Be radiant. Be charming. *Do not* be impertinent."

"Really, Richard," sighed Dominique, "If I'm such an embarrassment, send me back to the *Allegheny*."

Dominique hoped he wouldn't call her bluff. It took hours to curl her hair into perfect spirals. She was wearing her pearls and white rose perfume. She'd carefully selected a flax yellow gown, and it gleamed in the *Constitution's* lamplight. More than being a waste, if she spent another miserable night cooped up on the *Allegheny*, she might go insane.

Aubert pivoted and jerked her toward him. "Nonsense. You are my wife, and you belong at my side. But I've put up with rather a lot of your antics over the last few months. Flirting with brag players, sneaking off to smoke, frittering away ten dollars' worth of our private stores—I've born it all with grace. I've only got one shot at the tribute assignment, and I haven't the time for one of your mercurial moods."

"Mercurial?" Dominique tugged her arm free. "I've done nothing but support you since we left home. You're the one always busy with secret work."

"I am securing our future, and that isn't a wife's concern. Keeping her lips off other men, however, *is.*"

"I gave a sailor a harmless peck on the cheek!" objected Dominique.

"You bought the rabble off with trinkets."

Dominique decided to swallow her pride and turn up the charm. Maybe she could shake him out of this irritable mood. She slipped her hands around his back. "Richard, darling, I meant no harm. I only wanted the crew to see you as I do—a respected commander. A captain to be revered." She saw his eyes tracing down her corset, and she poured on the seduction. "A formidable...just..." She drew her lips closer, and his eyes slipped closed. "...potent man."

Aubert's fingers slid through her hair. He inhaled her

scent and kissed her hungrily. She could hear the desire in his breath as if he might take her right there on the dock. When he pulled away, he looked at her with intoxicated eyes. "You are…a maddening woman."

"That's why you married me, *mon trésor*," she said, showing him the line of her neck.

"God help me, it is," sighed Aubert. A smile cracked his lips. "Shall we, Mrs. Aubert?"

Dominique took his arm, and they boarded the *Constitution*. Two Marines flanked the gangway, wearing bright red coats and blue sashes, muskets shouldered. Aubert proudly escorted Dominique before a row of senior officers. She curtseyed and greeted each man. Guests of the party looked on curiously, whispering over champagne flutes. Servants roamed the deck with trays of lamb cutlets.

"Captain Aubert," said Commodore Edward Preble, gripping Aubert's hand. The captain of *Constitution* and commander of the U.S. fleet cut an impressive figure in his gold-trimmed admiral's coat. His close-cropped hair and booming voice suggested a man of granite will. "I've been looking forward to meeting the man who rid us of the Laffites."

"Thank you, Commodore," said Aubert. "But arresting a few smugglers is hardly cause for boasting. I was merely doing my duty."

"You're too modest, Captain," thundered Preble. "I'll need men of action to stop the Barbary Pirates." Preble's eyes wandered in Dominique's direction as if pulled by an invisible force. "And this must be Mrs. Aubert."

"Yes, of course," said Aubert. "May I present my wife, Dominique Aubert."

"It's a pleasure to meet you, Commodore," said Dominique with a regal curtsey.

The commander of the fleet took up her white-gloved hand. "Young lady, the pleasure is all mine." He planted a kiss. "You are a vision. Wherever did Aubert find you?"

"The frontier, Commodore." It was Dominique's sorest subject, but she could see Commodore Preble's fascination. She couldn't let an opportunity go to waste. "During the war, my parents were killed by Mohawks and Seneca at Cherry Valley. My sister and I were taken in by friendly Tuscaroras."

Aubert gave an uncomfortable sigh. "It's a long story, sir."

Preble blinked at Aubert, then at Dominique. "One I should very much like to hear. You lived among the Iroquois tribes? How intriguing."

"Richard rescued me, you see," said Dominique, "from a hard life on the frontier. Brought me back to civilization. He doesn't like to boast, Commodore, so I must say on his behalf: He's a man of great honor. It's why I fell in love with him."

"So he is," smiled Preble. "Please my dear, call me Edward." He looked at Aubert. "Captain, you're a very lucky man."

Aubert looked at Dominique, beaming from the compliment. "Aye, sir. I certainly am."

"Not so much lucky as determined," said a jovial French accent. The man approaching wore a white cut-across coat and the eternally blasé smile of a nobleman. "Richard Aubert always gets his prize."

A woman in a red gown hung on the man's arm. She was younger than her companion, with porcelain skin and effervescent eyes. In the same accent, she said, "Even as a boy, he had all the best toys." She bubbled with laughter.

"Ah, Captain Aubert," Preble said stiffly. "May I present the Marquis Sebastien Larocque, and his lovely wife, the Marquise Angele Larocque. Though, I suspect you're already acquainted."

"We are, Commodore," said Aubert. He accepted a kiss on each cheek, first from Angele, and next from Larocque. "Our families were close before the Reign of Terror."

"Oh, Richard!" said Angele, taking both of Dominique's hands, "your letter mentioned her beauty, but I had no idea." The marquise fawned over Dominique as if she were an adorable child. "It is so good to meet you, Dominique, my dove."

"The pleasure is mine," Dominique replied, hoping she wasn't blushing.

"The marquis owns a large merchant concern out of Marseille," said Preble. "He's kindly offered to resupply our fleet at a generous discount."

"I must admit to a little self-interest," said Larocque. He explained to Dominique, "Ours is but a small fleet. The French Navy is occupied with the English, so we find our convoys with scant protection. It speaks well of your young country that your Navy should offer us aid."

"Such a dashing man, your admiral," said the marquise, hooking her arm with Preble's. She ran a finger along his chin. "And such strong features. I should be very grateful for a dance."

Preble smiled, though more as if from indigestion than flattery. "Ah, yes. I'm sure I could be persuaded." His face lit up—perhaps with relief—when he saw the next guest approach. "Why, it's the man of the hour! Welcome aboard, Captain Bainbridge."

All eyes fell on the newcomer. The captain of the *Philadelphia* sauntered forward in formal naval dress, smiling proudly as he shook the commodore's hand. "It's an honor, Commodore Preble," said Bainbridge. "Captain Aubert, Mrs. Aubert," he said, greeting each of them in turn.

After a few more introductions, Preble said, "Only three days ago, Captain Bainbridge won an impressive victory. Under his command, the *Philadelphia* repelled a savage attack from the Barbary Pirates." Preble pointed toward a nearby wharf, where two new ships were docked. "The *Celia* and the *Mirborka*—his two prizes of war."

"Very impressive, Captain," said Aubert. His lips smiled, but in his eyes, Dominique saw chagrin.

"Good of you to say, Aubert," sniffed Bainbridge. "But really, it was a modest skirmish. I kept a cool head and applied sound strategy, just as our commodore would have done. If the officers of our fleet rise to similar caliber, and I believe they will, Tripoli will be defeated in short order."

"Well said," agreed Preble. He gestured to a servant, and soon they each held a glass of champagne. The commodore raised his flute. "A toast. To Captain Bainbridge. May his courage be an example to us all."

"Hear hear," said a chorus of voices. Aubert's voice came in last when the glasses were already clinking.

"Well, then." Preble swept a hand toward the *Constitution's* cabin. "Shall we find our seats?"

Over the next couple hours, the steward's crew served dinner to an assembly of officers, envoys, officials, and ladies. Most ate al fresco, but Dominique and her husband were among the honored guests in the cabin, at

Commodore Preble's table. They dined on a parade of delicacies, among them suckling pig, dark brown bread, oysters, chowder, and plum pudding. Dominique spent most of the time whispering or laughing with Angele, delighted to have the company of another woman after long weeks at sea.

After dessert, the dinner party moved up to the quarterdeck where the orchestra played a waltz.

"You really are a marvelous dancer," said Preble as he and Dominique glided to the music.

"Thank you, Edward," Dominique said with a shy smile. She'd been away from polite society for a month. It was exhilarating—and nerve-wracking—to be back. "As are you."

"Please," scoffed Preble. "I've stepped on your feet three times. But I appreciate you humoring an old salt."

They shared a chuckle. Dominique swept a spiral of hair from her brow.

"I can't imagine what it must have been like for you," said Preble. "To be orphaned on the frontier, alone amongst the Indians."

"It wasn't always so bad." Dominique felt her stomach in a vice. The memories were painful, but at the moment, useful. "Truthfully, I don't remember much about the attack. I used to have nightmares. I would wake up in the middle of the night, screaming. *Maman* Fawn would hold me and sing to me until I fell asleep. After a time, the dreams went away."

"They gave you a good home," said Preble. "You miss them, don't you?"

"I suppose I do," said Dominique. "Especially my brother, Grey Feather. But I wouldn't give up my new life with Richard."

"I imagine not," murmured Preble, his voice soft against the music of the quintet. "Still, you and your sister were lucky to be adopted by good people. Your Indian family will always be a part of you."

"Yes, they will," said Dominique, feeling herself blush. "I don't know what I would have done without Richard. He's a good man. He saw me wandering the market, destitute and alone, and fell in love. He said where other men saw dust, he saw a diamond."

"If Captain Aubert's choice in wife is any indication, he is a man of singular virtue." Preble gave Dominique a fatherly smile. His expression twisted suddenly into a grimace, and he doubled over.

"Commodore!" said Dominique. "Are you all right?"

"It's nothing," said Preble, waving her off. He managed to straighten himself again, but his smile couldn't hide his piqued color. "Just my stomach, dear. It acts up from time to time. I'll be fine. Could you forgive me if I rested a spell?"

"Of course," smiled Dominque. She curtseyed. "It was a pleasure."

"The pleasure was all mine," Preble said with a bow.

A while later, away from the dance floor, Dominique heard Angele's bubbly voice. "You are everything Aubert promised. And more."

"I'm...not sure what you mean," scoffed Dominique, turning to meet the marquise. She had heard Aubert mention his friends in Napoleon's court once or twice, but until tonight she'd known nothing about the marquis and his wife. Clearly, they already knew a great deal about her.

Angele flashed a mischievous grin. "He chose royalty, my dove. A woman of status and bearing. One at whose side he can climb the heights of power."

"You give me too much credit." Dominique shook her head, staring at the yellow lace on her slippers. "I'm just an orphan from the frontier."

"*Non, chère fille,*" cried the marquise. "You don't really think he brought you all the way from America for sight-seeing, do you? Look there."

Dominique followed Angele's pointing finger. She saw Preble and Aubert quietly chatting on the quarterdeck.

"My Sebastien just requested the services of brave Captain Aubert," said Angele. "Preble has agreed our convoy will join your tribute ship on the journey to Tunis. Your husband will be our guard. We couldn't have done it without your charm."

"Why did Richard want the *Allegheny* guarding the tribute ship?"

Angele gave a flighty giggle. "What does it matter? Leave the details to the men. You and I, my dove, we shall be like sisters. We're nobility, you and I."

"You perhaps," said Dominique. She was suspicious of the marquise's flattery. Still, Dominique had always dreamed of being part of high society. "I'm not."

"Are you sure of that?" The marquise winked. "Now then, shall we find a drink and a light?" She produced two small brown sticks from her purse. They looked to be tobacco rolled in brown paper.

"What are those?"

"Cigars!" squealed Angele, like a girl who'd swiped her father's liquor. "From the West Indies."

"You smoke?" said Dominique.

The marquise took Dominique's hand and spirited her away to new mischief.

Chapter 45

The USS *Philadelphia*
The Port of Gibraltar, British Imperial Colony
Tuesday, August 30th, 1803

"You don't look well, Mr. Sullivan," said Captain Bainbridge, scratching away at his log book.

The captain had never been more right. John stood with all the weight on his left leg, and still, his right calf throbbed. Cowdery had put the stitches in two days ago, but it felt like a phantom needle was hooking through his flesh. Every muscle ached. It hurt to cough, to laugh, to talk. Adding to his anguish, John forced himself to stand at attention before the *Philadelphia's* commander.

"I'll mend, sir," croaked John.

"So I hear," said Bainbridge, not bothering to look up.

John knew what he had to ask. He knew he shouldn't hesitate. But somehow, he struggled to find the words.

A breeze filtered through the broken stern windows, rustling John's hair. Street lanterns, taverns, and neighboring ships filled the harbor with light. Broken shards had been stripped from the window panes and blood holystoned from the deck. Still, scrapes and bullet holes marred every wall. Claw marks from a grappling hook disappeared under a red and gold rug. Dried blood wrote over Bach's signature on *Sonata Number 3*. Even with every candlestick burning hot and the furnishings exactly as before, the signs of carnage in the cabin weren't easily erased.

"You had a request, Midshipman," Bainbridge said, more a statement than a question.

"Aye, sir," John stammered, clearing his throat. "First I wish to congratulate you on your victory."

The captain's pen hissed on the paper.

"You led a brave defense of the ship," continued John. He'd already heard the captain's report from the other officers: An investigation discovered the galley explosion and rudder damage were untimely "accidents." A preposterous conclusion, but hours of interrogation had revealed no traitors. The captain wasn't about to report saboteurs he failed to catch, especially after nearly losing the *Philadelphia*. "Frayed rudder cables and a mishap in the galley almost gave the pirates a turn of luck. But your steady leadership inspired us all and won the day. All of this will be reflected in my log."

One of Bainbridge's eyebrows gave the briefest tick. "Your congratulations are noted."

"You should know I would report the same to any superior, including Commodore Preble. On a personal note, I wanted to thank you for the dismissal of the charge against me. I hope I lived up to your example during the action."

"Hmm," said Bainbridge.

If John had any chance to save Kaitlin, now was the time. "As my wounds were somewhat severe, and I will be less able in the month ahead, I thought I might ask your permission to take furlough. I could better recover ashore, where I would not be a hindrance to you or the *Philadelphia.*"

Bainbridge looked up through his eyebrows, pen stopped on a period. "There is no hindrance." The captain pecked the inkpot with his quill. "All the crew bore witness during the battle. You carried out my orders with distinction." The pen resumed writing. "Furlough denied."

John blinked. He'd just given Bainbridge everything— deference, a way to be rid of him, and an unspoken promise to corroborate his exact account of events. An account that was a total lie. "Captain, I only ask to take any burden you might bear…"

"My burden?" Bainbridge dropped the quill. He slammed the logbook closed. "You think I don't know why you're asking for furlough?" The captain tilted his head. "You think I don't know why you're on this ship? Why you bargained with Captain Aubert for an endorsement of your commission? And a surgeon's berth for your Negro chum?"

All at once, John felt as though the deck had turned to quicksand under his feet. His muscles were so weary, so leaden, he felt as though sinking. He meant to protest, but when he opened his mouth, he couldn't muster a word.

Bainbridge rose on his knuckles. "You're a sellsword and a smuggler. And to get this honorable posting, you stabbed your own pirate employer Pierre Laffite in the back. No honor among thieves, eh? If I grant furlough, you'll desert the service to go looking for your missing Irish kin. Do I have it about right, Midshipman?"

"Captain, you have my word—"

"Bugger your word. The word of a criminal?"

Bainbridge snorted. "I ought to flog every man jack of your division for that filthy little song. I should hang Chester Ryland for mutiny, letting you out after assaulting a fellow midshipman. And for all the good you're worth as an officer, I've a mind to revive the dread practice of keel-hauling!"

John could only stand there as if reeling from a punch. He hadn't thought of Bainbridge as a friend, but to hear such disdain...

"Lucky for you and your miscreant friends," continued Bainbridge, "circumstances put me in a difficult position. The crew regard your barbarity during the action as the heroism that saved the ship. They'll challenge any account of events that makes you a villain. So, you and your friends will live another day. You, Mr. Sullivan, will remain aboard your ship, as any *great hero* distinguished in battle should do, and your logs and reports will reflect your earlier compliments. Mr. Ryland has requested transfer to the *Allegheny*, and so I've graciously obliged. I've put him off the ship along with a few other ne'er-do-wells. The price we must all pay."

"Captain..." said John, his scratchy voice sounding pitiful. "Here in this cabin, over breakfast, you offered me a chance to prove myself. Yes, I've made mistakes, but you put your faith in me. If you will grant me this one request to help my mother and sister, who suffer on the Barbary Coast, I will reward that faith a hundred-fold. You will never know a more loyal officer."

Bainbridge squinted as if hard of hearing. "'Faith?'" The captain broke into a contemptuous laugh. "What you witnessed in this cabin, Sullivan, was a man barely holding down his *meal*." Bainbridge's face twisted in disgust. "It was so pathetic watching you grovel. Like a stray mutt begging for a master. I saw a filthy Irish rook with a reputation just *low* enough to win Ryland's trust. I offered you a place at my table in exchange for one honorable task. And you failed. Put faith in you? Your necessity to morale is the only reason I don't throw you overboard!"

John was speechless. Bainbridge had flattered him, and he'd fallen for it. He felt like a fool.

"I will grant you a day of shore leave, Sullivan," said Bainbridge, sounding official again. "If only to have you out of my sight a while longer. But then you will promptly resume your duties, or I will hang you for desertion."

Bainbridge sat down, opened his log book, and dipped his quill. "Now, get out."

Chapter 46

The USS *Allegheny*
The Port of Gibraltar, British Imperial Colony
Tuesday, August 30th, 1803

Dominique took another drag on her pipe. The momentary glow of the burning tobacco provided the only light in the cabin. Her fingers dug furiously through the papers in the drawer. As her puff receded, the darkness closed in again. She went to Aubert's coat hanging on the rack and rifled the pockets. The harbor lights shone through the stern windows. The reflections of waves played on the cabin ceiling. Sailors on the docks laughed and conversed on their way to taverns—or brothels. When her hand felt a leather-bound cover tucked in the inner pocket, Dominque pulled the book free. She took another swig of Bordeaux as she studied the embossed red journal. If she was to be cooped up on the *Allegheny* while her husband and Marquis Larocque caroused, why not indulge her curiosity?

Dominique laid down on the stern couch, the warmth of the wine flowing through her. She opened the red logbook and held it up to the wavering reflected light. She paged through personal log entries, navigational footnotes, mundane reminders. Nothing to explain Aubert's secrecy about this journal. She breathed in the woody scent of her pipe, took another drag, and pinched it in her teeth. As she reached the middle of the volume, an envelope fell out. She ran her finger along the edge, eager to read the contents. Then she noticed the fleur-de-lis in blue wax. Sealed. Of course. She weighed the prospect Aubert's ire against the allure of his secret.

The paper crackled as she tore it open. She could forge the seal again later. She held the letter up to the light. She stared in bewilderment. No pages of formal address and discussion. No embossed seals and elegant signatures. Just a few words in French, written on a scrap of parchment.

A,

Congratulations on securing the prize. Our agent in Paris has made contact. The number is five. The cost is ten percent. Paper ships. Hollow crews.

The Restoration is at hand.

L

Dominique's pipe hung from her lip. She read the note a few more times, trying to parse the meaning. "A" had to be Aubert. "L" had to be Larocque. But paper ships? Hollow crews? What on Earth was her husband up to?

Tap-tap-tap.

Dominique started and nearly tumbled off the bench. She scrambled to fold the paper, pipe ash spilling on the floor. She frantically stuffed the letter into the red book and jammed it under a cushion. She looked out the windows, trembling. The tapping came from the lower right pane. A hand waved at her. A face pressed against a square of glass.

Dominque's mouth fell open as she recognized the lithe figure clinging to the stern anchor cable. Dominique hurried to the window. She unhooked the latch pulled it open. "Melisande?!"

Melisande Dufort climbed aboard through the open window. She grinned and lay supine on the couch as if she were Cleopatra on a throne. Her dripping clothes soaked the cushions. "You were expecting someone else?"

Dominique stared at the surreal image of her sister. She wore the plain shirt, trousers, and kerchief of a Navy sailor. A moment ago, Melisande had been thousands of miles away, not to enter her life again for years. A phantom living only in letters and thought. Now, here she stood in the flesh. "But where did you come from? How did you get here?"

"Swam from the dock, climbed the cable. How else?"

"I mean how did you get *here,* to Gibraltar!" Dominique said, rolling her eyes.

"*Philadelphia*, my lovely." Before Dominique could react, Melisande sprang from the sofa and lifted her sister into a hug. "A little puddle like the Atlantic can't keep me from my big sis."

Despite Melisande being several inches shorter, Dominique needed a fair amount of effort to break free. Deep down, despite her irritation at her sister's antics, she was glad to see her. "Melly…you were on the *Philadelphia* all this time?"

"It smells like armpits and bollocks, but yes." Melisande looked from Dominique's vanity to Aubert's brag table covered in cards, to the French naval swords mounted on the port bulkhead. She sized up Dominique's dress, and her eyes went wide. "Wow, Dom. You look so beautiful. Am I keeping you from a ball?"

It was one of Dominique's older dresses—overdue for a wash. Dominique looked down at the worn laces of her corset, the frayed edges of her slip. She raised her chin and said, "Even when Richard is away, I feel it's important to present an air of cultivation." She snapped a striker over a taper. When the candle flared to life, she touched it to the bowl of her pipe and puffed until she had it going again. She sat down in Aubert's chair, crossed her legs, and shook out the taper. She prepared herself for Melisande's next biting quip.

But Melisande's eyes lit up, the way they used to when she was young and letting her older sister braid her hair. "You look beautiful."

The compliment took Dominique off guard. She whistled smoke. "Thank you." She proffered the pipe.

"Thanks," said Melisande, accepting it and taking a puff.

"Why did you follow me, Melly?"

"Who says I was following you?"

Dominique frowned.

"Okay, okay," Melisande admitted. She handed back the pipe, then dumped herself across the arms of a chair. "I missed you." She pulled a wad of tobacco out of her pocket and started a chew.

"I see you passed yourself off as a boy. You're terrified of the ocean. How did you even step off the dock?"

Melisande shrugged her shoulders. "Took me a couple days to work up to it. But it's not so bad...after the dry heaves go away."

"You shouldn't be here."

"Don't I know it," Melisande sighed. "So...how are

things with Mr. Fancy-French?"

"Fine." Dominique cast a furtive glance at the stern couch. A corner of the red book was sticking out from under the cushion.

"How was your journey? The two of you get along?"

Dominique picked up the wine bottle. She examined it for a moment, then took several gulps. "We're very happy together."

"Is that why you're sitting in the dark? Alone?"

"Jesus, Melisande." Dominique rubbed her temple. "That's what this is about, isn't it? You'll never let it go."

"I saw the bruise, Dom. The kind you only get from a fist."

"That was a year ago!" Dominique snapped. "I told you he apologized. It's none of your business."

Melisande jumped off the chair. "Of course it's my business. You're my sister. I'm not leaving until I know you're safe."

"You sailed three thousand miles out of spite for Richard. You have gone completely mad!"

"If he's such a great man, why did he drag you across the sea like his dunnage?"

Dominique bit hard on her pipe. "You know *nothing* about my life, and even less about Richard, so don't you dare lecture me."

"*Papa* Grey Fox didn't raise you to be some Frenchman's mule. To not even fight back."

"Grey Fox wasn't my father. Or yours. Can I never have my own life? Can I never have one good thing without you fucking it up?"

Melisande drew in her lip. "I dressed up as a man. Spewed into buckets. Left Grey Feather! To rescue *you*. To get you home, you ungrateful nag."

"To rescue *me*? Melisande, Richard wanted to book separate passage for me, but I demanded he take me aboard *Allegheny*."

Melisande's lip hung open, plump with tobacco. "You what?"

"You heard me. You don't know me, Melisande. You love who you *think* I am. All you've ever done is chase what brings you pleasure. You care about Melisande and Melisande only. Have you ever asked what *I* wanted? About *my* dreams? What makes *me* happy? No. You just want me to be your Indian sister. Another squaw in your little tribe. Well, I'm *not*."

For all of her strength, Melisande's face crumpled. She had deeply tender spots if one knew where to strike. "Dom, I…"

Seeing her sister on the verge of tears, Dominique nearly broke down herself. She hadn't meant to hurt Melisande. Despite her protests, she didn't want Melly to leave. In the next second, she might apologize and ask her to stay. "Out," Dominique commanded. "Now."

Melisande hesitated a second. Then she wiped a tear from her cheek, her expression turning to steel. "Fine." She swung onto the couch and slipped through the window. "Let him beat you to a pulp. See if I come running."

Dominique's lower lip quivered. Her resolve buckled. "Melly…"

But Melisande was already sliding down the anchor cable. She dropped into the water and was gone.

Chapter 47

The USS *Philadelphia*
The Port of Gibraltar, British Imperial Colony
Tuesday, August 30th, 1803

The lantern light spread through the darkness of the hold. John felt a strange deja-vu as the stench of bilgewater, and human excrement assaulted his nose. His feet landed in the gravel of the ballast, and he walked the aisle of chained prisoners. Eyes glinted into existence. John held up Chester Ryland's drawing of the manor and the tree. He showed it to the pirates, most of them still covered in smoke and grime from the battle. Few, if any of them, would know English. Fortunately, John had learned the language all slaves learn on the Barbary Coast.

"Look at this likeness," John said in Lingua Franca. "This is a place on the shores of Tunis. An ancient ruin with a sycamore outside its walls. The thief known as the Silver Hand dwells here."

A few chains rattled. A man coughed. But they looked on in silence. A bald man glared at John, cradling a festering slash on his arm.

"Do any of you know this place?" asked John, moving to a group of prisoners on the other side of the hold. A youth covered in gun soot recoiled.

Silence.

"Any man who can take me there goes free." John continued walking the line of pirates. "Any man. Take me there, and you go free."

As John reached the last of the prisoners, he sighed. Perhaps it had always been a long shot.

"I know that place," said a voice in the dark.

The words had come from a few steps to John's right—a group he'd just passed over. He backtracked a few strides. "Who said that?"

"I did," said an old man in the farthest row, his back against the hull, his waist soaking in slimy water. He looked old and weathered and was missing his right ear. Two bright eyes peered through a mess of salt and pepper hair. "I know that place."

The drawing crinkled as John held it closer. "You recognize this tree? You know this ruin?"

"Yes." The man sat among younger and more muscular corsairs, easily the frailest of the group. None of the others spoke.

"You can take me to this place on the shores of Tunis?" asked John.

"That place is not on the Tunisian shore," replied the man. "It's on a small island called Red Mortar Redoubt, a few miles from the city. And yes, I can take you there."

Strangely, John already believed him. But it felt foolish not to pretend otherwise. "How do I know you speak the truth?"

"It would surprise you how many times I've answered that question," the old man said, switching to English. He raised his shackled hands as if in supplication. "You're about to threaten me with death should I betray you. You will remind me that my fate is in your hands, and you will be right. Then, I'll remind you that I am your only guide. Rather than parse words, I suggest we leave it to fate."

John studied the man's slovenly face for a sign of deception. He might as well have studied a statue. If any other prisoners had an opinion, they kept it to themselves.

"Do exactly as I say," said John, reaching into his pocket and producing a key. He unlocked the shackles at the prisoner's feet. "The watch is about to change. We've only got one shot to sneak out of here. What should I call you?"

"Yesterday, I was a slave. Today, I am your prisoner. You may call me Varlick."

"Very well, Varlick. I'm—"

"I know your name," Varlick interrupted.

"You do?"

"We all do…Bloody Sully."

Chapter 48

Outside the Fortifications
The Port of Gibraltar, British Imperial Colony
Tuesday, August 30th, 1803

"Tell Fernando, a promise is a debt," said Barda, a contact of Pavia's. "Our debt is paid."

Melisande and Varlick were already in the skiff, sitting by the tiller. The gaff sail and foresail were still furled, the single mast bare. Two Basque men stood behind Barda on the pebbled shore. Their eyes searched the deserted patch of bay with ready muskets. Fortunately, a mile from the harbor, passersby were unlikely.

"There are food and supplies for a week," said Barda. Her weathered face and scarred eyebrow attested to a hard life. "After that, you are on your own."

"Thank you, *Doña* Barda," said John.

"*Nola bizi, hala hil.*" Barda nodded, a hand touching the wide brim of her hat. The three Basques set off down the beach without another word.

After watching them a moment, John turned toward the boat and braced both hands on the prow.

Melisande jumped out to help him push. "What did she say, Sully?"

John cast a look over his shoulder, but the Basques were gone. "She said, 'how you live is how you die.'"

Melisande stared at John for a moment, eyes aglow in the moonlight. Then she pressed her shoulder against the bow.

"That's far enough, John," said a voice in the boat.

A few feet behind Varlick, Ethan stood with a pistol aimed at John. He'd somehow stowed away under the spare sailcloth. John should have known Ethan would figure out his plan.

"Ethan," said John. "You know I have to do this, mate—argh…" A spasm of pain seized John's right leg. He trembled as he waited for the muscle to relax.

"Look at you, John," said Ethan, shaking his head. "You're in no shape for an open boat voyage. You can barely stand."

"I don't have a choice."

"On your behalf," Ethan continued, "I have lied, manipulated, and stolen. I helped you sedate a superior officer. I stood by and watched you become a man you never wanted to be, all in Kaitlin's name. And now, if I let you desert, you will hang. I wonder what she would have to say."

"I don't know, Ethan." John threw open his hands, too exhausted to bother with any more excuses. "If I ever manage to free them, maybe they'll say the cost was too great. That I'm a terrible man. But they'll be *free*. I've done things…" John lost his voice for a moment, tears clawing at his eyes. "I've done things I'm not proud of. I've asked of you things I had no right to ask. You're the best man I know—and I've let you down. But I don't know what else to do. I've got no choice but to try."

Ethan's eyes drifted to the beach, his brows so tightly

drawn they trembled. After a moment he looked at Melisande, gun still pointed at John. "And what about you, Melisande? You're going to let him drag you to the noose with him?"

"Come on, Fiddles," said Melisande. It was pleasant to hear her velvety, feminine voice again. "We both know I'm no sailor. I almost got us all flogged. I begged Sully to take me. I can't stay another minute in that stinky old boat. Me and Bluster-Britches would tear each other apart like angry cats."

Ethan looked at Varlick. "And you, old man? I remember rescuing you from a beating. What do you think they'll do if they find you escaping with deserters?"

"I am but a prisoner," said Varlick in his erudite accent. "My fate is not in my power."

"Damnit, John," said Ethan. "You're coming with me. I won't be responsible for your death."

"You know I can't, mate." John looked at Melisande and Varlick. They returned resolute expressions.

"Gambling I won't shoot?" suggested Ethan.

"I don't have to. The pistol isn't cocked."

Ethan looked at the hammer, flint safely folded all the way forward. He lowered the gun, tucked it into his belt, and said, "No. It's not even loaded." He shrugged, a sheepish smile touching his lips. He cinched his leather satchel tight against his hip, jumped out, and braced himself against the bow.

"Wait, what are you doing?" John protested.

"What does it look like?" Ethan widened his stance, ready to shove off. "I'm coming with you."

"No, I can't let you do that. You'd be a deserter too."

"It's that, or I turn you in," Ethan insisted. "I no longer know if helping you is right or not. I no longer know if you're a man I can follow. I certainly know this is insane. But if I let you go, wounded as you are, you'll never survive. God help me, but I can't bear to see you die. Even if it means I'm damned."

It was overwhelming. As John stared into Ethan's eyes, bright in the moonlight, he knew he was unworthy of such a friend. And yet, here Ethan was, like always, watching his back. John knew that if he spoke, he might shed tears. So, he nodded.

"Right," nodded Ethan. "Heave!"

The two men pushed the boat down a gentle slope of pebbles. It drifted into the calm water of the bay. They sloshed through the shallow water and hopped over the gunwales. Ethan took up one oar, John the other. They both looked at Melisande, and the three of them shared a quiet moment. The skiff and its four passengers drifted toward the moonlit sea.

Dipping his oar in the water, Ethan said, "Let's go find Kaitlin."

Part IV

Dead Reckoning

Chapter 49

The Lake of Tunis
Friday, August 26th, 1803

The thick wooden door squealed open. In the chambers of the ancient castle tower, a fire blazed under a vaulted mantle. The great hearth filled the room with light and shadow. The flames brought to life battles depicted on tapestries. Riders with pointed helmets and curved swords pounded over the desert. Spearmen with kettle hats and kite shields fell beneath hooves. Great deeds and bitter defeats long forgotten, alive now only in thread. Tiles of jade and lapis lazuli ran in sparkling rivers along the walls. Ocean air blew through the towering horseshoe windows. Curtains inscribed with golden Arabic letters flailed like ghosts in the night. The breeze carried the stink of the stagnant lake. But Declan Sullivan also caught a whiff of sand and sea—the only thing he liked in this room.

The butt of a musket jabbed Declan in the back. Thirty pounds of iron links scraped over the flagstones as his bare feet hobbled forward. Long years of practice had taught him the perfect length for each step—not short enough to test a master's patience, not long enough for the shackles to eat through his calluses. He stopped when he reached the black-lacquered table and its two chairs. As always, Declan knew what to do. And as always, he waited for the command.

"Sit," said Master Isitan.

As he had on dozens of other nights, Declan sat. The same silver tea set as always was arranged before him. A tray, two cups, and a single pot, fluted with ornate lines. A thread of steam floated up from a long spout. Two guttering candles provided the only other light. Incense filled the air with a sandalwood musk. Beyond the windows, Declan could make out a few minarets against a cerulean blanket of stars. Unlike any night before however, the other chair was empty.

"Where is Master Naim?" murmured Declan, worrying at the links chaining his hands. He stared at the crimson tablecloth, embroidered with stars and crescents.

Master Isitan's boots clicked on the stones as he circled to the other side of the table. His leather bandolier belt murmured against his saber sheath. "The left hand of the sultan will not be joining us tonight. One of his agents made contact, and he must visit the bey. He has sent me in his stead."

Declan's hand began to twitch as panic set in. "Every third night I am to recite for Master Naim. I am to tell every detail. I must not leave out a word."

"Yes, slave, I know," said Isitan. "And normally, you would. Tonight, you will recite for me."

Declan's breathing quickened. "Every third night, I am to recite for Master Naim. I am to—"

"Peace, old fool," said the soldier. When Declan quieted, Isitan settled into the opposite chair. After a deep sigh, he asked, "Do you know why you recite your story every third night?"

"I recite for Master Naim." It was the only answer Declan could think of. "Every third night." A pointless thing to add, he somehow knew, but he couldn't resist.

"Look at me, slave," commanded Isitan.

Only the fear of disobedience could outweigh the fear of looking, so Declan lifted his gaze. Isitan regarded Declan with cold amber eyes. The commander had the same short cropped hair and curled mustache of the other *Nizam-I Djedid* soldiers. Two of them stood a couple paces behind Declan. Isitan straightened his cardinal red coat, perfectly fitted to his lean, youthful frame. The rows of gold buttons on his chest glinted in the candlelight.

"Where I come from," began Isitan, "Master Naim is known by another name...Pour the tea."

The manacles clattered on the table as Declan picked up the teapot. An earthy aroma steamed forth as he filled each cup. As he always did, he poured one for Master Naim—Master Isitan, tonight—and one for himself.

"Where I come from," continued Isitan, "they call him 'The Chronicler.' Do you know why?"

"No, Master."

"Any scribe can record words. Any courier can carry a letter. Any soldier can issue a threat. But to send a message with all the emotion of the sender, and to make the recipient truly understand...one must have knowledge. Knowledge of the sender. Knowledge of the receiver. Knowledge of a great many things. And that knowledge must tell a story. By guiding your recitation every three days, Master Naim is crafting a work of art. A chronicle. You are merely his pen and parchment. Do you understand, slave?"

"No, my lord."

Isitan gave a dry chuckle. "Of course not." He took a long sip of tea, straightened the gilded gorget around his neck, and leaned back in his chair. "Now then. Begin the chronicle. Tell every detail. Leave out not a word."

Chapter 50

The Skiff
The Mediterranean Sea
Wednesday, August 31st, 1803

The sun was a smudge in the sextant viewfinder, the lens shade dulling the white-hot light to amber. John Sullivan struggled for balance as the skiff crested a wave. His muscles ached as he fought to keep the instrument steady. The Mediterranean heat wrung sweat from his brow.

"It's all right, John," offered Ethan. "Let me have a go."

"I've almost got it," snapped John. He carefully turned the dials, the angle of the mirrors bringing the horizon and the noon sun together. The sun wobbled, slipped left, then finally met the edge of the world. "There!" cried John. "Got it—" He doubled over against the rail, wracked with coughing.

Ethan hopped over a thwart and took the sextant. He offered an arm to hold him up, but John waved it away.

"I'm fine," said John. The boat leaned on the starboard tack, its course southeast for Tunis, the opaque sea nearly spilling over the port side. The trapezoidal gaff sail and triangular jib snapped in the wind, fanning out like fins. A four-knot wake washed behind the boat. John coughed again, feeling needles in his ribs.

"I told you, damnit," Ethan said. "You need *rest*. I can handle the readings. But only *you* can plot our position and chart a course."

"Relax, Fiddles," chided Melisande with a mouth full of tobacco. She had the double duty of manning the tiller at the stern and keeping an eye on the shackled prisoner aft of the mast. A loaded pistol sat across her lap, ready should Varlick make a wrong move. "A good chew and Sully will be in ship-shape. Won't you, Sully?"

John coughed.

"He doesn't need a 'chew,'" said Ethan. He picked up his medical bag from its place amidships, nestled in a canvas sack. "Five days since I put your stitches in, and you haven't had more than a few hours' sleep." He sat down by John at the bow. "Shirt off."

"Tell this headwind to change directions," said John as he stripped off his coat and shirt. His whole body ached, every muscle felt stiff, and his wounds throbbed worse than ever. As if he'd been chewed on by a pack of dogs. He longed for rum but couldn't risk dulling his wits. "We can't miss a single tack. Every day we're out here, we risk being spotted by the Navy. Or pirates."

Ethan began unwrapping the bandages wound around John's torso. "I thought that's why we're on this northern latitude. To stay away from the coast and avoid pirate hunting grounds."

"Aye, but there's always a risk of finding them outside the usual shipping lanes. Agh…" John winced as Ethan peeled a patch of old gauze off of his back.

"Sorry, mate."

"It's fine," John said through clenched teeth. Another

patch, glued to the cut with dried blood, burned as it came away. "Besides, at this pace, a few days and we'll reach our target longitude. Once we make Red Mortar Redoubt and Katie and Mam are safe, I'll take all the rest you want."

"Never mind if you drop dead in the meantime." Ethan bent close and sniffed John's wound. "No foulness. The cut looks clean. It's closing nicely. Turn around."

"See?" Melisande hawked tobacco juice. The brown glob broke apart on a wave. "I haven't seen the wound that can kill Sully."

"*Yet,*" said Ethan. After a similar examination of the bullet hole in John's side, he added, "You're on the mend, John, but you can't keep overexerting yourself. God forbid you trust Melly and I with a little seamanship. You know, I do recall some of what you taught me. Give me your leg."

"I trust you, mate," said John as Ethan rolled up his pant leg and began unwinding the bandage on his calf. "The truth is, the closer I get…the harder it is to sleep."

Ethan paused in his ministrations for a moment, then nodded.

"*La taqtal 'akhi,*'" said Varlick.

John, Ethan, and Melisande all looked at Varlick in unison. It was the first time their prisoner had spoken in days. Varlick sat cross-legged, his shackled hands resting in his lap. His communications usually consisted of little more than nods or grunts. He'd shown no signs of resistance or subterfuge. Rarely had he moved. He ate his share of hardtack and salt pork without complaint. He slept when told and obeyed the odd command to haul a line or tie a knot. But he was always watching his captors.

His clothes may have been ragged, his face gaunt, his hair and beard unkempt, but his eyes were sharp.

Startled as he was to hear Varlick speak, John recognized the words. "What did you say?"

"Actually, you said it," Varlick replied to John. "'*La taqtal 'akhi.*' You uttered that phrase over and over in your sleep. Perhaps that is why you struggle to rest."

"Impossible," snapped John. "I don't know what that means."

"No?" said Varlick with a frown. "Strange you should dream in Arabic."

"What does it mean?" asked Ethan.

"A common insult. Something you heard in the battle, Midshipman Sullivan? Or as a slave?"

"I don't care what it means," said John, glowering at the prisoner. "And I'm not a midshipman anymore—no longer bound by the Articles of War. I would tread lightly if I were you."

"That's right, Scruffy," put in Melisande. She didn't look up from her antler-hilted dagger as she ran a whetstone along the edge. "Sully's in charge, and I've got ways to remind you if you forget."

Varlick raised his open palms, the iron cuffs rattling. "I meant only to help. I know what it is to be a slave."

"Maybe," said John, wincing as Ethan cleaned his calf with a wet cloth. "Maybe not."

Varlick scratched pitifully at the ribbon of flesh where his right ear should've been. "We have a common goal, Sullivan. A far more valuable thing than trust."

"That's a load of bull," Melisande said with a wry smirk. "A warrior is only as good as the man watching his back. I trust Sully with my life."

"Indeed," agreed Varlick. "You must both trust

Sullivan a great deal to follow him into desertion. If your fleet catches you, your lives are forfeit."

"We're not following him anywhere," snapped Ethan. "We're choosing to help a brother in his time of need. You have no idea who we are. What we three have been through together." He looked up from his work, exchanging a look with John, and then Melisande. "We may quarrel sometimes, but we're family."

Ethan's smile spread to John, and then to Melisande.

"Of course, you are right," said Varlick. "A man must fight for his family. I only hope it is not too late for yours, Sullivan."

John shot Varlick a hard look. "I *will* find them and I *will* bring them home. Believe it."

"I do. Bloody Sully."

"Damn right," said Melisande, spitting another wad over the side.

"Killing slavers is bloody work." John gave a cold smile. "But I don't mind. Did it bother you…watching me run those pirates through?"

"There is an old saying on the Barbary Coast," said Varlick. "'He who acts like sheep, the wolves will eat.'" Varlick looked at his shackled hands with a rueful smile. "I know which I am. Otherwise I would have escaped years ago. What good fortune that a wolf came along."

"Men aren't livestock," asserted Ethan, jerking the gauze on John's leg a little too tight. "Even if they're treated as such. The strong preying on the weak? That's no way to live."

"There I disagree, young Ethan," Varlick said. "Most of us work our whole lives to prosper, only to find we were being fattened for slaughter. My master was very wealthy a week ago. Then Bloody Sully butchered him with his own sword. Did you escape your own master in such bloody fashion, Sullivan?"

"I didn't kill my captor," said John. "He steered my family's ship into a reef. It was pure luck I survived. Ilyas must have drowned in the sinking."

"Did that cause you sorrow?"

"I never feel sorrow for dead slave masters."

At that, Ethan grinned.

Varlick rubbed at his mangled ear. "While I was steward to Master Harrak, he used me very cruelly—I was not sorry to see him die. But before him, I was house servant to a kind merchant for many years. He regretted having to sell me to pay off his creditors. It felt like losing family."

"Ilyas Naim was no family to me—he showed me the kindness of stealing my home and destroying my family. He was worthless fucking rot, and it gives me great pleasure to know he went to a watery grave."

Varlick gave a wry smile. "Harrak used to say, 'there is no pleasure greater than the death of an enemy.'"

"He was right," said John. "That's just how it felt when I 'butchered him with his own sword.'"

For a moment, Varlick and John shared a silent look. There was something knowing in Varlick's eyes—and a sadness. As if he felt concern for John. Or pity.

"Sully!" cried Melisande, rising to her feet. She raised a finger towards the bow.

Everyone in the boat looked east, dead ahead. Cords of pain tightened in John's neck as he craned for a view. For a moment, John only saw a few wisps of cloud drifting behind a blue horizon. The endless waves and nothing else. But then, movement. He groaned as he fumbled over the thwarts, tugging the spy glass free from his belt. His elbow banged painfully into the rail as he held up the glass.

At the very edge of the horizon, John could make out the faint outline of a triangular sail. Then another inched into view. His heart began to race. "Sails! Two points off our starboard bow."

"A merchantman?" said Ethan hopefully.

"No. Ketch-rigged by the look of her. That means pirates."

"Are you sure?"

John snapped the spyglass shut and scrambled aft. "Doesn't matter. By the time we're sure, it'll be too late. They may have seen us already. Melly, hard to port!" He began unwinding the main sheet from the belaying pin. The skiff pitched hard as Melisande jerked the tiller all the way to the right. "Ethan, man the weather sheet. Prepare to come about."

"Reverse course?" Ethan said as he grabbed the rope tethered to the jib sail. "We'll be sailing the wrong way. We could wind up right under the bow of the *Philadelphia* if she's looking for us. Why not tack south? Get around them?"

"We're close-hauled in an open boat, Ethan. Our only hope to outrun them with the wind at our backs. We sail for all we're worth."

"For how long?"

"Until the wind changes or we lose them."

Melisande looked at the distant vessel with a deepening frown. "And if the wind doesn't change?" asked Melisande.

John hauled on the mainsheet. "Pray."

Chapter 51

Declan Sullivan's Chronicle
The Quarry of the Bey, Outside the Port of Tunis
One Year Ago

Dreams were my only escape. I didn't know how long I'd been a slave. A year? A dozen? Every dawn begins a struggle to survive until sunset. Every hour begins the patient wait for a mouthful of water. Every second begins another swing of the pick. Time is a luxury. Desire a futility. Freedom a distant memory. But at night…at night I could dream.

In one of my favorites, I would be walking the deck of my ship, after the forenoon watch. I'd see my two boys— Isaac ten, John five. Isaac would tease Johnny that he was too little to climb the shrouds. Johnny would dash for the rigging, only for Isaac to drag him back, kicking and fighting. Sometimes I would dream of Katie, tugging on my coat until I watched her dance. Most nights, though, I dreamt of Nora.

I awoke to a wooden truncheon on iron bars. Dust danced through the faint rays of sun. I stared up at the hollowed-out limestone of my cell. It was part of a warren of old tunnels burrowed deep in the mountain. All the useful minerals had been mined from this shaft long ago. My joints clicked and popped as I struggled to rise. I scratched patches of flea-chewed skin. Scabs rubbed raw, then scabbed over again. This day began the same as every other.

"Up, rats," barked Master Jabbour in Lingua Franca. I looked up to see the round, bearded face of our overseer. He walked the row of cells, banging and shouting. His attendant Janissaries followed, pistols stuck through sashes, scimitars at their belts. Jabbour unlocked the cells. "Up, rats. To work."

The long walk toward the light of day gave my joints time to get moving. I shuffled a half-step at a time to start, crutch digging into my shoulder. My gait hadn't been right since my last *bastinado*. Too many strokes of the cane on the soles of my feet had left me permanently hobbled. When my seized muscles began to unwind, I moved into a brisk limp. I marched with a line of poor souls to a long day of breaking stone.

"Come, lads," I would say as cheerfully as I could. "Many hands make light work." I was the foreman of my group. If I failed to motivate with words, Jabbour would motivate with the whip.

A few minutes later, I led them into the light of dawn. Each man would take a wedge of bread with a little oil, which he greedily devoured on the way down the slope. Every slave knew better than to reach the bottom with half-eaten food. As I crunched a sprig of straw in my biscuit, I looked across the only sight I had known for years. A sunbaked caldera, sunk into barren, russet mountains. Jagged ridges where blocks and boulders had been chipped away to build the walls and towers of Tunis.

Nearly naked slaves from every corner of the world swarming over the gravel hills like ants. Each emaciated man dragging a length of iron chain by the ankle.

My first task was to shine the overseer's shoes. Every sunrise and sunset, Jabbour would sit in his tent and complain of his plight. I would listen and polish his boots.

The rest of the day consisted of the purgatory of the slave. Lift the pick. Swing the pick. Lift the pick. All a man could do was focus on the next stroke. His only break came when he had to carry the chunks to a cart. A slave had to move fast enough to avoid the whip, but slow enough not to collapse. His only hope was to see the dusk.

At noon that day, I saw my boatswain's son, Patrick, trembling as he lifted his pick. The metal head wobbled behind his head for a moment, then dropped to the earth. The nineteen-year-old fell to a knee. Flies collected on his baggy eyes. The sun had long since blistered, peeled, and tanned his freckled face. Today, he was ghostly pale. Jabbour was cursing at another slave and hadn't seen. I dashed to Patrick's side and threw his arm over my shoulders.

"On your feet, Paddy!" said I. My old boatswain had died of sunstroke in my arms. Before he passed, I swore I'd look after his son. I didn't mean to fail in my promise. "It won't do for Master Jabbour to catch you idle, now will it?"

Patrick's head lolled to the side, his eyes barely open. He'd taken sick the night before. Some fever was making its way through the camp. Six men were dead from it already.

"Come on, Paddy boy," I coaxed, patting his cheek till

he opened his eyes. "That's the way. I'll bring you some water."

"Da?" murmured Patrick, looking at me with vacant eyes.

"That's right," I lied. "It's me. It's your da."

Crack!

Jabbour chopped his truncheon into the back of Patrick's legs. The boy crumpled into the dirt, too weak even to cry out.

"Lazy cur!" spat Jabbour, beating the delirious lad.

"Master, please," I begged. I threw myself onto the boy. "He's ill. Mercy. We'll produce his share, I swear."

The overseer paused mid-swing, and from his glare, I could see I might be next. "I want *twice* his share." He gave the lad a parting kick and swaggered off.

We all worked a little harder that afternoon. Sooner or later, each of us knew we would need a mate to carry our load. Later, as I hobbled from man to man with a bucket of water, the sound of a great horn blared from the manor house. I looked up the mountainside, along the white walls at the cliff's edge. Janissaries jogged along the ramparts, bowling each other over in haste. One of them rode out from the gates. I watched the horseman race down the narrow winding path to the quarry floor, the horn still blaring. He spurred his horse straight towards me, and I nearly bolted. But a slave learns that punishment is always worse when you run.

The young man reined in his mount. He had the white kaftan and tall felt hat of Ildemir's barracks. He came up just short of Master Jabbour. "*Sidi* Ildemir wants to see this one." The Janissary nodded in my direction.

Master Jabbour's face screwed up as he looked at me. "This rat?"

"Both of you. At once!" snapped the rider, before spurring his horse back up the hill.

I had only seen the inside of the manor a few times. When I hobbled into the inner courtyard a half hour later, every step sent a shudder of pain from my knees to my spine. To the eyes of a slave, it was a limestone enclosed paradise. The cool courtyard air washed over my weary body like a salve. Blue awnings shaded flowers and shrubs. A pair of colorful finches chirped in a domed cage. *Corbaci* Ildemir, appointed minister of Hammuda Bey's quarry, stood near a long table. An ornate wedge of gold-plated copper on his hat marked him as the commander of his Janissary regiment. His wife lazed on a couch beneath the fronds of two date trees, green silk covering her long, slender body. She and two servant girls wore a veils covering all but their eyes. One girl served her from a tray of grapes while the other poured tea.

Ildemir scowled at Jabbour with an arm tucked behind his back, fist opening and closing. "Three times, Jabbour. *Three. Times.*"

Jabbour dropped to the floor, bowing as though at call to prayer. "*Sidi* Ildemir, I swear I have—"

"Three times I have been robbed!" boomed the voice of the Janissary leader. "You promised me this Red Heart's head on a spear! In as many nights, this thief has stolen my priceless sixteenth-century *kilij* from the Siege of Vienna, the golden bridle given me by the Bey of Tunis, and now my wife's ruby pendant. The last he stole right out of her chambers!"

Bahar sighed, her veil fluttering. She observed her fingernails.

"*Sidi*, I have scoured the quarry," Jabbour groveled. "Given dozens of these rats the *bastinado*. Doubled my patrols. No one has seen this thief."

Ildemir swatted a silver chalice from the table. "Then your men are bigger fools than you!" he shouted over the clattering cup. "The mountain is to the south and east, the cliffs to the north and west. Walls surrounding the entire quarry. Only one gatehouse allows entrance, and I've tripled the guard. Incompetence is the only possible way a thief could sneak in and out of here three nights in a row."

"*Sidi*, if you'll permit me—"

"Bah," growled Ildemir, hand swatting the air as if at a fly. "I'll deal with you later. Get out of my sight."

Jabbour's mouth worked for a moment, then he bowed. As he left, his eyes promised me future horrors. My heart sank as I turned to follow.

"Not you, Captain Irish," said Ildemir.

When Jabbour had gone, I asked, "yes, *Sidi* Ildemir?"

Ildemir smiled, wagging a finger at me. "You play the quiet cripple, but you're a clever one, Captain Irish. Your workers are the most efficient in the quarry, and there's nothing that goes on in that pit you don't know about. I want you to help me catch this thief."

"*Sidi*," I said, my terror rising. "I have never heard of this 'Red Heart' before. Nor have my lads."

"Perhaps not, but I think you can be of some use."

Arched wooden doors swung open on the courtyard. A young man in a simple traveling kaftan stepped out. He had short dark hair and a tan complexion, and he looked no older than seventeen. He came alongside Ildemir, leather-gloved hands clasped together, eyes alert and cocksure.

"This is Aruna," said Ildemir, gesturing to the newcomer. "He is an esteemed member of the guild of thieves known as the Silver Hand. Bahar suggested I engage his services against a rival thief. He will sniff out our Red Heart. Aruna, this is my quarry foreman, Declan. He's been a very dependable sort over the years."

"Very good," said the young man, looking at me. His accent sounded of India.

"Get him whatever he needs, Declan," said the Janissary commander. "I won't be made a fool by a common burglar!"

"Of course, *Sidi,*" I said, bowing my head.

"Bring the thief to justice swiftly, and your men will have a day of respite, food, and drink."

Extra rations. A day of ease for my men. At that moment, I would have considered any task, no matter how debased. "Yes, *Sidi* Ildemir."

"But fail me, Captain, and I shall have to turn the matter of punishment over to Jabbour." Ildemir's eyes lingered on me a moment. Then he went into the house, Bahar and her handmaidens in tow.

Aruna gestured to an empty chair at the table. So young—not a line on his face. For a moment, I thought of my sons.

I worked my aching knees forward and hobbled to a chair. The other handmaiden came alongside and poured two cups of tea. I could see a rumor of freckles beneath her veil, and I felt a pang in my heart. Another enslaved girl, not even fifteen years old—but at least Ildemir was a gentle master. Bahar would not have her servants mistreated. The girl glided away before I could glimpse her eyes, leaving Aruna and I to our tea.

"I have many questions," said Aruna in a jovial tone. "I hope you have many answers, friend."

"Of course, Mr. Aruna," I said. "But my men are innocent."

"I will be the judge of that!" snapped Aruna. Then, his tone became friendly again. He leaned close and said, "and please, call me Rune."

Aruna—or "Rune" as he liked—questioned me for hours. The name of every slave. How he became a slave. His health. What he talked about. Whether he chafed under the yoke of slavery or accepted his fate. Miserable as it was to inform on my mates, it would have gone worse for us all if I resisted. It didn't help that the cool air, fresh water, and plates of fruit made me want to stay forever. The shadows were long in the courtyard when Rune's questions were finally done.

"Very good, Captain Irish Declan," smiled Rune. "I will now inspect the grounds for myself. You may return to your cell. I will send a guard to escort you." He reached out as if to shake hands.

Before my hand could reach his, Rune flicked his fingers, and a gold piece appeared. I stared. It might as well have been a treasure trove—enough to buy new clothes and extra food for the lads, and perhaps a Christian burial for Patrick. Rune winked and flicked the coin in the air. By the time I caught it, he was on his way out of the courtyard. "My kindest thanks indeed, Captain Irish Declan."

For a moment, I didn't even register that I was alone. I was still rapt by the sight of the gold coin. But then I looked around the empty square in panic. A quarry slave alone in the *corbaci's* house? If a guard saw me, I'd have my feet whipped.

Before I could rise and hobble out of the courtyard, a small, warm hand alighted on my own. It was the servant girl, looking at me through the slit in her veil. "Declan, wait."

I stared, her brown eyes bringing me the calm of an oasis pond.

"I have a message from the Red Heart," she said in Lingua Franca. "A thief who has come to set you free."

"What? No! You're in league with the thief!" I stumbled out of my chair, only to lose my balance and flop on the floor. The girl kept ahold of my hand, kneeling close.

"Declan," she said, "Nora is safe."

I froze, barely able to breathe my next words. "Nora..."

"She is free, and she waits for you."

"No, this is a trick..." I said, shaking my head.

"'Awake, dear heart, awake. Thou hast slept well.' The words you etched on her watch."

I blinked, tears welling in my eyes. "Nora...she's...safe?"

"And if you trust the Red Heart, tomorrow you will both be free." The servant girl extended her hand. "Will you help me?"

Slowly, I took her hand. A tear fell on my cheek. I nodded.

"Good. Now listen carefully. There isn't much time."

Chapter 52

The Skiff
The Mediterranean Sea
Saturday, September 3rd, 1803

Thud…thud…thud-thud.

The sea had moods. That was one thing John Sullivan had learned in all his years before the mast. No single day on the water felt exactly the same. Three days ago, when a distant sail appeared on the horizon, the day had been bright, the wind stiff, the sun hot. John might have called the mood energetic. Today, he called it morose. It was sometime near noon, but a blanket of clouds covered the world in dismal twilight. The ocean surface was an ashen wasteland. There wasn't a breath of wind. The boat sat motionless on an empty sea. He stared at the limp mainsail—useless as a shirt on a clothesline. A white-bellied cormorant had landed at the top of the mast. The bird looked askance at John with a menacing red eye. John felt an overwhelming urge to shoo the animal away, but he was distracted by a fit of coughing.

Thud…thud-thud.

Melisande's grapeshot hit the deck again. She was sitting on a thwart aft of the mast, legs stretched out along the bench, back against the port side. In her hand, she held a crooked stick of driftwood with a net of twine at the end. She used the net to scoop up the iron ball, toss it in the air, and catch it again. Apparently, the stick, which she'd fashioned in her boredom, was used in an Iroquois game called "lacrosse." Every time Melisande missed her catch, the bouncing iron made John's headache a little worse.

Thudda-thud-thud-thud.

"Must you do that, Melly?" John barked.

"Yes!" agreed Ethan from his seat near the stern. He had his straw sailor's hat drawn over his face. "I'm trying to nap."

Varlick offered no opinion. He dozed in his usual cross-legged pose.

Melisande shrugged and tossed the ball in the air again. "No. I s'pose not." She flipped the ball in the air, stretched out her arm, and nearly lost her balance making the catch. It landed in the net with a soft *thwip*. "But I gotta stay sharp."

As if to agree, the cormorant shrieked and flapped its wings. Now it turned its other eye on John. He considered fetching his pistol.

Another toss. *Thud…thud-thud.*

"Damn it, Melly!" shouted John. He jumped out of his seat, ready to seize the infernal stick and throw it in the sea. But a spike of pain lanced through his chest and he doubled over in a fit of hacking. Every cough burned his lungs and rubbed his raw throat. His breath sounded like a codger on his deathbed.

Ethan snatched the hat off his face and jumped up. "John? Are you all right?"

By now, John knew what to expect. His friend's

mothering became more oppressive by the day. Unable to speak through his coughing fit, he threw up a hand.

Melisande caught the ball again and set the stick down. She looked concerned. "Come on, Sully. Enough of that."

After a few more gasps, John managed to whisper, "I'm fine." But he wasn't. Stars swarmed John's vision. His legs felt like lead. His muscles ached to the bones.

"You're not," said Ethan, stepping over the water casks and bundles of provisions. "Your skin is pale. Clammy. I told you to rest, but you won't *listen.*"

The light touch of Ethan's hand on John's forehead felt like a hammer blow. John tried to suppress his wince. "I can't. Three days becalmed since we lost that ship, and I have yet to take our position. I can't afford to miss a break in the clouds."

"God, mate, you're burning up." Ethan pulled his kerchief from his pocket and dipped it in seawater. He placed it against John's forehead. "Damn it, John! I told you this would happen."

"What, Fiddles?" Melisande asked, a slight quaver in her voice. "What's wrong with him?"

"He has a fever," Ethan replied. "Because instead of resting and healing from his wounds, he's been exhausting himself every day for a week!" Gesturing to John's bedroll at the bow, Ethan said, "Now, sit."

John looked ruefully at the sextant, then toward the sun. The sky might as well have been a granite roof. He would get no measurements today. Fatigue made it easy to give in, and John settled onto his blankets. The cormorant crowed and flapped its wings.

"Melly and I will watch the sky," said Ethan as he held a canteen of water to John's lips. "If I see the slightest patch of sun, you'll be the first to know. Now, *rest*."

Staring into Ethan's intense eyes, John felt transported to an earlier time. A time when he felt safe. When Isaac would tuck him into his hammock as a boy. John hadn't thought of his older brother often in recent years, but at this very moment, he missed him dearly. The best friend he ever had. Dead now. They were so alike, Ethan and Isaac. How had John never realized? Somewhere deep in his soul, John felt an iron grip loosen. He reached up and clasped Ethan's forearm.

The frustration melted from Ethan's face. He squeezed back, caught off guard by the gesture.

"Okay, mate," said John. "You win."

Ethan smiled. "And it only took a week to wear you down."

John smiled as his eyelids drooped. God, but he *was* tired. He hadn't realized until now. Before his eyes closed, he caught one more glance of the large seabird roosting above the sail. The grim creature crowed, beat its wings, and launched into the gray.

Chapter 53

The Skiff
The Mediterranean Sea
Sunday, September 4th, 1803

Ethan Auldon bit off a chunk of hardtack, filling the quiet afternoon with crunching. The skiff and its passengers drifted on a windless, placid sea. It felt like a day of lazy fishing on the pond, except there were no sounds. No buzzing insects, warbling birds, nor croaking frogs. He was lucky to hear a fish nip the water. At least the clouds—and some spare canvas stretched from mast to rail—offered shelter from the sun. But there was no escaping the humid heat.

Ethan looked over at his patient, finally sleeping under a parcel of canvas stretched over the bow. He had dozed off while sitting upright against the keel, arms folded, face clammy and pallid. One thwart over, Melisande snored with an open mouth, a string of tobacco hanging down her chin. She had her lacrosse stick in one hand, grapeshot in the other, and her cheek jammed against the hull. Ethan didn't understand how those two could sleep in such odd positions.

"They look very peaceful, don't they?"

Ethan looked to his left, once again caught off guard by Varlick's voice. The old man looked at Ethan with alert, penetrating eyes. "Yes," said Ethan affably. He slowly fished the pistol out of his ditty bag and laid it across his lap, where Varlick couldn't see it. "A rare state for those two."

Varlick smiled as he looked at John and Melisande. "The beauty and vigor of youth."

"I suppose." Ethan thumbed the pistol hammer to half-cock, just in case.

"Forgive my nostalgia," said Varlick, looking off toward the horizon. "I had children once. A son and a daughter. Some nights, I would rise and go to their bedsides. I would watch them sleep for hours, often until dawn."

"My father used to do the same," said Ethan. He recalled the image of Seth Auldon sitting in his chair by the fire, pipe between his lips, Ansel and Judith tuckered out after a story and asleep on the floor. Ethan missed his late father terribly.

"Then he knew the most beautiful sight in the world—the face of his sleeping child."

"Where are they? Your children?"

"It hardly matters now." Varlick laid his head back against the rail, looking at the ceiling of canvas. "That was a very long time ago."

"I see," said Ethan, not feeling right to pry. He bit off another hunk of bread.

"You worry about young Sullivan." Varlick said, looking at Ethan. "Fear not. I believe your care will see him through."

"I hope so," said Ethan, crunching on a kernel of wheat.

"A doctor's apprenticeship, the respect of your comrades, your freedom—you've given up rare fortunes to come to his aid."

"And he worked at my family's tavern for free, walked miles with me in a blizzard, and even fought a duel to save me. That's what friends do."

"Ah." Varlick raised his eyebrows. "So, it was *Sullivan* who freed you from slavery."

"What?" said Ethan through a half-chewed chunk of bread. "How could you know about that?"

"I saw it in your eyes. The day we met. When I was at the mercy of your soldiers, and you came to my aid. Of course, I wasn't certain until just now."

"I was born free! I was abducted—against the law—and held prisoner for three weeks. I was never a slave."

"Does it comfort you to believe there's a difference?"

"I don't know," said Ethan, looking bitterly at the pistol. "Maybe there isn't. All I know is that John wouldn't smuggle slaves for the Laffites and the Tindalls—and they tried to hurt me in retaliation. John didn't just risk for me—he risked for what was right. That's why I'm risking everything for him. I don't expect you to understand."

It looked like Varlick might argue the point, but instead, he shrugged. "Of course, you are right…Still, I wonder. Why a duel?"

"Because it was the only way John could secure my freedom."

"No, I mean why would Tindall choose a duel? Sullivan's reasons are clear enough. But what would Tindall have to gain?"

Ethan had to admit—that gave him pause to think. John had said Clyde refused an offer of money, claiming it was too low to replace the slaves John set free. Goading the elder Tindall into issuing a challenge had been the only way to win Ethan's freedom. But Clyde Tindall imagined himself a cunning businessman. Why throw all that away for pride? Had John told the whole story? Ethan narrowed his eyes at Varlick. "And why are you so interested? What do you care about our lives?"

"And who else should I take an interest in out here?"

Ethan shook his head. "I see you watching us. Listening to us. Always quiet. Always agreeable. Then when one of us turns our back, you're talking to the other. You want something."

"You're right, young Auldon." Varlick pulled his folded legs closer. "There is something I want. For God to deliver us safely to Red Mortar Redoubt."

"An interesting choice of words, for a man that looks east every morning, but never prays."

"Perhaps I am a Jew. Or a Christian."

"Aboard the *Philadelphia*, you refused salted pork along with the other prisoners. And you never take a ration of grog."

Varlick tilted his head, scrutinizing Ethan for a moment. At length, he said, "Your insight continues to impress. I must be a Muslim, then."

Ethan shook his head. As his gaze drifted north, he noticed a dark bank of clouds. He fished for his spyglass, adding as an afterthought, "In fact, I get the feeling you don't believe in anything anymore."

"Your first miss, young Auldon." Varlick looked to the mire gathering in the sky. "I believe."

A bolt of lightning crackled in the distance.

Chapter 54

The Skiff
The Mediterranean Sea
Monday, September 5ᵗʰ, 1803

"What do you want?" cried John, clawing at his face. Warm drops were falling on him—drops of blood. He felt them drenching his clothes. Saw the face of the scrawny boy staring at him with wide, vacant eyes. Heard the boy say again, *"La taqtal 'akhi."* The rain of blood was falling too fast now, too fast to wipe away. "No!...No!" A hand touched John's shoulder, and he recoiled. "No, don't touch me. You're dead. You're..."

"John, it's me," said a soft voice. "It's only a dream."

John blinked the water from his eyes. The blur resolved into the face of Ethan, rainwater pouring off his brows. Rain cascaded down the limp sails, gathering in a pool on the canvas awning. Angry clouds leeched all color from the day. John found himself sitting in six inches of water, as warm as tea gone cold.

"Get up, mate!" Ethan said, shouting over the roar of rainfall. "It's a cloudburst. We're taking on water."

John struggled to his feet, shaking off the fog of sleep. Falling water had turned all the world into a blur. He couldn't tell where the sea ended and the rain began. In the absence of wind, the drops fell like balls of lead. They raised great clouds of mist as they pocked the ocean surface. The boat was collecting water like an open cistern.

"Bail!" cried John, shocked into action. He hurdled over the thwarts to one of only two buckets on the skiff. He tossed one to Ethan. With the other, he scooped water surging around his feet. "Bail for all your worth!"

Ethan sloshed to the starboard side and set to work, tossing bucket after bucket into the sea.

"Sully," said Melisande. "I haven't got a bucket!"

"Use the chamber pot," John said, pointing at their shared wooden privy.

Melisande wrinkled her nose. With a sour look, she emptied the pot over the side and started bailing.

"Sullivan," Varlick yelled over a crackle of thunder. Cascades of water flattened his hair and beard. He held out his shackled hands, blinking drops from his eyes. "Free my bonds. I can help."

John stared at the prisoner's wrists, separated by only a single link of iron. "No. You'll have to manage."

"Don't be foolish!" he argued. "The weight alone will slow my efforts. Look around you! If this keeps up, all four of us may not be enough. You need my help."

Thorns of light cut across the clouds. The report exploded through the sky. Reluctantly, he fished the key from his breeches. He paused with the key in the lock. "Mark me, Varlick, if you try anything—"

"Yes, yes, you'll run me through," muttered Varlick. "Now shall we get to work?"

John's eyes narrowed. Misgivings or not, he had no choice if he wanted to stay afloat. With a sigh, he turned the key. The lock clicked, and the manacles came undone. Varlick scooped up a food bowl and went to work bailing. He showed surprising speed for a man of later years. John followed suit, the slash across his back screaming with pain.

As if to defy the efforts of the four voyagers, the sky announced another bone-shaking strike of lightning. The downpour thickened. They tossed bucket after bucket, bowl after bowl. In a gale, the rain might have swirled and stung. But in the windless calm, it fell with a sheer, punishing weight. Water emptied, only to be refilled. A stalemate fought from minute to minute. The minutes gathered into an hour.

In what seemed like a moment of divine mercy, the rain began to slow. By now, they were all exhausted, their muscles on fire, but they couldn't stop. This was their chance to gain. To turn back the tide. They bailed even harder. Every so often, John would give a gesture to trade implements. He would use the bowl or the chamber pot for a while, then switch again. None of them had spoken a word since beginning their battle with the elements. Gradually, the stagnant pool at their shins began to retreat. Finally, it fell to their ankles.

And then the sky thundered again, and the next wave came down. Hour after hour it went. Four defenders under siege. A motionless boat, the sole island in an infinite pond. The difference between life and death a matter of inches, rising, then falling, then rising again. In a rare glance at the ocean as he tossed a bucketful, John caught a flash of movement a few yards away. A dolphin arced through the wall of falling water, then gracefully slipped into the sea. Another jumped, and then another, one in a spiral, the other with a flop. As John willed his tired arms to empty another bucket over the side, he realized with great envy the dolphins were playing. As the four passengers in the boat continued their fight, they spared a glance every now and then for the sleek gray animals sailing through the air. It was a moment of surreality—two of God's creatures watching one another from opposite sides of fate. One indulging in a delightful frolic. The other barely clinging to life.

When the last gloomy light of day started to fade, the rain slowed. The torrent became drizzle. The drizzle became a drip. Another terrible hour of work finally reduced the water in the boat to a few puddles. After an eternal day of exhausting labor, John finally decided the danger had passed. A weak wave of his hand served as the order to rest. All four of them dropped their buckets and bowls and collapsed into a chorus of panting. For a long time, no one spoke. Night fell, and they could only see each other in faint silhouette. Silence enveloped the sea. The only sound was the drip of wet sails.

John shivered violently, his soaked clothes hanging off him. Trembling made his muscles ache, but the cold wouldn't let him stop shaking. He exploded into a fit of coughing.

"John," murmured Ethan, crawling over to him. "Mate, you're going to freeze."

John didn't resist as Ethan pulled off his wet shirt.

"God, what I would give for a fire," lamented Ethan, looking around at their sodden supplies. "We have to keep you as warm as we can. Melly, water."

It took a moment for Melisande to reply, and when she did, she sounded half awake. "You got it, Fiddles." She clamored over to the water casks. They left them uncorked during the rain, and now they were full—at least one benefit of the downpour. Melisande held a cup out to John with a leaden arm.

John drank greedily, then collapsed between thwarts. He felt the warmth of skin against his back as Ethan pulled him close. The arms of his friend circled around him, a blanket driving out the damp cold. John shivered so fiercely, he worried he might injure Ethan with a stray elbow. He felt embarrassed, as though he'd asked for an outrageous favor.

"It's all right, mate," said John through chattering teeth. "There's no need—"

"Forget it," Ethan replied. "You need to get warm if this fever is to pass."

John felt another body come close. He detected the familiar odor of exertion, but also a hint of something softer. Like picked clover. It was Melisande, her naked back pressing up against his chest. He felt her rump come close. The feminine shape against his body caused him to flush with heat. He felt a stirring in his loins. He angled his hips away, mortified that she might feel his sudden arousal.

"Quit squirming, Sully," complained Melisande. "You aren't the only one cold on this boat."

"Right. Sorry," John chattered. It felt like the height of impropriety, laying there, pressed between the half-naked bodies of his two closest friends. But he couldn't deny the comfort of their warmth. Considering they were adrift in the Mediterranean, it occurred to him that concerns over propriety were also ridiculous. "Well, this will make a charming story for the Sawduster."

"No one will ever hear of this," muttered Ethan.

"We'll never speak of it," agreed Melisande.

"Right," added John.

"It'll be a song," suggested Melisande. "*The Trials of Fiddles and Melly, and Sully's Eager Janissary!*"

Ethan and Melisande chuckled.

"Very funny," grumbled John.

On the other side of the boat, Varlick sat cross-legged in his usual spot. Even in the dark, John could feel the old man's stolid gaze.

Chapter 55

The USS *Allegheny*
The Mediterranean Sea
Monday, September 5th, 1803

Rain pelted the cabin skylight. Dominique and Angele shrieked as a chittering mechanical statue skittered over the planks. It was a miniature replica of a Greek statue, sculpted of silver and gold filigree, and hollow inside. The sculpture was a nude, drunken faun, reclining on a bed of wolf pelts. Inside his hollow likeness, there were mechanical sprockets and a reservoir of wine. The marquise's strange device charged in random circles. Each woman jumped when it cut a sudden path in her direction, only to giggle when it danced away. When the gears wound down, Dominique found the supine man splayed before her. A flash of lightning illuminated the *Allegheny's* cabin, momentarily brightening the cloudy day.

"Drink!" cried the marquise. She drummed her thighs. "*Le Faune Barberini* wants you, my dove."

"Oh no," laughed Dominique as she picked up the heavy contraption. She seized the muscular chest of the ancient Greek and pulled. A soft click and the torso of the statue flipped sideways, revealing his lower half to be a spout. Wine swashed in the cavity of the sculpture. As Dominique brought the figurine's loins to her lips, she fell apart giggling. "I can't. I can't."

Angele smirked at Dominique through her eyebrows. "Rules are rules. Besides, you know you want to."

"No, I couldn't possibly," Dominique giggled through her hand. Heady with wine, she drank, the faun's loincloth touching her bottom lip.

Angele clapped with delight. "Wonderful, wonderful!"

Allegheny's decks sounded as if under a waterfall. In the becalmed sea, the ship felt oddly still. Dominique drank to the music of rain on the stern windows. A little life was left in the statue, and it shuddered. She started and gushed Bordeaux all over her face. She dropped the bizarre machine on the deck like a wriggling snake. The two of them laughed hysterically.

"I certainly hope you ladies aren't becoming wanton over there," said Marquis Larocque with a grin. He sat at Aubert's mahogany card table, across from the captain, a hand of brag fanned before his face.

"Or overly intemperate," said Aubert, shifting one card behind another. His smile belied his gruff tone, and he took a sip of brandy. He and Larocque were already as drunk as their wives.

"On the contrary, my love," cooed the marquise. She slipped a foot free of her burgundy gown and slid it toward Dominique. A silk-stockinged toe gently caressed Dominique's foot. "We are becoming positively amorous."

Dominque took in a sharp breath, taken off-guard by Angele's intimate touch. Perhaps it was the coziness of the cabin against the bleak day. Or the heady warmth of the wine. But Dominique didn't find the caress at all unpleasant.

Larocque took a drink from his own snifter, then pinched his pipe between his teeth. "What do you say, *Capitaine*? Shall we…join them?"

Aubert puffed on his pipe, adding to the haze of smoke. He flashed a look at the two women, and Dominique was surprised to see the intrigue in his eyes. But then he fished a few coins from the rail. "Later, perhaps. When our game is done." He dropped his bet on the blue felt.

"As if you need more of my money," groused Larocque.

Dominique felt the warmth of Angele's body as she drew close. The marquise lowered her voice to a murmur. With the battering of the rain and shouts of sailors outside, her words didn't carry to the card table. "How long has it been, my dove?"

"Richard's been very busy lately," said Dominique, brushing the hair from her eyes. "And it's not easy being captain of a 'hen frigate.' It's been difficult for both of us." She looked into Angele's drunken eyes. "But it's been so wonderful having you and the marquis pay us visits. Really, you've been the kindest of friends."

"Oh, *chère*." Angele puffed out her lips and pulled Dominique into a hug. "My heart weeps for you, cooped up on this stinky hunk of wood. How fortunate we met. Soon, my dove, our worries will be a thing of the past."

"What do you mean?" Dominique whispered, glancing at Aubert. He and the marquis were too busy drinking and posturing over their bets to overhear their wives. She thought of Aubert's red book. The mysterious letter to

"A" from "L." Paper ships. Hollow crews. "Are you talking about…the Restoration?"

In her tipsy state, Angele practically squeaked the words. "Where did you hear that?"

"Nowhere!" snapped Dominique, heart beating faster. "I mean, I've heard rumors…about events in France."

Angele had a sly grin. "All you need to know, my dove, is that one day soon, the republican upstarts will be swept away. Bonaparte will be gone, and France will have a king again. When that day comes, Richard intends to stand at the heights of power with you at his side. I told you, my dove. We're nobility."

"But, how can you say that? Isn't Sebastien a member of the *Sénat conservateur*?"

"Pish," scoffed Angele. "We play our part. Living off the crumbs from Consul Napoleon's table. I was younger than you the day I watched the rebels break down our doors. Plunder all of our fine things. They dragged my mother and father off to the guillotine. Didn't even allow them noble funeral rites."

"That's terrible," whispered Dominique. "Richard doesn't like to talk about his exile. His family fled to England, but he had fought the English in the French Navy, and he couldn't bear that humiliation. So, he chose Pennsylvania."

"You see what the peasants have done to us, *chère*? Just what the savages have done to you. Taken everything. All that's left of my family is our name. But that's all about to change." Angele took another sip. Lightning flashed in her eyes.

Dominque looked at the gray sky, dumping sheets of water on the ocean. "How?"

"Sebastien and I have held our tongues. Bided our

time while the rabble tear apart our beloved France. Let us just say, soon it will be we who rule." Angele took up Dominique's hand. "After all, it is your birthright."

Dominique leaned closer, eyes locked with Angele's. "What do you mean? My father was a fur trapper."

"How much do you really know of your father, Marcel Dufort?"

"Only a few childhood memories, some rumors…"

"What do you think keeps your husband so busy late into the night? He's been reclaiming your past. Dufort was the name of a proud and powerful house before the Revolution."

Dominique's heart raced. "You're saying my father was a noble?"

Angele leaned close, her lips parting to reveal the secret.

There was a rapping at the cabin door.

"Who is it?" called Aubert, not bothering to look up from his cards.

"Begging your pardon, sir," said the voice of the *Allegheny's* newest officer. "It's Lieutenant Ryland."

"Come."

The roar of the rain filled the room. Lieutenant Chester Ryland, recently transferred from the *Philadelphia*, tracked a torrent of water over the threshold. A puddle formed under his oilskin coat. Dominique caught the smell of cold and damp. The whole room felt darker as if invaded by the cruel storming sea.

Ryland saluted. "Lieutenant Kimble's compliments, sir, and he reports all pumps running at capacity. Calm seas and no wind, but we're taking on water. We've ordered every available hand to pass buckets from the bilge."

"Very good," said Aubert. He pushed a coin stack

towards Larocque. "Five is the bet…Will that be all, Mr. Ryland?"

The wet lieutenant looked around the room. "Sir, I wondered if you might like to come above decks."

"I would not. Assuming the men are doing their duty and my officers have the matter in hand. Am I wrong in that assumption, Lieutenant?"

"No, sir. I only meant…"

Marquis Larocque looked over at Ryland with lazy eyelids. "Are you telling us we should abandon ship, *Monsieur* Ryland?" He blew smoke through his nostrils.

"No, My Lord," replied Ryland with a slight stammer. Aubert had directed all the crew to refer to the marquis with proper honorifics—a practice uncomfortable to Americans.

Aubert grumbled, "Then why are you dripping all over my golden fleur-de-lis carpet?"

The Larocques and the Auberts shared a chuckle at Ryland's expense. Ryland's eyes found Dominique's for a second, and she realized how petulant she felt for laughing. He looked like a man on the brink of desolation.

"Sir," said Ryland with a defeated salute. He retreated from the cabin and closed the door.

"Bit of a quibbler, your lieutenant," said Larocque.

"Bainbridge's refuse," sneered Aubert. "But I was able to rid myself of a few agitators in the bargain. On balance, I'd rather have ignorant layabouts than energetic troublemakers. I'll pay to see. I have a run."

Dominique couldn't help but feel a tinge of guilt. Every man aboard was cold, wet, and exhausted, and here she was indulging in Bacchanalian revels.

"*Merde!*" swore Larocque, slapping his cards on the

table. "Just a pair. Are you happy, Aubert? You've emptied my pockets again. Now then, how about a nightcap?" He looked over at Angele, who flashed him lustful eyes.

"Yes, finally!" said Angele. "Enough of your boring cards. Let me show you my marvelous machine."

Aubert continued to sort his winnings into neat stacks.

Larocque rippled his eyebrows at the marquise. "Sweet wife, I have not only seen your machine, but I've also wound it a time or two."

"Sweet husband, you've mostly fiddled with the levers." Angele nearly tipped over giggling.

Dominique flushed red. She'd never heard any woman talk like this in Pennsylvania. Except for Melisande, of course.

"Marquis, Marquise," said Aubert. He stood with all the formality of a naval captain concluding dinner with his officers. "It's been a wonderful evening. Thank you for joining us. If I could beg your indulgence, I would like to be alone with my wife."

"Ah," said Angele, raising an eyebrow in Dominique's direction. "Just so."

"Come, dear wife," said Larocque, putting on his coat. "We wouldn't want to wear out our welcome."

Dominique helped Angele up. The *Allegheny* tilted, and the drunken marquise nearly fell over. Dominique caught her, and Angele burst into laughter all over.

"Oh my," said Angele as she let her husband's arms slip around her. "The wine goes straight to my head. And my machine."

Husband and wife both laughed at that one. They half walked, half stumbled as Aubert escorted them out.

"My officers have prepared the wardroom for you,"

said Aubert. "I'll have a cutter row you back to the *Minerva* in the morning."

"After Jean-Christophe's famous croissants, of course?" said the marquis.

"Of course," said Aubert as he closed the door.

For a moment, Dominique and Aubert listened to the fading voices of the two nobles. Then Aubert's boots clunked over the carpet. He looked Dominique up and down as if seeing her for the first time. She could see the red in his eyes from the brandy—and the desire.

Dominique took off her wine-stained sash. "You didn't need to send them away so early. We might have played a game."

Aubert came up behind her. His hands flowed over her bare shoulders. "I don't want their games. I want you." He pressed his nose to her neck and inhaled.

"Angele told me something. About your research…" Dominique turned around and looked up at her husband.

Aubert's eyes roamed over her for a moment, then he pressed his mouth to hers. She could taste the brandy and pipe smoke on his tongue. The smoke she didn't mind. "*Mon chaton…*" he whispered.

Aubert was happily drunk. His first good mood in weeks. She knew she shouldn't dash his spirits, but she couldn't get the question out of her mind. She pulled away from his kiss. "Did you…" Her eyes looked up into his. "…research my father's history?"

Aubert's eyes went slack with frustration. "You ask me this now? Can we never have a pleasant evening? Will nothing ever please you?"

"Richard, *mon trésor*," said Dominique, pouring sugar on her tone. She looked at him with inviting, submissive eyes. "I want to be close to you. I miss you. It pains me that you feel you must conceal your work."

"Everything I do, I do for your own good. And besides, you shouldn't be letting the marquise fill your head with loads of nonsense."

"But Angele has been a friend. A good friend."

"To the marquis and his wife, we're a means to an end. As they are to us. They're not to be trusted."

Dominique felt a quiver of disappointment. She wanted to believe in Angele's friendship, and she wasn't ready to give up on it yet. "She said you knew something about my parents, and I believe her. If you do, I have a right to know."

Aubert let his arms fall from her shoulders, giving up on romance. He sighed. "I haven't finished my research. I am waiting to hear from several contacts in Paris. To speak on your parents would be premature."

"Richard, how can I—"

"*But*," Richard interrupted. "Since you asked, I have spent the last year collecting documents on France's peerage prior to the Reign of Terror. I discovered correspondence, heraldry, and records of lineage that lead me to conclude your father was the first son of Count Achille Dufort, who was executed alongside your three uncles. Your mother was the daughter of Baron Luc Lafaille. On the day of the attack on Cherry Valley, your parents died without title, having renounced their claims. But as your father's kin later perished under the guillotine, their title was posthumously restored. You are the daughter of the Count and Countess Marcel Marius Dufort, and a countess of Provence in your own right."

Dominique stared at Aubert in disbelief.

"I told you when I asked for your hand, Dominique. Only a woman of the highest stature belongs at my side.

Only a woman of the most impeccable quality. I will reclaim my rightful title. I will avenge what was stolen from my family. And I will wield power again in my beloved France. I want to share that future with a woman who has no equal. That woman is you."

Dominique's mouth fell open. She couldn't move. Couldn't even speak. The last muddy rays of sunset provided the only light. A cloudburst added energy to the rain. It sounded as if gravel were falling on the windows.

Dominique threw herself against Aubert. The captain stumbled back with the impact, blinking in surprise. He opened his mouth to say something, but her lips cut him off. She bit as she kissed him. Her hands clawed at his back.

Aubert didn't question her sudden lust. He tore off his shirt, fighting to keep their lips locked. Dominique dug her hands into his chest, squeezing his muscles. Aubert tore at the laces of her bodice, and her breasts slipped free. He planted a hand on her bosom, her nipple between his fingers. She chewed at his lips, and he flinched at her ferocity. He slipped a hand under her skirts and found the warmth between her legs. She gave a soft moan. There was a flicker of lightning as pleasure rippled through her body.

Aubert hauled Dominique off the floor. She wrapped her legs around her husband as he carried her to the card table. He swept the felt clean, coins clattering against the bulkhead. He kissed ravenously and unlaced his breeches.

Dominique shrieked as his manhood entered her. She closed her hands tight around the back of his neck, and he began to thrust. She flopped on her back, breasts shuddering as her husband thrust again, and again. The table bucked, legs scraping the floor. Dominique's moans rose above the driving rain.

A mad chittering filled the cabin—the sound of a rattlesnake shaking its tail.

Aubert and Dominique broke off their lovemaking, jumping in fright. Dominique threw her arms around her husband, and Aubert looked around as if to grab a pistol. They searched for the source of the sound.

On the carpet, Angele's bizarre mechanical statue had found a third wind and was buzzing around the floor. After a couple seconds, it came to a stop.

The Auberts stared at the odd device for a heartbeat. Then they burst into laughter.

"A marvelous machine, no?" chuckled Dominique, imitating the drunken Angele. She smiled into her husband's eyes.

"Perhaps we should fiddle with the levers," smiled Aubert.

They shared another laugh, and then laughter gave way to kissing. The table legs went back to scraping. Rain pelted the windows. The sea boiled under a deluge.

Chapter 56

The Skiff
The Mediterranean Sea
Tuesday, September 6ᵗʰ, 1803

"How long has he been like this?" worried Melisande Dufort. She squatted on a thwart, looking over Ethan's shoulder.

The young surgeon's apprentice had an ear to Sullivan's chest, listening to each rattling breath. Sullivan lay on a bedroll, head nestled at the bow. Melisande had never seen Sully so sickly and frail. His cheeks were gaunt and drawn, his skin jaundiced. Dark circles sagged under his closed eyes. The boat had dried since the rain, but Sullivan's clothes were soaked with sweat. He shivered and mumbled in his sleep. Melisande was powerless to help him, and it terrified her.

Ethan drew the pile of weather-treated peacoats over Sullivan. "Since the middle of last night," replied Ethan. "He's getting worse."

"Goddamn it," cursed Melisande. She glowered at the glassy water. Pouted at the bleak sky and the suffocating heat. Another day of misery. Would it *never* end? "Where is the fucking wind? I've never gone three days without wind in my life!"

"Four," corrected Ethan, like a typical know-it-all doctor.

"Ugh," growled Melisande. "Four. What do we do, Fiddles? What does Sully need?"

"For a start," said Ethan, "you can stop breathing over my shoulder. It makes it impossible to concentrate."

Melisande exchanged a glare with him. She felt a sudden urge to scream at him until her voice went hoarse. To claw his eyes out. Four days idle in the humid heat had frayed their nerves to a breaking point. Her pestering wasn't helping anything. She knew she was doing it, but she couldn't stop. One thing she knew about herself— nothing drove her mad like standing still. Even so, Auldon didn't deserve any of that—he was just trying to help. So, she hid her rage behind humor. "*Somebody* woke up with fire ants in his britches."

"All we can do is keep him warm, nourished, and his thirst slaked. The rest is in God's hands."

Melisande felt her pulse quicken. "What does that mean?"

Ethan sighed. "It means there's nothing more I can do, Melly. I hear water in his lungs. He's coughing up livid sputum. I smell no foulness in his wounds, so my guess is pneumonia. Or, a fever in the blood. If Dr. Cowdery were here, he'd know which."

"Come on, Fiddles. You're the smartest bloke I know. You don't need The Doc. You just need to think."

Ethan groaned, rubbing his sore back. "It doesn't matter. John's driven himself to exhaustion. We have to hope his fever breaks."

"And…" Melisande said, almost too afraid to hear her own question. "If it doesn't?"

"He will die," Ethan admitted.

"But…" Melisande's lower lip trembled ever so slightly. Crazed a moment ago, now on the verge of tears. What was wrong with her? Was she losing her mind? She heard her voice crack. "But…you said his wounds were mending. And he looked so strong just a few days ago. How can he be so sick?"

"Because he didn't fucking listen to me!" shouted Ethan. His voice echoed across the still water. "Like he never does. I told him he needed rest." Ethan stomped over the benches and threw his medical bag down. "I told him this would happen, but he ran himself to death. Damn him for a stubborn ass!" Ethan flung himself down against the bulkhead, drew his knees up close, and stared at his feet.

Melisande raised eyebrows at the surgeon's mate. "Wow, Fiddles. I don't think I've ever seen you lose your temper."

Ethan looked away from her.

"I think I like this side of you." Melisande settled down onto the thwart. She crossed one deerskin-clad leg over the other. "He is a stubborn ass, isn't he?"

Despite his best efforts to sulk, Ethan smirked.

"What do you think, Scruffy?"

Varlick's eyes slid over to Melisande, then back to the horizon.

"Yeah, that's what I thought," she said, hawking spit over the side.

The hours continued to roll by in slow, miserable minutes. Melisande busied herself sharpening her copper knife, then her throwing knives, then her antler-hilted boot knife. After that, she choked down another hunk of dry sod commonly known as "hardtack." Then she spent an hour—or was it two?—practicing with her lacrosse stick. When Ethan pleaded with her to stop, she put it down and watched him attend to his duties. Ethan's most important daily chore was to drop a triangular slab of wood over the side and then pay out a length of rope attached to the so-called "chip log." By counting each knot in the rope as it spilled overboard, Ethan could record the skiff's speed. As he did every day, he notched the result in the wood beneath the gunwales. The rest of the time he spent checking, double checking, and triple checking the supplies. All the while, Sully slept. Any of Melisande's previous notions of boredom fell utterly short of her current predicament.

The boat hardly rocked. The water barely stirred. The clouds hung as low and solid as a clay roof. All Melisande wanted was one little ray of sun. One little swatch of stars. One glimpse of the moon. At times, she wondered if there was even a world left out there. Could there really still be cities bustling with activity? Clan mothers sitting around longhouse fires? Trading posts abustle with gamblers and whores? What if all the world had simply vanished, and this lonely plane of sea was all that remained? Perhaps they were dead and hadn't come to the realization. Four souls adrift in the afterlife.

On top of all the misery of being stranded on a boat, in the middle of nowhere—on the ocean—Melisande felt her guts cramping. Now she understood her anger at Auldon a few hours before. It was her courses coming on. They always stoked her emotions like a wildfire. The afternoon was late when Auldon finally gave her the watch and went to sleep. She made her way over to her little corner at the stern and dug some raggings out of her dunnage. She squatted over her privy bucket as if to relieve herself, then paused. She cast a glance over at Varlick.

The former Turkish slave reclined in his usual spot, eyes closed, under the shadow of the sailcloth. He gave Melisande the creeps. Even with eyes closed, it felt like he was always watching.

"Keep those eyes closed, Scruffy," warned Melisande.

For a moment, she didn't think he would respond. But then Varlick said, "I have no interest in your private business."

"Good," replied Melisande. After another moment of careful scrutiny, she unlaced her breeches.

A few minutes later, Melisande settled back against the starboard rail. She pulled the brim of her straw hat over her brow and tried to forget the pain tying her stomach in knots.

"You are a remarkable young woman," said Varlick. He spoke in a soothing, grandfatherly tone.

Even if Melisande happened to find his voice disarming, she feigned annoyance. "You're not my type, Scruffy."

Varlick grunted. "Please, my dear. You are young enough to be my daughter."

"Now that's settled…" muttered Melisande, picking at a sliver of salt pork in her teeth.

"I meant your resolve. I can see the toll this journey is taking on you. Yet you endure hardship with hardly a word of complaint. I wonder if you even realize your own strength."

"Don't go flattering me, old man." Melisande pulled the brim of her hat up an inch. She expected to find Varlick looking at her, but he was in the same position, eyes closed. "On second thought, go ahead. I ain't got any better plans."

Varlick chuckled under his breath. "You proved your bravery on that gunboat. What would your shipmates think if they knew it was a woman fighting beside Bloody Sully?"

Melisande smirked with pride. Of course, she didn't trust this stranger, but what was the harm in a little fun? "*Now* we're talking. Dominique could learn a thing or two from you."

"Your sister?"

"Who else?"

"Ah," nodded Varlick. "Indeed. Our brothers and sisters should be dearest to our hearts, but it is they with whom we fight most bitterly."

"I'm not the one fighting—I love Dominique. But she hates me."

"I am certain that is not true."

"Oh? And what's it to you anyway?"

"I am as stranded as you are," shrugged Varlick. "I saw no harm in a little conversation."

Fair enough, thought Melisande, pursing her lips. "My sister is a brat. Not much else to tell."

"I sense there's a great deal more to tell. It's written on your face. There has been resentment between you. Jealousy. She recently let you down."

Melisande sat up a bit. How the hell did he know that? She hadn't said a word about her fight with Dominique in Gibraltar—not even to Sully. "Not that I aim to discuss it with *you*."

"Then do not," said Varlick with a sigh. He tilted his head back as if to take a nap.

Melisande huffed and crossed her arms. She tapped her foot for a moment, then blurted out, "Dominique married a husband that beats her. She's stubborn and selfish and wants to be a fairy tale princess living in some French castle. I'm not jealous of anything—I'm trying to knock some sense into her. But she's too stuck up to see it. She doesn't want my help? Fine. I've had enough of the princess. At least Sully appreciates my talents."

"Has it ever occurred to you that Dominique is jealous?"

"Of who? *Me?*" Melisande scoffed so hard, she nearly blew snot. "She can't *stand* me. Thinks I'm all rustic and crude. Thinks being pretty is about poufy dresses and jewels. She's always looked down her nose at me. What could she possibly be jealous of?"

"You truly don't see it, do you? Your strength, your courage, your mettle—they reflect her own self-doubts like a mirror. Your sister sees in you what she lacks in herself. To escape your shadow, Dominique has no choice but to seek a different path."

"What a load of bull," laughed Melisande. But even as she rolled her eyes, she found herself intrigued. What an absurd idea. Dominique? Envy *her?* And yet, there was so much it would explain… "Forget it, Scruffy," Melisande retorted, snapping out of her moment of vanity. "You don't know me, and you don't know my sister. Whatever our problems, they're between us."

"Perhaps."

Melisande folded her arms, annoyed. She found herself disappointed that Varlick didn't press the conversation. It turned out, hearing about Dominique's burning envy pleased Melisande a great deal. Still, better to keep this stranger out of family matters. Especially when she knew the real truth. Her eyes drifted over to Sullivan, shivering in his fitful sleep. The truth was, if

Dom knew what was good for her, she never would have broken Sully's heart.

"Ah," smiled Varlick.

Melisande looked at Varlick, seeing that his eyes had followed hers.

The old Turk turned his eyes on her. "How long have you been in love with him?"

Melisande nearly toppled off her thwart. "What?!"

Varlick stared at her, face immutable.

"Me? In love with Sully?" Melisande laughed, but it sounded forced to her ears. "Have you been drinking seawater, old man? Sully and I are friends. Besides, he's not my type."

"A sailor? Irish?"

"A *man*."

Varlick raised an eyebrow.

"That's right, Scruffy. You heard me. I like lovers with long hair, shapely little bums, and big beautiful breasts. Got that?" She got to her feet and pantomimed a sensual caress of her own bosom. "With all the curves of a goddess."

If Varlick was shocked, he didn't show it. "A bold admission."

"Yeah? You don't like it? Well, you can piss off." Melisande plopped back down and pulled the knife from her boot. She fished her whetstone out of her satchel and started sharpening.

The only sound was the ring of the blade on the stone. After a moment, Varlick added, "And yet, you feel something."

Melisande grimaced as if tasting something sour. Varlick was getting on her nerves now. She felt like grabbing her warclub and knocking him out if only to have one hour of him not watching. And because a small part of her feared he was right.

Chapter 57

Declan Sullivan's Chronicle
The Quarry of the Bey, Outside the Port of Tunis
One Year Ago

"Good. Now listen carefully. There isn't much time." The servant girl reached into the folds of her dress and produced a small iron key. She closed it in my palm. Through the slit in the veil, I could see she was perhaps thirteen or fourteen. The confidence in her voice belied her youth.

"What shall I unlock?" I asked.

"Nothing. Leave that to the Red Heart. Tomorrow, when you shine Jabbour's boots, slip the key into the pouch at his belt."

"What if he catches me?"

"A man's pocket is easier to lade than pick," she said, her eyes smiling. "You can do this. I know it." She gave my hand a squeeze. "You just need to be a little brave."

"Who are you?"

"A friend of the Red Heart," she said. "Now go! Hurry."

A door opened on the courtyard behind me. My heart

skipped a beat when I saw two Janissaries marching into the square. I turned to warn the girl away but found she was already gone.

"Come along, dog," said one of the soldiers. "Holiday is over."

As I rode a horse-drawn cart down to the quarry, I watched the setting sun turn limestone hills crimson. I felt the weight of the mysterious key in my pocket. I imagined a hundred terrible ways Jabbour would punish me—or my men—when he caught me trying to sneak it into his belt. Had I gone mad? Maybe I had found some worthless key buried in the sand, hallucinated a mysterious girl, and dreamt up her plan for escape. As I crawled into my cell among exhausted, filthy bodies, I lay awake and wondered what to do.

When at last I fell asleep, I dreamed.

Her sienna hair is dark with sweat. Her cheeks are pale, her eyes exhausted, but she's beaming at me. She's even more beautiful than the day we met. Nora rests in my captain's hammock as the midwife hands her a tiny bundle, swaddled in plaid. Under the folds, there's a tiny face splotchy with blood.

"Declan," says Nora. "Meet your wee daughter."

I am filled with wonder. "A daughter?" The infant makes a soft coo. Her eyes are swollen closed. Her hand opens, arm wiggling. I touch an index finger to her palm. "Hello, little one. I'm your Da." The babe's hand closes on my finger, and Nora and I chuckle with delight. "Nora, you're a marvel. She's so beautiful. What shall we call her?"

"Let's call her Kaitlin, after Saint Catherine." Nora smiles at me, and I've never been more in love. "Our first child born at sea."

"I'm sorry I couldn't get you home to Belfast, my heart."

Nora plants a kiss on my lips. She gently rocks our baby girl. "We are home."

A wooden truncheon raked the iron bars. When we awoke, one of us didn't rise. I walked to Patrick, curled up on the floor, and shook his shoulder. "Paddy boy, up now."

Patrick rolled over, revealing pallid skin and empty eyes. I'd watched him grow up beside my own sons on the deck of the *Wandering Hart*. My boatswain, and now his boy, were dead.

"Have two of your rats haul him out before he starts to stink," sneered Jabbour on the other side of the bars. "Then, my boots, Irish."

My men and I began another long journey through the tunnel, toward the sweltering quarry. Two of the men carried Patrick's body. As I did every day, I said, "Come, lads. Many hands make light work."

A few minutes later, the portly overseer dumped himself into his tall chair. He sat under the shade of a tent, monitoring the quarry slaves. On any other day, the glare I gave Jabbour would have earned me a dozen *bastinados* on the soles of my feet. But today, the overseer smiled, gloating over Patrick's death. That was the moment I decided to plant the key.

I set to work polishing his boots. A series of wagons trundled by, pulled by donkeys. Boxes and casks filled each cart—the baggage of *Corbaci* Ildemir's wife. She was probably leaving for the city to tend to their estate.

"You know," said Jabbour. He bit into a date, juice gushing on his fingers. "I remember when Ildemir's haughty whelp was running around here, barking orders, telling me my business. He hated me, that brat, thought he'd be the end of me. But now he's off to fight in Tripoli's war against those colonial mongrels, and here I am. I outlasted him, and I'll outlast this thief."

As the overseer spoke, I looked up at his belt. I could see the leather pouch at his side where his kaftan parted. I reached into my pocket for the key.

"What are you looking at?" muttered Jabbour, a fleck of date caught in the corner of his mouth. "Get to work, Irish rat."

I yanked the hand from my pocket, pretending to fumble for more polish. I whipped the rag across his toes.

"That smug bitch of his…" griped Jabbour. "Looks at me like I'm no better than you slave dogs. Bahar thinks she can hire a thief to do my job? Humiliate me in front of her husband? Just look at all that junk." He waved at the long train of wagons on the road. "She travels like a sultan's wife. And when she decides to flee with this robber on the loose, I'm the one charged with carting her rubbish. One day, it'll be her that's treated like a donkey…" Jabbour yelled at a Janissary tossing a rolled carpet onto the cart. "Careful with that, fool!"

I knew I had my opportunity, if I could keep Jabbour distracted. "Do you think this Aruna from the Silver Hand will succeed?"

Jabbour looked down at me, eyes narrowing to slits. For a moment, he said nothing. Then he turned his attention back to the plate of dates on the table beside him. "I think I'm going to humiliate that Silver Hand brat, and you're going to help me. Or that sickly pup of yours won't be the last to die."

The overseer jumped out of his seat to yell at two slaves carrying a chest to the cart. One had lost his grip, and the trunk had fallen. "You filthy rats! Drop one of our lady's chests again, and I'll have you crushed under a pile of stones."

The kaftan fluttered in the breeze. My eyes were level

with Jabbour's purse. With a trembling hand, I withdrew the key, tugged the purse string, dropped it inside. Just as I tugged it closed, Jabbour spun and glowered down at me.

"You!" he shouted. "What do you think you're doing?"

And just like that, I was caught. Sweat trickled down my temple. My body shook with fear. "Please…" A pitiful plea—and all I could manage.

"You're not finished," said Jabbour, plopping back into his chair. "Don't be trying to sneak off before the job is done. There!" He pointed to a smudge on his heel. "I want to see my reflection."

I never polished shoes with such joy in my life. A few minutes later, as I put my finishing touches on Jabbour's boots, the sound of horse hooves pounded up to the tent. I turned to see *Corbaci* Ildemir drawing his mount to an expert stop. Aruna—or Rune as he called himself—brought his horse up alongside.

Jabbour put on his most obsequious smile. He walked out to greet them, hands outstretched. "My *sidi,*" he said as Ildemir and Rune dismounted, "How very fine to see you this morning."

"Yes," sniffed Ildemir as he tugged off his riding gloves. "A fine morning indeed. Aruna has caught our thief."

I watched Jabbour's face fall. The overseer shook his head. "Already? But how? He hasn't even searched the town. Or the neighboring farms. The Red Heart must have taken shelter somewhere."

"He has," said Rune with a grin. He folded his hands as if taking a merry stroll. "Here, in the quarry."

"What?" Jabbour burst into a grating laugh. He held

his belly for effect. "My *Sidi,* I hope you have not paid this charlatan in advance."

Ildemir's mustache twitched. "That is not your concern. Now then..." The Janissary turned to Rune. "I came as you asked, Silver Hand. Where is the thief you promised?"

"Ah," crowed Rune. "But to reveal that, I must first ask you to open your wife's wardrobe chest." He swept a hand toward the largest trunk on the baggage train—a monstrosity of mahogany. A heavy iron lock hung from the latch.

Ildemir sighed, his annoyance growing. He stepped toward the chest, fishing in the leather satchel at his belt.

"You see, after Captain Irish Declan's kind help yesterday," Rune pontificated, "I was able to put several of the most useful slaves to work as my eyes and ears. In the night, they spied your thief moving his ill-gotten loot."

Ildemir patted another pouch on his belt, frowning. "I seem to have...misplaced the key."

"Oh, that is a shame. Because your stolen goods are inside this very chest. May I suggest: break the lock."

Ildemir shot a stern look at Rune.

The thief simply shrugged.

The Janissary commander walked over to a pile of rocks, picked up the pick leaning against them, and returned to the chest. Jabbour knit his brows, curious in spite of himself. Even I couldn't resist wondering if Rune was right. Ildemir brought the pick down in one clean swing, and the iron lock thudded into the dust. He gestured to two slaves, and they hurried over to the chest. They set it at the commander's feet and flipped open the lid.

Ildemir's mouth fell open. He reached into the chest and brought out a golden necklace inset with a large red ruby. "My wife's necklace...and my sword...and bridle. You mean to say...the thief was hiding here the whole time? That the stolen goods never left?"

"Indeed," said Rune. "You said it yourself—very difficult to get in or out of this mountain quarry. Easier to stash the goods, then smuggle them out in a chest no one would dare search. Very clever."

"And your men saw the Red Heart last night?"

"Oh yes. That is him." Rune pointed a finger straight at me.

Ildemir looked in my direction. I wanted to bolt, but it's always worse to run. So, I stood there, knees buckling, as Ildemir stomped forward. But he stopped in front of Jabbour, a few paces away. "*You?*" he said, glowering at the overseer.

"Me?" whined Jabbour. "*Sidi*—it's impossible. I've stolen nothing. This Silver Hand vermin is lying."

"I most certainly am not," Rune breezily proclaimed. "My spies saw him use the key. Perhaps if you check his belt..."

Ildemir looked at Rune, then back at Jabbour.

"*Sidi*..." said Jabbour with a nervous laugh.

Ildemir reached for Jabbour's belt. He yanked the pouch free, pulled the string, and stared inside. He glared at his hireling, then pulled out the iron key. "You..." he breathed. "You...stole from my chambers? From my *wife?*"

"That...that..." stammered Jabbour. The blood drained from his face. "That's not mine. I don't know how that got there."

"You traitorous cretin! Guards!" bellowed Ildemir. A

pair of Janissaries marched up without another order and seized Jabbour.

"*Sidi* Ildemir! Please! You must believe me. I have only ever been loyal to you. *Sidi!*" Jabbour's shouts faded as the soldiers dragged him away to the slave cells.

For a moment, Ildemir watched. At length, he turned to Rune. "I never liked that man. And my son always warned me not to trust him. I should have listened. Well done, Aruna."

Rune bowed humbly. "It was a great honor to serve you on behalf of the Silver Hand. Our rival has been eliminated and your treasures restored. Now, there is only the small matter..." and here he bowed lower, "...of payment."

"Of course," said Ildemir, his lips eking out a smile. "Thirty percent of the value of the treasure, as agreed. My purser will see to you."

"The Silver Hand thanks you most humbly, but..."

"Yes?"

"It is a rare service indeed to perform such a feat in a single night. If I recall the lovely Bahar's generous offer, our quick resolution entitles us to...a bonus?"

"Yes, yes, of course," grumbled Ildemir. "Name it."

"A small token really. My master is a great admirer of youth and beauty. We ask that you grant us one of your wife's servant girls. And this slave."

Rune pointed at me. I pointed at my own chest as if to ask, *me?*

"Him?" asked Ildemir. "He's crippled. What possible use could he be?"

"Ah ha," Rune musically laughed. "I am afraid that is the business of the Silver Hand. Are we agreed?"

Ildemir narrowed his eyes. He gave a slight nod, and

the bargain was struck.

Three hours later, I sat on the back of a cart, riding through the open gates of the quarry. After years spent in a hole in the earth, I rolled onto the open road as easily as a lord from his manor. Sitting beside me was the veiled servant girl who had given me the key. Her eyes were smiling again as she watched the Janissaries fading into the distance.

"There never was a 'Red Heart,' was there?" I asked.

"Of course there's a Red Heart," she said in English. That's when I heard something familiar in her accent. "It just wasn't Jabbour. The Hand and the Heart were pursuing the same treasure all along." She turned her twinkling eyes toward me. "You, Declan."

"'Hand and Heart.'" I smiled at her. "Fitting. Two parts that go together. So who is he, this Heart of yours?"

The girl gave a small laugh. She stared at her pointed silk shoes, dangling above the passing road. "Not 'heart' like what beats in your chest, Declan. 'Hart.' Like the stag."

My eyes widened. My breath shortened.

"And not 'he.'"

With that, she reached up to the delicate clasp by her cheek. There was a soft click, and the veil fell to the dust.

Chapter 58

The Skiff
The Mediterranean Sea
Wednesday, September 7th, 1803

There was a faint whisper.

John.

"Mother?" murmured John Sullivan. He had the vague idea that there was something important he had to do, but he couldn't recall what. Nor could he recall where he was. His mind wandered in the dark.

Now a child's voice called from far away. *Johnny.*

"Katie?" He became aware of anguish. His body wracked with pain. His soul filled with sorrow. What was it he had to do?

John, whispered Nora.

Johnny, called Kaitlin.

Son, said Declan.

John opened his eyes on a sight of wonder. Thousands of stars—millions—filled his vision. The North Star blazed like a torch. The midnight sky was a mural of light.

"Sextant!" John whispered. He remembered he was in the skiff. The clouds had cleared, and he needed to take their position. He threw the peacoats off and looked for his sextant by starlight. Ethan snored beyond the next thwart. Varlick lay asleep against the gunwale. Melisande slept upright at the stern. John's hand touched cool metal.

Pressure throbbed in John's skull as if it might burst. He couldn't breathe through his stopped-up nose. Sweat covered him like a patina. He crawled to the gunwale and held up the sextant. He had to concentrate.

The sea was as smooth as glass. Not a wave. Not a ripple. The water reflected a perfect twin of every star. It was like looking at the floor of Heaven.

What had he been doing?

"Sextant," John whispered again. He fumbled to remove the sun filter. He held the looking glass up to his eye. He scanned for the North Star. At last, Polaris filled the lens. He began turning the dial, and the Pole Star descended toward the horizon.

John.

"What?" John murmured. He let the sextant lower from his eye. There was something…out there.

On the water, John saw a figure. He leaned forward for a better look. A good distance to starboard, a great red stag stood on a bank of stars. Four hooves were planted on the surface of the sea. The deer's lips grazed near a violet nebula, ears flicking back and forth. The buck reared its head and looked in John's direction, displaying a set of regal antlers. Its eyes reflected spirals of celestial light. John felt wonder and terror in equal measure. This was no ordinary hart, but a powerful spirit of the wilds.

The sextant slipped from John's grasp. *No!* The fog in John's mind cleared for a moment, and he scrambled to catch it. But it was too late. The navigational tool splashed into the water and began a swift descent to the bottom of the sea. John should have cursed his misfortune, but a flash of movement drew his eyes. Spooked by the sound, the stag reared on its mighty legs and bolted. It galloped away on the starlit sea.

"Mother?"

Where the stag once stood, Nora Sullivan sat with legs tucked under her. In her hands, a storybook. Sitting in her lap, Kaitlin—a little girl with red curls and a blue dress. Nora read softly while Katie brushed her dolly's hair. A man approached them, a tumbler of whiskey in his hand, with short red hair and a curly beard. Declan Sullivan stood behind his wife, one hand caressing Nora's shoulder, a thumb in the pocket of his waistcoat. A fourth figure walked up behind Kaitlin, taller than all of them. A young, handsome, confident man in an officer's coat. Isaac, the family's ever watchful protector. The ocean surface supported the family like a floor of glass.

"What..." said John, choking on the word. "What are you all doing here?"

Distantly, John realized this was a dream. Or a mirage. The fever playing tricks. And yet, they looked so real.

"Mam!" John called, his throat on fire. He had to get their attention. They *had* to see him. "Mam! Katie! I'm here. It's me...John."

But they didn't look at him. They couldn't hear him. Because they weren't real. In hundreds of years, among thousands of slaves, how many ever came back from the Barbary Coast? And what remained of the few that did? Any sane man in John's place would count himself lucky to have escaped. He would move on, start a new life, and mourn for those left behind. But not John. He spent every day scraping, planning, and fighting. He threw away an inheritance. He threw away his dignity. He threw away his first love. For a fantasy.

The family on the field of stars rose to their feet. They stood as though posing for a portrait. Declan behind Nora, Isaac behind Katie. They were waiting for him.

"Wait!" John cried. "Don't go…"

They were a mirage, because John's quest was a mirage. It always had been. He was becalmed at sea, a deserter from the Navy, trusting a Barbary slave to lead him to his family. He was a fool.

"I know why you're here," John said, a tear running down his cheek. "You're here…because you're dead." John bent over the rail and wept until his ribs hurt. When he fell silent again, he threw a leg over the gunwale, then another. He looked up at his family on the water with a renewed purpose.

"Wait for me," he cried. "I'm coming."

Ethan Auldon's eyes snapped open. Someone was speaking with an Irish accent.

"Wait for me—I'm coming!"

Ethan rubbed his eyes, looking around in the darkness. His heart leaped when he saw the sky filled with stars. For a moment, he could only think of getting the sextant. Then John's voice drew his attention to starboard.

"Wait!" John pleaded. He no longer sounded like a Pennsylvanian. "I'm coming. Wait!"

"Oh my God," Ethan murmured.

John was climbing over the side of the boat, calling out to someone. Ethan followed his gaze, trying to figure out who the hell John was trying to hail. Nothing but the calm starlit sea. No ships, or boats, or lights. No one at all. John already had his feet dangling over the side. In the next second, he would be in the water.

"John!" Ethan dashed across the boat. He grabbed John's waist and hauled him back to safety.

"No!" wailed John. He fought and thrashed. "Let me go! I want to go with them. They're dead. They're all dead."

"Sully!" cried Melisande, coming to Ethan's aide.

"Help me pull him aboard," Ethan said. "He's delirious."

Ethan and Melisande wrestled John down into the boat.

"Let me go," demanded John. "I want to go to them. They're dead, and I have to go to them."

"There's no one out there, Sully," Melisande argued.

"Kaitlin's alive, John," said Ethan. He finally had John in a bear hug, holding him down like an anchor. "You've got to listen to me, mate. You're delirious. You can't give in to despair. You must keep faith. Katie's alive."

John's strength ebbed. "They're gone, Ethan. They're all gone."

"You don't know that, John," said Ethan.

"We're going to find them, Sully," said Melisande. "You've got to fight."

"I failed them," John murmured, eyes searching the stars. "I took too long. I wasn't strong enough."

"Listen to me, John," said Ethan, his voice becoming stern. "You want to blame yourself because tragedy makes more sense when it has an author. But what happened to your family isn't your fault. It happened because sometimes, bad things just happen. That's all there is to it, John. You're going to get through this delirium, you're going to stop this self-pity, and you're going to fight. Because we've come too far together to quit. Do you hear me? I won't *let* you quit."

John looked up at his friend as if seeing him for the first time. He nodded. "Okay, mate. Okay."

Ethan put a cool rag over John's forehead. Melisande put a canteen to his mouth. After a few minutes, John settled. Finally, he nodded off to sleep. Ethan pulled the coats over him again.

"You did a good job, Fiddles," said Melisande.

"Thanks, Melly." Ethan's eyes drifted toward the North Star.

"I've never seen Sully like that. What was he doing anyway?"

Ethan was lost in thought for a moment as he considered. "The sextant!" Ethan cried. The stars were out—a chance to find their position. He dug through John's supplies. "Where is it?"

"Don't bother," murmured Varlick. "I awoke and saw Sullivan drop the sextant in the sea."

Ethan and Melisande stared at Varlick, speechless. There were stars everywhere, and not a single one they could read.

Chapter 59

The Skiff
The Mediterranean Sea
Thursday, September 8th, 1803

There was a gentle swaying. Then wind whispering on canvas. Warmth on John Sullivan's skin, then cool drops. He awoke and put a hand up against the rising sun. A spray of surf came over the bow and wet his hair. John sat up on his elbows, blinking sleep sand from his eyes. He was laying under a pile of blankets, feet pointed aft, head below the triangular jib sails. Emerald waves rolled under a cloudless sky.

Ethan sat a couple thwarts away, back to John, measuring out the portions of salt pork and biscuits. Varlick stooped over a cask, to the right of the mast, hands unshackled. He ladled water into a wooden, drum-shaped canteen, then corked the spout. Melisande sat in her usual Siren pose, back against the bulwark, legs stretched along the thwart. To John's curiosity, she held Nora's watch on her palm, hunter case open, examining the inscription. The jib sails were turned to windward, but the mainsail was eased—allowing one to collect the breeze and the other to let it spill. With the rudder lashed hard into the wind, the skiff yawed back and forth, going nowhere.

John's first attempt to speak ended in a rattling wheeze. When he was able to get his vocal chords going, he sounded like an old man. "Why are we heaved-to?"

Varlick looked up from the water cask. Ethan glanced over his shoulder. Melisande sprang off the bench.

"Sully's up!" she cried. The deerskin-clad woman skipped from thwart to thwart and landed squatting beside John. She swept a tuft of black hair out her eyes, beaming. "I knew you'd pull through!" She knocked him on the shoulder.

"All right, all right," John smiled.

"First thing's first," declared Melisande, producing a rum flask from her vest pocket. She plucked the cork with her teeth and jabbed the spout between John's lips. "Get a good pull, now," she said.

John gulped for his life. His scratchy throat fought back, and he spluttered spirits all over his chin.

"That's it, Sully," said Melisande. She re-corked the flask, then pulled a pouch from her other pocket. "You've been down for two days. Can't have you wasting away. Open up."

"Melly—" A wad of tobacco cut John off as Melisande stuffed the leaves down his lip. He offered a muffled protest. "Me—wy...umf..."

"What's that?" said Melisande. "Another drink?" She wiggled her flask.

John waved his hand in surrender. "No, Melly, I'm fine. Thank you." He had to admit, a chew hit the spot.

Varlick was watching in silence. Ethan stayed busy with the food rations.

"How do you feel?" asked Melisande.

After a deep breath of the fresh sea air, John said, "Good." It was true—for the first time in over a week, his wounds weren't throbbing. He could move without muscles seizing up. The feverish ache in his bones had gone. Though he still had a painful cough, he felt like himself again. "Hungry. Really hungry."

"Good timing," said Melisande. "Fiddles was just setting out breakfast. You can have my ration."

"Thank you, Melly. A single ration will do."

"Nonsense! We need Bloody Sully back in fighting form. Oh, and I have this." Melisande pulled the watch from her breeches pocket and held it out to John. "I kept it safe for you."

John looked at the silver watch, then at the delight in Melisande's eyes. For a moment he just smiled, wondering how he'd ever met anyone so extraordinary. He took the watch, feeling its weight. "It couldn't have been in safer hands."

Melisande flitted over to where Ethan had parceled out the food.

John slipped the watch into his pocket. He staggered to his feet and made his way over to Ethan. His friend didn't look up. "I see we've got the wind back."

"I see you're awake," said Ethan, handing Varlick his share of food.

"Why are we hove-to?" John asked.

"We don't have a course," said Ethan as he handed a serving to Melisande.

"Sure we do, mate. East. I'll take our position at noon and make any needed corrections."

There was a pause. Melisande inspected her bread for weevils. Varlick scrutinized the flapping mainsail.

Ethan faced John and held out a ration. There were

dark circles under his eyes. His jaw was a rigid line. "You don't remember."

John accepted the food and bit off a hunk of hardtack. "Remember what?" John said as he chewed.

Ethan plopped down on a bench, looking toward the southern horizon. "Last night, in your fever dream, you dropped the sextant overboard."

"What?" John said through a wad of bread.

"We were all still exhausted from the rain."

"I only nodded off for a second," said Melisande defensively.

"It hardly matters now," Ethan went on. "You woke up in the middle of the night, John, yelling and carrying on, thinking you saw someone on the water. You almost jumped overboard before we caught you. You're lucky you didn't drown. I think you must have meant to take a reading, and somehow dropped the sextant."

John swallowed heavily. He sat down on the gunwale, nearly dropping his salt pork.

"So, you see, John," Ethan went on, "we have no way of knowing where we are. We sailed miles off course to evade a possible enemy, we drifted for days on a becalmed sea, and we're lost on the Mediterranean with only a few days of food left. We have no idea where we are. And do you know why?"

Varlick scratched at his beard. Melisande rubbed the deck with her toe.

"Because you're a stubborn fool," Ethan said.

There was nothing to say. Ethan was right. John had never been good at rest—at standing still. At rest, John could feel the tension. The tension that stretched every moment of his life taut. He felt like a man hanging onto the yard by the footropes. No choice but to climb or fall.

He reached into his pocket and opened Nora's watch.

Awake, dear heart, awake. Thou hast slept well.

In five years, had John *ever* slept?

"Come on, Fiddles," piped Melisande. "Don't be so hard on Sully. He'll get us out of this."

"And just how exactly?" snapped Ethan. "We have no way to navigate, and we're low on supplies."

"I'm sorry, mate," murmured John.

"Well I'm not for sitting around," Melisande declared. "I say we sail straight south. We'll run into some Barbary land or other. I'm tired of all this tossing about at sea anyway. Get some land under my legs, and I'll find us a way to where we're going."

"That would be dangerous," said Varlick in his most silken tenor. "The Janissaries do not take kindly to trespassers on their shores."

"Varlick is right," Ethan agreed. "Our only choice is to sail north, where we're sure to run into a French or Italian port. We can re-provision, buy new instruments, and start fresh."

"No!" said John, jumping to his feet. "We've already delayed too long. Who knows how much time my family has left. Besides, we risk getting caught for desertion. Or meeting a pirate vessel. Or another storm. No, we press on."

"Hear, hear," said Melisande. "Scruffy, you know the way to the island. How hard can it be to steer us in the right direction?"

"I can point us toward the island," said Varlick. "But only if I know where we are. We cannot risk a guess—the closer we get to Barbary Coast, the more danger we face. Wandering around, looking for a bearing, we'll end up slaves—again."

"Our only chance is to sail to a friendly port," said Ethan.

"So, we give up and start over?" John leaned over the rail. He looked at his own frowning reflection in the green water. "That's not like you, mate."

"Then you figure it out."

John shoved off the gunwale and rounded on Ethan. "Look, I said I'm sorry, didn't I? You were right, and I was a fool. I should have taken better care of myself. I was stubborn. I admit it. When this is done, I'll grovel on my knees if you want. But right now, I'm asking for your help."

"I *am* helping. By advising you to sail north." Ethan crossed his arms and squinted into the distance.

"Ethan," murmured John, "I know I've ruined things. But Kaitlin is innocent. Maybe she deserves a better brother than me—but right now, I'm all she's got. *We* are all she's got. I'm not asking you to help me. I'm asking you to help her. Please, mate. I need you."

Melisande looked from Ethan to John, to Ethan again. Her knuckles were white on her ball of grapeshot. Varlick watched with his usual alacrity.

"I've done all I can," murmured Ethan, picking at the notches on the bench.

"Fine," retorted John. He looked at the prisoner. "Varlick, if we land on the Barbary shores, can you guide us?"

"Yes," replied the disheveled old man. "I know those lands well. I may even be able to talk us past the Janissaries, but it will be dangerous."

"All right," John nodded. "Melly, take the tiller."

"I've done all I can!" Ethan repeated, jumping to his feet.

The others in the boat returned a puzzled stare.

Ethan smiled. "I've done all *I* can. I've kept the chip log every day. Noted our course and speed. Recorded my readings in these notches. But there's something *you* can do, John. If you can't use the sun and stars to plot a course, use my readings."

John knit his brows. "You're talking about dead reckoning."

Ethan gave a cocksure smile.

"Dead reckoning?" asked Melisande. "Whatever that is, it sounds bully! Let's do it."

John explained, "Dead reckoning means working out our current position by using our last known fix. We'd have to work out where we started, then calculate where we've travelled since then. But that would mean mapping our entire course for the last…"

"Six days," offered Ethan.

"Which means plotting our flight from the unknown ship, and then all those days of aimless drifting. I don't know anyone who could manage that feat."

"Bloody Sully's not just anyone," said Melisande.

"I appreciate the vote of confidence, Melly," John replied. "But there's the currents to account for. Even when we were becalmed, they could have carried us far. I don't know them."

"Perhaps I could help," said Varlick, drawing all of their attention. "I know the currents well. I have sailed this sea for many years."

"There you have it," said Ethan.

"*If* we can trust old Scruffy," said Melisande.

Varlick raised his shackled hands as if in supplication. "I have no reason lie. My fate is entwined with yours." He fixed his eyes on John. "To guide us into a reef would mean my death."

"Draw for the ace, win with the deuce," said John. He turned toward the bow and watched the wind-swept waves. His hand found its way into his pocket. He produced the Islanded Lion, holding it up between forefinger and thumb. He flicked it into the air. He caught the spinning coin and turned to his friends. "Let's get to work."

Chapter 60

The Skiff
The Mediterranean Sea
Thursday, September 8th, 1803

The sun was already low when it came time to ask Varlick's help. John fought to keep the navigational chart smooth. A canteen and compass pinned the map to the thwart. The occasional gust tugged at the edges. Ethan had kept it dry by sealing it in a cask. John carefully retraced one of the penciled numbers at thirty-seven degrees north, ten degrees east. He pinned the legs of his calipers to a line. Straining his eyes in the dusk, he walked them back along a zig-zagging path.

"Remember, boys," Declan says, pacing with hands behind his back. His boys sit on boxes forward of the Wandering Hart's *wheel, scribbling on their slate boards. "A good navigator trusts the arithmetic and his instincts."*

The sea had moods, John's father had always told him. She kept secrets no map could tell. John had plotted three days of travel, advanced from the moment they fled a stranger on the horizon. Tacking east and west. Wearing around to the north, then coming about to the south. A dozen other course changes to follow the wind. The most complicated calculations he'd ever done. Did he have it right? His instincts told him he did. He looked over at the unkempt old man sitting by the mast. He watched Varlick pick at a bloody scab on his maimed ear and wondered if he could trust this man.

As John motioned Varlick over, he knew he was taking the biggest gamble of his life. For the first few minutes, Varlick and John sat across from each other, the thwart between them like a table. Varlick looked over John's course, examined the extrapolated position, and began scribbling notes. He picked up John's calipers and walked the points along the Tunisian coast.

Without looking up, Varlick said, "When you see her, what do you imagine your first words will be?"

John's pencil paused on the fortieth parallel north. "What?"

"To your sister, Kaitlin. When you find her."

John resumed writing. "I don't know. I hadn't given it much thought. It's hardly the business of a stranger."

"I know what I will say. To my daughter. Should I ever see her again."

"Hmm," said John, feigning disinterest. The truth was, his first and last thoughts every day for five years had been of his family. Father. Mother. Brother. Sister. Their fate. Living to see them again. But until Varlick's question, he hadn't really imagined the first conversation after his mission succeeded. Would they even recognize him?

"I would tell her I was sorry," continued Varlick. "For spending so many years away. For missing her childhood. For not being the father she deserved. For failing her. Your compass, please." Varlick offered the calipers in exchange.

"How…how did you fail her?" asked John, taking the calipers and sliding over the compass box.

"I chose a life of service," said Varlick. He studied the compass on his palm. "A life of danger. And sacrifice. And in the end, I wound up a prisoner. I squandered my chance to be a father. And I shall never get another."

"You speak as if she's still alive."

"She is, as far as I know. Somewhere." Varlick placed the compass back in its box. "Our present speed?"

"Three knots," Ethan called out.

"You may see her again," said John. "When we reach Red Mortar Redoubt, I'll keep my end of the bargain. You'll go free. You're not my enemy."

Varlick gave a wry smile. "A kind sentiment. But I'll never be a father again, nor will I ever be free. Men like us can never go back."

"What do you mean 'us?'"

"Even if you find your mother and your sister, do you really think it will be the end of your war? That you'll be the man of peace you were before that fateful day? How will you explain all you've done in their names? How will you tell Kaitlin about Bloody Sully?"

Melisande's carving knife paused on her piece of driftwood. Ethan looked up from his anatomy book. They both watched John and Varlick.

"I did what I had to do," said John. "If I'm a killer, it's what the Barbary Pirates made me. I am the work of *Re'is* Ilyas Naim."

"Given the chance, would you undo his work?"

John leaned close to Varlick. "I'd give anything to undo that day."

"Go back to the dreary life of a merchant's son?" Varlick said. "The look on your face when you butchered

Re'is Harrak tells a different story. A wolf can never choose to be sheep. You may hang your sword over the mantle, Sullivan, but it will never be far from your reach."

"I'm not like Naim," insisted John. "I'm not like the Barbary Pirates. I came here to right a wrong. To free my kin. I never wanted any of this."

"And yet, your very reason for taking up the sword gave you the strength to wield it. The Barbary Pirates built the crucible that forged Bloody Sully. A part of you must feel gratitude."

"Don't listen to him, John," said Ethan. "You are not a prisoner of fate. Every man has a choice."

John looked at Ethan for a moment. He took out his mother's watch and flipped open the case. He ran his thumb over the inscription. "There did come a day that I was grateful to Ilyas Naim," said John. He stared at the black tine of the minute hand, creeping toward *XII*. "I'd been teaching him navigation for a month. He treated me kindly. Gave me better food and more freedom than the other slaves. We loved to talk. Of ships. The sea. Even Shakespeare."

A calm fell over the boat as John spoke. The water plunked against the hull. A gull called. Ethan and Melisande listened intently.

"He would tell me of the Black Sea," continued John. "I'd always wanted to see it. I would tell him of the West Indies and my time there as a boy. I'd been so lonely since becoming a slave. I felt grateful to have a friend again. Even one that owned me."

"There is no shame in wanting friendship," Varlick said softly.

"Oh yes there is," said John, turning a bitter smile seaward. "One day, the first mate told me what the rest of the free crew already knew. The real reason Ilyas bought me, rather than my father. A deal my mother struck with him the first night after he took the *Wandering Hart*. He would make me his navigation tutor. And in return she…" John sighed, eyes closed against the horrors of the past. "She gave herself to him." John looked up at Varlick.

"Sully…" whispered Melisande, lacrosse stick nearly slipping from her hand.

Ethan sank onto a thwart.

Varlick didn't speak. After a moment, he turned his attention to another calculation.

John went on. "So, when Ilyas wanted my help plotting a course to the Sicilian coast—to plunder and enslave, of course—I drew a line through a dangerous reef near Sicily. Father had charted it only a year ago. Ilyas had no idea it was there." John snapped the watch closed. "By the time the *Wandering Hart* sank into the sea, I had climbed onto a small rowboat. I saw Ilyas Naim not far away, floundering and crying out for help. He couldn't swim. I could have saved him. I even felt like I should. Which is why I let the sea take him. I watched him flail, and gasp, and beg. And I was glad when he went under for the last time."

Varlick's pencil scratched on the chart.

"That is the only gratitude I have for the man who stole my freedom," John continued. "Destroyed my family. Raped my mother. And when I get to the Barbary Coast, I will have that very gratitude in store for every pirate I meet."

"The death of an enemy," mused Varlick, glancing up from his calculations.

Silence descended on the boat again.

John scribbled a few more notes and said, "I'm done. I've accounted for your currents as best I can. Check my work."

"Very well," agreed Varlick. He bowed close to the page. "You will forgive me—my eyesight is not what it once was."

"Take your time."

Varlick alternately whispered and hummed to himself as he traced John's path. His face hovered from point to point, his eyes straining in the light of sunset.

"'*La taqtal 'akhi*,'" quoted John. "You never told me what it means."

"I thought you knew."

"I told you I didn't," said John. He picked up his calipers and checked a southeasterly line for a third time. "But I am curious why you were so keen to bring it up."

Varlick looked up at John through his eyebrows, the dusky light gleaming in his eyes. "It means, 'surrender, villain.'"

"I don't believe you."

"Why not?"

John wanted to say he didn't trust Varlick, but that wasn't the reason. He sensed the words meant something else, though he didn't know why. "The Barbary Pirates brought this war on themselves. What they've done to innocent travelers at sea—it is unforgivable."

"A wolf does not seek the forgiveness of sheep."

"You sound as if you admire your former masters."

"I understand them—in a way you do not. We all have our reasons for inflicting slaughter. Your countrymen have theirs. You have yours. I had mine. What is forgivable, what is deserved—small matters in the end."

"What were your reasons?"

"My plotting is done."

John's brows knit together.

Varlick planted his index finger on the chart. "Here. I've plotted all the currents along our path. I have checked all your work. Our fix is as close as it's ever going to be." He rose, stepped over to Ethan, and offered his wrists.

Ethan reached for the manacles. "Right. It's getting late."

"No," said John. "That won't be necessary."

"Are you sure?" Ethan asked, frowning at John.

"We've come this far," said John. "He could have done us harm any number of times, but he's only ever offered to help."

Varlick gave a deferential nod, then returned to his usual place amidships.

Ethan tossed the shackles onto a coil of spare cable, then came to sit across from John. He leaned close and whispered, "Are you sure about this? About *him*?"

"I thought you trusted him more than me," John pointed out. He ran through his course again, re-checking each correction.

"There's something off about him. He's been whispering in all our ears since this journey began. Learning about us. And yet, what do we really know about him?"

"I trust him," said John. "Besides, soon, it won't matter. I've reckoned our position." He pushed the chart closer to Ethan.

The surgeon's mate followed the meandering course of the skiff all the way to a final "X." It lay a little west of Sicily, a little north of Tunis. "That close? We could make the island in a day."

"If the wind holds. You still with me, mate?" John extended his hand across the thwart.

Ethan looked at his feet for a moment. John wondered if he would refuse. But then Ethan accepted John's hand. "Always, mate."

"Well then," declared John as he got to his feet. "Melly, tiller hard to port. Varlick, let fly the jibs. Ethan, sheet home the mainsail. Best speed to Red Mortar Redoubt."

Chapter 61

Declan Sullivan's Chronicle
The Quarry of the Bey, Outside the Port of Tunis
One Year Ago

There was a soft click, and the veil fell to the dust. For a moment, I couldn't breathe. So much of the servant girl's face had changed, but so much was familiar. The little trail of freckles across her cheek, bronzed by years in the sun. Her red locks of hair, longer, but still curly. The light in her cognac eyes as she smiled.

I nearly fainted and tumbled off the cart. I caught myself on one of the planks. "Katie? Can it be you?"

Her smile lit up like a sunrise. A tear ran down her cheek, and she hurried to wipe it away. "It's me, Da."

I couldn't believe my eyes. The last time I had seen her, she'd been a little girl. Had that much time really passed? She would later tell me it had been four years, and she had just turned thirteen. "Katie? My Katie?"

She nodded, the tears flowing fast now. "Aye, Da, it's me. It's your Katie."

"Kaitlin, my darling!" I said as I pulled her close, shedding tears of my own. "Oh my God, my child." I kissed the top of her head again and again. "Katie, my child. My precious child."

"It's me, Da," she repeated. "It's me."

Rune cast a glance over his shoulder. I could see his smile in the corner of my eye. He turned his attention back to the reins.

"Praise the Lord," I said. "I thought I'd never live to see you again. This is a miracle."

We held one another for a good while. When we were both composed enough to continue our conversation, the questions came too fast for me to ask them all. "Are you all right? Have you been harmed? How did you find me?"

"Da," laughed Katie. "Slow down. I'm fine. I promise."

"More than fine," Rune proclaimed from the box seat. "Your daughter became the most skilled apprentice in the Silver Hand. Even better than me, the magnificent Aruna *Taigar Pair*—the Tiger Foot. And now, she's a skilled thief with a name all her own."

"All right, Rune!" said Kaitlin, her cheeks flushing red. She brushed her hair back as she looked at him, a starry look in her eyes. I could tell she fancied him. "Don't embarrass me in front of my da."

"It's true," Rune said with a shrug.

"So," said I, "a thief, eh? 'The Red Hart?'"

"It's nothing," Kaitlin said. She looked away bashfully. "I needed a name other than Silver Hand."

"And I say keep it," said Rune. "A name well earned."

Kaitlin chuckled. "I don't know about that…"

"And you snuck around that quarry all this while?" I cried. "You did all that stealing from the Janissaries? My God, you stole that key from Ildemir's chambers! Are you daft?"

"Da," said Kaitlin, her smile fading. "I knew what I

was doing. Besides, I had to. I couldn't leave you. Please, don't be cross."

"I…I'm not cross. I could never be cross with such a brave lass."

Her smile returned.

"Rune's right," I said. "I like the name."

"You do?" Kaitlin said with a grin. For a moment, she was my little girl again, wanting me to be proud of her.

"I do." I smiled and pulled her close. She put her head on my shoulder—the way she used to when I read bedtime stories to her. We were quiet for a long while as the cart trundled across the desert.

The Lake of Tunis
Friday, September 9th, 1803

"Why have you stopped?" asked Master Isitan.

The fire had burned to low embers. The heat of the night suffocated the room. With no breeze, Declan could smell the fetid lake more than ever. "Master, I have told this story so many times. Why must I tell it again?"

Isitan was leaning on his arm, fist pressed into his cheek. He straightened his posture and poured another cup of tea. "Because those were The Chronicler's orders. Every night, you tell the story, and leave out not a detail."

Declan stared into the inky liquid in his silver cup. It looked as deep and dark as a well. "It causes me such pain. How much longer must I suffer?"

"Not long. Master Naim will return soon." Isitan touched the curved dagger laying on the table. He ran a finger along the razor edge. "In the meantime, our imperative work must continue. Should we falter, there will be consequences." Isitan's eyes flashed to Declan's. "Do you understand, slave?"

The truth was, any torture would have been preferable to telling another word of the story. At least then, Declan could hope that his body might give out under the strain. He could finally have release. But his longing for death had to remain secret. The masters had to believe in his will to live. His fear of the lash. Or else they might unearth the truth—his last forlorn hope.

"I understand, Master."

"Good. Tell us of the day you reached the island. Leave out not a word."

Declan Sullivan's Chronicle
Red Mortar Redoubt, Island off the Coast of Tunis
One Year Ago

The gates of Red Mortar Redoubt opened, and I passed into a magnificent manor. It was on a mesa, surrounded by cliffs, on an island protected by reefs. Travelers on the sea would think it was a barren pile of rocks too dangerous to approach. But for the thieves, it was a hidden Garden of Eden. Three stories enclosed a courtyard filled with grapes on lattices, rows of date palms, and hedges of flowers. Ivory fountains bubbled with water. The walls were a patchwork of ancient stone, most of them built of the same rose-colored mortar. Everywhere I looked, there were youths of all ages. There were men and women tending the gardens, the grounds, and the children.

"*This* is where you've been living?" I asked Kaitlin.

"The lair of the Silver Hand," Rune proudly proclaimed, taking in a lungful of air.

"The grandmaster of the guild saw my skill," said Kaitlin. "He bought me from the bey. He made me Rune's apprentice."

"Remarkable!" I said, smiling at my daughter. "And these children…?" I asked.

"Most are thieves in training," said Kaitlin. "Some were born to thieves who live here."

My daughter led me to the foot of another large sycamore, though not as grand as the one outside. An older African man stood there wearing a richly embroidered kaftan and silk turban. He stretched out his arms as I approached. "Declan Sullivan. Welcome, my friend."

"Ibrahim?" I said, recalling the slave broker who once consoled my captive family. "You are…"

"The Grandmaster of the Silver Hand," he boomed. Then, with a wry grin, he said, "but please—just Ibrahim to you."

"You…rescued my daughter from the Bey of Tunis?"

"I did nothing of the kind," said Ibrahim. "She showed potential, and like any good investment, I acquired her. She has since earned her place. Her mission to secure your freedom was a reward she requested in return for her loyal service."

"All the same, I owe you a great debt."

"Be careful to whom you indebt yourself," Ibrahim said, wagging a finger. "Especially in the company of thieves. Please, enjoy the garden. You are a guest in my home. I will give you a moment to say your farewells."

Before I could reply, Ibrahim was walking away,

leaning on his cane. He disappeared into the manor.

"What does he mean 'farewells?'" I asked Kaitlin.

Kaitlin looked at her feet, the way she always did when nervous. "Da, I have to go. But you'll be safe here."

"Go? Go where? I thought we were free."

"You are. I still owe Ibrahim one final job. It was part of the bargain."

"You mean another burglary?" I felt my heart pounding in my chest. "No! I've only just gotten you back—I won't have you in danger again. I'll speak to Ibrahim. We'll settle this. We'll—"

"Da!" Kaitlin interrupted. "This is something I have to do. I'll be all right, I promise. I do this all the time. It's easy." Her eyes brightened the way they used to when she would climb a tree or jump a brook. "I'm the Red Hart, and the Red Hart never gets caught."

I gave a heavy sigh and pulled her into a hug. "All right, love. But *please* be careful. You come back to me, you hear?"

"I promise, Da."

"Declan?"

Kaitlin and I looked down the cobbled garden path. A woman was approaching. A few strands of gray in her sienna hair. A new line or two under her eyes. The most beautiful woman I'd ever seen. The love of my life.

"Nora?" I said.

Nora's first steps toward me were slow, tentative. As if we shared the same fear—that either of us might wake. But then her steps quickened. I caught her in my arms. We held each other for a while without words.

"My love," she whispered in my ear. I could feel her tears wetting my neck.

"My dear heart," I whispered back.

I felt the arms of our daughter closing around us both. We stood there, the three of us, lost in that embrace.

It was the last day I would ever know joy.

Chapter 62

The Skiff
Red Mortar Redoubt, Island off the Coast of Tunis
Friday, September 9th, 1803

It began as little more than a pile of rocks on the horizon. Clouds towered above the distant island like palaces carved in marble. As the skiff drew closer, the rocks became sheer cliffs. A few miles away, the barren place came to life with flocks of birds nesting in the cliff face. Their harsh caws echoed across the water, scraping the ears. One or two of them flew over the boat, gliding on black buzzard-like wings. Their wild neck feathers and long beaks reminded John of the cormorants on the Lake of Tunis.

"Waldrapps," said Varlick from his seat at the tiller. He had insisted the island approach was dangerous, and that he take the helm. John reluctantly agreed. "There is an unusual number of them. Barbary Pirates and Tunisian sailors keep well clear. They believe the birds are harbingers of evil spirits that inhabit the island."

"Are they?" asked Melisande from her place amidships. She and Ethan were staring at a trio of waldrapps circling the mast.

"They're birds," snapped John. But his dismissive tone belied his own dread. He leaned over the bow, watching for rocks, trying not to notice the winged shadows.

"Of course," agreed Varlick. "But I have found that men give their superstitions life."

"Legends are drawn from a measure of truth," said Ethan. He shuffled to the port side and dropped a sounding line. "I'm sure the reefs surrounding the island have been the doom of many ships."

As if to prove Ethan's point, John called back to Varlick, "Hard to starboard!"

The ship lurched as Varlick threw the tiller hard over. They all had to brace themselves as the skiff pitched to avoid the tip of a rock jutting out of the water.

John looked back at Varlick, his heart pounding.

"Well spotted," said Varlick with a wry smile.

The boat took a circuitous path to land. A shore of white sand wreathed the island. The beach sloped gently into clear teal water. But the tranquil coast was a mirage. John saw ring after ring of submerged reefs, like the hungry jaws of Charybdis. Only a small boat like theirs could make the approach, and then only with great care. Ethan took sounding after sounding, his quick orders averting disaster more than once.

There were many smaller shoals and patches of land apart from the main island. On the largest of these stood the foundation of an ancient watchtower. Most of it had likely crumbled centuries ago. Its blocks turned from red mortar at the base, to sandstone at the middle, to granite at the top. A crumbling stair, patched with rotting wood, spiraled around the wall, disappearing into a doorway in one place only to reappear elsewhere. Where the roof should have been, a massive sycamore tree grew as if it had been potted in the tower. A canopy of leaves spread across the entire patch of sand like a great green dome. The roots snaked through cracks and traced down the wall like ivy vines. When the four travelers, at last, splashed into the surf and towed the boat ashore, they paused a moment to stare up at the patchwork edifice.

Paper crinkled as John unrolled Ryland's drawing. He looked down at the sketch of a treetop visible above a manor wall. "That's the tree," said John, looking up again. "The one in Ryland's drawing. This is what he saw."

"It is said," began Varlick, "Red Mortar Redoubt was an outpost of Saladin during *ḥurūb al-faranǧa*. You call them the Crusades. Before that, a Roman watchtower. Before that, a lighthouse of ancient Carthage. And who knows how many others."

"I don't understand," said John, shading his eyes as he studied the cliffs. The watchtower and this miniature island it stood on had no connection to the larger whole. "This tower must have been abandoned for decades. There's nothing else here. I don't see any wall, any other signs of life."

"So it appears," said Varlick. "That is why the Silver Hand chose it as their base. You will see." He swept a hand toward the tower. "Please."

John's calf smarted as he limped forward. His wounds had settled from searing pain to dull ache, and he was stronger every day. But the moment he started up the spiral of steps, he had a coughing fit.

Ethan put a hand on John's back. "You all right, mate?"

"I'll be okay," John managed to gasp.

"Take it slow, all right?" Ethan admonished.

For once, John decided to take his friend's advice. He

stepped inside the first door. Ethan followed, pistol in hand, with Varlick behind him. Melisande brought up the rear, hand on her warclub. Narrow shafts of daylight streamed through arrow slots. Where stone steps had collapsed, there were rickety wooden posts hammered into the wall. A mountain of crumbled earth rose to half the tower's height, blocking the passage in places—the remains of walls built, razed, and built over again. From the mound rose the trunk of the elder tree, thicker in diameter than any tree John had ever seen. The gnarled wood smelled of a forest floor.

"I don't like it here, Sully," said Melisande, looking skittish. She twirled a throwing knife between her knuckles. "This place is haunted by restless spirits. Carried on the wings of those birds—they can't reach the Sky World."

"It's all right, Melly," said John. His eyes traced upward. The canopy of leaves colored the light like stained glass. "Just a little further, and you'll see. It's only an island. No spirits, just a hideout for a guild of thieves. Katie was here. I can feel it." John grimaced as he nudged his throbbing leg forward.

They picked their way ever higher. Once Ethan nearly slipped when a piece of stair crumbled away, but John caught his arm. Not a minute later, Ethan called out to John, bringing him to a stop. A wooden step was missing in front of him—a missing step that might have sent him tumbling down the tower. John nodded his thanks and stepped over the gap.

At the top of the stairs, they emerged onto a wooden platform. The platform formed a walkway around the tree trunk. Opposite the stairs, an archway stood empty, looking out onto the cliff. The adjacent walls had crumbled long ago. They had to duck under branches as they crossed the width of the tower.

"This is the entrance," said Varlick as they reached the skeletal archway.

"Here?" said John, looking doubtful.

Varlick smiled. He pulled an old torch sconce flanking the doorway.

Heavy chains clattered below their feet. John, Ethan, and Melisande looked over the tower edge in astonishment. A series of pulleys hidden on the far wall were paying a thick cable. At the bottom end, a massive block of stone—a counterweight—plunged into the sea between tower and cliff face. There was a sound like ramshackle wheels as a catwalk extended from the archway to a narrow crevice in the cliff. Only then did John notice a subtle path, and the rumor of rose-colored walls beyond.

"Shall we?" said Varlick, again pointing the way.

"You take the vanguard this time," ordered John.

Varlick nodded. "As you wish."

The four of them crossed the bridge, Varlick in the lead. Ethan stayed close to John, ready to catch him if his bad leg lost its footing. Melisande eyed the waldrapps nesting in the rock face. Their calls were more deafening than ever.

"It must be a great relief to be so close to the end," mused Varlick.

John frowned as he limped off of the bridge and onto the narrow stone path. "It will be. When my mother and sister are safe. Not a moment before."

"You dreamt of them again last night," said the old Barbary slave as he followed the winding path, barely wider than a man. "Perhaps after today, you will sleep more soundly."

"That's no concern of yours."

"No," murmured Varlick. "I suppose not. Here we are."

They rounded another bend in the path and emerged onto a wide, flat mesa. A cobbled path led straight to a red wall of sandstone. At the center, a double wooden gate reached to the top of fifteen-foot ramparts.

John's heart hammered now. Emotions churned in his gut. This was the place. Where Ryland had seen Kaitlin. The end of a five-year journey. Behind those gates, the answer to his family's fate. He could hear the calls of the waldrapps, more distant now. He should have felt relief. Even joy. But staring at those great doors, he felt too afraid to take a step.

Ethan came up on his right side. "We're with you, mate. We'll go together."

Melisande came up on his left. "That's right, Sully. Together. We didn't come all this way to spit off the cliffs."

John nodded. He took a step forward, and then another. Then he was limping as fast as he could. He was about to lay his hand on the gate when he heard Varlick behind him.

"'*La taqtal 'akhi.*'"

"What?" said John.

Varlick came alongside him, shoulder touching the iron bands of the door. "The words you said in your sleep. As you have done every night."

John wanted to deny it, but he just stared into Varlick's eyes. He thought of the scrawny boy's face.

John sees hate. No, he wants to see hate. But there's fear in the *boy's eyes when he says, "*La taqtal 'akhi.*"*

John cleared a lump from his throat. "What does it mean?"

"In your heart," said Varlick, speaking softly, "you already know, don't you?"

"John," said Ethan, snapping his friend out of his momentary trance. "We can discuss this later. Look at the gate."

As John studied it more closely, he realized there would be no need to knock. The two doors weren't flush. One was open a crack.

"Why wouldn't they be locked?" wondered Ethan.

"Something doesn't feel right, Sully," said Melisande shifting from foot to foot.

John thrust himself into the gate. It groaned inward, its massive hinges resisting all the way. He stumbled over the threshold, and the breath vanished from his lungs. He was standing in a great courtyard, bereft of life, paved in ash. Everywhere he looked, he saw the withered twigs of burned plants. Shriveled vines. Bushes of dead thorns. Piles of charred wood from burned furniture or lattice. A series of cobbled paths snaked through the wreckage to a derelict fountain—once three concentric waterfalls—now poisoned pools. Soot stained the marble and sandstone of the three-story manor enclosing the square. At the center of it all, another sycamore stood burnt and stripped of leaves, like a twisted grave marker.

"Can't be," whispered John. He limped forward, his feet kicking up ash. He coughed, the dust irritating his lungs. "It can't be."

"What happened here?" gasped Ethan.

"Sully…" said Melisande, a hand over her mouth.

John clawed at his hair, turning circles, eyes roaming

over the wreckage. "No, it can't *be*."

"In your heart," said the smooth voice of Varlick behind them, "you've always known, Sullivan. You dream of those words because some truths transcend language. You saw their meaning in the eyes of the boy you killed."

John rounded on Varlick. He pulled the pistol from his belt and let it hang at his side. "What?

Something was different as Varlick stepped easily through the ash, arms folded behind his back. *He* was different. No longer did he stoop like an arthritic old man. No more did his eyes cower toward the ground. He walked with a posture of military confidence. He looked at John with unflinching command. "I was watching when you thrust in the blade. I heard the boy's pitiful squeak. '*La taqtal 'akhi,*' he begged, but you ignored his plea."

John leveled the pistol at Varlick. "What the hell happened here?"

A bittersweet smile crept over Varlick's lips. "That is not for me to tell."

"Sully!" cried Melisande, drawing her war club and pistol.

A storm of tramping boots and rattling metal filled the square. John looked up to see soldiers filing out along the rooftops. They wore bright crimson coats, the same color as their felt hats. They had bright blue trousers, loose about the thighs. Unlike the Janissaries, their double-breasted buttons, stiff collars, and gold highlights suggested a more European style uniform. Bayonets gleamed from their muskets in a neat row as they assembled, muzzles trained on John and his party. There were at least thirty of them up above. A dozen more filed out of the burned manor and into the courtyard.

John aimed two pistols in opposite directions. Ethan switched his pistol from target to target. Melisande thumbed the edge of her throwing knife in one hand, pointed her pistol in the other. The three of them came back to back.

A fit, confident soldier, perhaps five or ten years older than John, walked down the middle path leading to the squalid fountain. Unlike the simple red coat and white belt of the others, his jacket had intricate gold embroidery. He carried a long, curved saber. His hand rested on the gilded ivory hilt. "Lay down your weapons," the soldier commanded in English, with a hint of a Turkish accent.

"Strange," said Varlick as he strolled past John. "All that time together in the boat, and you never really asked my name. My *full* name."

"What the hell is this, Varlick?" shouted John. "Who are these men?"

The soldiers' leader proclaimed, "*I* am Commander Isitan, and *we* are the *Nizam-I Djedid*. We serve the will of the sultan, and his chronicler." Isitan looked to Varlick, then to John.

The pistol wobbled in John's hand. He had to act. Had to fight. But for the first time since his quest began, he had no idea what to do.

"You never asked me who planned the attack on the *Philadelphia*," said Varlick. "You never asked who paid your sailor, Thomas Prince, to cripple the ship. Would you like to know how many pieces of silver I offered?"

"Prince!" spat Melisande. "I knew I hated that little shit."

"You led the attack!" said John, training the pistol on Varlick.

493

"Planned it. Directed it. Watched you bathe yourself in blood to win it." The mysterious man that had guided John and his friends to Red Mortar Redoubt took a step forward. His arms fell to his sides. Even with the tangle of hair covering his face, the change in his demeanor made him a man ten years younger. He stood a full foot taller than John, something the young midshipman hadn't noticed until now. He walked with ease and vigor. His eyes were sharp as daggers. "All for one prize. You."

"Who are you?"

"My name is Varlick Naim. Chronicler of Constantinople. Left hand of the Sultan. Father to Ilyas Naim, the man you watched drown. My son, whom you murdered."

"Lay down your weapons," repeated Isitan.

"What do we do, Sully?" said Melisande, her voice cracking.

"John…" whispered Ethan.

John stared at Varlick Naim. The father of his former master. He recognized the joy in his enemy's eyes. The same joy John had felt when he charged the decks of the Barbary gunboat. When he shot Clyde Tindall. When he watched Ilyas drown. And he knew immediately that it was all true. He lunged forward, ignoring the lance of pain in his calf. Guns rattled, and hammers cocked as the *Nizam-I Djedid* aimed at John. The muzzle of John's pistol hovered a few inches from Naim's nose.

"Order them to drop their weapons!" John shouted.

Naim smiled. "You always have a plan, don't you, Sullivan? Always so sure of your talent. So certain you can win. The day comes for each man when he must taste defeat."

"Do it, or I'll hollow out your fucking skull!" shouted John. "Do it!"

The soldiers laid fingers on triggers, but Naim raised a hand, and they relented. He took another step, allowing the cold metal of John's pistol to kiss his forehead. "My orders are already given," he said. "Fire that weapon, and you will watch your friends die in slow torment. You will never know the fate of your mother. Or your sister. And just as befell the Silver Hand, whatever survives you in this world, will burn. Fire your weapon—and my victory will be complete."

John's nostrils flared. His finger trembled on the trigger. He roared, a tear running from his eye. For a moment, be knew he was about to fire. But then the pistol fell away. He sank to his knees, staring into the dirt. "Lower your weapons," he breathed.

Ethan and Melisande did as ordered, and the soldiers rushed over to seize them. Isitan took Melisande's pistol, club, and knives. Ethan handed over his weapons, his medical bag, and his cutlass.

Naim squatted down in front of John and slipped the pistol out of his hand. "I saw you on that gunboat, Bloody Sully. I heard the words. *La taqtal 'akhi.*"

In the shock of defeat, in a fog of despair, John looked up at Naim. He felt as powerless under that gaze as he was on the *Wandering Hart* five years ago.

"It means, 'Don't kill my brother.'" After a moment, Naim rose to his feet and set off toward the gate. He said to Isitan, "Shackle them and load them into the boats. You will find their skiff beached near the tower."

The soldiers seized John's arms and hauled him to his feet. As they pulled *Ace* and *Spade* from his belt, he looked at Ethan and Melisande, their eyes full of fear. They could read the defeat in John's eyes, and he knew it.

A gun butt jabbed John's back. The *Nizam-i Djedid* marched the three *Philadelphia* sailors toward the gates of Red Mortar Redoubt.

Chapter 63

The USS *Allegheny*
Off the Coast of Italy
Friday, September 9th, 1803

Dominique stood on the deck of the *Allegheny*, blowing smoke rings toward the distant USS *Minerva*. The two-masted sloop lay anchored on crystal clear water. One of *Minerva's* boats was rowing ashore to replenish the water casks. The *Allegheny* watched from the mouth of the bay, dutifully protecting the treasure-laden ship, along with the Larocques' two merchant vessels. The *Minerva* was carrying a quarter million dollars in tribute to Bey Hammuda of Tunis—a tempting target for enterprising rogues. The marquis and the marquise had taken up residence on the treasure ship, and Dominique wished she could row over and have lunch with Angele. She took a drag, listening to the tobacco sizzle in her pipe.

"Smoking on the sly, eh?" said a man's voice.

Dominique coughed a cloud of smoke. "Not at all, I was just—"

"It's all right." Lieutenant Chester Ryland said. He joined Dominique near the bow. "Only teasing. Your secret's safe with me."

"Ah," Dominique said, looking past the friendly officer for other onlookers. There were a few crewmen going about their duties, but since the day she served them breakfast, they'd become her co-conspirators. She proffered the pipe to Ryland. "Care to?"

"Well, thank you kindly," said Ryland with a sly grin. He took a few puffs as he looked over the harbor. "Odd time to take on fresh water, with Tunis so close. Seems the marquise insisted." Ryland handed the pipe back.

"Angele is very particular about her comforts," said Dominique. "At least my husband is happy to indulge one wife on this journey. The other, I think, he finds a burden."

"Well, speaking only for the crew, you're thought of with great affection."

"I am?" asked Dominique, the pipe stem pinched in her teeth.

"They were a bit unsure of you when you first came aboard, but since then, you've shown yourself to be hardy at sea. I'm not sure what you did, but it impressed them."

Dominique continued to puff.

"Sailors usually think of women at sea as bad luck," Ryland went on. "But on this ship, they're calling you the 'Lady of the *Allegheny*.'" Ryland leaned a little closer, nudging her with his shoulder. "Like King Arthur's Lady of the Lake. You're the spirit of their beloved ship, which is named after a beloved American river. Isn't that charming?"

"Me?" Dominique scoffed. "How about that."

"I can see why he cares for you."

"Richard?"

Ryland opened his mouth, then snapped it shut. "May I?" He reached for the pipe, and Dominique handed it to him. He took a few puffs. "There's something I must tell you. We have a mutual friend aboard the *Philadelphia*."

It was plain he was talking about Sully. Dominique didn't reply.

"No need to say anything," said Ryland. "Just listen. He's deserted the Navy to search for his family on the Barbary Coast. Sullivan told me his plan, and I agreed to help him if I could. That's why I transferred to this ship. I knew the *Allegheny* was bound for Tunis. My plan is to bring him in and speak for him at his court-martial. We'll claim any sailors with him went under duress. I'll do whatever I can for Sullivan, but he knows his odds won't be good at trial."

Dominique felt a flutter in her heart. As much as she didn't want to admit it, she couldn't bear the thought of Sully swinging from a noose.

Ryland must have read the look in her eyes, because he said, "Sullivan wanted you to know: He did what he had to do to set Kaitlin and Nora free and bring Melisande home to you. And he has no regrets."

The pipe nearly fell out of Dominique's mouth. "Melly's...with Sully?"

"Aye. Should he not get a chance to say it himself, he wanted me to tell you he's sorry for the trouble he brought you and your sister. He hopes you can forgive him for the promise he broke."

Dominique remembered her last conversation with John. *Get going, Sully. Do what you're going to do. Then you can be done with this city and out of our lives.* She felt a rising panic. A growing horror that those might be her last words to John Sullivan. On that day, she had needed him gone. Needed him not to exist. Because she made her choice and couldn't go back. A necessary cruelty. Or so she once thought. "Thank you, Mr. Ryland. But John Sullivan is in my past. Captain Aubert is my future."

"Of course," said Ryland, tipping his bicorner hat. He started to walk away when a call came from the crosstrees.

"Ships to port!" cried the lookout. "Two points abaft the beam!"

Ryland yanked the spyglass from his belt. He panned the lens across the horizon, then let it fall from his eye. "Beat to quarters!" he shouted. "Weigh anchor. Pass the word for the captain!"

Dominque looked toward the mouth of the bay, where five ships were rounding the point.

The ship erupted with noise. Orders shouted from man to man, up into the rigging, and to the decks below. A drummer sounded the alarm. Sailors swarmed out of every hatch, climbed the rigging, or manned the guns. Gunners took off their shirts to avoid cotton in their wounds. The ship's boys raced down into the hold, ready to carry loads of shot and powder. Men with long muskets ascended to their perches in the main and fore tops.

"Mrs. Aubert," said Ryland, "Come with me. We need to get you ashore immediately. Bosun Toule, launch the jolly boat."

"Belay that order, Mr. Ryland," said Captain Aubert as he strode toward them. He sounded as calm as a man reading from the morning newspaper. "My wife remains aboard with me. Report." Aubert studied the approaching ships through his spyglass.

"I count five ships rounding the point, sir," said Ryland. "Two ketch-rigged, three gaff-rigged. Flying Tripolitan colors. Guns already run out. They'll be on us in minutes. Sir, I recommend we transfer your wife to the *Minerva,* recall the shore parties, and provide cover while they escape."

"I see you have a firm tactical grasp," said Aubert. The nearby gun crews watched the conversation. "I also see that your recent near miss on the *Philadelphia* has left you timid. Mr. Kimble!"

"Sir!" replied Lieutenant Kimble with a crisp salute.

"Loose our sails and make our course south-by-southwest out of the bay." A smirk tugged at Aubert's lips. "What do you say, boys? Shall we teach these brigands a lesson?"

The crew let go an excited cheer.

"Shall we show these jackals how *Alleghenies* fight?"

An even louder cheer.

"Then blow your matches!" cried Aubert, getting hurrahs in reply. He handed back Ryland's spyglass. "There you have it, Lieutenant. The men are for attack."

Ryland rubbed his temples. "Captain, there are five of them."

"Five smaller, poorly armed, poorly equipped, ships. Mr. Ryland," tutted Aubert, "I am not a milksop like your former commanding officer. Unlike Bainbridge, I know how to win a sea battle."

"Then if you mean to take the offensive, at least let me get Mrs. Aubert to safety ashore."

"No!" snapped Aubert. "She is safer at my side. I want Bosun Toule to take her below with four Marines. They'll keep her safe on the orlop deck, below the water line, where a shot is less likely to penetrate."

"As you wish," murmured Ryland. His eyes were baggy. Exhausted.

"Dominique," said Aubert. "With me."

Dominique felt light headed. Foggy. Her heart was beating so fast, she thought it might tire and give out. She followed her husband aft, eyes drifting to the warships sailing toward them. She had never been so terrified in her life. "Richard…" said Dominique as they approached the quarterdeck hatch. "Richard…stop, please…"

Aubert sighed and paused on the first step down. "Dear, you will be fine. You must trust me."

"But what if Mr. Ryland is right? Shouldn't I go ashore? What of the danger?"

Aubert gave a quick glance around the deck, took Dominique by the shoulders, and shuffled her aside. He whispered, "There is no danger. You will be just fine."

"How can you say that?" cried Dominique. "We're outnumbered five to one!"

"I will not have my *wife* question my command." Aubert rolled his eyes as if lecturing a child. "There is no danger because I say there is none. It's been arranged."

That was the moment when Dominique put her finger on it. Aubert wasn't just confident—he had *no* fear. As if he knew the outcome. She recalled his red book and the mysterious letter inside.

A,

Congratulations on securing the prize. Our agent in Paris has made contact. The number is five. The cost is ten percent. Paper ships. Hollow crews.

The Restoration is at hand.

L

"'Arranged?'" Dominique pressed. "You and Marquis Larocque…Richard, what have you done?"

"I have done nothing…" said Aubert, a redolent look

in his eye, "…That wasn't necessary to secure our future." Aubert jerked his head to the right. "Bosun Toule!"

The bosun ambled up to the captain and his wife. He looked at them silently, his mutton-chop sideburns as dark as his scowl.

"Take my wife below," ordered Aubert as he looked into Dominique's eyes. "No harm is to come to her."

"Aye, captain," said Toule.

"Richard," whispered Dominique, drawing close to Aubert's ear. "I don't like that man."

"Of course not. He's repulsive," Aubert whispered back. "More so than the rest of these revolutionary yokels. But he's loyal and useful to his betters. You'll be fine with him." He nodded to the stoic bosun and headed aft to command his quarterdeck.

Dominique found herself alone with Bosun Toule's scarecrow stare. The bosun bid her follow with a wave of his cane. She waited till he turned around and started down the hatch. After a few hesitant steps, she followed him into the darkness.

The walls of wood thundered around Dominique's ears. She curled up against the barrels, head buried in her knees, hands covering her ears. A tremor went through her body every time a cannonball struck. She jumped with every boom from an *Allegheny* gun. There was no way to hide from the cacophony. Every impact stung her eardrums. The rare moments of quiet were even worse. Minutes spent waiting for the next explosion of violence. She'd open her eyes, and there would be Toule, staring at her in the lamplight of the spirits room. She'd grown nauseous on the smell of the beer and rum. She analyzed every shout from the sailors on the higher decks, desperate for a sign it was over. It went on for hours. The shrieking of a wounded sailor echoed through the lower decks.

A scream echoes from the yard outside. Maman *is pulling Dominique by the hand, trembling.* "Down here girls," *says* Maman. "Everything will be all right."

Baby Melisande is squalling against Maman's *shoulder. Their mother lets go of three-year-old Dominique to throw open the cellar door.*

Dominique doesn't want to go into the dark. Tears stream from her eyes. "No, Maman! *There's monsters,* Maman!"

A crash comes from somewhere else in the chapel. A door is bursting from its hinges. Scary sounds are coming from the men who follow. Maman *puts a hand over her tear-streaked mouth.*

The stack of rum casks shook, straining against the ropes lashing them down. More cannonballs thundered against the hull. The ship lurched, and the lantern banged into the ceiling. Dominque made herself a tighter ball. She tried to fight the memories off, but they kept coming. The smoke from *Allegheny's* guns became the burning houses. The shouts of the sailors became the war cries of Mohawks. The moans of wounded sailors became women screaming. Men pleading. Children crying. Dominique screamed, tears pouring down her face. She bawled like a girl, rocking back and forth. The last time she knew this kind of terror, she had been three years old.

"Stop!" Dominique screamed. "Make it stop. Make it stop!"

A hand brushed her shoulder.

Dominique recoiled like a trapped animal. Bosun

Toule's paw was reaching for her. "Get away from me!" she shouted over the cannon fire. "Don't touch me. Don't ever fucking touch me!"

Toule knit his brow, as if more puzzled than offended. He retreated to his corner. The four Marines exchanged awkward glances. Toule had been trying to comfort her. She'd rather take solace from a hissing alligator.

The thunder stopped. The shouts faded. Dominique looked up at the planks overhead. Another lull in the action. Soon, the terror would begin anew.

Then the sound of cheers erupted and spread throughout the ship. Feet padded over the planks. Hip-hips and hoorays resounded through the ship.

Toule maintained his implacable scowl. "Seems our boys won the day, miss." He offered a hand to help her up.

Dominique didn't take it. "It's over?"

"I'll send the Marines to make sure it's safe, but that sounds like victory."

Dominique climbed to her feet. "No. Get me out of this miserable cellar."

"Cellar, miss?" puzzled Toule.

"Get the hell out of my way!" shouted Dominique. The five men all stepped back.

A few minutes later, as Dominique emerged from the lower decks, she felt the low sun wash over her like a balm. All around the deck, sailors were smiling, shouting cheers, or clapping each other's backs. Dominique followed their gaze to starboard, where the enemy ships lay scattered, one of them smoking. The nearest was at least half a mile away. The ship rolled over a wave, and the image of five fleeing pirate ships tilted in and out of view.

"We beat them, Mrs. Aubert," cried an elated Lieutenant Kimble, grinning like an excitable boy. "We beat them into retreat! You should have seen the captain. Your husband was amazing—outnumbered five to one, and he led us to victory easy as you please."

Dominique looked aft to the quarterdeck. Behind the ship's wheel, a group of officers and sailors were chattering in a circle around Richard. She couldn't hear their words but she could read their faces. Aubert basked in a shower of praise. He was stoic, confident, poised—as if delivering impossible victories was a boring pastime.

"You must be so proud, Mrs. Aubert," said Kimble. "Your husband is a great man."

"I'm just glad it's over," replied Dominique, mustering a smile. She ought to have felt as euphoric as Richard's crew, but she felt drained. Detached.

"Helm," Aubert's voice called out. "Wear around and take us back to into the bay. I think we'll find our charge waiting safe and sound."

There was a round of victorious laughter.

"A shame we couldn't capture one," said Kimble. "But with Captain Aubert in command, there'll be no shortage of prize money!"

Dominique feigned another smile. She wanted to be alone, but she couldn't bear to go below decks. She slipped away to her usual spot by the bow, trying to keep out of the way. Her hands trembled so badly, she couldn't get the tobacco into her pipe.

A while later, when *Allegheny* rounded the point and sailed into the bay, they should have found the *Minerva* floating right where they left her. Instead, the *Allegheny* crew lined up along the rails and stared in shock. The tribute ship was gone. In her place, clusters of broken planks and torn sailcloth. A single boat filled with some thirty crew rowed toward the *Allegheny*. Among them, Dominique could make out the Larocques' garish tailoring. During the hour it took the boat to reach the port side, the men shared murmurs of dismay.

"Oh, Richard, it was so awful," wept Angele as she climbed over the side. She threw herself into Aubert's arms, crying into his coat. "I was so afraid."

Aubert gave her a rigid pat on the back. "Marquis Larocque, what happened?"

"A pirate ship, Captain," the Marquis declared as he climbed aboard. His voice had all the drama of a town crier. "A craven, dastardly bunch lying in wait. While you pursued the others south, they sailed around from the north side of the island. We were caught by surprise. The next thing we knew, shots were smashing through our hull. Water flooding in from everywhere. The ship sank in minutes."

"Sank?" said Kimble. "So quickly? Why would pirates aim to sink such a prize?"

Larocque shrugged his shoulders. "I doubt they meant to. A lucky shot. The pirates had lookouts on land—they signaled their ship to flee when they saw the *Allegheny* victorious. You arrived not a moment too soon, Captain Aubert!"

"What of *Minerva's* captain?" said Lieutenant Ryland. "And the rest of the crew?"

"Oh, *terrible!*" wailed Angele, wetting Aubert's coat with fresh tears.

"I regret, they went down with the ship," said Larocque, bowing his head. "They fought gallantly, *Capitaine*! We would not be alive, but for their brave sacrifice. They did your country proud."

A murmur of horror whispered over the deck.

"Now, now, peace men," admonished Aubert. "Let us get our survivors aboard and salvage what we can. There will be time for revenge. We won't let these pirates escape. Let us be grateful for those we have recovered."

"Angele," said Dominique. "How could so many drown?"

"Oh, Dominique," sobbed the marquise. "My dear friend, I'm so glad to see you. It was so terrible. So terrible…"

"It's over now. You're safe." proclaimed Aubert. Turning to his officers, he said, "Mr. Ryland, launch a boat to recover salvage. Mr. Kimble, prepare a damage report, and then ready the ship for action. I intend to hunt these dogs down. Pass the word to Chef Jean-Christophe—slaughter two of my hogs. I want fresh meat, biscuits, and a double ration of rum for every man aboard. That'll put fire in their bellies."

A half-hearted cheer went up. It had the hard edge of anger.

Aubert said, "Mr. Ryland, when you begin your sweep—" A cry from the crosstrees cut him off.

"Ship ho! Fine on the port quarter!"

Everyone aboard craned for a look. One of the pirate ships was rounding the south point of the bay, its sails ruddy in the light of dusk. Not one of the ships they'd fought. This one was larger. With more sails. A sleeker hull. And many more guns.

Chester Ryland reacted first. He calmly unfolded his spyglass.

"Well, Mr. Ryland?" There was something different in Aubert's tone. Dominique heard no more of the bravado. There was an edge. An edge of fear.

Ryland snapped the glass shut. For a moment, he stared while the crew awaited his answer. "I recognize the ship," Ryland said, his voice forlorn. "It's the *Wolf of Tunis*."

"Twenty…erm, twenty-two guns, right?" stammered Aubert.

"Twenty-four," Ryland corrected.

"Twenty-four or forty-four," cried Lieutenant Kimble. "I say they're no match for our captain!"

Kimble's declaration inspired a smattering of huzzahs. The men didn't want to cheer—they wanted to fight.

Larocque chuckled nervously. "No doubt, no doubt, but, Captain Aubert…should we really push our luck?"

Dominique read the fear in Larocque's eyes. In Angele's eyes. In Aubert's. Something was terribly wrong. "Richard," she murmured. "Run. Please. Run."

Her voice must have carried because a few of the officers and crew turned worried glances on the captain.

Aubert looked at her soberly. For a moment he didn't speak. Then he turned to his first lieutenant. "Mr. Kimble, clear for action!"

The crew scrambled back to their posts. Lit slow-burning cords. Carried packets of shot and powder. It was all starting again.

Dominique felt someone's eyes on her, and she looked over her shoulder. She locked eyes with Chester Ryland. They shared a look like prisoners denied reprieve.

Chapter 64

The Abandoned Fort
The Lake of Tunis
Saturday, September 10th, 1803

John had been sitting in a dark cell for hours. He had no word of his friends' fate. No answers to any questions. Naim's men had rowed John, Ethan, and Melisande to an island in the middle of the Lake of Tunis. It was the second time John had come to this city in chains. But instead of making landfall and being marched to the bey's palace, the boat brought them to an island. In the middle of the fetid body of water, an old Spanish fort decayed on a barren patch of rock. Crumbling but sturdy walls enclosed a fortified dock, which led into a courtyard filled with slave pens. The pens were mostly empty, the windows of the barracks dark, and the ramparts guarded by a skeleton crew. Until recently, the place must have been abandoned. The *Nizam-I Djedid* had taken Ethan and Melisande to parts unknown.

In the bowels of this forgotten stronghold, the silence was the worst. Unlike any other jail or dungeon, there were no voices. No calls or shouts. No banging, no snoring, no clattering bars. Only the stillness of a crypt.

The light of a flickering torch strained through a tiny square of iron bars in the cell door. John sat on a wooden cot opposite, on a decomposing mattress of straw. A bucket in the corner was his only other comfort.

A shadow fell over John's chest. A key clattered in the lock. He saw a soldier's face blocking the grating in the door. It swung inward and slammed against the limestone wall. Two of the *Djedid* entered with torches and took up positions on either side of the open doorway. They were clean-shaven, their uniforms identically immaculate, their movements precise. Both looked at John with professional indifference. Somewhere down the hall, a pair of boots clicked on the stones. One slow, measured pace after the other. They drew closer until finally a figure stooped under the door. A man John hardly recognized.

It was Varlick Naim—but not even a trace of the old man remained. Gone was the matted beard, wiry hair, and threadbare robe. Now, a fit man in his early fifties towered over the guards. His dark beard, with a dash of gray, was cropped short. His hair was cut, oiled, and brushed. Thin lines of black traced along the edges of his eyelids. His green eyes, verging on yellow at the center, gleamed like jade. Only his mangled ear suggested the beggar of a day ago.

Naim wore a flowing kaftan of fine linen, a ladder of golden rope running down his chest. Where his kaftan parted at the sides, a long elegant sword hung on his belt. It had a wooden handle and bronze crosspiece—no ornate filigrees. The austerity of the Turkish *kilij* didn't fool John—it was a fearsome weapon. His boots were polished but splashed with dust. The pouches on his hip were well worn from travel. His belt looked like Parisian suede, but the buckle was beaten tin.

"Naim," said John as he sat up. His wrists chafed at the shackles, which were bolted to the wall. *Don't ask him,* a voice pleaded in John's mind. *Whatever you do, don't ask.* "Whatever your grudge with me, this feud is between us."

Naim's head tilted. He watched John but said nothing.

"Ethan and Melisande had no part in your son's death," John continued, barely able to hide his contempt. Had he been free with a sword to hand, he would have driven it through Naim's stomach. But if his friends had any chance to survive, he had to get through to this man—even if it meant groveling. "Let them go. Let us settle this like men. As a matter of honor."

The *Djedid* stood stock still. Naim raised his chin a degree. Again, the sultan's agent said nothing.

"Revenge?!" snapped John, tugging at his chains. "Is that what you want? It's yours. A duel. You and me, to settle this for good—no one else. Have you forgotten that Ethan defended you against those Marines? That Melisande helped free you from the *Philadelphia's* hold?"

Nothing.

John despaired. He'd always been good at reading people. Aubert and his arrogance. Laffite and his greed. Tindall and his pride. But this man confounded him. His face betrayed little more than detached curiosity. He studied John like a scientist might examine a cadaver.

Don't ask, thought John. No matter how desperately he wanted the answer, he couldn't tip his hand. "Naim, I didn't mean for Ilyas to die, but I could see no other way to escape. Any man in my place would do whatever he could to regain freedom. And despite your son's part in attacking my vessel—he was kind to me. I came to feel...fondness for him. Whether you can hear this or not, I am sorry for your loss." John set his jaw. "But I did what I had to do."

For the first time, Naim broke eye contact. He looked at the floor and took a step forward. "The day my son told me *Sheik* Arslan had expelled him from study, I cursed him for a fool and a disappointment. We argued bitterly." Even Naim's voice had changed. His English was fluent, his Arabic accent regal. He continued, "Ilyas wanted adventure and romance. Not scholarship and legacy. I sacrificed everything to give him opportunities I would never have, and he slapped them away. I told him to go to *Sheik* Arslan, fall on his mercy, and promise any recompense necessary to return as his pupil. If he did not, he was to leave my house and never return. The next day, Ilyas was gone. That was five years ago."

Naim took another step forward. "The following night, I went into his room. I gathered all of his childhood things. The rug from the foot of his bed, his abacus, his collection of miniature soldiers. Everything. I cast it all into a heap and set it ablaze. The bonfire devoured every memento. Such was my rage, I smiled as it all withered in the flames. The last of his possessions was a stallion carved of wood. I made it for him the day he was born. It was his favorite childhood toy. He'd left it on his bed for me to find." Naim gave a rueful smile. "An expertly chronicled message. I hesitated to throw that last vestige of my son onto the pyre. But at last, I did."

Naim twisted the emerald ring on his finger, staring into the gem. "I have few happy memories of Ilyas' childhood. I rarely saw him. When I did, it was usually at night. I would tuck him in and watch him fall asleep with the stallion in his hand. In the end, I could not bear to watch it burn." Naim let go the ring and showed John his right palm. Melted skin stretched from wrist to fingertips.

There was a neat lip around the ring where the heated metal had branded his flesh. "No force is more empowering and more crippling than love for one's child."

"Naim," John murmured, "Ethan, Melisande, my mother, and sister—they didn't kill Ilyas. It was me—only me. Let them go. Hold *me* responsible."

Naim smiled. He folded his arms under his kaftan.

John shook the chain tethering his hands. "What do you want from me?" John shouted.

The *Djedid* didn't react. Naim's face didn't so much as twitch. His stare was carved in granite. He turned to leave the cell.

Don't ask. Whatever you do don't ask. This was a high-stakes game. Like brag, it depended on strategy. On hiding one's true desire. But John could stand it no longer. "Naim…"

Naim stopped, angling an ear toward John.

"You said…" John murmured, staring at the flagstones. "…If I killed you, I wouldn't know the fate of my family. Please…can you just tell me if they're safe?"

The Chronicler of Constantinople jerked his head at one of the *Djedid*. "Bring him," he said and continued out of the cell.

The soldiers escorted John behind Naim. After a march through the lonely halls of the fort, up a winding stairwell, under a fallen-in chunk of tower, they came to the door of a small chamber. It opened on a suite— perhaps for the lord of the castle in a time long past.

A grand hearth almost as tall as John arced across one side of the room. Across from the door, silk curtains stirred in horseshoe windows. John could make out the lake and beyond that the staggered blocks of Tunisian buildings. Fire and torchlight winked like constellations across the city. The moonlight from the windows illuminated a grand tapestry of an ancient battle between Saracens and Crusaders. A table with two chairs sat in the center of the room. On the table, steam rose from a silver tea service. An earthy aroma mingled with the swampy odor of the Lake of Tunis.

Two of Naim's soldiers stood beside a door on the other side of the room, muskets shouldered. Isitan took up a position beside the table.

"What the hell is this?" said John, glaring at Naim.

The agent of the sultan didn't respond. Instead, Naim walked to the wall of tapestries and seated himself in a tall wooden chair. He sat with hands curled around each armrest as if he were the sultan himself, ready to observe some grand contest.

"Come," Isitan encouraged, his open palm beckoning toward the table. "Sit."

John looked at Naim but found the same inscrutable stare. Naim's eyes fixed on his captive like the dour statue of a god. John's chains grated on the stone floor as his feet shuffled forward. When he sat down, Isitan unlocked the shackles on his hands, and then his feet. Two *Djedid* soldiers stood a couple paces away from the table, muskets cocked and shouldered. John looked around, puzzled. The opposite door squealed open.

Two more *Djedid* escorted a slave into the room. A man in a dirt-caked, blood-stained smock hobbled toward the table. John leaned forward in his chair, trying to get a look at the newcomer in the light of the hearth. The prisoner walked with head bent toward the floor. A long tangle of gray and red hair obscured his face. He took tiny steps, his right foot dragging the left. His bare feet were lumpy and curled as if badly broken some time ago. Something about this prisoner caused John to sweat, his pulse to quicken.

The soldiers sat the newcomer across from John. The prisoner grimaced, his bones clicking. Every motion appeared to cause him pain.

"What is this?" John repeated, looking at Naim. "Who is this?"

Naim's eyes were hard as marble.

The prisoner's head lifted slightly. Greasy hair draped over the man's visage. He had a burn on the lower half of his face, as if a hot iron had been laid on him from nose to jaw. One timid eye darted between dangling locks, avoiding John.

"Slave," said Isitan to the invalid.

"Yes, my lord," murmured the captive, a rattle in his breath.

"You come with a chronicle for this man, do you not?"

"Yes, my lord. I carry a chronicle on behalf of Master Naim. I have practiced its telling many nights."

"Yes," said Isitan. He took up the teapot and filled first the prisoner's cup, then John's. "The time to deliver your message has come. You will recite your story to this man, as The Chronicler commands."

"Yes, my lord."

"Do you recognize this man?"

The prisoner's eye flashed up toward John's, then retreated again. "No, Master Isitan."

Isitan filled a third cup. One of the soldiers brought the tea to Naim, who sipped it in the shadows.

"Oh, I think you do," said Isitan. His voice turned hard. "Look at him."

The prisoner started, then looked into John's eyes. There was a moment of pure vertigo. The man had a face like aged rawhide. The bridge of his nose skewed right, as if broken and never set. His eyes were milky. Filled with fear. And yet, under all of it, John could see the shadow of the man that had once been. A young, vibrant captain. A man easy with confidence, quick to laugh, slow to lose his temper.

John felt sick to his stomach. "…Da?"

The man's eyes flicked down. Declan Sullivan stared at the silver teapot.

"Da?" John repeated, hearing his voice breaking. He felt tears brimming at his eyelids. "It can't be."

"Do you hear that, Declan?" said Isitan. "This man is your son. John."

Declan looked at John again. Tears ran from his eyes. He looked to Naim. "Master, am I to give this man your chronicle?"

Naim replied with a single incline of his head.

"Chronicle?" said John. "What chronicle?"

"Now then, slave," said Isitan, taking up a position in front of the windows. "Begin the chronicle. Tell every detail. Leave out not a word."

Chapter 65

Declan Sullivan's Chronicle
Red Mortar Redoubt, Island off the Coast of Tunis
One Year Ago

It was the last day I would ever know joy.

Together, Nora and I bid farewell to our daughter. We watched with heavy hearts as she passed the gates of the courtyard on one final mission. Our hosts showed us to a room in the manor with a small hearth and a balcony overlooking the garden. For most of those hours, we barely spoke. We could see the questions in one another's eyes but lacked the courage to ask. Mostly, we just held each other. Sometimes we cried. Other times we lay together. After the sunset, we made love.

I wish I could tell you it was the idyllic reunion of my dreams. That all our troubles were behind us, and life was good again. But our time together felt like two wounded animals licking each other's scrapes. We held one another and trembled as though huddling together for warmth. The emotions we shared—not through words, but through touch, and through our eyes—left us exhausted. We fell asleep by the light of the high moon.

In the morning, I reached for my wife, only to find her side of the bed empty. I saw the balcony doors open. The tail of Nora's dress fluttered near the curtains. I got up and joined her on the small terrace.

"Such a beautiful place, isn't it?" I said, circling my arms around her waist. We were watching four children splashing through one of the pools. "I'm so grateful Kaitlin found this refuge."

"Aye," murmured Nora. She felt rigid in my arms. Her stare was long and distant. "But it's still a cage. And tonight, our Katie risks her life while we're safe and sound."

"I know," I said. It felt shameful—a daughter fighting in her father's stead. "I hate it. But when it's done, we'll all be free. And we can leave these terrible shores together." I bent to kiss her neck, but she flinched. "What is it?"

"I'm sorry," said Nora, leaning on the rail. She closed her eyes, chin quivering.

Years ago, on the deck of the *Wandering Hart*, she had been so full of fire. So full of laughter. So eager for adventure. To see her now—trembling, quiet, distant…it broke my heart all over again.

"You've nothing to be sorry for," I said. "We all need time to heal."

Nora nodded, eyes shut tight.

"On the journey here," I continued, "Kaitlin told me her letters to Peter went unanswered. But when she wrote to your mother, she received word of John."

"Katie told me the same. Our boy escaped. To America."

"Can you believe it?" I smiled. "Johnny is free. Safe. When Katie returns, we'll be free to sail to Philadelphia together. Our family…" I trailed off, my voice choking up at the thought. "…whole again."

"It'll never be quite whole," said Nora.

She was right, and the words hit me like daggers. Our son Isaac was gone forever. "Aye…"

Something in me knew I was losing my love. I would have said anything to ease her pain. Done anything to bring her back from the darkness. But I had no more power to save her than to save myself. "It's all right, my love," I said, reaching for her hand. Slowly, she entwined her fingers with mine. "We'll find our way back to each other. We have time."

Drops fell from Nora's eyes. She didn't look at me, but I felt her hand squeezing mine.

I turned toward our room, deciding to give her some time alone, but she held fast.

"Declan." Nora faced me, her eyes watering, her brow trembling. "I love you. I always will. I need to know you believe me."

"Of course I believe you," I said. "I love you with all my heart. All that I am is yours."

Nora nodded, eyes downturned. "I need some time to myself." She pecked me on the cheek, then left me alone on the balcony.

I ended that day alone in our bed. Nora had been gone the whole evening. Not knowing when she might return, I nodded off. I woke to a warm touch. The window cast my wife's face in starlight. Before I could say a word, she drew close, and we kissed. That night, we were like we were before—passionate. Infatuated. In love. Afterward, we lay awake in each other's arms, hands interlocked. After watching the stars awhile, Nora spoke.

"Declan, my love."

"Yes, my heart," said I.

"I have a son."

"Aye, we do," I smiled, kissing her head. "He waits for us in America."

"No," she murmured. "I'm not speaking of John. I can't go with you to the Colonies."

I realized what she was saying, and it knocked the wind out of me. My heart broke to imagine the shame she must have felt—the burden she carried. Did she worry what I thought of her? Did she think she might be less in my eyes? That thought wounded me more than any other. I wanted to take her in my arms, but I resisted the urge and listened instead.

"You must understand," sobbed Nora. "It wasn't my choice. I never wanted a child with any man but you."

I could feel my breathing quicken. As the horror of her words sank in, I scrambled for something to say. Anything to console her. To let her know, I could never feel betrayed by a wrong visited upon her. I would have given anything to take her pain upon my own soul, that she might be spared.

"I only ever wanted to escape my captor. I thought I could leave the child behind..." Nora broke into sobs. "But he's just a babe. An innocent boy. *My* boy." She cupped her hands over her mouth, weeping.

"Shh," I said, running a hand over her hair. "It's all right, love. There's no need to make any decisions tonight. Let's rest. We can talk in the morning."

Nora nodded, burrowing deeper into my arms. I held her as she cried. My wife needed me, and I couldn't fail her. Or I would lose her. As we drifted to sleep, I reassured myself that everything would be better in the morning. We would find a solution.

The sunrise was not to come.

"Declan, wake up."

I opened my eyes to the dim glow of dying coals. A hooded figure hovered over my bed, shaking me awake. I started and retreated. In the delirium of sleep, I thought a master was about to drag me off to a *bastinado*. "No, please, Master, mercy…"

"Declan, Declan," whispered the man in a young, gentle voice. "It is all right. It is me, Aruna."

The Indian accent registered. My eyes adjusted, and I could make out the outline of his face. "Rune? I…what is it?"

"Katie sent me. You must come with me now."

"Katie?" I said, relief washing over me at the thought of my daughter safe. "She's back, then? Her mission succeeded?"

"No," said Rune, the embers lighting his distraught frown. "Something went terribly wrong. We must all leave the island now—soldiers are coming." Rune must have seen the panic on my face, because he added, "Katie is safe. She's guiding the children's escape. Now come, Captain Irish Declan. Time is short."

I nodded, and the adolescent thief whisked me away through the darkened hallways of the manor. We gathered as many stragglers as we could along the way. Out the windows, I could see torchlight beyond the walls.

"This way," said Rune. "It's not much farther."

We crossed the courtyard with a group of children. A young African woman was standing in the door to the kitchens, waving the children in. A boy, no older than nine called out to her in a language I had never heard.

"Nafi, hurry," she called.

Nafi stumbled on a root from the sycamore.

"Up you go, laddie," said I, helping the boy up.

Nafi hurried into his mother's arms. She shooed him through the door, pausing to look at me. "Thank you," she said and disappeared inside.

We heard an explosion, a splintering of wood. I looked back to see the iron lock on the gate breaking apart. There was smoke—probably from a grenade. The doors screeched open, and two columns of soldiers came storming in. There were dozens armed with muskets and torches. They didn't look like the Janissaries—they wore red tunics and blue breeches. They moved with familiar uniformity—like the soldiers of England—but their felt hats were Ottoman. They fanned into the courtyard, some of them kicking down doors and charging into the house. Their torchlight spread from window to window.

"Hurry!" cried Rune. He led me through the kitchens, down a dark set of stairs, to the very back of the wine cellar. A cabinet of wine bottles was pulled away from the wall, revealing a hidden tunnel. The women and children were hurrying inside. Rune took a burning lantern off a sconce. "This way."

By the time I followed the last of the fleeing families into the passageway, I could hear the soldiers stomping through the house. Furniture crashed. Glass shattered. Rune pulled the wine cabinet shut behind us. We traveled underground for what seemed like miles. With my slow hobbling, most of the others were far ahead. When my toe struck a chunk of rock, I fell painfully to my knee. I felt a small hand tugging on my own.

It was Nafi, the little boy I'd helped before. I smiled. "Thank you," I said in Lingua Franca. "You must not stay, laddie. Go. With your mother. Hurry."

The boy hesitated, let go of my hand, and then hurried

away. Rune took my arm over his shoulder, and we were off again.

"Who are those soldiers?" I asked. "The bey's men?"

"No," said Rune quietly. I could hear the fear in his voice. "They're not Bey Hammuda's men, and they're not Janissaries. They're…something else."

"What happened?" I demanded.

"Kaitlin and I were about to lift a priceless piece of art from the bey's palace—something Ibrahim long coveted. We planned the job for months, her and I. It should have been simple. But it was a trap…set by these soldiers. We narrowly escaped."

"You promised to look after Katie!" I said, wincing as threads of pain pulled from my hips to my ankles. "You got careless."

"Never!" protested the young man, frowning at me in the lamplight. "I took every precaution. But there was a man…"

"What man?"

"An agent of the Ottoman court. Someone dangerous. As we escaped the palace, he called out to us. He swore to find Kaitlin. He knew her by name."

"What? How?"

"I don't know. I only know your family is in great danger. We raced here as fast as we could. Not fast enough…"

Rune trailed off. I decided to pass the rest of the journey in silence. The pain in my clicking joints had become excruciating. Sweat soaked through my shirt.

We exited the tunnels through a trap door in the earth onto the flat, desolate mesa. The moonlit sea stretched away in every direction. An orange glow drew my eyes to the north. Some two miles across the mesa, a column of flames rose from the compound. The soldiers set the entire manor ablaze. Here, at the other end of the island, stood a collapsed stone building. There were no walls— just fragments of columns like the bones of a rotting carcass. On the other side of the ruin, a wooden bridge extended beyond the cliff. It connected to a log tower and several flights of steps leading down to the beach.

"Da!"

I turned around just in time to catch Kaitlin throwing her arms around me. "Katie, darling," I said. "Thank God."

Kaitlin was dressed all in black, with a kaftan of leather over loose breeches. Her belt was lined with odd metal tools, coiled ropes, and buckled pouches. She wore a leather cowl over her hair. She reminded me of the mysterious traveler in stories, appearing in the sleepy village where nothing ever happens. "I was so worried about you and Rune."

"We're all right, love. We're..." I trailed off when I saw my beautiful wife walking toward us in the moonlight. "Nora," I said, barely above a whisper.

"Declan," Nora replied, joining me and our daughter in an embrace. "I'm so sorry. I was going to leave, but I had to turn back. I couldn't lose you and Katie and Johnny again. I just couldn't. I'm so sorry," she said, shedding tears.

"It's all right, love," I said. "We'll make it right somehow. We'll find a way."

"Come, Sullivans," said Rune, beckoning from the steps of the crumbled tower. "We must get to the ship."

Kaitlin was the first to break away. She jogged toward the steps into the ruin, pausing to wave us on. "Mam, Da, come on."

"Is this *really* our Katie?" asked Nora with an incredulous smile.

"You know, she gets it from you," I teased.

Nora and I shared a smile, then hurried after our daughter into the ruin. It was like a house with its walls knocked out. Kaitlin led us through a crumbled doorway on the opposite side, then onto a wooden platform. I went dizzy as I gazed over the edge of the mesa, down a seventy-foot cliff, into the tossing sea below. I found myself looking out over a deep fjord, mostly surrounded by rocky cliffs. This cove had calm waters, sheltered from the sea.

A bridge led from the platform on which we stood to a square wooden tower twenty strides away. It was built of crisscrossing planks atop a lone column of cliff, apart from the rest of the mesa and only about forty feet high. A long wooden stairwell spiraled down the wooden tower, around the lone pillar of land, and onto a small spit of beach. A dock extended from the beach, where a ship waited far below. It was a small ketch-rigged schooner. Little points of light illuminated the refugees of Red Mortar Redoubt as they climbed aboard.

"Run ahead with Nora and Kaitlin," I said to Rune. "I'll be along."

The young Silver Hand thief was on the other side of the bridge near a pile of four wooden kegs. He carefully threaded a fuse through the top of one, then let out the slack. "I have to ready the charges. We'll blow the bridge to slow down the soldiers."

"No," I insisted. "I'll take too long. Get aboard and go! Leave a boat for me if you have to. Get those sails unfurled! I can lay the charges."

"We're not leaving you, Da!" said Kaitlin, her hand

pulling on mine.

"I'll be right behind you both," I said, smiling at my wife and daughter.

"Very well, Captain Declan," said Rune. He had a torch in one hand, the spool of fuse in the other. He turned toward us. "I'll leave a torch so you can light—"

The arrow landed in Rune's chest with a soft *thwip*. The boy froze on the other side of the bridge. He looked down, staring wide-eyed. A four-inch shaft of wood, fletched with black feathers, poked between his ribs. "Ugh…" he wheezed, before dropping to his knees and sprawling on his side.

"Rune!" screamed Kaitlin.

Someone had fired the bolt from behind us. We all turned around to find the ruin filling with torchlight. A tall, lean man with dark hair and a short beard stood a few strides away, still aiming a repeating crossbow. Four of the soldiers were coming up the steps behind him. The strange man wore a long kaftan and a curved Turkish sword. He looked out of place among the soldiers—as if he should have been sipping coffee in an Ottoman embassy, not leading a military assault. Two of his soldiers dropped to a knee, muskets trained on my family. The two behind held torches in one hand, pistols in the other.

"It's him!" whispered Kaitlin. "The man that almost caught us in the palace. The sultan's chronicler."

"For two long years," said Varlick Naim, taking slow, menacing steps toward us, "I have searched for the kin of my enemy." He spoke in a pleasant tone as if he had come to discuss philosophy, not threaten murder. "One by one, I found each of you, only to arrive too late. Now," he spread his arms wide, crossbow aiming at crumbling stone. "I have all three."

I stretched my hands in front of Nora and Kaitlin, edging them behind me. "What enemy? We're no enemies of yours."

"We only wish to go in peace," added Nora.

The man continued to draw closer, a wry smile tugging at his lips. "So it is with every soul I visit. But I am a humble chronicler of the sultan. I can do no more than record and deliver his word. So rarely do his messages bring tidings of peace."

I took a step back, desperate to keep my family away from this malevolent man. "We have nothing to do with your sultan, or the Bey of Tunis, or anyone else in your empire."

"I am afraid," said Naim, tracing small circles with a raised index finger, "tonight is not for the business of the Ottoman Court. I am here on my own account. I have a chronicle I must deliver. To your son."

"John?" said Nora, her voice trembling. "Our son has no quarrel with you. He's half a world away. He's done nothing."

Naim smiled, now only a stride away. He tilted his head as if an idea had just occurred to him. "You know? I believe that is all true. Now." His brows drew down over his eyes as he raised the crossbow again. "Come with me, or I shall slay you all where you stand."

"Please," said Nora. "Whatever wrong we have done you, give us a chance to make it right. There is no need for bloodshed. What chronicle would you have us deliver?"

"It is not in your power to deliver," said Naim. "Some chronicles one writes upon a scroll. Others, one writes with flesh."

Naim drew close now—pushing us to the edge of the bridge.

"Please," I said, "Spare our daughter. She's innocent."

"I know," said Naim. "You are all innocent. If you weren't, you would be of no use." He gestured to his soldiers, and they marched forward, pulling manacles from their bandoliers.

"Wait!" said Nora. She stepped in front of Naim, standing her ground as he towered over her. "All right. We'll do as you command. We won't fight. Please, just let us have a moment with our daughter—to explain. Please. As a gesture of honor."

Naim's eyes rolled to me, then to Kaitlin, clutched in my arms. He looked at Nora and inclined his head. "Out of respect for your courage. One moment."

Kaitlin ran forward, throwing herself into Nora's arms. Nora knelt down with her, stroking her hair. "Oh, Kate, my love," sniffled Nora.

For all her newfound maturity, Kaitlin trembled. "I'm scared, Mam."

"Don't be afraid, Rabbit," said Nora, tears running fast now. "Remember how we used to call you that?" she smiled. "It was Johnny started that, wasn't it?"

Kaitlin nodded.

"Remember how we used to scold you for running?" Nora said. "You'd fly so fast, so dangerously—just like a rabbit. No one could catch you."

"I remember," murmured Kaitlin.

"Good," nodded Nora. She pulled away and looked Kaitlin in the eye. She whispered, "Now fly, Rabbit!"

Nora flung herself against Naim. Before the sultan's agent could react, her teeth were on his ear. Naim shrieked as Nora bit the earlobe free, leaving behind bloody ribbons.

"Run, Kaitlin!" I shouted to our daughter.

And fly Kaitlin did, sprinting the distance across the bridge in mere seconds. There was a musket shot. And then another. Just as Kaitlin reached the safety of the tower, the kegs ignited.

I watched in horror as the bridge disintegrated in a blaze of fire. The flames billowed into the enclosure of the watchtower. The bridge fell away in a rain of smoking planks.

"Katie!" I screamed.

"Hold your fire, fools!" cursed Naim.

Fire was engulfing the wooden tower now. I could find no sign of my daughter. I called her name again and again. I looked behind me and saw Nora lying on the ground, blood soaking through her dress. I crawled to her, cradling her in my arms. I watched as Naim rounded on the two soldiers who had fired. He drew his curved sword. In one clean stroke, he opened their throats. He watched as his own men dropped and suffocated on the stone, blood gurgling out of their sliced gullets. The two behind took a terrified step back. Naim glowered at his dying troops, his eyes filled with fury.

I pressed a hand to the growing patch of red on Nora's stomach. Her skin had gone waxy. Her dress was soaked with blood. "Nora!" I cried, arms trembling.

Nora's eyes drifted toward mine. "Declan, my love."

Her blood bubbled up between my fingers. "Nora, oh my love. Stay with me."

"Did she—" said Nora, forcing the words through shallow breaths. "Did she make it? Did she—get away?"

I closed my eyes, terrified the burning tears would

betray me. "Aye, love," I lied. "She did. You should have seen her. She was so fast. So brave."

"Always told her—not to run," said Nora, a smile tugging at her eyes. "Declan."

"Yes, love?"

But then Nora's breathing slowed. Then halted. And she was gone.

"Oh God," I wailed, hauling her body close to mine. "Oh, my wife. My beloved Nora."

I heard the boots of Varlick Naim clicking as he approached. "Those imbeciles cost me my revenge."

I looked up at the hateful bastard that had just murdered my wife and daughter. I was glad to see blood from his ear running his kaftan red.

"You're going to wish they hadn't." Naim dropped to a knee. His yellow-green eyes burned like a fire. "For I shall have to craft a new chronicle."

Chapter 66

The Abandoned Fort
The City of Tunis
Saturday, September 10th, 1803

"I am all that's left," said the broken slave after telling his story. "Isaac. Nora. Kaitlin. They're all…gone." Declan broke down into pitiful sobbing. "Gone…"

John sat in paralyzed shock. Surviving the streets of Philadelphia. Gilroy's message in the rain. Extorting the truth from Ryland. Nearly dying on the journey to Red Mortar Redoubt. All come to nothing. His family was gone. Already dead for a year. And in their place, this crippled ruin of a man, barely capable of independent thought. It couldn't be.

"It's a lie," John breathed, eyes burning with tears. "It isn't true."

"No!" cried Declan. He looked at John with the crazed expression of a man shown the noose. "It's true! I swear. Every word. I serve The Chronicler. I would never bear false witness in his name."

In the shadow just beyond the firelight, Naim watched in perfect stillness, his eyes agleam.

"The what?" whispered John, biting the words off

with his teeth. "I don't give a damn who you think you serve. You've just told me that Mam is dead. That you saw Katie…burned. Do you understand what you've told me, Da?"

Declan trembled, his body shaking as he wept. "I'm sorry, son. I failed them. I failed you, Johnny. I failed all of you."

Isitan stepped up to the table and poured each of the prisoners more tea.

John's face screwed up in disgust. "You 'failed?'" A log popped on the fire. "You gave up when you should have fought. When the pirates came to drag my mother and sister away in chains, you didn't 'fail.' You *surrendered.* Like a coward."

Declan sobbed like a child scolded to the point of hysterics.

"You're a coward," John said. "You're a coward, and you killed them!"

In the shadows, Naim crossed one leg over the other. He rubbed a thumb under his chin.

"I'm sorry," Declan whimpered. "Oh, Nora, I'm sorry. My poor Katie. My poor child…"

"'Your poor Katie?'" whispered John, staring at his father in disbelief.

In a flash, John's hand was on the hilt of Isitan's dagger. He tore it from the sheath and sent the table tumbling. The silver rang on the stones as John lunged for his father. Declan didn't even raise his hands in defense as John seized him and pitched him to the floor. The *Djedid* soldiers snapped into action, pointing their muskets at John. But John didn't care—he piled onto his father and pressed the curved blade to his father's throat. He heard Isitan's sword sing out of its sheath.

"Wait," ordered Naim, rising from his chair. Isitan and his men took a step back.

"It's your fault," John shouted into his father's crying face. "All of it. It should be you that's dead—not them. It should be you burned to cinders. You're pathetic."

Declan's eyes were closed. John expected him to fight or to plead. But he just lay there, limp. Slowly his eyes opened, bloodshot with tears. As if with great effort, he lifted them to meet John's. "Yes," he sobbed. "You're right, son. It should be me." He lifted his chin, allowing the knife to press more evenly across his gullet. "This is what I deserve."

Naim walked toward the two men with slow, measured paces.

John pressed the knife harder. His fingers kneaded along the grip. "All your fault," he repeated. "All of it."

As he looked into the eyes of his broken father, he wanted to feel hate. For years he had convinced himself that Declan was to blame. Tragedy made more sense when it had an author. But at that moment Declan was neither father, nor captain, nor slave. He was just a man. A man who had lost everything he ever loved. And he was also Da. The man that read to John as a boy. The man that first helped him climb the rigging without fear. The man who first taught him to lead. And all John felt was sadness.

John exploded to his feet and thrust the dagger at Naim. But Naim was already gone, and John's failed lunge left him fumbling on hands and knees.

Isitan hurdled over Declan, sword raised to attack John. A word from Naim stopped him.

"No," ordered Naim as he watched John rise into a crouch. "Don't interfere."

John tossed the dagger from hand to hand. He circled right, then switched left.

Naim took short, calm steps, patiently waiting for John to strike. He didn't even draw his sword.

John exploded forward. He hooked the blade toward Naim's side. But Naim wheeled out of the way, moving entirely too fast for a man of his years. The sultan's agent moved like water slipping through fingers, his body gliding more than twisting, his feet dancing more than jumping. Even so, John's lungs burned with exertion—before the fever, he would never have lost his wind so quickly. John swiped again, but again Naim simply wasn't there. Even if John's bum leg and seizing back hadn't slowed him, John had never fought a faster opponent. John twitched forward, feigning a lunge. When Naim stepped right, John pivoted and drew an arc straight for Naim's throat.

With a slight tilt of the head, Naim allowed the dagger to narrowly miss the artery in his neck. He caught John's strike in the crook of his arm. Before John could react, Naim's fingers closed on John's wrist and twisted it almost to the point of breaking. John felt his arm folded behind his back as easily as if his muscles were made of stuffing. Naim swept John's feet out from under him.

Cold stone pressed against John's cheek. The dagger he'd been holding a moment ago appeared in the corner of his eye.

Naim brandished the blade close to John's temple as he held him to the floor. "For just a moment, I actually thought you might put your own pitiful father out of his misery. How pleased I am that you chose me for your enemy. It will make these coming days so exquisite."

John grunted and fought, but the slightest twitch from

Naim and his arm threatened to dislocate. He spat and hissed, helpless as a rabbit in a snare.

John felt Naim's breath hot on his ear as The Chronicler whispered, "I had planned for you to bear witness to your family's end—how disappointing to settle for Declan's retelling. Oh, but you gave me so much more in those long days at sea. All I had to do was let you talk. Let your friends talk. Now, I have your *new* family. You gave me everything."

A draft from the windows kicked up the fire. John's eyes widened to the sound of crackling flames.

"You still have so much," said Naim, "that I have yet to take."

All at once, the weight on John's back was gone. He coughed milky phlegm onto the flagstones. His chest spasmed until he thought his ribs would crack. He couldn't even resist as the soldiers dragged him up by the arms.

"Take him back to his cell," commanded Naim. "We have a long day tomorrow."

As the *Djedid* led John back down the spiral stairways, he moved like a man sleepwalking. He felt numb. Unable to think. Somewhere, in the foggy reaches of his mind, he knew he must plan an escape. He knew Ethan and Melisande would depend on him. But the thoughts were like badly remembered rumors.

His family was dead. Another pair of shackles dragged on the castle floor behind John. He looked over his shoulder at Declan, hobbling along with another pair of soldiers, hunched over and staring at the ground again. He should have felt rage. Or sadness. Or self-pity. But John felt nothing. None of it seemed real.

The *Djedid* led John back to the same cell as before.

They pitched him inside, Declan tumbling to the floor after him. The soldiers slammed the door closed, wrapping them in near darkness. The key ground over the tumblers and the guards marched away. For a moment, John stayed on hands and knees, trying to catch his wheezing breath. He stared at the small square of torchlight flickering on his straw bed. In the faint light, he could make out his father's shape huddled in a corner.

"Johnny," Declan said. "There's something I must say…"

"Shut up," murmured John. "I don't care." He crawled onto his bed. All he wanted was to sleep. To sleep and think of nothing.

His father's neck collar rattled as he shivered. "I'm sorry, Johnny…I'm sorry…"

"I don't want to hear it, Da. I want…" The moment John's back landed on the mattress, a sharp pain lanced up between his shoulder blades. Something hard under the straw? But he hadn't felt it before. With a grimace, John dumped himself off the cot again. He lifted up the mattress. He blinked.

A large, jagged chunk of sandstone sat on the boards.

"How did that get there?" wondered John.

A shape on the underside of the mattress drew John's eyes. The square of light from the cell door shined on a patch of bright crimson. John squinted, studying the shape.

"What is it?" wheezed the voice of his father from the corner.

John's eyes narrowed. A shape in red paint, like the face of a horse. The red silhouette also had a pair of horns. No, not horns John realized. Antlers. It was the head and antlers of… "A hart!" cried John.

"A what?"

The mattress slipped from John's fingers and flopped back down on the cot. John spun around, sitting on the cold floor, eyes searching in the dark. "A *red* hart. Painted beneath my mattress while I was away. A rock to tell me it was there."

A smile spread across John's face. His heart pounded in his chest. He felt strength surge through his body.

"Da!" said John, looking at his father in the dark. "The Red Hart—it's her symbol. She's telling us she's here to help." A laugh of pure joy burst out of him. "Katie is alive!"

Chapter 67

Red Mortar Redoubt
Island off the Coast of Tunis
Saturday, August 14th, 1802

Kaitlin Sullivan woke up coughing on water. Her lungs burned as she gasped for air. She turned over on hands and knees, the world still a blur. Cool sand drained through her fingers. The light of the moonlit sea crept into her vision, and she found herself on a beach at the edge of the island. The memory of the jump came back to her. Her father's wails of sorrow. The explosion and the swim. Pulling Rune to shore. She became aware of another body lying nearby.

"Rune!" she cried, crawling over to where he lay on his back. His eyes were closed. He wasn't moving. The crossbow bolt still jutted from his chest, the breeze rustling its fletches. "Rune," she whimpered, on the verge of tears. "Wake up. Please."

Aruna lay still. Soot from the fire was smeared over his round, youthful face. A trickle of blood ran from a cut in his cheek. A wound matted a patch of his black hair.

Kaitlin panicked and shook him. "Rune! Wake up. Rune!"

Rune's eyes flew open. He coughed and gulped for air. With each breath, the arrow in his chest made a sucking sound. "Katie," he gasped.

"Rune!" Kaitlin smiled, her relief bubbling over. She laid a hand on his smooth cheek, a thumb rubbing his eyebrow. "You're okay."

"Katie..." he wheezed. His eyes drifted closed, then opened again. "You have to...You have to listen to me."

A thundering split the quiet on the water. Kaitlin looked southeast. A couple miles out to sea, flashes lit up the night. Cannons firing from a ship. Each time one of the iron muzzles ignited, Kaitlin caught a glimpse of the *Lake Runner*, dwarfed by the larger two-masted vessel. She could hear the timbers breaking apart, the screams of her fellow thieves echoing toward her. The soldiers had caught them, and they were ripping the vessel apart.

"No!" cried Kaitlin, tears running down her cheeks. Another shot lit the sky like a lightning bolt, and she saw the *Lake Runner* roll over. Another shot and the ship was vanishing beneath the waves. "No..."

"Katie," said Rune, his breath quick and shallow. "Listen to me. There's a boat. Hidden in Carthage Cove. You remember where we used to fish?"

Kaitlin nodded, sniffling.

"You have to go now." Rune laid his hand over hers. She entwined her fingers with his. "It's small enough for you to handle. Get to Tunis. Find one of our tavern contacts—someone you can trust. You keep to the shadows, and you survive."

"Not without you," she said, squeezing his hand in both of hers. "I won't leave you."

"Katie—" A cough interrupted. Rune spoke in ever shorter bursts. "I can't go…with you. I'm not…going to make it."

Kaitlin's face twisted in despair. "You can't leave me alone," she sobbed, burying her head in his chest. "You have to live."

"Listen to me," her mentor wheezed. "Where I'm…going, you can't follow…You're going to live…and you're going to be free because…you're the Red Hart." He mustered a faint smile.

"I don't want to be the Red Hart anymore." She squeezed his hand in both of hers. "They're all gone. Our home is gone. I don't *want* to stay. I want to go with you—to the next life."

"It's not your time, Katie," said Rune. He'd begun to shiver. "You have more to do in this place. Your brother…is on his way. He's…going to need your help."

"John? But how?"

"I sent a man named Gilroy with…your message. John will come…he will help you…"

"But that's why we decided not to send it!" cried Kaitlin. "You promised."

"You forgot the first lesson…I taught you," Rune grinned, shrugging. "Never trust a thief."

A tear ran off Kaitlin's chin. She gave a faint smile. "I remember."

The bolt in Rune's chest was sucking more air. A pink foam bubbled from the wound.

"Rune?" whimpered Kaitlin. "Please, don't die, Rune. You can't. You can't because…"

Rune smiled at her, his grip tightening. "The body dies, but the *Ātman* lives on…we'll meet again…"

"Please, Rune. You can't go, because…"

Rune's grip relaxed. Red froth ran down his chin. His eyes drifted away from hers and fell still.

The cry just came out of her. A pitiful, childish wail of sorrow. Kaitlin's tears spilled onto Rune's chin. "No," she sobbed. She squeezed his languid hand in both of her own as if to stir him back to life. She lay her head on his chest. "Because…I love you."

She collapsed under the weight of her own despair, crying into his still heart. She bawled like she hadn't since she was a little girl. Her arms encircled his body and pulled him close if only to feel his warmth one last time. How could she let him go? For a while she lay there like that, weeping. In the end, it was the clatter of weapons and scrape of boots that pulled her away.

Kaitlin looked down the beach. Distant torchlight moved under the shadow of the cliffs. At least three soldiers were coming toward her. She looked down at Rune's still face, gazing eternally into the stars.

"I love you, Rune," she sniffled. She bent down and pressed her lips to his, her tears falling on his face. The first and last time they would ever kiss. "Goodbye."

An hour later, with the sound of shouting men drawing closer, Kaitlin Sullivan dragged Aruna's hidden boat out from under a tangle of weeds. She paddled into the surf and set a course for Tunis. Just as she cleared the last ring of submerged reefs, she looked back to where she'd been. The torches were swarming over the cove. High above the mesa, ruddy light glowed under a belly of smoke. She turned away from the burning redoubt. And so began her midnight journey on the starlit sea.

When she finally made landfall outside Tunis, she stumbled out of the surf and collapsed in exhaustion. She lay on the sand for a half hour, unable to do anything but cry. When she had no more tears left in her, she pulled herself to her feet and headed for the city walls. It was easy enough to find one of her secret tunnels and sneak back into the blocks of tenements. She wended through abandoned alleys, vacant merchant stalls, overgrown gardens. Eventually, she climbed by eve and ledge onto the rooftops. Here, she could traverse the whole of the city unseen, as she had a thousand times. She ended her travels in her favorite spot. In the hour before dawn, her feet dangled over the crenellations of the tallest minaret.

For a while, Kaitlin sat on the narrow, round tower, just staring out across the staggered rooftops and the lake beyond. All the tears were dry now. Every sob spent. Rune was gone, and she had a choice to make. Kaitlin had never asked for Tunis to become her city. A place she had come to in chains. A place of fear and despair. But over the years, this place had become something different to her. A land of opportunity. A lock to be picked. A maze to be outsmarted. It was an odd feeling, Kaitlin decided, to discover the city she had so long wanted to escape became the place where she first fell in love.

Time to decide. She rose, feet gripping a pyramidal block of stone. At her back, the walls of the tower. In front of her, a hundred-foot drop. She had only to step off and follow Rune into the next life.

Your brother is on his way, Rune had said. *He's going to need your help.*

Kaitlin reached into the pocket of her breeches. A stick of sanguine chalk rested on her palm. With perfect balance, she pivoted and squatted before the inner tower. Her tongue poked from her lips as she sketched a shape on the sandstone. A shape she had drawn many times. When she was done, she stood and admired her work.

Satisfied, she slid the chalk back into her pocket and produced a brass oil lamp from her satchel. Carefully, she uncapped a flask and filled the reservoir, struck a few sparks from a flint, and watched as a flame grew from the long spout. A lantern to guide Rune's soul to his next life.

"Goodbye, Rune," Kaitlin whispered. "We'll meet again."

She cinched her belt, drew her black cloak over her shoulders, and checked the rope grappled to the rampart. She turned back toward the ledge. Behind her, the lamp lit the red-chalk image of a stag's face and antlers. The silhouette of a solitary survivor of the forest. A powerful spirit of the wilds whose glowering visage on the *Wandering Hart* once terrified her. Now, a spirit she felt watching over her, lending her strength. With the lightest jump, she sprang off the crenellations. The rope sang under Kaitlin's gloves as she rappelled down the side of the tower. She landed on a rooftop ledge, surrounded by windows, some still flickering with light. She tugged the rope, and the slip knot loosened. She tugged a few more times, and it came free. The grapple landed in her outstretched hand. She coiled the rope and tucked it into her satchel. Kaitlin cast one last look out toward the sea, her red hair flying up in the breeze. She drew the dark cowl over her head, then dashed off along a ledge.

The sleeping citizens of the capital took no notice of a dark-clad figure silently moving under their windows. The agile thief slipped from shadow to shadow, vaulting over low walls, traversing alleys on clotheslines, scaling cracks in the stone. The tears were dry. The sobs quiet. There would be time to grieve, in a quiet moment when there was nothing else to occupy the mind. For now, despair slept under a thief's hood.

The approaching dawn spread shallow pools of light across the city of Tunis. In the inky depths beyond, the Red Hart flitted beneath a shoal of stars.

John Sullivan and Company return in

Blood & Oak:
Wolves Will Eat

FREE GIFT!!
The Art of Blood and Oak

Join my Readers' Group email list at
www.bloodandoak.com/gift and get a FREE Art Book!

"The Art of Blood and Oak" brings this classic high seas
tale to life with original commissioned art. The artbook
is delivered in easy-to-print PDF format. You'll also get
exclusive behind-the-scenes details about the
characters and the world. Yours FREE!

Glossary

Aft
Towards the stern.

Amidships
The middle section of a vessel.

Ballast
Heavy material (such as gravel or stones) that is placed in the hold of a vessel to provide stability.

Bar Shot
Cannon balls linked with a solid bar used to damage rigging and masts.

Belfry
The ship's bell and the wooden frame the holds it, usually located forward of the main mast and aft of the foremast. Used to keep time.

Bow
The front of a vessel.

Bowsprit
A spar projecting forward from the bow used as an anchor for the forestay and other rigging.

Brig (Prison Aboard a Ship)
An interior area of the ship used to detain prisoners.

Brig (Type of Ship)
A vessel with two square-rigged masts.

Bulwark
The extension of the ship's side above the level of the weather deck (or spar deck).

Carronade/Smasher Gun
A short, smoothbore, cast iron naval cannon, used as a powerful, short-range anti-ship and anti-crew weapon.

Chain Shot
Cannon balls linked with chain used to damage rigging and masts.

Clew
The lower corners of square sails or the corner of a triangular sail at the end of the boom (sometimes shorthand term for "clew-line").

Clew-line
Used to truss up the clews, the lower corners of square sails.

Crew Deck
On USS *Philadelphia*, the deck located below the gun deck and above the orlop deck. The crew's hammocks and dunnage, the sick berth, the officers' quarters, and the wardroom are all located on this deck.

Crosstrees
Two horizontal struts at the upper ends of the topmasts of sailboats, used to anchor the shrouds from the topgallant mast.

Footrope
Ropes fastened along a ship's yards for sailors to stand on while setting or stowing the sails.

Forward
Towards the bow.

Frigate
Generally, a sailing warship with a single continuous gun deck, typically used for patrolling, blockading, etc., but not in a major line of battle.

Furl
To roll or gather a sail against its mast or spar.

Gangway
An opening in the bulwark of the ship to allow passengers to board or leave the ship.

Grapeshot
Small balls of lead fired from a cannon, analogous to shotgun shot but on a larger scale. Similar to canister shot but with larger individual shot. Used to injure personnel and damage rigging more than to cause structural damage.

Gun Deck
On the USS *Philadelphia*, the deck located below the spar deck and above the crew deck. The main complement of cannons, the galley stove, the livestock manger, the head, and the captain's cabin are all located on this deck.

Gunwale
The top edge of the side of a boat.

Halyard

Ropes used for hoisting a spar with a sail attached.

Kedge

A technique for moving or turning a ship by using a relatively light anchor known as a kedge. The kedge anchor may be dropped while in motion to create a pivot and thus perform a sharp turn. The kedge anchor may also be carried away from the ship in a smaller boat, dropped, and then weighed, pulling the ship forward.

Long Gun

A cannon with a lower caliber and longer barrel than carronades, best for hitting targets at long range.

Mast

A tall upright post, spar, or other structure on a ship or boat carrying a sail or sails. The foremast is the mast farthest forward, the mainmast is the tallest mast and is aft of the foremast, and the mizzenmast is the mast farthest aft.

Orlop Deck

On the USS *Philadelphia*, the lowest deck on the ship. The surgeon's cockpit, the brig, the spirits room, powder room, cable tier, and various other cargo compartments are located here. Beneath the individual compartments is the hold, the very bottom of the ship, filled with ballast.

Piling

Heavy posts throughout a ship, which serve as support columns.

Port
Towards the left-hand side of a vessel when facing forward.

Ratlines
Small ropes fastened across a ship's shrouds like the rungs of a ladder, used for climbing the rigging.

Reef (Reefing)
To temporarily reduce the area of a sail exposed to the wind, usually to guard against adverse effects of strong wind or to slow the vessel.

Sheet
A rope, attached to the clew, used to control the setting of a sail in relation to the direction of the wind. The sheet is often passed through a tackle before being attach to fixed points on the deck.

Shrouds
Standing rigging running from a mast to the sides of a ship to support the mast sideways. The shrouds work with the stays, which run forward and aft, to support the mast's weight. They also form the ladder which allows sailors to climb into the rigging.

Skiff
Generally, a small boat, sometimes equipped with a sail, manageable by a small number of crew.

Sloop
A small to mid-sized sailboat larger than a dinghy, with one mast bearing a main sail and head sail and located

farther forward than the mast of a cutter.

Sloop-of-War
Generally, any sailing warship bearing fewer than 20 guns (sometimes referred to as a "sloop").

Spar
A wooden pole used to support various pieces of rigging and sails.

Spar Deck
A ship's uppermost deck, exposed to the sky. Also known as the weather deck.

Starboard
Towards the right-hand side of a vessel when facing forward.

Stay
A strong rope supporting a mast and leading from the head of one mast down to some other mast or other part of the vessel; rigging running fore (forestay) and aft (backstay) from a mast to the hull. The stays support a mast's weight forward and aft, while the shrouds support its weight from side to side.

Stern
The rear part of a vessel.

Swivel Gun
A small cannon, mounted on a swiveling stand or fork which allows a very wide arc of movement, and loaded with small caliber shot or grapeshot. Primarily used as an antipersonnel weapon.

Tack

A leg of the route of a sailing vessel when tacking.

Tacking

Zig-zagging so as to sail directly towards the wind.

Taffrail

A rail at the stern of a boat or ship.

Thwart

A bench seat across the width of an open boat.

Wear ("Wearing Ship" or "Wearing Around")

Tacking away from the wind in a square-rigged vessel.

Weather Deck

A ship's uppermost deck, exposed to the sky. Also known as the spar deck.

Weather Gauge

The tactically superior position over another sailing vessel with respect to the wind.

Yard

The horizontal spar from which a square sail is suspended.

Yardarm

The very end of a yard.

Acknowledgements

All my life, I've loved tall ships, the sea, and the age of fighting sail. Crafting this adventure has been a labor of love. On this journey, I was overwhelmed by the outpouring of love and support I received from family, friends, and colleagues.

I wish to thank my friend and fellow writer Jesse (aka "The Jackal"). You encouraged me to take a risk on something new and stuck with me to the end. To bestselling author Rebecca Forster, you have been a true friend and mentor, and I'm forever in your debt. I am also enormously grateful to those friends who took the time to read my work and give me my first feedback: James, Tom, and Sorya. Thank you for always being there for me.

To all of my family: Thank you for always believing in me and nurturing my love of adventure. To all of my friends: Thank you for your steadfast encouragement, feedback, and moral support.

I would also like to thank the Maritime Museum of San Diego. Your commitment to preserving the Age of Sail provided an amazing source of research and inspiration. I'm also deeply grateful to the Redondo Beach Writer's Group. Your feedback, friendship, and discourse became the best part of my week.

The following professionals lent their exceptional talents to the production of this book:

Jenny Jensen: Editing for Style and Narrative.
jennyjenseneditor.com

Pablo Fernandez: Cover Artwork.
pablofdzart.com

Kerem Beyit: "Blood & Oak" Title and Logo Artwork.
artstation.com/kerembeyit.

H.O. Charles: Cover Design.
hadleighdesign.com

Formatting and interior design by
WriteIntoPrint.com

Your Face is Rad Photo Studio: Author Photography.
yourfaceisrad.com

Finally, my admiration and gratitude to our republic, the United States of America, founded on the principle that freedom is the birthright of all humanity; and to her defenders, our sailors, Marines, soldiers, airmen, law enforcement officers, and first responders, whose legacy is a storied one.

About the Author

Garrett Bettencourt always loved telling stories, from the illustrated travels of a shipwrecked boy when he was eight, to a novel of pirate adventures when he reached high school. His love of adventure and the unexplored gave him a passion for space, science, history, high fantasy, and the ocean. His penchant for all things nautical led him to spend two and a half years researching the early U.S. Navy. The result is book 1 of Blood and Oak, an epic series of swashbuckling high seas adventures.

Garrett currently lives in the desert city of Scottsdale, Arizona, but still dreams of the sea.